A Wife's Courage

A Wife's Courage

The Battersea Tavern Series: Book 3

Kitty Neale

ORION

First published in Great Britain in 2023 by Orion Books,
an imprint of The Orion Publishing Group Ltd
Carmelite House, 50 Victoria Embankment
London EC4Y 0DZ

An Hachette UK Company

1 3 5 7 9 10 8 6 4 2

Copyright © Kitty Neale 2023

The moral right of Kitty Neale to be identified as the author
of this work has been asserted in accordance with
the Copyright, Designs and Patents Act of 1988.

A CIP catalogue record for this book is
available from the British Library.

ISBN (Mass Market Paperback) 978 1 4091 9767 6
ISBN (eBook) 978 1 4091 9768 3

Typeset at The Spartan Press Ltd,
Lymington, Hants

Printed and bound in Great Britain by Clays Ltd,
Elcograf S.p.A.

MIX
Paper from
responsible sources
FSC® C104740

www.orionbooks.co.uk

I

Battersea, London
12 June, 1944

Maureen Fanning looked straight ahead as she trudged through Battersea, pushing her few belongings in a perambulator. Her husband, Brancher, walked beside her, with one hand shoved into his trouser pocket and the other holding a roll-up. His confident swagger irked Maureen. It was Brancher's big mouth and bad temper that had got them thrown out of their lodgings. Now they had to go cap in hand and ask her grandparents to accommodate them for a while.

For a while, Maureen thought, silently seething. For a while would more than likely turn into several months. Brancher had lost his job again and God only knows when he'd find another! But Maureen wouldn't moan at him about it. She'd keep her mouth shut, as usual, and, hopefully, save herself from having to listen to yet another tirade of abuse. She supposed she should be grateful that at least her husband didn't beat her. He'd push and shove her, and sometimes he'd throw things in her direction, but he'd never actually whacked her. She could put up with shouting, though Brancher's words always cut her deeply. Indeed, his words could hurt just as much as a slap around the face and the pain would linger for longer.

'I don't know why you insist on keeping that bloomin' pram. It ain't like we've got a kid, and we ain't likely to ever have one again. You *baron* cow,' Brancher spat. He took a long, angry draw on his roll-up before throwing it into the gutter.

Maureen's jaw clenched as sharp grief stabbed at her heart. Brancher had done it again: in one sentence, he'd managed to reduce her to tears. It wasn't as if she needed reminding of the baby she'd lost two years earlier. There wasn't a day that passed when she didn't think about the child that she'd birthed. She'd been six months gone when her waters had broken and a wrenching pain had ripped through her stomach. In a flood of blood and agony, the tiny, perfectly formed boy had been born, but he hadn't opened his eyes or taken a breath. He was with the angels now.

She dashed away her tears, hoping that her husband hadn't noticed her crying. She was sure that he got some sort of sick pleasure in seeing her upset.

'Give me a couple of bob,' he demanded loudly.

Maureen stopped walking and, with a heavy heart, she fished in her cloth bag for the small purse that held their money. She knew that there was barely enough in there to last them for more than a few days. But she wouldn't dare argue with him. Instead, her voice little more than a croak, she asked, 'What do you want money for?'

'The pub,' Brancher answered bluntly.

She wasn't surprised that he was going to put their cash behind the bar. He'd always liked a good drink, but alcohol made him even more intolerable than usual and would bring out his jealous streak. She'd lost count of the number of times that, after a few pints, her husband had accused her of flirting with other men or of having an affair. The idea of even looking at another man seemed preposterous to her – she wouldn't have the guts!

'Sorry, but that'll have to do you,' she said, hoping he wouldn't demand more.

Maureen handed Brancher a couple of coins, half of the money that was left in the purse. He looked at the meagre amount in his hand and shrugged. 'I'll see ya later,' he said, and then sloped off.

She watched him strut away. Her stomach knotted at the thought of him turning up later at her grandparents' with a belly full of beer. She hoped that he'd hold his tongue in front of them and not lay into her with another verbal slating. She cringed at the thought of her grandparents hearing Brancher throwing abuse around. And it was very likely that they would hear every vile word that would spew out of his mouth. After all, Brancher was never quiet. Half deaf, he was prone to shouting instead of talking. Maureen felt ashamed of never standing up for herself. But as Brancher had told her on numerous occasions that she was useless, she believed him. After all, she'd proven how useless she was when she hadn't even managed to keep their baby in her womb for nine months.

Once her husband had turned the corner, Maureen carried on towards her grandparents' home. She felt a flutter of excitement at seeing them both, though her delight was marred by the thought of Brancher showing her up. As she drew closer to their terraced house, she realised that it had been a month since she'd last visited. Her gran was bound to ask why she hadn't been sooner. What could Maureen

3

say? She couldn't tell them the truth; that she'd been too exhausted to call in because she'd been working three cleaning jobs that paid the rent and for Brancher's booze. Her gran would be furious and would probably give him a right telling-off! Brancher wouldn't stand for that, but it wouldn't be her gran he'd turn on. No, it would be her. Maureen's mind whirred. She could fib and tell her gran that she'd been under the weather. Yes, that would do. She'd fob her off with a tale about having a summer cold.

Maureen knocked on the front door. A wide smile spread across her face in anticipation of seeing her dear gran. When no one answered, she knocked again and called through the letter box, 'Gran, it's me, Maureen.'

She was pleased to hear her gran call back.

'Let yourself in, pet. The key is under the pot.'

Maureen left the pram under the front window and went inside to find her gran sitting by the empty hearth with her feet up on a pouf.

'Hello, dear, what a lovely surprise,' Renee greeted.

'Hello, Gran. How are you?'

'I'm all right, but my old legs aren't working too well, that's why your granddad left the key under the pot. He knew that if anyone called, it would take me forever to get to the door. Anyway, I'm glad you're here, it's smashing to see you. Your granddad will be back soon. You haven't got to rush off, have you?'

'No, not at all,' Maureen answered. She sat on the corner of the sofa and nervously twiddled a strand of her chestnut-brown hair, suddenly feeling apprehensive about asking if she and Brancher could move in.

'What's bothering you?' her gran asked.

The perceptive old woman could read her like a book, so there was no point in beating around the bush. 'Me and Brancher haven't got anywhere to live, Gran,' she answered, embarrassed, looking down at her scuffed and tatty shoes.

'Why? What happened to the flat you were renting in Wandsworth?'

'The landlord wants to sell the place, we had to leave,' Maureen lied.

'Didn't he give you notice to find somewhere else?'

'Yes, a bit, but it's hard to find anywhere. So many families have had their homes bombed, there's a real shortage of decent housing.'

'What are you going to do?'

'I – erm – I was wondering if we could move in here? Just until we find somewhere.'

'Of course you can. It'll be lovely having you around.'

Maureen leapt from the sofa and rushed to her gran's side. She placed an enthusiastic kiss on the woman's papery cheek. 'Thanks, Gran, thanks so much. I've got our things outside; I'll fetch them in.'

As Maureen went to turn towards the door, she felt her gran grab a hold of her hand. 'There's something you should know,' she said, her tone serious. 'It's your granddad. He's becoming ever so forgetful.'

'Well, he is getting on a bit.'

'It's not just that. I think he's losing his marbles.'

Maureen wasn't overly concerned. Her gran had always been a worrier. She doubted very much that there was anything wrong with her granddad other than old age. 'I'm sure he's fine, but I'll keep an eye on him,' she assured. If anything, Maureen was more concerned about her gran's legs, especially as it appeared that she was struggling to walk. Her grandparents had aged a lot this past year, yet Maureen hadn't noticed until now. A wave of guilt washed over her as she thought that she should have visited them more often. Perhaps living with them was the best thing that could have happened ... just as long as Brancher behaved himself.

'Well, I never!' Winnie Berry exclaimed when she set eyes on Brancher Fanning. 'I haven't seen you in my pub for ages.'

'Hello, Mrs Berry,' Brancher boomed with a wide smile. 'This place ain't changed a bit. I knew I'd get a welcome smile in the Battersea Tavern. I'm glad to see you're still the landlady. You're looking well.'

Len, who was sat at the end of the bar in his usual place, turned on his stool. He scowled when his eyes set on his grandson-in-law. 'What do you want?' he growled.

'Half a mild, thanks, Len.'

'You cheeky sod, that's not what I meant and you know it. What are you doing here in Battersea?'

'Maureen is round at yours, so I popped in for a quick drink.'

'Shouldn't you be at work?'

'Yeah, I'd love to be, but I got laid off.'

'Give the supervisor a load of lip again, did you?'

'No, Len, it weren't like that.'

'Yeah, I bet. It never is, is it?'

Winnie went to pour Brancher his drink, leaving him and Len to catch up. It was no secret that Len didn't think much of Brancher, but Winnie had always put it down to the pedestal on which Len had placed his granddaughter. In the old man's eyes, no one would have been good enough for Maureen. Especially someone like Brancher who was full of himself and liked a good few pints. But Winnie didn't see what was so wrong with the bloke. He'd been one of her regular customers since he'd been old enough to drink. Though Winnie hadn't seen him since he'd moved to Wandsworth with Maureen.

'How are you, love? And Maureen, is she well?' Winnie asked as she placed his drink on the bar.

'Yeah, thanks, Mrs Berry, can't complain. But I was just telling Len about how I lost my job.'

'Oh no, that's a pity.'

'Yeah. I got laid off. Mind you, there's plenty of house-building going on so I should be able to find a labouring job easily enough.'

Len stood up and knocked back the last few mouthfuls of his stout. 'I've heard enough of his rubbish. He's a bleedin' sorry excuse for a man. I'm off home to see … erm … err … I'll see you tomorrow, Win.'

'Yes, see you, Len,' Winnie replied with a weak smile. She'd noticed that Len had lost track of what he was saying again. The man never said much, but just lately, when he did speak, he sometimes muddled his sentences. *Poor old bugger*, she thought. None of them were getting any younger!

'I'll be home in a bit, Len. I'm just gonna finish me drink,' Brancher said, picking up his glass.

Len didn't answer and marched out of the pub.

'I don't know what his problem is,' Brancher said, sighing heavily.

'Don't worry, love, it's not personal. After Maureen's mother died, Len became very protective over Maureen and her brother. He'd be the same with anyone the girl had married.

7

I reckon that even if you were royalty, Len would still give you a hard time.'

'I suppose so. But I've been married to Maureen for nearly five years now and he ain't come round. He's never going to like me, is he?'

Winnie smiled. 'Probably not, but Len's a miserable bugger and doesn't like many people.'

Brancher drank his half pint quickly and then wiped the back of his hand across his mouth. 'I'd best get off.'

'Don't be a stranger.'

'I won't. I'm hoping to be in here a lot more. Maureen is asking Len and Renee if we can move in with them. I'll be seeing you.'

Carmen, Winnie's barmaid and lodger, came to stand beside Winnie. 'Was that Brancher Fanning?' she asked as the door closed behind him.

'Yes. He might be moving in with Len and Renee.'

'Blimey, I've not seen him in years. He used to knock about with my Errol when they were kids.'

'He's a few years older than Errol, isn't he?'

'Yes. Errol used to look up to him. He's a nice lad.'

Winnie agreed. Brancher was nice, though she thought he must be nearly thirty years old by now, hardly a lad. And though Winnie liked the fella, Len never had a good word to say about him. According to Len, Brancher was a skiver for not doing his bit and fighting against the Germans. But Winnie knew that Brancher had hearing difficulties, which also explained his loud, booming voice.

The door opened again and Winnie beamed with delight when she saw her four-year-old granddaughter running in.

'Nanny, nanny,' Martha squealed excitedly. 'I stwoked a puppy. He licked my face and it tickled me.'

Winnie's heart melted at the beautiful sight of Martha's sparkling blue eyes and rosy cheeks. Her blonde hair glistened in the sunlight that streamed in through one of the windows. She looked so angelic, the apple of Winnie's eye. She was grateful that Martha took after her mother, Rachel, and bore very little resemblance to her father, David. Rarely a day passed when Winnie didn't think about her son David, but he had left a bitter taste in her mouth. She would never forgive him for the terrible things that he'd done.

Winnie pushed memories of him from her mind, and smiled down at her granddaughter.

'Sorry, Win,' Rachel said as she hurried in behind Martha. 'I tried to drag her round to the back door, but she wriggled out of my grip, the little madam. She will insist on coming in the pub.'

'It's all right, love. She's just been telling me about a puppy.'

'Yes, there's a litter of them out the back of the corner shop. Cute little things.'

'They need a home, Nanny. Can we have one? Please, Nanny,' Martha asked. Her little hands held on to the brown painted bar as she enthusiastically jumped up and down.

'I've already told her "no",' Rachel mouthed.

'We can't have a puppy, love. We haven't got a garden for the puppy to play in.'

'Please, Nanny. I've always wanted a puppy,' Martha pleaded, her head cocked to one side.

Winnie smiled and rolled her eyes. 'Oh, all right then, I suppose so,' she said. 'But you'll have to take the puppy out every day and look after it.'

'I will! I pwomise! Thanks, Nanny. I luff you!'

'You're too soft with her,' Rachel scoffed.

'I know. I can never say no to her. She's got her old nan wrapped around her little finger.'

'Can we go and get the puppy now?' Martha asked her mum, excitedly.

'Come on then,' Rachel answered with a sigh. 'But no running ahead of me this time. Keep a hold of my hand.'

' 'Ere you are, love,' Winnie said, and went to the till. She took out several coins and handed them to Rachel. 'Use this to get whatever the puppy needs.'

Once Martha had skipped off holding her mother's hand, Carmen turned to Winnie and said ruefully, 'You're lucky to have your granddaughter living here with us. It's nice that you're so close.'

Winnie felt sorry for Carmen. The woman had a strained relationship with her own daughter, Cheryl, and saw little of her new grandson. And since Carmen's son, Errol, had been released from prison, no one had seen him in Battersea, though Winnie thought that Errol's absence was a good thing. Carmen had no family of her own to speak of but had become an integral part of Winnie's life and the Battersea Tavern. They lived in the flat upstairs: Winnie, Carmen, Rachel and Martha. And although Rachel's mother, Hilda Duff, didn't live with them, she spent a lot of time upstairs too. And there was also Winnie's adopted daughter, Jan, a nurse, married to Terry. Jan would visit whenever she could, but her work at St Thomas' Hospital kept her busy. Though they weren't all blood related, as far as Winnie was concerned, they were one big, happy family.

'I do feel very blessed,' Winnie said. But as she spoke, her stomach twisted with nerves. So far, her *family* had escaped the atrocities of the damned war. They'd had their run-ins and lucky escapes – Jan had been buried under rubble when a bomb had landed on the nurses' home and Carmen had nearly lost Cheryl when Balham underground station had been flooded. But, unlike so many other unfortunate families, Winnie wasn't left to grieve the loss of her loved ones. Granted, her husband, Brian, had been killed, and so had Carmen's husband, Harry. But neither women were upset about being widows. In fact, the opposite was true!

She wondered how much longer her luck would last. The war had been raging for years now. Surely it had to end soon. Troops had landed in Normandy and were fighting the enemy back through France. She gritted her teeth as she hoped with every sinew of her body that Hitler would be defeated and her family left unscathed.

2

The following morning, Len plodded back from the corner shop with his daily newspaper tucked under his arm. He was in no rush to get home to read it. He already knew what the headline would read – *Pilotless bombs attacked East London in the early hours of the morning.* Len had heard the news bulletins on the wireless. His blood had run cold when he'd listened to the announcer reporting on the rockets sent by Hitler. The Germans were in France, just across the Channel and close enough to launch their deadly weapons. Len was sure that the rockets were sent in retaliation for the British, American and Canadian troops landing in France a week ago. It had been a massive operation and the resilient Brits had been swept up in a wave of euphoria. Now though, they were going to pay the price of Hitler's wrath.

Len drew in a long breath. As if things weren't bad enough, to make matters worse, he would have to sit and look at Brancher's face across the breakfast table. His lip curled in disgust. What Maureen saw in Brancher would remain a mystery to Len. He found the man to be brash and loud, with a lazy streak and no ambition. Not nearly good enough for

Maureen. But his granddaughter seemed to love her husband, so he supposed that he'd have to put up with the bloke.

Arriving back home, Len ambled through to his kitchen in the back of the house. Renee was sitting at the table and sipping a cup of tea. Maureen had some bread under the grill and the kettle was on the stove. And there was Brancher, sat on a seat with his feet up on another and smoking a roll-up.

'Shouldn't you be out looking for work?' Len barked. He pulled his newspaper from under his arm and whacked it across Brancher's boots. 'My kitchen chairs are made for backsides, not feet,' he scowled.

'Yeah, I will look for work, Len, but I can't on an empty stomach,' Brancher replied. He pulled his booted feet off the seat and ran his hand through his greased black hair.

Len watched in disgust as Brancher then wiped his hand on the tablecloth. 'Oi, wash your bleedin'… thingy, erm, hand, at the sink. I don't want that hair pomade stuff on Renee's clean linen.'

Maureen rushed over with a dishcloth and rubbed the tablecloth. 'Sorry, Granddad. Brancher's got a bad habit of doing that. I don't think he even realises what he's doing.'

'Don't apologise for me,' Brancher growled.

Len saw Maureen lower her eyes and the colour drain from her face. She walked back to the stove, her back rod-straight. He was surprised that his granddaughter had allowed Brancher to talk to her in that tone. He was about to stick up for Maureen and have a go at the man, but Renee suddenly cried out.

'Pilotless bombs!' she shrieked. 'Oh, Len, have you seen this?'

Maureen came to stand behind Renee and looked over her

gran's shoulder at the newspaper spread on the table. 'Good grief! Whatever next?'

'What are you on about?' Brancher asked and snatched the paper towards him. 'Rockets... the Jerries are firing rockets at us from France,' he blurted, sounding aghast.

'Yes, I heard it on the wireless this morning. But there's no need to panic. The RAF will shoot 'em down, pilot or no pilot.'

'But, Granddad, it says here that one witness said they heard the engines, humming, and then it cut out and went deathly quiet until there was a huge explosion. The rocket falls out of the sky and you can't hear it coming!'

'The Hun got lucky, that's all. Now our boys know what to expect, they won't let no more rockets through,' Len reassured her.

'Bloomin' clever though, eh? Pilotless bombs, who'd have thought it,' Brancher said, his hazel eyes wide.

Len didn't like the fact that Brancher appeared to be impressed with the German's invention. He slammed his fist down hard on the table. 'Don't you give them murdering bastards any credit,' he ground out through his gritted teeth.

'I ain't, Len. I was just say—'

'Nothing. Don't say nothing,' Len interrupted. His nose wrinkled at the smell of burning toast and he looked over his shoulder.

'Oh, blimey,' Maureen said and dashed back to the stove. She quickly forked the blackened bread from under the grill and onto a plate. 'It's ruined,' she moaned and blew on it.

'It'll be fine,' Renee assured. 'Just scrape it. Do it over the sink, mind.'

'But it's burned to a cinder, Gran.'

'Have you seen the queues for a loaf? We can't afford to waste bread. Like I said, give it a scrape and it'll do.'

Len wasn't hungry anyway. The thought of rockets flying over from the continent had turned his stomach. Though he'd play it down in front of Renee. As it was, his wife lived on her nerves. He didn't want to give her something else to worry about.

Maureen placed a plate in front of him and gave another to Brancher, both with two slices of scraped toast on them. Len peered at the plate, suddenly feeling confused. What was Maureen doing here? Why was she giving him his breakfast? His heart raced. Renee, where was Renee? And why hadn't Renee given him his breakfast? He looked up, relieved to see his wife at the other end of the table.

'Are you all right?' she asked.

Len gulped. 'Er, yeah. Yeah, I'm fine,' he lied. 'I'm not hungry,' he added, pushing his plate away. He grabbed the newspaper and pretended to read as his mind tried to work out what was happening to him. These lapses of memory seemed to be happening more often. One minute, he'd be perfectly lucid and then the next, he wouldn't know his arse from his elbow. It had happened the other day on the way back from the Battersea Tavern. He remembered saying goodbye to Winnie and then he'd found himself in a street that he didn't recognise. He had no idea how he'd got there. Luckily, once the fog in his head had cleared, he'd managed to find his way home. But Len had to admit to himself that it had worried him. And he wondered if Renee had noticed. If she had, she hadn't said anything. Or maybe she had and he'd forgotten!

Brancher reached across for Len's plate. 'I'll have that if it's going begging.'

Len didn't respond. He kept his head in his newspaper, gripped by his worries. The thought of going doolally terrified him. He'd seen it happen to his father and his father's brother. Both had lived to a ripe old age but had become drooling wrecks who didn't know who they were, or recognise anyone else. They hadn't been able to feed or clean themselves and were totally reliant on their wives. Len feared the same fate. He'd rather be dead than live in that state. And it wouldn't be fair on Renee. The woman could hardly walk. She'd never be capable of caring for him and he wouldn't expect her to.

Maureen's voice broke into his thoughts.

'I'll be doing all the cooking from now on, Granddad. Do you fancy a nice stew later?'

'Long as you can manage not to burn it,' Len answered and forced a chortle.

He smiled tenderly at his granddaughter, though his insides were churning and his mind in turmoil. He hoped against all the odds that his moments of confusion were merely old age creeping in and that he wasn't turning into a dribbling replica of what his father had become. But if the truth be told, deep down, Len knew his fate, though he was yet to accept it.

'I can't believe it, flying bombs without pilots! It's really scary,' Rachel said with a shake of her head.

She was sat in the front room with Winnie and Carmen while Martha was in her bedroom with the new puppy. Martha had again asserted her independence and was getting herself dressed. She'd shown herself to have a stubborn streak and insisted on doing everything for herself. Rachel couldn't wait to see what clothes her daughter would choose to wear today.

Carmen checked her reflection in the mirror over the fireplace. Her once ebony black hair was now almost completely white. Rachel mused that maybe the stress of the war had taken the colour out of Carmen's hair. The woman was about the same age as Winnie and though they looked nothing alike, Rachel thought that they were similar in many ways. She admired the fact that they were both strong and were good at putting on a brave face. And neither Carmen nor Winnie were afraid to speak their minds.

Carmen turned away from the mirror, saying, 'I thought we'd pretty much seen the back of Hitler's bombs, but these rocket things are a whole new kettle of fish.'

'Well, we got through the Blitz, so we'll get through this,' Winnie said firmly. 'This is just Hitler retaliating 'cos of our troops landing on the beaches in Normandy last week.'

'Maybe. But, Rachel, you really ought to think about sending Martha to the countryside, somewhere safe,' Carmen suggested.

Rachel leapt to her feet. 'No, I won't hear of it,' she answered adamantly.

'I don't blame you for wanting to keep her with you, but Carmen has a good point,' Winnie joined in. 'We don't know how many of those rockets Hitler has or how many he's going to send over here. Don't get me wrong, I don't want my granddaughter away from home any more than you do, but perhaps evacuating Martha is something to consider?'

'No, Win. There's no way and that's final,' Rachel snapped.

Carmen cleared her throat. 'Excuse me, young lady, but there's no need to bite Winnie's head off.'

'You're right, I'm sorry.' Rachel hadn't meant to sound so aggressive, but she felt passionate about keeping Martha with her. She'd nearly lost Martha once before when the girl had been a baby and Lucy Little had kidnapped her. Lucy hadn't been of sound mind and had stolen Martha to run away with David. Unfortunately, though no one knew what really happened on the platform of Clapham Junction railway station, Lucy had been killed under a train. Winnie blamed David, her own son, for Lucy's death. It had been a terrifying day for Rachel, one that she'd never forget. And now, she couldn't stand the thought of her daughter being away from her. No one knew how much longer the war would last, it could be months or even years! All the more reason to keep Martha at home.

Martha came clumping into the room, with her puppy jumping around her ankles. Rachel tried not to laugh at the sight of her daughter wearing a back-to-front dress and balancing in a pair of Rachel's high-heeled shoes.

'I'm dwessed, Mummy,' she said proudly.

'I can see that.'

Winnie also looked as though she was trying not to laugh. 'And you look as pretty as a picture, love. Have you got a name yet for your puppy?' she asked.

'Yes. His name is Cake because he's the same colour as cake and cake is my favewit. I luff cake and I luff my puppy.'

'You've clearly given it a lot of thought,' Rachel said. 'Now, go and put your own shoes on and we can take Cake for a walk.'

Martha clumped back out of the room, calling, 'Come on, Cake.'

'She's special, bless her,' Winnie giggled in Martha's wake.

'Yes, she really is. I'm popping up the Junction to get her a new pair of shoes. She's almost grown out of the ones on her feet. I can't keep up with her, she's shooting up so fast. Can I leave Cake with you?'

'Of course you can, love. Go in my purse and get a few bob. I'll treat her to a new pair of shoes,' Winnie smiled.

'Thanks, Win. That's ever so good of you. She's a lucky girl. When I was her age and had grown out of my shoes, my gran used to cut the ends off.'

'Me an' all. That's how things were. But Martha won't know what it is to be poor or hungry. I shan't have any granddaughter of mine with an empty belly or ever wanting for anything.'

'Just as long as you don't spoil her,' Carmen remarked. 'It's none of my business, but I do think you're too soft with the girl. *Spare the rod, spoil the child.*'

'I'm her nan, I'm allowed to spoil her.'

'And I won't have anyone spank my child!' Rachel said indignantly. 'Anyway, I'll take Cake for a quick walk and then I'll see about her new shoes. See you later.'

After walking Cake to the end of the street and back, Rachel popped the puppy back indoors and then headed to Clapham Junction. Martha held her hand and was chatting keenly about what shoes she wanted, and about Cake's wet nose and then she started jabbering on about the new ribbons that Carmen had given her. Rachel wasn't really paying much attention to her daughter. Instead, she was thinking about the pilotless bombs that had landed in Hackney, flattening a railway bridge and houses and leaving several people dead. She shuddered, terrified of the thought of Battersea coming under attack again. As it was, the borough bore the deep scars of the Blitz. So many families had lost their homes. Kids now played on the bombed ruins where houses had once proudly stood. The odd raid still occurred from time to time, but nothing like a few years ago when they'd endured the continual nightly bombing for months and months. Martha had been too young to remember it. But Rachel would never forget the fear. Or how they'd slept in their clothes, ready to flee to shelter. The fires, the damage and the death: it had felt like it was never going to end and now the thought of going through it all again left her feeling terrified and exhausted.

Martha's high-pitched squeal brought Rachel back to the moment.

'Nanna Hilda,' the girl called.

As Rachel looked across the street, she felt Martha's small hand yank free of her own. 'MARTHA!' she bellowed.

Rachel stood rooted to the spot in terror as she saw her daughter running towards the kerb.

Quickly glancing sideways, she spotted a car hurtling down the street in their direction. Fear for Martha's life spurred her into action and she reached out for the girl, but Martha had stepped into the road. Rachel dashed after her, praying that she'd be able to grab her to safety from the oncoming speeding car. As Rachel went to step off the kerb, her ankle went to one side and she stumbled before falling to the ground in a heap. Oblivious to the pain in her leg, she cried in panic, 'MARTHA!'

Scrambling back to her feet, Rachel noticed a dark man who had seemed to appear from nowhere. In one swift move, he scooped Martha from the road and carried her to the pavement. The car passed, its horn blaring. Martha began to cry. And then Rachel felt strong hands gently pulling her arms, helping her to stand. She looked to her side to see another dark-skinned man assisting her.

'Mummy … Mummy …' Martha whimpered.

Rachel reached out her arms to take her child from the exotic-looking stranger who had saved her daughter's life. But she winced as a sharp pain shot through her ankle.

'You're hurt, miss,' the man who had helped her to her feet said. 'Lean on me.'

She was grateful to take the weight off her swelling foot. And now Hilda had rushed across the street and was taking Martha from the other man's arms.

'Thank you. Thank you so much,' Hilda gushed. 'I don't know what would have happened if it weren't for you acting so quickly.'

'It was not'ing, ma'am.'

'It was very heroic!'

Martha buried her head into Hilda's shoulder, gently sobbing.

'I've a good mind to slap her legs,' Rachel said angrily.

'Don't tell her off, darling. She's upset enough as it is. That must have been an awful scare for her,' Hilda pleaded as she stroked the back of her granddaughter's head.

'She could have been killed!' Rachel spat, her panic turning to anger.

'But she wasn't.'

'Fine. You're right. But it was only thanks to these two kind gentlemen. I don't know what to say. I'm so grateful to you both.'

The man who had been holding Martha spoke. 'Is your leg OK?'

Rachel, still leaning on the other man's arm, placed her foot on the ground. 'Ouch,' she yelped. 'No, it's very painful.'

'Are you far from home?'

'Not too far.'

'Perhaps we can help you back?'

Rachel shot a desperate look to Hilda. Surely they could manage between themselves. But Hilda shook her head, saying, 'I think you're going to need help, sweetheart. I'll take Martha and you'll have to hop along with them.' Then she turned to the two men. 'I'm Hilda, Hilda Duff. And this is my daughter, Rachel, and my granddaughter, Martha.'

'Pleased to meet your acquaintance, ma'am. My name is Alberto King and my good friend there is Clinton. Now, don't you worry about a t'ing. We'll get you home.'

As Rachel hobbled along with Alberto on one side and leaning on Clinton's arm on the other, she was pleased to hear that Martha had stopped crying and was instead telling her nanna all about Cake. But then Rachel cringed when Martha asked loudly, 'Nanna, why are those men black like coal?'

'Shush, don't be rude,' Hilda hissed.

Alberto laughed. 'Martha can ask me anyt'ing she likes about my black skin,' he said. 'What would you like to know, little lady?'

'Why is your skin black?'

'Because I come from another country far, far away from England. Where I lived, the sun was always hot and shining. Everyone has black skin to protect them from burning.'

'What's the name of this country?' asked Hilda.

'British Honduras. It's in central America. It's on the other side of the world.'

'Are you with the American army?' Hilda asked.

'No, ma'am. Clinton and me were tree cutters and worked for the Forestry Commission. We volunteered to come to Scotland to fell trees. About nine hundred of us came across. Our unit was disbanded last year. Some were repatriated and went home, but we stayed. But it's cold in Scotland so we decided to move further down South.'

'Yes, Scotland is freezing. I was given three uniforms and used to wear them all at the same time, and I slept in them,' Clinton added.

Alberto laughed. '*Two coats Scotland, one coat London*. That's what we heard, so here we are!'

'You came all the way from British Honduras to Scotland to fell trees. What on earth for?' Rachel asked, astonished.

'The wood is needed to shore up your coal mines and for your houses that need rebuilding. Most of the Scottish lumberjacks are away fighting, but the country still needs wood and lots of it.'

'Does your skin feel the same as mine?' Martha piped up.

'Yes, little lady, touch,' Alberto replied softly, his voice deep. He held his hand to Martha, who stroked his palm.

'If I fall over and gwaze my knees, wed blood comes out. Is your blood wed too?'

'Oh yes, my blood is as red as a bus.'

'Can I feel your hair too?'

Alberto leaned down and Martha touched the top of his head.

'It's soft and curly,' she said with a smile.

'Thank you,' Rachel mouthed to Alberto.

'It's fine. She's curious. At least she isn't scared of us.'

'Scared?' Rachel asked, confused.

'Yes. When we first arrived in Scotland, many Scots had never seen black men before. They ran from the streets and into their homes, some were screaming.'

'Goodness! Well, we are quite familiar with seeing coloured men in London. There weren't many around before the war, mostly working at the docks, but there's an awful lot of American troops in town now.'

'And from what I've seen, they aren't always treated well by their fellow white soldiers,' Hilda mumbled with disgust.

Rachel knew all too well about the divisions between the black and white American GIs. She'd seen it first-hand in the pub. There had been a couple of occasions when the white American soldiers had demanded that the black troops be refused service and thrown out. But Winnie wouldn't stand for it. Unlike some public houses in London, she refused to put any signs up excluding blacks or Irish and welcomed everyone into the Battersea Tavern.

'This is home,' Rachel said, nodding her head towards the pub.

'It was nice meeting you, little lady,' Alberto said to Martha and held out his hand to shake hers.

'Aren't you coming in for a drink? On me. It's the least I can do,' Rachel offered.

'Thank you, but I don't think that's a good idea,' Clinton answered.

'Please come in and see my puppy,' Martha implored. 'His name is Cake.'

'Yes, come in,' Hilda parroted. 'We insist.'

Rachel saw Alberto and Clinton exchange a worried

24

glance. '*Everyone* is welcome in the Battersea Tavern,' she assured them.

The men nodded and Martha beamed with obvious delight. She took hold of Alberto's hand and almost dragged him through the door. Rachel hopped in, holding onto Clinton's arm.

When Winnie saw them, her eyes almost popped out of her head. 'Oh, blimey! What's happened to you?' she asked.

'I've twisted my ankle. This little madam ran out into the road and nearly got run over. I chased her, but I fell over. But, thankfully, Alberto and Clinton here saved the day.'

'Stone the crows! Well, thank you very much, gentlemen. What can I get you to drink? Anything you like, on the house. And I'll throw in a slice of pie with that too.'

'Would you mind helping Hilda to get me upstairs first?' Rachel asked Alberto.

'No problem. And I can say hello to Cake.'

Martha smiled up admiringly at Alberto. Rachel had never seen her daughter quite so enamoured with anyone. Luckily, Alberto seemed to be a patient man who had a kind way with children.

Upstairs, after raising Rachel's foot onto the sofa, Hilda said she'd put the kettle on. 'Would you like a cup of tea or would you prefer a drink downstairs?' she asked Alberto.

He had the puppy on his lap. Cake was excitedly licking Alberto's chin, which had Martha in fits of giggles. 'I'll have a cup of tea, t'ank you.'

'Take Cake with Nanna Hilda to the kitchen and give him some lunch, there's a good girl,' Rachel instructed.

Once alone, Alberto whispered, 'T'ank you for rescuing me from the killer pup.'

'I think my daughter and her puppy are rather taken by you.'

'She's a pretty little girl, just like her mother.'

Rachel felt herself blush. It had been a while since anyone had paid her a compliment.

'Her father ... is he away?' Alberto asked.

'Erm, no. She doesn't have a father.'

'Oh, I see. I'm sorry, it's none of my business. But does that mean that you don't have a man?'

Rachel had just rested her head back on a cushion but snapped it forward at Alberto's direct question. Her eyes stretched wide and she stuttered, 'I, erm, er, I ...'

'Would you like to be the queen to Alberto King?' he pushed with a cheeky glint in his eyes.

Rachel, astonished, wasn't sure how to answer. She hadn't looked at Alberto in *that* way. But now, studying his strong jaw and dark eyes, his smooth skin like chocolate and broad shoulders, she began to notice how attractive he was and butterflies flitted in her stomach. But she hadn't entertained the thought of a man since David had abused her and left her pregnant with Martha. In fact, she'd resigned herself to a life without one.

'I'd be honoured if you would consider allowing me to court you. I'm a simple man. I don't have jewels and furs to offer. But I will always be kind to you and your daughter and treat you both well.'

His polite manner threw Rachel and she inadvertently found herself nodding her head in agreement.

A wide smile spread across Alberto's face, revealing his brilliantly white teeth. 'You must rest now. Alberto King will come back tomorrow to see his queen.'

Alberto walked over to the sofa, took Rachel's hand and kissed the back of it. As he walked away, Martha came skipping into the room, with Hilda following.

'You off? You haven't had your tea yet.'

'I will be returning soon,' he answered, before looking over his shoulder and slowly winking at Rachel.

'Oh, righto. I'll see you out,' Hilda said.

She walked Alberto to the top of the stairs and then rushed back into the front room.

'What was all that about?' she asked.

Rachel told Martha to take Cake to her bedroom. Once the girl had gone, she said to Hilda, 'I can't believe what I've just done ... I think I've agreed to be his girlfriend.'

'Really? Do you like him then?'

'Yes, I do. He's ... I don't know, he's ... different. The way he speaks, his dark eyes, his skin. I suppose I got a bit caught up in the moment. But he's so dishy!'

'He is, but have you considered the problems that you're bound to encounter?'

'What do you mean?' Rachel asked.

'His colour, Rachel. People round here can be ever so prejudiced.'

'Ha, is that all? I'm not worried about that. I've had to listen to gossip and whispers since the day Martha was born. I know what people say: I'm labelled a slut and my child a bastard. But it's helped me to develop a thick skin, so I'm not in the least bit bothered about what they might say about me and Alberto.'

'Well, it's your lookout. And you know that I'll support you.'

'Thanks.'

'I must say, I'm a tad surprised. I was beginning to think that you'd given up on men.'

'Not half as surprised as me! This was the last thing that I was expecting. Oh, gawd, I hope I haven't made a mistake and rushed into this. What do you think? You could chase after him and tell him that I've changed my mind.'

'You like him, don't you?'

'Yes, I think so.'

'Then give him a chance. You've nothing to lose.'

Rachel thought for a moment. Her reputation was already in tatters. No decent man in Battersea would court her. And it wasn't as if she'd said she would marry Alberto. It was only a date. 'No, I've nothing to lose.'

'There you go then, there's no need for me to go running after him. Right, now that's settled, I'd better get going. I've got a mountain of sewing repairs to do for the army and then I'm on fire watch duties tonight. Will you be all right on your own?'

'Yes. Winnie and Carmen will be up soon.'

'All right, sweetheart. I'll drop in and check on you to-morrow. Make sure you rest that leg.'

Once alone, Rachel rested her head back again and closed her eyes. She ignored the pain from her throbbing ankle and pictured Alberto's dreamy face. She had a boyfriend! After all these years, she'd finally dropped her guard and agreed to date a man. But although Alberto didn't yet know it, they would be taking things very slowly, very slowly indeed.

Clinton had almost finished his drink and wondered what was keeping Alberto. His friend was only supposed to be helping Rachel up the stairs.

'I'm ashamed to admit that I've no idea where British Honduras is,' Mrs Berry said. 'Show me on here,' she added, spreading a global paper map across the countertop of the bar.

Clinton studied the countries and then placed his finger in the centre of his homeland.

Mrs Berry took a moment to look. 'Blimey, next door to Mexico, that's miles away. Mind you, there's been times when I wish that I could leave here and start a new life somewhere else. Not halfway round the world though! How did you get here?' she asked.

'It was a long journey. We had to travel to New Orleans by boat and then on to New York. From there, we were in the bottom cabins of a big boat that took us to Scotland. I spent two weeks praying to the Lord that we'd make it across the Atlantic without being torpedoed by German U-boats.'

'It was ever so brave of you to volunteer to join our war effort.'

'It's our war effort too, Mrs Berry. British Honduras is a crown colony and we don't like the idea of our motherland being harmed.'

'Good for you. What will you do now that you're in Battersea?'

'Find lodgings and work. We have fine references and we're honest men,' Clinton said, though he wasn't telling the entire truth.

'There's a nice, clean house on the Westbridge Road. Mrs Crosbie runs it. I'll write you a note of recommendation.'

'I'd really appreciate that, t'ank you. We weren't sure how men with our skin colour would fare in London, so we're grateful for any help.'

'No problem, love.'

Alberto finally came back downstairs, but when Clinton saw the smug look on his friend's face, his heart sank.

'Is Rachel all right?' Mrs Berry asked.

'Yes, she's resting.'

'Thanks for what you did today. I'll get you a drink and that slice of pie.'

Mrs Berry walked away and Clinton leaned in towards Alberto. 'What are you playing at?' he asked in a whisper.

'What?'

'Don't pretend to be innocent. You've been upstairs trying to charm Rachel, haven't you?'

Alberto smiled, which told Clinton all he needed to know.

'We're supposed to be keeping our heads down. We agreed, no women. If we get caught—'

'Calm down, Clinton. We're not going to get caught,' Alberto answered, waving his hand dismissively.

'What about Rachel?'

'What about her? She couldn't resist my good looks. I had to ask her out.'

'You didn't *have* to do anyt'ing.'

'Look, I'm just dating her, that's all. She's a beautiful woman and you know I have a weakness for a pretty face.'

'Yes, and look at the trouble that's caused. Just don't get too close to her. We don't want anyone to find out about—'

Again, Alberto interrupted. 'I know. Take it easy, Clinton. There's no need for Rachel or anyone else to ever know.'

Mrs Berry came back with a slice of pie for them both. She refilled Clinton's glass and placed a drink on the counter for Alberto.

Clinton held his glass aloft. 'To new friends,' he said and clinked glasses with Alberto.

'To new friends,' Alberto parroted and flashed a smile at Mrs Berry.

Clinton thought that they could be on to a good thing in Battersea. Mrs Berry had already offered to help them secure accommodation. The man on the newspaper stand at Clapham Junction train station had said there were plans to regenerate large areas of London and much of the borough would need new housing built. It seemed that finding work wouldn't be a problem – just as long as the colour of their skin didn't prove to be an issue. Battersea appeared to offer opportunities. But they had to be careful and keep up their guard. The last thing Clinton wanted was for their murky past to catch up with them and ruin everything.

3

Len scowled at the sight of Brancher swanning into the pub. 'This your idea of looking for a job, is it?'

'Give a bloke a break, Len. I've been traipsing the streets all day. Me feet are killing me.'

'All day? It's only bleedin' lunchtime.'

'Yeah, I know, and after lunch, I'm going to try me luck in the factories along York Road.'

'You do that.'

'I've never fancied working in a factory, but beggars can't be choosers.'

'That's right, they can't. I suppose you want a drink?'

'Thanks, Len, I wouldn't say no.'

Len tapped a coin on the counter to get Winnie's attention. 'Get him a … erm … er …'

'Half please, Mrs Berry,' Brancher said, finishing off Len's sentence.

Len grimaced, feeling frustrated with himself. He'd found himself struggling with words more and more lately and supposed it went hand in hand with his lapses in memory. But even simple everyday tasks were becoming challenging.

Yesterday, he'd forgotten how to turn on the kitchen tap and then he'd got himself in a state over his shirt buttons. Not to mention the worrying event last week when he'd gone to make Renee a cup of tea. He had no idea how it had happened, but he'd turned on the gas and hadn't lit it. By the time his foggy mind had cleared, the kitchen had stunk and he'd had to open the windows to freshen the air.

As Winnie went to one of the pumps, Brancher stepped closer to Len. 'Who are them darkies down there?' he asked, nodding his head towards the other end of the bar and glaring menacingly at the men.

Brancher may have thought that he'd whispered his enquiry to Len, but there hadn't been anything hushed about his voice.

Winnie placed his drink on the counter and with a stern face, she said slowly, 'They are *my* customers and *my* guests. Alberto and Clinton are new to the area. How about you show them a bit of Battersea hospitality, eh?'

Brancher puffed out his chest and had a look on his face like he was chewing a wasp.

Len scowled at him. 'Wind your neck in. They've done more for this country than you ever have. You oughta be over their thanking 'em and shaking their hands.'

'No chance. You don't know where their hands have been, dirty bastards. They wouldn't allow 'em in my local pub in Wandsworth. Good job an' all.'

'Oi, you can pack that in right now or you'll be out that door with my foot up your backside!' Winnie barked. 'I won't have talk like that in my pub, Brancher Fanning.'

'I've known you for years yet you'd throw me out over a couple of darkies? That ain't on,' Brancher huffed.

'My pub, my rules. If you don't like it, then sling your bleedin' hook.'

'You won't be missed,' Len added.

'All right, I'll keep my opinions to myself. But I'm warning you, Mrs Berry, you'll lose customers if you start letting their sort in here.'

'Right, that's it. OUT! Go on, get out of my pub and don't come back until you've learned some civility.'

'What? What did I say?'

'You heard,' Len spat. 'Off you trot.'

Brancher gulped down his beer and slammed his glass down on the counter. 'It's a bloody disgrace when a man can't drink in his own local without having to look at a couple of stinking negroes,' he growled, and then stamped out of the pub.

Winnie folded her arms across her chest. 'Well, I'd have expected better from him,' she said, sounding disappointed.

Len looked at the woman, his mind blank. *Expect better of who?* he thought.

'When you get home, you can tell Brancher that I shall be wanting an apology from him.'

Home ... where was home? And Brancher ... what was Brancher doing at his home? Apology for what? Len's mind whirled and he found himself feeling nauseous. What was going on? He was in the Battersea Tavern, he knew that. And Winnie Berry was talking to him, he knew that too. But what was the woman talking about? It made no sense. Home. For the life of him, he couldn't think where home was. Fear gripped him as bile rose, burning at the back of his throat. His heart began pounding so fast in panic that he could hear the blood rushing in his ears.

'Are you all right, Len? You look as white as a sheet.'

'Yeah … er … I ain't feeling too clever.'

'Come with me,' Winnie said as she hurried around from behind the bar. She ushered Len into her small kitchen, urging him to take a seat. 'I'll put the kettle on.'

'There's no need to go to any bother.'

'It's no bother, love.'

Winnie filled the kettle and put it on the gas to boil. Len's brow furrowed as he tried to make sense of the situation.

Minutes later, Winnie handed him a cup of tea. 'The colour is coming back into your cheeks. Are you feeling a little better?' she asked.

Len gratefully accepted the drink and took a few sips. Then he remembered and it all became clear. He'd had another one of his episodes. They seemed to be coming more frequently. He slowly began to put the fragmented pieces in his mind back together. 'I'm feeling much better, thanks, Win.'

'Good. You sit there for as long as you need. I've got to get back to the bar. Carmen isn't working today.'

'Yeah, of course. I'll head home. I'm fine now.'

But Len wasn't fine. And he was worried that he'd forget where his home was again. This wouldn't do. He couldn't allow his muddled mind to get the better of him or affect his confidence. One way or another, he'd try his best to carry on as normal. But he wasn't sure if he'd be able to hide the truth about his deteriorating illness for much longer.

Maureen read the letter from her brother aloud to her gran for the fourth time that day. And Stephen's words had the same effect on her gran each time. She would smile through her tears, say how proud she was of Stephen and how much she missed him, and then she would close her eyes and ask God to keep him safe.

'I wonder what it's *really* like to be in the jungle,' Maureen mused.

'Well, according to your brother, it's hot and humid and there's spiders bigger than your hand! I wouldn't fancy that.'

'No, me neither, Gran. It's strange to think of Stephen on the other side of the world in Burma. I suppose it's the middle of the night there now.'

'Maybe. If the sun is out here, it can't be shining there too. I just wish this war would end so that our Stephen could come home.'

'Yes, me too, Gran.'

Maureen looked towards the front-room window and saw Brancher walking past. Her pulse quickened, not because she was excited at the sight of her husband but because she feared humiliation. She jumped to her feet and dashed into the passageway, hoping that Brancher would be in a good mood. When he came through the front door, Maureen's body tensed at the sight of his surly face.

'Hello. You're home early. Cup of tea?' she asked nervously.

'Don't you start, woman. I've had enough of your granddad watching my timekeeping.'

'Come into the kitchen, I'll put the kettle on and make you a sandwich,' she coaxed, wanting to get him out of earshot of her gran.

Once in the kitchen, she quietly closed the door. Maureen filled the kettle and then thinly buttered two slices of bread.

'We've had a letter from Stephen,' she said, trying to lighten Brancher's mood.

'The *hero, our Stephen*. Just because your brother is fighting in Burma, it don't make him special,' Brancher spat sourly.

'I know, I was just saying.'

'Well, don't. I couldn't give two hoots about your brother. Him and your granddad have always looked down their noses at me. And what was Stephen doing before he got drafted, eh? He was nothing but a labourer, the same as me.'

'Actually, he was a site foreman,' Maureen muttered under her breath.

'What did you say?'

'Nothing. I was just moaning about the lack of butter.'

Brancher pulled out two seats at the table, one to sit on and the other to rest his booted feet on. Maureen wanted to remind him that her granddad didn't like him using the chairs as a footrest, but she kept her mouth shut and instead asked, 'Macon all right for you?'

'Not that fried mutton again. It's all fat and nothing like real bacon.'

'It's not too bad with a bit of salad cream.'

'No, I'll have cheese.'

'But there's only a tiny bit of cheese left in the larder. I'd better not use the last of it.'

'First come, first serve. Your granddad can have the Macon.'

Maureen's jaw clenched and she gritted her teeth as she reluctantly fetched the cheese from the larder. If her gran or granddad asked about it, she'd fib and say that she ate it.

Brancher tucked into his sandwich and spoke with his mouth full. 'That Mrs Berry in the Battersea Tavern is allowing coloured blokes in her pub. And your granddad don't seem to mind. He was quite happy to have a drink with two darkies in there.'

Maureen didn't respond. She wasn't sure what to say. She didn't see the problem with men of colour drinking in the pub. She'd heard about the segregation in America and how the black and white soldiers were treated differently. But it made no sense to her. After all, they were all fighting the same war. Surely it was the Jerries and the Japs who were the enemy, not the coloured folk from America.

Brancher finished his lunch and slurped back his tea. He belched loudly and then banged his feet down heavily on the floor. 'Right, that's me done. I'll see you later,' he said. He walked across the kitchen and kissed Maureen on the cheek. 'I'm gonna try me luck at the factories.'

'Good luck,' Maureen called after him.

The front door closed and she finally relaxed as the tension left her body. Thankfully, her husband hadn't been too confrontational.

Maureen went back into the front room with a smile on her face.

'Has he gone off again to look for work?' her gran asked.

'Yes. He's going to try at the factories.'

'At least he's trying, I suppose. What *really* happened in Wandsworth?' Maureen could feel her gran's eyes boring into her. She knew it would be pointless to fib. Her gran would see right through her lies. She grabbed a piece of her hair and began winding it around her finger.

'There's no need to worry, pet. Whatever you tell me will be strictly between us.'

A tear slipped from Maureen's eye, but she didn't try to wipe it away or hide it. And once the first tear fell, more followed until she found herself bawling. 'Oh, Gran, it's been awful,' she cried.

'I knew it. I knew you weren't happy. You used to be so gay and carefree. Now you're like a little mouse who's scared of her own shadow. What's that man done to you?'

Maureen sniffed and drew in a juddering breath. 'It's not all his fault,' she said.

They heard the front door open.

'Quick. Go and wash your face. Don't let your granddad see you upset. We'll talk later.'

Maureen fled through to the kitchen just in the nick of time. She splashed cold water on her face and then blew her snotty nose into her hanky. She hadn't expected to react like that in front of her gran, but once she'd allowed herself to cry, it had been like the floodgates had opened. Now she was regretting revealing her sadness to her gran. Renee wouldn't let the matter drop and Maureen knew she'd have to tell her everything. But the shame of it burned deep inside. God, she wished she'd kept her feelings to herself. But most of all, she wished she'd never married Brancher Fanning.

4

On Wednesday morning, Winnie was pleasantly surprised when Rachel walked into the kitchen. 'I didn't expect to see you up and about,' she said.

'My ankle feels as good as new.'

'Pleased to hear it. Is Martha still sleeping?' Winnie asked.

'Yes, she's out for the count and so is Cake. They look adorable cuddled up together.'

'I thought you said that Cake isn't allowed in Martha's bed.'

'He wasn't in her bed. Martha must have got up in the night and crawled into Cake's. I didn't have the heart to move her, so I threw a blanket over the pair of them.'

'Aw, bless her. I bet that was a bit of a squash, but she loves that pup.'

'Good morning,' Carmen chirped.

Winnie smiled. 'Morning, love. You sound perky.'

'I am. After those rockets the other morning, I thought we'd all be sheltering in the cellar last night. Instead it was nice to get a good night's kip without hearing Moaning Minnie wailing her head off.'

'Hmm, I hate to say this, but don't get too comfy in your

40

beds. I've no doubt that there will be more of those bombs coming our way soon,' Winnie warned. She didn't like to put a dampener on Carmen's mood, but they had to be realistic.

'I know,' Carmen sighed, shrugging. 'But it's good to make the most of the peace while it lasts. I can see I'm not the only one in a good mood this morning.'

Winnie followed Carmen's gaze and saw that Rachel was sat at the table, daydreaming into her cup of tea with a soppy grin on her face. 'Three guesses what she's looking so happy about.'

'That'll be Alberto King,' Carmen answered. She sat beside Rachel and nudged her arm. 'Oi, we're talking about you.'

'Eh?' Rachel said, looking up.

'Thinking about Alberto, was you?' Carmen teased.

Rachel flushed pink.

'He's dark and mysterious. I can see the attraction.'

'Can you? You don't think I'm mad?' Rachel asked.

'No, not at all. If I were twenty years younger, we could have double-dated with Alberto's friend.'

'You'd have had to get through me first,' Winnie said with a chortle.

Rachel's eyes lit up. 'Really? You both would have dated a coloured man?'

'I don't see why not. Let's face it, my Brian was an 'orrible bloke and Carmen's husband weren't any better. He led her a right merry dance. At the end of the day, love, the colour of a man's skin isn't a measure of the man,' Winnie replied.

'Winnie's right. It's what's inside that counts. If Alberto is good to you, it doesn't matter if he's black, brown, yellow or green with purple spots. Having said that, I'm sure there will be people queuing up to give you their spiteful views on the matter.'

'But that sort of gossip has never bothered Rachel, has it, love?'

Rachel sat bolt upright and folded her arms. With a determined look, she answered boldly, 'I'm past caring about what other people think.'

'Good,' Carmen said. 'But don't let him take any liberties with you. You're an unmarried mother, so he might be of the opinion that you're a loose woman.'

'If that's what he thinks, he'll be in for a shock. Just because I have Martha but no husband that doesn't mean I don't have any morals.'

'And you make sure you stick to them,' Winnie reminded her.

'I will.'

'Any idea where he'll be taking you today?' Carmen asked.

'No, none. I might suggest a walk in the park. It's a glorious day. Cake will enjoy the exercise and Martha loves the big barrage balloon.'

'That's a smashing idea. Fresh air doesn't cost anything either.'

'I'll leave you two to have a natter,' Winnie said. 'I'm just popping to the corner shop for a new mop head. I'm hoping to beat the queues.'

'Please don't buy Martha any more sweets, Win. I found two sticky boiled sweets in her dress pocket yesterday, covered in fluff.'

'All right, if you say so. But it won't feel right to leave the shop without a bag of goodies for my granddaughter.

Mr Coggins always keeps a few aside for me. He don't half charge a fortune for them though. Mind you, I suppose I'm lucky to get my hands on any sweets at all.'

Just twenty minutes later, as Winnie walked to the shop, she found that her thoughts had drifted back to worries of impending air strikes from the enemy. She understood why Rachel refused to send Martha away to safety, but every night and day spent in London was a gamble with their lives. Battersea was her home, and the pub and her customers meant a great deal to Winnie, but she wondered if her and her family would be better off upping sticks and heading to somewhere that wasn't Hitler's target. Moving out of London had seemed an almost inconceivable thought, something that Winnie had never before considered, but now she was willing to give it some serious thought. And the more she thought about it, the more the idea appealed.

The bell rang above the door of the corner shop when Winnie ambled in. 'Good morning, Mr Coggins,' she greeted. 'I'm looking for a new mop head.'

'Good morning, Mrs Berry. I've several over here,' he replied and showed Winnie to a large wicker basket in the corner. 'I've got some broom heads in too. I've not been able to get any new ones for a while. I can do you a special price for a mop and broom head together?'

'Go on then, I'm sure my old broom could do with one. I don't suppose you have any paint for the bath? Our line has worn off, so I need to paint on a new one. If I don't indicate what five inches of water looks like, Rachel will fill it right up.'

'We can't have that, Mrs Berry. Even the bathtubs in

Buckingham Palace have the five-inch water mark painted on. It's important that we conserve our coal and not waste it heating water gratuitously. I don't have any paint for sale, but I have half a tub in my shed. I'll drop it in to you this evening.'

'Thank you, Mr Coggins, that would be very much appreciated. And how is Mrs Coggins?' Winnie asked. She wasn't fooled by his generous offer. She knew full well that Mr Coggins had a fancy for Carmen. The man seemed to find any excuse he could to call into the pub and Winnie was sure it was just so that he could leer at her friend.

'She's well, thank you. You'll find her in the kitchen experimenting with a recipe that she heard on the wireless on the Kitchen Front broadcast. Would you like to see her?'

'No, but please pass on my regards.'

'Will this be it for today? No sweets for Martha?' Mr Coggins pointed to the sweet jars behind him, all empty except one that had a measly few toffees at the bottom.

'No, not today.'

'Can I interest you in a carrot stick for the girl? With the lack of sweets, I'm finding that these sticks are a good replacement for the children.'

Winnie surveyed the carrots on lolly sticks. They didn't look very appealing, though a carrot stick might appease Rachel's request of no sweets for Martha. And Winnie had to admit that during these times, buying sweets for her granddaughter was very indulgent, especially as Mr Coggins' prices were extortionate. But, just like many food items, sweets were hard to come by. *Damn this war*, thought Winnie, pursing her lips. 'Go on then, just the one carrot stick,' she said.

Winnie heard the bell above the door ring and she glanced over her shoulder, pleased to see Len walking in.

'Hello, love,' she said with a smile.

Len frowned and seemed to look straight through her.

'Are you all right?' Winnie asked.

He didn't answer. His eyes began to dart around the shop and he looked quite frantic.

'Len ... Len ... What's wrong?' Winnie placed her shopping basket on the floor beside her and reached for his hand.

He was quick to pull back from her and Winnie saw a look of fear in his rheumy eyes.

'What is it, Len? What's bothering you?' she gently asked.

Len spun around. Then back the other way. He seemed to be in a panic. Winnie went to reach out to him again, but he turned and fled out of the door.

'Keep my things,' Winnie called to Mr Coggins as she ran from the shop in Len's wake.

Outside, she looked up and down the street before spotting Len on the other side of the road. She found it distressing to see the man huddled on the ground against a wall with his arms wrapped over his head. Winnie hurried over and crouched beside him.

'Tell me what's wrong, Len. I can't help you if I don't know.'

He looked at her and slowly unwound his arms from over his head. 'Who are you?' he asked.

Winnie tried to hide her shock. 'I'm Winnie. Winnie Berry, the landlady of the Battersea Tavern.'

'Do I know you?'

'Yes, love. Do you know who you are?'

Len went quiet and frowned as he thought. He eventually nodded.

'Good. Shall I help you to get home?'

Again, Len nodded.

'Come on then,' Winnie said, holding out her arm for Len to take.

As he stood up, Winnie felt engulfed in sadness. Poor Len had lost his mind. She'd seen it happen to other men. Mostly when they'd returned from the trenches of the Great War. Shell shock, they called it. Men rendered unable to walk or talk, living in a constant state of fear, their minds turned to mush. And she'd also heard about the institutions that were full of people who'd gone mad. When she'd been a young woman, the stories of the lunatics in the asylums had been rife. She assumed that this was what was happening to Len.

They hadn't taken more than a few steps when the man stiffened and stopped walking. 'Winnie, what … where …'

'It's all right, love. You had a bit of a funny turn. I'm just helping you home.'

Len immediately let go of Winnie's arm. 'I'm quite all right, thank you very much. I don't need any help.'

Winnie was delighted to see that he was acting and sounding more like his old miserable self, but she was still profoundly concerned about him. 'It's no bother,' she said.

He looked at her suspiciously and took a deep breath. 'What happened?'

'You came into the corner shop and seemed a bit confused. I don't think you recognised me. Or yourself.'

Len hung his head. 'Please, keep this to yourself, Win.'

'This isn't the first time, is it?'

He slowly shook his head.

'Oh, Len, you have to tell Renee.'

'No. She mustn't know.'

'But you need help.'

'I'm fine.'

'You're not. What if I hadn't been in the shop when you came in? Anything could have happened to you.'

'I don't want Renee or anyone else finding out. It's my business and I'd like to keep it that way,' he said, sharply.

Winnie sighed, frustrated. But Len was right, it was his business and nothing to do with her. 'All right, have it your way. But I'm not happy about this.'

'I'm going to get my paper. I'll see you later.'

Len turned and headed back to the shop, leaving Winnie stood in the street and shaking her head at the stubborn old man. He was too proud to admit that he had a problem. But he'd made his feelings more than clear and there was nothing that she could do. Yet she'd known Len for donkey's years, so maybe she could have a chat with him later and try to persuade him to change his mind about telling Renee. Though she had a feeling that she'd be wasting her breath.

With a heavy heart, Winnie trudged back to the shop too. She had a carrot stick in her basket and couldn't wait to see the peculiar look that Martha was likely to give it.

Clinton pulled on his shirt over his vest and looked daggers at Alberto. He couldn't believe that his friend would risk ruining their new life in London. 'I still t'ink that you should call it off with Rachel,' he urged.

Alberto was sat on the edge of his single bed. He leapt to his feet with an angry look in his eyes. 'Stop going on about it! I'm doing no harm.'

Clinton walked over to the window and peered down onto the street. He'd been pleasantly surprised to find that the house and room recommended by Mrs Berry was more comfortable than he'd expected it to be. They each had their own bed with clean linen, a bathroom in the house with running hot water and the promise of a cooked meal every evening. It felt luxurious in comparison to their accommodation in Scotland. And today, to top it all, they hoped to find jobs. Yet Alberto was willing to throw it all away. 'Have you thought about the consequences of what might happen if we mess this up?'

'I'm only taking the woman out. I won't be telling her our life stories. Stop worrying, man. I won't tell her anyt'ing that could link us back to what happened in Scotland.'

'But she's a woman and you know what women are like. She'll want to know everyt'ing about you. I know you, Alberto, you run your mouth off without t'inking about what you're saying. You could slip up. You might say somet'ing to arouse her suspicions.'

'For God's sake, you worry like an old woman! Enough now!'

Clinton knew that there'd be no changing Alberto's mind, so he reluctantly dropped the subject. He could only hope that his friend wouldn't reveal their secrets.

Later that morning, after a few hours of tramping from factory to factory and inquiring for work at every building site and warehouse, Clinton had become disheartened at their fruitless search. 'This is useless,' he moaned. 'With so many men away fighting, you'd t'ink that there would be plenty of jobs going.'

48

'There probably is, but not for men with black skin,' Alberto answered. 'Come on, I've had enough for today. I t'ink I'm ready for the welcoming hospitality of Mrs Berry.'

'You mean, Rachel.'

'I can't deny it: Rachel will put a smile on my face.'

They started towards the Battersea Tavern, Clinton with a heavy heart, but he noticed that Alberto had a skip in his gait. They'd been the best of friends for years, but Alberto's carefree ways and lack of responsibility irked Clinton. His heart dropped even further when they rounded a corner and came face to face with the man who'd been thrown out of the pub yesterday. Clinton braced himself, expecting trouble.

When Brancher saw them, a thunderous look came over his face and he snarled in their direction. But Brancher had a woman walking by his side. A pretty young lady, plain but with huge doe eyes that set on Clinton. If she hadn't been with the menacing man, he would have offered her a smile.

Brancher expanded his chest and his chin jutted forward. As he stamped towards them, he seemed to be taking up all the pavement. The woman lowered her eyes and walked just behind him, scurrying to keep up with his pace.

Clinton and Alberto stepped to one side, allowing Brancher to pass. But Clinton was disappointed when Brancher stopped right in front of them and eyed them up and down with contempt.

'You shouldn't be allowed on our streets,' Brancher growled.

Clinton kept his head down. He'd come to London for a fresh start and a new life, not for trouble.

The man spat on the ground at Clinton's feet. 'Sod off back to your own country. We don't want your sort 'ere.'

Clinton didn't react, but he saw that Alberto's fists were clenched at his side.

Brancher stepped closer towards him, so close that Clinton could smell the stale tobacco on his breath. 'Dirty gits,' the man hissed. Then he turned to the woman, saying, 'Come on. We don't want to be near 'em for too long. They stink.'

When Brancher marched on with his woman following, Clinton let out a sigh of relief.

'What's his problem?' Alberto spat angrily.

'Leave it. He's not the first and he won't be the last.'

Clinton glanced over his shoulder. As the man walked away, he appeared to be having a go at the woman. She looked back, briefly catching Clinton's eye before snapping her head forward again. In those couple of seconds, Clinton had seen fear in her eyes and felt sorry for her. He'd encountered men like Brancher before and knew that they were bullies. He suspected that the woman led a miserable life, controlled by her husband, too afraid to answer back, just like Clinton's mother had been. It had been a blessing when his father had died. Finally, his mother had her freedom and had been released from the constraints of oppression. But the man's death had left the family in poverty. Clinton did what he could to financially support his mother and two sisters, even breaking the law when he had to.

His heart hammered. The worry of the police catching up with him was never far from his mind, neither was the dreaded thought of being locked away in a British prison.

'They're taking liberties, them two; walking round Battersea like they own the place. Blacks, Jews, Irish and Gypsies, filthy, the lot of 'em. Thieving scum,' Brancher ranted.

Maureen's short legs had to almost run to keep up with him. She dared not lag behind her husband, not when he was in one of his dark moods. As it was, he was already shouting and she didn't want to give him cause to become even angrier.

'I'm warning you, Maureen. You'd better not have anything to do with them darkies. If I hear about you talking to 'em in the pub, there'll be trouble. Have you got that?'

'Yes, Brancher,' Maureen answered flatly. She thought it was a good job that he hadn't noticed her looking back at the black man. Christ almighty, Brancher would have done his nut if he'd seen her! Yet she hadn't been able to stop herself from stealing a glance; the man had been so mesmerising.

'And another thing, watch what you wear in the pub. I won't stand for any of Mrs Berry's customers leering at you.'

'Yes, Brancher,' Maureen repeated. Though she had no idea what clothes she had in her wardrobe that Brancher would consider to be unsuitable for her new job in the Battersea Tavern. All of her outfits were plain and sensible, just how Brancher liked them to be. She didn't possess anything that could be interpreted as racy.

'Don't tell your granddad how much you're earning. It's none of his business and I don't want to be coughing up more than we have to for our keep.'

'Yes, Brancher,' she said again.

'Good. Now go home and get my lunch ready. I'll be back in an hour.'

Maureen didn't ask Brancher where he was going, but she doubted that it would be to look for work. He'd have no urgency to be in employment, not now that she had a position in the pub.

Mrs Berry had seemed reluctant to agree to Brancher's proposal at first, but he'd soon convinced her that she'd get twice as much work out of Maureen for what she was paying. He'd persuaded the woman to take Maureen on a trial basis. They'd agreed an arrangement where Maureen would clean the pub three mornings a week and do two shifts behind the bar. But Brancher had had to apologise to Mrs Berry for being gobby in her pub the day before, and having to say sorry had set off his bad mood.

Indoors, Maureen found her gran with her feet up on the pouf.

'Hello, pet. Any luck finding work?'

'Yes. I'm going to be doing the cleaning in the Battersea Tavern, and a couple of lunch times behind the bar.'

'Really? Well, I'll be blown. There's three women in that pub so I'm surprised that Winnie would want a cleaner.'

'To be honest, Gran, I'm not convinced that she does, but Brancher managed to talk her round. I start tomorrow morning. I won't get paid for a week so, erm, I was wondering…'

'What, pet?'

'Do you think that you could lend me some money, please? Just a few bob to tide me over,' Maureen asked sheepishly. She hated to ask, but, with empty coffers, she had no choice. 'I'll pay you back as soon as I get my first wage packet.'

'I'll have a word with your granddad, but I think he'll agree that we can stretch to a few bob and we won't want the money back. A little treat.'

'Thanks, Gran, but I'd like to pay—'

'Your granddad should be home soon. He can give you a bit from our savings and I don't want to hear another word about it.'

Grateful tears welled in Maureen's eyes. 'Thank you. Thank you so much,' she gushed.

'Go and pour us both a cuppa and then we can finish off that conversation we started yesterday.'

'What conversation?'

'The one where you was about to tell me why you're so unhappy.'

'Oh, that. It was nothing, Gran,' Maureen fibbed. 'I was just upset because we'd lost our home and Brancher had lost his job. But things are looking up, I feel better now.'

Her gran looked at her suspiciously with narrowed eyes. Maureen knew that the woman didn't believe her. But before her gran could question her further, Maureen made a hasty retreat to the kitchen.

As she took the knitted tea cosy off the teapot and held her hand against it to feel if it was still warm, she fought to stop herself from bawling. The tears of joy that had pricked her eyes just moments earlier had now turned to tears of sorrow. She couldn't possibly pour her heart out to her gran and tell her what had been happening in Wandsworth. It was far too painful to say out loud and she'd rather keep her shame to herself.

5

Rachel brushed away an ant that was crawling up her leg. 'I don't like insects,' she said to Alberto.

'Would you rather we find a bench to sit on?'

'No, this patch of grass is fine and Martha likes it here. She loves looking at the pigs. The pig farm, the allotments, the shelters, they're all new additions to the park. Before the war, this was all grassed. It's changed so much; I hardly recognise the place.'

Another ant crawled over Rachel's leg, which Alberto flicked off. 'The ants are tiny in England.'

'Are they much bigger in Honduras?'

'Oh, yes. Huge. And big spiders too.'

'Do you miss home?'

Alberto looked thoughtful. 'Sometimes.'

'What do you miss?'

'The sun,' he answered with a laugh.

'What about your family?'

'I don't have a family. They were all killed.'

'Oh, Alberto, I'm so sorry.'

'It was a long time ago, nearly thirteen years. September

1931. I'll never forget that day, I still remember it like it was yesterday.'

'Do you mind me asking what happened?'

'Mother nature at her fiercest. She took away my brothers, my sisters and my mother and father.' A far-off look came over Alberto's face as he explained, 'It started off as a wonderful day. Everyone was happy, we were going out to join the celebrations of the Battle of St. George's Caye. We were looking forward to the parade and the marching band. My mother and my father had dressed us in our finest clothes, but my trousers were patched over the knees and hung four inches higher than my ankles. We were a poor family but rich in love. I was the eldest at seventeen and I had five brothers and two sisters. They were all hopping with excitement, man, it was so good to see. We stood with the crowds on the streets, but then the rain came. I tell you, it was *heavy* rain. But it would stop and then start again until the winds came too. We heard that the parade had been cancelled and that a hurricane was on its way. So, my mother and my father ushered us inside a large, wooden church. We sat in there huddled together for an hour or two as the hurricane tore through the town. The building rattled and shook. My sisters were crying, but my mother sang to them. She was a resilient woman, though she must have been scared to death too. Then, just before the storm died down, part of the church roof was blown away. I remember looking up and being petrified ... Rachel, that wind was so strong, I thought it would suck me right out through the roof!'

Rachel could imagine how terrifying it must have been. She'd felt the same when bombs had landed nearby and rattled the cellar of the pub.

'Once the wind had stopped, my father told my mother to stay in the church with the children while he took me outside to see the damage and what we could do to help. I couldn't believe my eyes! Buildings had collapsed, many had roofs missing. The street was littered with debris. We helped as many people as we could, some with wounds, and led them to the church, where my mother and some of the other women were ripping their skirts to use as bandages. Back outside, further up the street, a man was screaming for help. His son was trapped under a fallen tree. We rushed to help, but then the ground began to shake. I could feel it vibrating right through my body, from my toes up to my head. And then there was a low, rumbling noise, getting louder and coming closer. I didn't understand what was happening. My father told me to run. *Run as fast as you can*, he yelled, but I just stood there ... until I saw the water. It looked like a small wave at first, coming straight towards me. As it came nearer, I realised what it was: a tidal wave was about to engulf me. Man, I ran then. I ran as fast as my legs would carry me. But you can't outrun the sea. I saw my father being taken away. There was nothing I could do to save him. The look on his face: he knew that he was going to die.'

Rachel gulped. 'How did you save yourself?' she asked.

'I climbed a tree and held on for dear life, praying that the roots would stay in the ground. As the water rushed in, all sorts of things passed me by, bodies too. I don't know how long I was in that tree for. I just wanted to get back to the church to be with my family. But eventually, when I did return, they were all dead. Everyone in the church had been killed, swallowed by mud or drowned. I'd sent people to that church for shelter. It took me a long time to come to terms with that. But thousands were killed that day. It turned my stomach to see the vultures in the trees, sitting there, waiting. I was offered money to collect the dead, a few cents a body. It was a terrible job, but I had no money, and so I did it. The next day, I was stood in line for food rations and realised that there was nothing in the town for me. I left. Just walked away and never looked back. I ended up meeting Clinton. He was a lumberjack and got me a job felling trees too. That day changed my life.'

'How?'

'It brought me here, to you,' Alberto smiled.

Their eyes locked and Rachel could feel herself blushing. But the moment was interrupted when Martha plonked herself down in between them.

'Cake says he wants to play hide-and-seek,' Martha chirped.

'Oh, *Cake* wants to play it, does he?' Rachel asked sardonically.

'Yes, and Cake said that me and Alberto have to hide together and you have to find us, Mummy.'

'Come on, little princess,' Alberto said, jumping to his feet. 'I t'ink I know a good place to hide where your mummy will never find us.'

'Close your eyes and count to ten,' Martha instructed as she slipped her hand into Alberto's.

'Off you go then,' Rachel said and squeezed her eyes shut. But not before taking a peek at her daughter skipping alongside Alberto. Martha giggled happily and gazed up at him with adoring eyes. It was clear that the child liked him – Rachel thought that her daughter had very good taste. After all, she liked Alberto too. In fact, she liked him very much indeed.

Sat in the front room upstairs, Winnie rubbed her aching bunion. 'Ooo, it's good to take the weight off my feet,' she said wearily.

'I know what you mean,' Carmen agreed. 'Are you sure you've made the right decision about Maureen doing a bit of cleaning and a couple of shifts?'

'What do you mean?'

'Well, we're managing perfectly well between us. I've got to speak frankly, Win, I think you're wasting your money.'

'Maybe. But let's face it, we'll both appreciate an afternoon off and neither of us enjoys cleaning. To be honest, when Brancher started badgering me to give her a job, I agreed more for Maureen's sake than my own. I reckon she could do with the earnings.'

'You're not a flippin' charity, Win.'

'I know, but it's not costing me much.' In truth, Winnie had given Maureen a chance more for Len's benefit. If her suspicions were right about the man's illness, then Winnie thought that the family were going to need all the help that they could get.

'Nanny ... Nanny ...' Martha squealed as she ran into the room. She clambered up onto Winnie's lap as she excitedly relayed her adventures in the park. 'We played hide-and-seek and Mummy couldn't find me and Alberto. And Alberto helped me to climb up a big tree. He picked me some flowers too, Mummy's putting them in water.'

'Sounds like you had a wonderful time.'

'I did. Alberto is my best fwiend.'

'I thought Cake was your best friend?'

'Cake is my second best fwiend,' Martha explained earnestly.

Rachel swooned into the room, grinning. Winnie recognised that look and was pleased to see it on the girl's face. She hadn't seen Rachel looking so happy for many years; in fact, not since Rachel had been dating Arnold had she appeared this ecstatic. Unfortunately, the girl's happiness with Arnold hadn't lasted long. A wealthy fella, he'd swept her off her feet, only for Rachel to discover that Arnold had been using her to win back his rich and posh ex-fiancée. Winnie had felt awful about the whole sorry affair and still felt guilty for encouraging the relationship. After all, Rachel had her doubts about dating a man above her class, and, as it turned out, she'd been right to question Arnold's motives. *Poor Rachel,* thought Winnie. The girl had let her guard down and had ended up with a broken heart. She hoped that it would work out better for her this time.

'Martha, go and wash your hands and face, there's a good girl. And then take Cake to his bed. Your pup is exhausted after running around the park.'

Winnie ruffled Martha's hair, saying, 'Off you go, love, do as your mum says.'

As Martha trotted off, Winnie turned to Rachel, keen to hear about her time with Alberto. Carmen's eyes were firmly fixed on the young woman too.

Rachel flopped down onto the sofa and glanced at one woman and then the other. 'What?' she asked.

'Well, how did it go?' Carmen probed.

'We had a smashing time. He's so well-mannered and such a gent. And so interesting. It was fascinating to hear about his life in British Honduras.'

'You'll be seeing him again, then?' Winnie asked.

'Yes, very soon and I can't wait.'

'You could invite him for dinner with us on Sunday. Jan will be here, it will be nice for her to meet him.'

Rachel looked hesitant before answering, 'What, to be scrutinised by you two?'

'We wouldn't scrutinise him, would we, Carmen?'

'No, of course not,' Carmen answered.

Rachel rolled her eyes. 'Who are you trying to kid? Yes, you would. You'd interrogate the poor bloke. But thanks for the offer.'

'I promise you, me and Carmen will be nothing but polite. Bring him here for his dinner, I insist. Jan will be upset if you don't, you know that she'd love to meet him.'

Rachel sighed. 'All right, I'll invite him. I'm sure Martha will like that. She's quite taken by him, you know.'

'I noticed. She's taken a real shine to him. I suppose she's missed having a father figure in her life,' Winnie said and her mind drifted to thoughts of David. She missed her son more than she'd ever admit and hoped that he was safe and well. But she also hoped that he'd never show his face again in Battersea.

Later that night, in bed, Winnie tossed and turned as sleep evaded her. She'd tried to stop images of David from creeping into her mind, but her memories seemed to be playing in her head like a film reel on a loop. David had been such a sweet child and had been no bother. Or had he always been selfish and she had been blinded by love? Had she spoiled him? Was it her fault that David had turned out so bad, or did he naturally take after his father? She doubted that she'd ever understand the reasons for David's vile behaviour. He'd violated Rachel and manipulated poor Lucy Little, the young woman now dead. There were no excuses for what he'd done and she'd never forgive him. And she'd never stop loving him, even though she didn't want to

A sound from downstairs pricked her ears and made Winnie's heart race. She sat bolt upright and held her breath as she listened for any unfamiliar noises. There it was again: someone was in the pub; she was sure of it!

Winnie threw her legs over the edge of the bed and then fumbled in the darkness for her dressing gown. Slowly opening the bedroom door, she popped her head out, her eyes searching up and down the passageway.

Carmen had slipped out of her bedroom too, tying the cord of her dressing gown around her waist. The woman jumped when she saw Winnie.

'Did you hear something?' Winnie whispered.

'Yes. I think there's someone downstairs.'

Carmen went to the top of the stairs and peered down into the blackness. Winnie tapped her on the shoulder and then ushered her into the kitchen. She quickly and quietly riffled through a drawer and then held out a knife, whispering, 'We don't know who is down there or how many of them there are.'

'Shall I wake Rachel?'

'No. Follow me.'

Winnie led Carmen back to the top of the stairs and began to slowly creep down. She could feel a breeze wafting up the stairs and knew instantly that the back door was open. With her heart thudding and her clammy, trembling hand gripping the long bread knife, she edged down, quietly closing the back door. Then she tiptoed along the downstairs passageway to the door that went through to the pub. Holding onto the doorknob, she glanced over her shoulder at Carmen. Even in the darkness, Winnie could see that Carmen's eyes were wide with fear. 'Ready?'

Carmen nodded.

Winnie pulled the door open, stepped inside and shouted, 'Who's there?'

Silence met her.

Her eyes flitted around. 'The police are on their way,' she lied.

Still, silence.

'I'll turn the lights on,' Carmen uttered, her voice shaky.

As the pub illuminated, Winnie blinked and tried to quickly focus her eyes. There didn't appear to be any intruders and everything looked as it should behind the bar. But Winnie had a strong feeling that a thief had fled the scene. 'Someone has definitely been in here,' she said gravely, 'I hope they've gone.'

'Check the kitchen, Win,' Carmen said. 'I'm right behind you.'

Winnie felt braver with the lights on and marched to the small back room. Bracing herself, she flicked on the light switch, sighing with relief to find the kitchen empty. But there were obvious signs here that the intruder had been searching for money. Cupboards and drawers were open, including the oven door. Winnie's heart sank and a sob caught in her throat. She had a suspicion about who the intruder was.

'What's going on?' Rachel asked.

Her voice made Winnie jump.

'We think someone broke into the pub,' Carmen answered.

'Oh no! Why didn't you wake me?'

Winnie turned to look at her. 'We didn't want to worry you, love.'

'Did you see who it was?'

'No. The back door was open. Whoever it was is long gone now and empty-handed.'

'What, they didn't even take any booze?' Rachel asked, her eyes bleary.

'No. He was looking for money and thought he knew exactly where to find it.'

'What do you mean?' Carmen asked.

'I always used to keep the pub takings hidden in here. First a teapot, but it got robbed so then I used to hide the money in the oven. But that got robbed too.'

'Oh, no, Winnie … It couldn't be … could it?' Rachel asked, her jaw dropping.

'I think so. Who else would have known where my hiding places were? And I bet the sly git has got a key to the back door.'

'Who?' Carmen asked, her eyes darting from Winnie to Rachel. 'Who are you talking about?'

'David,' they answered in unison.

'Your son, David?'

Winnie swallowed hard. 'Yes, I'm afraid so. I think my David is back.'

'You have to go to the police, Win,' Carmen said firmly.

'And tell them what? That my son let himself in through the back door and went through my kitchen cupboards. I hardly think that they'll take that very seriously or even consider it a crime.'

Carmen tutted, shook her head and, pursing her lips, she

said, 'But what if it weren't David? What if it was a lunatic? We could have been killed in our beds while we slept.'

'No, it was David, I'm sure of it.'

'I still think you should go to the police.'

'Carmen's right,' Rachel added.

Winnie lifted the kettle from the stove and filled it at the sink. 'We might as well have a cuppa,' she said.

'Sit down, I'll make it,' Carmen offered and pulled out a seat at the table for Winnie.

Winnie eased herself down, resting her elbows on the table and her face in her hands as she fought to hold back tears of despair. She felt Rachel's hand on her shoulder.

'Are you all right, Win?'

'No, love, I'm not. I can't believe that he's come back to rob me again.'

'I know how you feel, Winnie,' said Carmen. 'I'm the same about my Errol. I still feel awful about him hitting you. You love your children, but some have the ability to fill us with shame.'

'Cor, you can say that again.'

'But it might not have been David,' Rachel gently reminded her.

'It's unlikely to have been anyone else, but whether it was David or not, I'm going to the police.'

'I think that's a very wise decision,' Carmen assured.

Winnie glanced up at her two friends, who were looking back at her with eyes full of sympathy. 'I'm sorry about him,' she said, guilt gnawing at her heart.

'You've got nothing to be sorry for,' Carmen assured.

'Yes, I have. I raised a rat of a son and now he's affecting all our lives. Look at us, having a cup of tea at half past two in the morning, scared out of our wits.'

'You were a good mother, Win. It isn't your fault,' Rachel assured.

Winnie offered the girl a weak smile, but it didn't reach her eyes. No matter what anyone told her, she would always feel responsible for her son's failings. 'I need to get bolts put on the inside of the door then, key or not, David won't be able to get in again. I'll ask Bill to do the job. He'll probably pop in this afternoon once he's packed up his market stall. And Flo won't mind lending her husband out to do me a favour.'

Carmen put a cup of tea on the table in front of Winnie. 'Good idea. I think that we'll all sleep a lot sounder if we know that the doors are bolted. And Bill's a good egg, he'll happily oblige, especially if you bung him a couple of bob. I reckon their dress stall must be struggling now that everyone seems to be making do and mending.'

'Rachel, you should get yourself back to bed, love. You've got a date with Alberto tomorrow. You'll need your beauty sleep,' Winnie said, trying to keep her voice light.

'Are you sure that you're all right?'

'Yes, love, I'm fine. Go on, off you go.'

Rachel nodded and yawned before trotting back off to bed.

Carmen sat at the table. 'You're not going back to bed, are you, Win?'

'No, love. I couldn't sleep now. But don't you dare think about sitting up all night with me.'

'I couldn't sleep either. I'll keep you company if you don't mind?'

'To be honest, I'd be glad of it,' Winnie replied, this time, her smile reaching her eyes.

'We can sit and put the world to rights, eh? A good old chinwag.'

'Sounds good to me, Carmen, thank you.' Winnie felt grateful that she wasn't facing a long night alone and wouldn't be left to wallow in her own pitiful thoughts about David. Carmen understood better than anyone how it felt to have a son who'd turned out to be a disappointment. And they'd both had husbands who had let them down too. She reached across the table and placed her hand on top of Carmen's. 'I've always said that there's more to a family than just sharing the same blood. You, Rachel, Martha, Jan and Hilda, you're my family, and bugger the likes of David.'

'Yeah, bugger the likes of David and Errol,' Carmen agreed. 'I just hope this ain't an omen.'

'An omen?'

'Yes, an omen. I hope Errol doesn't show his rotten face an' all. That's all we need, the pair of them back in Battersea.'

'Gawd, I hope not too. But they can chuck what they like at us and we'll sling it right back at them. We're stronger together, Carmen, and we won't let them bring us down.'

Once again, thoughts of moving away from Battersea crept into Winnie's mind. She could sell the pub and buy a big house in the country, a place where David and Errol would never find them. The idea appealed to Winnie, though she wasn't convinced that Carmen, Rachel and Hilda would be so keen on a quiet, rural life. In fact, the closest that any of them had experienced to country living was a day out in Battersea Park and that was hardly comparable!

6

When Maureen breezed into the kitchen, Len eyed his granddaughter up and down with pride. He thought that she looked very smart for her first morning at work in the Battersea Tavern. Granted, it was only a cleaning job, but he knew that Maureen would do it well. That was just the sort of young lady that she was: honest and hard-working. After Maureen's mother had died, he and Renee had raised Maureen and her brother to take pride in all they did and to always work to the best of their abilities. He thought it was such a shame that Maureen had chosen a husband who didn't share their same values. *The lazy git*, he thought to himself, eyeing Brancher with contempt as her good-for-nothing husband followed Maureen into the kitchen.

'Any tea in the pot?' Brancher asked.

'Yes, it's brewing,' Renee answered. 'Are you all set for work today?' she asked Maureen.

'Yes, Gran, but I'm a bit nervous. Mrs Berry can be quite a fierce woman when she wants to be.'

'She only ever gets out of her pram when it's called for. You've no need to be nervous of Winnie. And have you got a spare hankie up your sleeve and a packet of matches in your pocket?'

'Yes, of course I have, Gran. Your pearls of wisdom have come in handy. I don't smoke, but there's been plenty of times when I've needed a match to light the gas or a candle.'

'I'm glad you've listened to your old gran. I've always told you, keep a hankie up your sleeve, a packet of matches in your pocket and never leave the house without clean drawers on,' Renee chuckled.

Len felt the dreaded fog descending again as his wife's words floated over his head. He glanced around the room from one face to another, his pulse racing. Renee, his wife. Maureen, his granddaughter, and Brancher, her husband. Thank goodness he could remember their names. They were talking about Winnie, the landlady of the Battersea Tavern. That was all clear, but what was the silver coloured object on the table? The thing with a round bit at the end. He knew what it was, but he couldn't recall the name of it or its purpose. *Think, Len, think,* he urged himself, anger bubbling inside.

'I'll be doing the washing when I get home. Do you want to give me that shirt, Granddad, and put a clean one on?' Maureen asked.

Len gawped at her blankly, feeling confused. Hadn't he put a clean shirt on this morning?

Renee added, 'Yes, Len. It's not like you to wear the same shirt for days on end. Go and get changed, let Maureen wash that one for you before it walks itself to the laundry basket.'

'Yeah, er, all right,' he answered, confused, and scraped his seat back.

As he trudged up the stairs, he heard his wife call out, 'And change your socks while you're up there too. Gawd only knows how long they've been on your feet.'

The sound of his family's voices drifted up the stairs as Len walked into the bedroom. He stood still for a moment, trying to recall why he'd come upstairs. It couldn't have been to get his coat; that was over the newel post downstairs. He looked down to the floor and saw that he had his shoes on. So what was it? Why was he standing in his bedroom? Frustrated, Len turned and went down to the kitchen, the smell of bread toasting making his stomach grumble.

'Why haven't changed your shirt?' Renee asked. 'There's freshly ironed ones in the wardrobe.'

'Yes, Granddad, I put three in there yesterday,' Maureen added.

'I don't want to change my shirt,' he snapped. 'This one is perfectly good. Stop getting on at me, the pair of you, like old fisherwomen,' he barked.

'I think someone woke up on the wrong side of bed this morning,' Renee said sarcastically to Maureen, nodding her head towards him.

'That's it, I've had enough of this,' Len moaned.

He turned on his heel with a huff and marched out of the kitchen, along the hallway and out of the front door, slamming it shut behind him. As he steamed down the street, he tried to gather his muddled thoughts.

'Buggering hell,' he seethed, annoyed at himself. He knew what was wrong: his brain was turning to mush. And now he was worried that his wife and granddaughter suspected the same. 'I'm a stubborn old git, I won't allow this to beat me,' he mumbled aloud. 'And I won't let my family down. I'll do better. I'll have to do better. My Renee must *never* know what's happening to me.'

In the wake of her grandfather losing his temper and storming out of the house, Maureen's grandmother let out a long sigh, saying, 'See, I told you he's getting forgetful. Now do you see what I mean?'

It wasn't the fact that her granddad seemed forgetful that worried Maureen, it was more that he'd so easily become angered. She'd never seen him react like that before and had found it rather upsetting. Though she felt far from assured herself, she tried to offer her gran some reassuring words. 'Don't worry, Gran, I'm sure he'll be back home soon with his tail between his legs.'

'Huh, that's if he can remember where he lives. I'm telling you, Maureen, it's a lot worse than he's letting on. His father went the same way and his uncle too. But you know what your grandfather is like ... I don't think he's ever seen a doctor in his life.'

'Oh, I don't think he needs the doctor, Gran. Getting old and forgetful isn't a disease.'

'It is in your granddad's case. He's got a diseased brain. It's called mania and in my day, when I was young, they used to lock up people like your granddad in asylums. Bleedin' awful places, they were.'

'Ha, the miserable old codger has lost his marbles,' Brancher sneered.

'Oi, you, watch your mouth,' Renee spat.

'I've got to get to work,' Maureen said quickly, hoping

70

to get Brancher out of the kitchen before he said anything unpleasant to her gran. 'Are you going to walk me to the pub on my first morning?' she smiled at him.

'I suppose so, but you needn't think that I'll be making a habit of it.'

'See you in a while, Gran, and stop worrying.'

'Yes, see you, pet, and good luck.'

Outside, Maureen was pleased that her husband seemed to be in a good mood, for a change. She wouldn't risk changing it by asking if he was going to look for work today. Since they'd moved back to Battersea, Brancher had been disappearing for hours at a time but never said where he'd been. Maureen was sure that he hadn't been spending his time searching for a job. She thought it was more likely that he'd been in a pub.

'Give us a light,' he demanded, a roll-up stuck on his bottom lip.

Maureen offered him the packet of matches from her pocket and smiled as she thought of her gran's wise words: *always keep a hankie up your sleeve and a packet of matches in your pocket.*

When they reached the Battersea Tavern, Maureen stood outside nervously, shuffling from one foot to the other.

'What's the matter with you, woman?' Brancher asked.

'I dunno … I'm just a bit jittery.'

'Don't be daft. You're only doing a bit of cleaning. Even you can't mess that up!'

'Wish me luck.'

'Just get in there and do your bleedin' job. And remember what I told you: no talking to them darkies or larking about with any of the customers. I'll be in later to check up on you.'

Maureen's shoulders slumped. She didn't need reminding about how to conduct herself. After all, Brancher had her well trained in the way he liked her to behave. Everything that she did or said was always preceded with the question: *what would Brancher think?* Maureen had forgotten what it felt like to have an opinion of her own.

Brancher walked off without bidding her goodbye or wishing her luck. She supposed she shouldn't have been surprised. In fact, she would have been more surprised if he'd shown her an open display of affection. He'd never been one for offering tenderness, not even during their lovemaking. Maureen shuddered at the thought. Thankfully, she only had to endure him clambering on top of her about once a fortnight nowadays. And she was grateful that it was normally over quickly. There was nothing pleasant about the act, no warmth or passion. Just several thrusts and grunts from Brancher while she laid back and winced at how uncomfortable he felt inside her.

The pub door flew open, startling Maureen and leaving her stood on the pavement open-mouthed and wide-eyed.

'What are you doing standing out there? Come in, love. Did you knock? I didn't hear you,' Mrs Berry said, ushering Maureen through the door.

'Oh, I, erm, was just about to knock ...'

'Are you ready to get cracking or do you want a cuppa first?'

'No, thank you. I'd like to get started.'

'All right, love. I've left a bucket behind the bar. You'll find cleaning cloths, brass polish and carbolic soap inside. I suggest that you start behind the bar and work outwards, but it's up to you. I'll leave you to find your own routine. There's tea in the kitchen. Help yourself. I'll need you to have finished by opening time. Is that all right?'

'Yes, Mrs Berry. Thank you.'

'And then we can get you started behind the bar. You can do a shift today with me and Carmen. We'll show you the ropes so that you're not dropped in at the deep end when you do your scheduled shifts.'

'Oh, OK. I wasn't expecting to be working behind the bar today.'

'Is that a problem?'

'No, Mrs Berry, not at all.'

'All right, love. I'm just popping up to the phone box and then I'll be upstairs. Just give me a shout if you need anything.'

Maureen could feel her heart beating fast, but she didn't really know why. Mrs Berry had been very welcoming, even offering her a cup of tea. But the thought of working behind the bar had sent her into a bit of a spin. She'd thought that she had a couple of days to prepare herself before having to greet customers and pull pints. And she hoped that Brancher didn't get the hump because she wouldn't be home to make his lunch. If she'd known that she was going to be late home today, she would have prepared him something this morning. The thought of bar work felt daunting enough without the added worry of upsetting her husband. But, she reasoned, at the end of the week, she'd be bringing home a wage packet and surely that would appease Brancher.

'I've left Maureen downstairs to get on with the cleaning. I must say, it's quite nice to be a lady of leisure,' Winnie said as she sat at the kitchen table with Carmen and Rachel.

'You're hardly a lady of leisure, Win,' Rachel quipped.

'I am for the next couple of hours. And, to be honest, after that fiasco last night, I'm glad of the rest.'

'Did you telephone the police station?' Carmen asked.

'Yes, love. They're sending someone round later.'

'Did you tell Maureen to stay alert?'

'No, I didn't want to scare the life out of her on her first day. She's quite the little mouse, bless her. Funny though, when she was a youngster, she used to be full of beans and have a lot more confidence.'

'Well, maybe working behind the bar will bring her out of her shell.'

'I hope so. She'll need to be able to hold her own to deal with some of my customers,' Winnie said before yawning widely.

'You're shattered, Winnie. Why don't you go and get a few hours' kip, eh? I can show Maureen what to do,' Carmen offered.

'No, love, I'm fine, thanks. Anyway, I need to be awake for when the copper comes to see me.' Winnie was grateful for the offer and, under normal circumstances, she may have accepted it. But even if she did take to her bed, she knew she'd never get to sleep, not while the thought of David being back in Battersea was hurtling through her mind. She'd never been a woman to run away from her difficulties, but she couldn't help feeling that a new life far, far away would be the answer to her problems. 'But I wouldn't say no to a fresh cuppa,' she said, masking her thoughts.

Hours later, Winnie had fixed a welcoming smile on her face and had opened the pub doors. Maureen was standing stiff-backed behind the bar, anxiously ringing her hands.

Winnie hoped that the girl would soon relax into her new role.

'How's your granddad?' she inquired.

'He's fine, thanks, Mrs Berry.'

Either Maureen was keeping her family business to herself or Len still hadn't told them about his problem.

'Talk of the devil,' Winnie said, flicking her head towards the door as Len ambled in.

She noticed that as he walked towards the bar, he seemed taken aback to see Maureen standing behind it.

'What are you doing there?' he asked his granddaughter.

'Working, Granddad. Mrs Berry and Mrs Hampton are showing me what to do.'

'Working? In here?'

'Yes. Why do you sound so surprised?' Maureen asked, her brows knitting together.

Winnie stepped in. 'Morning, Len. Maureen's done a grand job of the cleaning this morning. She wasn't down for a shift behind the bar today, but me and Carmen thought it would be a good day to get her started. Your usual to drink?'

Len nodded, still looking baffled.

'Get your granddad a bottle of stout and his tankard off the shelf there. Then Carmen can take you down to the cellar to show you where we keep the stock.'

Maureen scurried to get the drink and the tankard and plonked them down on the counter.

'You have to remove the lid off the bottle,' Winnie instructed.

'Oh, of course, sorry,' Maureen answered quickly.

Once Carmen had led Maureen to the cellar, Winnie leaned over the bar towards Len, pleased to see that he didn't look quite as confused. 'You didn't remember that your Maureen is working here now, did you?'

'No, Win, I didn't. Do you think that she noticed?'

'No, I don't think so, love. But don't you think that it's time to talk to Renee?'

'Leave me be, Win. I told you, I don't want anyone knowing. It's none of your business or anyone else's.'

'All right, don't bite me head off. But I think that you're making a big mistake.'

The door opened again and a mature, uniformed policeman walked in. Winnie's face broke into a genuine smile.

'Hello, Sergeant Bradbury. Fancy seeing you here! I thought you were stuck with a desk job these days?'

'Good morning, Mrs Berry. Yes, I was, for years, but the shortage of bobbies on the beat has brought me back out onto the streets. I'll be glad when this war is over and we can get back to some normality. My old bones aren't used to riding my bicycle.'

'Sit yourself down, I'll get you a drink.'

'That would be most welcome, thank you, but just a glass of water. I won't drink when I'm on the job.'

As Sergeant Bradbury sat at a table and removed his helmet, placing it on a seat beside him, Winnie asked Maureen to bring them both a glass of water. She then joined the policeman at the table, surprised to see how much his hair had thinned and greyed. The last time that she'd seen Tommy Bradbury, he'd had a thick mop of coppery hair, though that had been about five years ago.

'You're looking well, Mrs Berry,' he said, his grey-blue eyes holding her gaze.

Winnie felt a flush of embarrassment and looked down at

her hands on her lap. 'Can't complain. And call me Winnie. Christ, how long have we known each other? Must be nigh on twenty-odd years and you're still calling me Mrs Berry.'

'Just being formal, Winnie. After all, I am in uniform. And it works both ways, you can drop the *Sergeant Bradbury*.'

'Well, I must say, it's about time that you popped your head in here. It's been far too long since you came in for a drink.'

'If you remember, Winnie, the last time I was here, I wasn't made to feel very welcome.'

Again, Winnie felt herself flush as she recalled her husband being none to friendly towards Tommy. For some reason, Brian had got it in his head that Tommy had a thing for her. Winnie thought the idea of Tommy fancying her was ridiculous, but, nonetheless, Brian had a *quiet* word in Tommy's ear and Winnie hadn't seen him since. 'Brian's dead, Tommy. He was killed by a bomb.'

'Oh, blimey, Winnie, I'm so sorry.'

'I'm not,' she said, the words slipping out before she had a chance to stop them. 'I mean, yes, I'm sorry that he's dead, but Brian and I had separated a while before he was killed.'

'I see. And you're managing all right?'

'Yes, you know me, Tommy.'

'I do. You're a fine woman, Winnie, and if you don't mind me saying, I always thought that you was too good for Brian.'

Winnie found herself lowering her eyes again and her cheeks burning. It had been quite some time since a man had flattered her.

'So, I hear you had a bit of bother here last night?'

'Yes, Tommy, that's right. Someone broke in and had a rummage through my downstairs kitchen. He was obviously looking for money. But, as far as I can tell, nothing has been

77

taken. You can imagine the fright it gave us though. There's only me, Mrs Hampton and my four-year-old granddaughter and her mother, Rachel, upstairs.'

'Mrs Hampton, you say?'

'Yes, that's right.'

'Mrs Harry Hampton?'

'Yes, Carmen.'

'Hmm, I assume you are fully aware of the Hamptons' reputation?'

Winnie glared at Tommy with annoyance. Always protective of her *family*, she wouldn't allow anyone to bad mouth them. 'Of course I'm aware. Anyway, Harry's dead and Errol hasn't been seen in Battersea for a while now. I hope you're not suggesting that Mrs Hampton is in anyway *unsavoury*?'

'No, I'm just surprised, that's all. I had many a run-in with Errol and a couple with Harry too. I heard about Errol attacking you.'

'He did time for it.'

'I know. Anyway, about this break-in … do you know how the intruder gained entry?'

'I found the back door open, so I'm assuming that's how he came in. And I suspect that he might have a key.'

'I see. Apart from yourself and the ladies abiding here, who else has a key to the back door?' Tommy asked.

'I hate to say it, but I suspect my son, David, might still have a key. I've not seen him in years.'

'Hmm, it won't come as a shock to you to know that his name is known to us at the station. He's wanted for questioning about the death of Lucy Little.'

'I know. And it wouldn't be the first time that he's stolen from me. Whoever was in here last night went through my kitchen and David knows that it's where I used to hide the takings.'

'I don't think that we should jump to conclusions based on that. To be honest, Winnie, most pub landlords hide their takings in places that they think are unusual, but a seasoned robber will know this. I've even known money to be stolen from the privy, the kettle and under a sofa cushion.'

'Really? I haven't kept the takings in the oven since David stole them a while back, but I used to. And in a teapot before that.'

'I'd suggest that you use a bank, or at least a safe. Is there anything else that suggests to you that your son was here last night?'

'Only the fact that the back door was open and he might have a key, which would explain why there's no smashed windows or anything.'

Tommy pulled a small notepad from his pocket, licked the end of a pencil and began to scribble down some notes. 'And you're sure that the door was locked before you went to bed?'

'Yes, I'm quite sure.'

'Could the intruder have come through the cellar?'

'I don't know, I doubt it. Not with the back door being open like that.'

'He may have left via the back door but come in another way,' Tommy suggested.

'Oh, I hadn't thought of that.'

'I only ask because we've had a spate of robberies lately. Of course, the blackouts don't help. But it appears that pubs are being specifically targeted and, on two occasions, the culprits gained entry via the trapdoors. Do you mind if I take a look?'

'Please, be my guest.'

Winnie didn't believe that anyone had broken in through the trapdoors. They were only ever opened when the draymen came with deliveries and Carmen always double-checked behind Winnie that the doors were secured.

'No sign of a break-in that way,' Tommy said as he sat back at the table, adding, 'and you're sure that nothing is missing?'

'I'm pretty sure.'

'I know David, I'll circulate his description and I'll ask around if anyone has seen him in the area. In the meantime, if he does return, please inform me immediately.'

'I will, Tommy, and thanks.'

'You should change the lock on the back door too.'

'I'm going to have a word with Bill who works on the market and ask him to fit me some bolts.'

'No need. I can do that for you and change the lock too, if you like?'

'That's not part of your job now, is it?'

'No, Winnie, but I'm off shift early today. I can pop back in at about four o'clock.'

'If you're sure you don't mind, I'd be grateful.'

'It'll be my pleasure. I'll see you later then. Keep your eyes and ears peeled for anything suspicious.'

'Will do, and thanks again, Tommy.'

Winnie watched Tommy place his helmet back on his head and tuck the strap just under his bottom lip. She could never understand why they didn't wear the straps under their chins. It seemed daft to her. Her eyes stayed on him as he walked away with a slow and confident swagger, leaving Winnie with a warm feeling. It had been nice to see him and she was looking forward to him calling in again later.

'Was that Sergeant Bradbury?' Carmen asked.

'Yes. He'll be back later to change the lock on the back door.'

'He felt Harry's collar a few times and Errol's too. I was surprised to see him, I assumed he would have retired by now. It's reassuring to know that he's still doing the rounds in Battersea. He's good at his job, not like some of these youngsters who are still wet behind the ears.'

'Er, sorry to interrupt,' Maureen said awkwardly, 'but that fella over there wants a half a lager and I'm not sure how to pour it.'

'It's easy, you'll soon get the hang of it,' Carmen answered, leading Maureen to the pump.

Winnie smiled over at Len, who grimaced back at her. He clearly still had the hump with her for trying to interfere in his business. But, right now, she had her own family business to be worrying about. If David was back in Battersea, it would only mean one thing: trouble.

'I told you we would find work. Our perseverance paid off,' Clinton said, feeling smug. Alberto had suggested that they should give up trying to find employment in Battersea and look elsewhere, maybe over the bridge in Chelsea, but Clinton had insisted that they keep going. And now they had both secured jobs in the boiler rooms at Battersea Power Station.

'I t'ink we should go to the Battersea Tavern to celebrate,' Alberto suggested.

Clinton thought out loud, saying, 'Any excuse to see Rachel.'

'Once we start work, I won't be seeing as much of her. I might as well make the most of it while I can.'

Mrs Berry welcomed them into the pub with her friendly smile. 'Good afternoon, gentlemen. Your usual?' she asked.

'Yes, please, Mrs Berry. We have good reason to be drinking today,' Clinton said.

'Oh yes, why's that?'

'We will be starting work at Battersea Power Station on Monday,' he answered with pride.

'That's wonderful, I'm really pleased for you. You'll do all right in there, I hear that they treat their staff well. What's it like inside? I've always wondered.'

'You wouldn't believe it! It's like a cathedral, and so clean.'

'The boiler rooms aren't so clean,' Alberto added. 'And that's where we'll be.'

'Do you want me to give Rachel a shout? I'm sure she'd love to hear your news.'

'Yes, t'ank you, Mrs Berry.'

As the landlady went to shout for Rachel, Clinton glanced around, hoping that he wouldn't see Brancher. He was surprised when the man's wife emerged from the cellar. She appeared equally shocked to see him and quickly dropped her eyes.

'You have a new barmaid?' Clinton asked Mrs Berry, indicating to the shy woman.

'Yes, that's Maureen. It's her first day.' Then she turned to Alberto and told him, 'Rachel said to go upstairs.'

Alberto threw Clinton a self-assured glance before sauntering off. But Clinton wasn't really taking much notice. He had his eyes on Maureen. He couldn't stop looking at the woman, though she seemed to feel uncomfortable under his long stare.

'I've got a bit of corned-beef hash left over from last night. Do you fancy a bit, Maureen can warm it up for you?'

Clinton had never heard of corned-beef hash, but he felt ravenously hungry. 'I'd be grateful, t'ank you, Mrs Berry.'

She gave out her instructions and Maureen scuttled past Clinton. His eyes followed her but she didn't look up. He wondered if she was scared of him or maybe she was prejudiced, like her awful husband. And then Clinton's heart dropped into his boots when Maureen's husband sauntered in.

Clinton wanted to avoid any nastiness and turned his back to him. But he could guess that the man was glowering.

He heard Mrs Berry serving him. 'Hello, Brancher. Have you come to see how your Maureen is doing?'

'She'd better be doing a good job.'

'Of course she is. She's in the kitchen, she'll be out in a tick.'

Clinton could feel his jaw tighten. Brancher had put him on edge and made him feel uncomfortable.

Maureen appeared, and Clinton noticed that when she saw her husband, the blood drained from her face and her eyes widened with what appeared to be fear. Holding a hot dish with a tea cloth, she tried to pass the corned-beef hash to Mrs Berry.

'Give it to Clinton, love, and don't forget to ask him if he wants any salt.'

Maureen stood ramrod straight with her feet rooted to the ground.

'Go on, he won't bite,' Mrs Berry urged before ambling off to the other end of the bar.

Clinton could see Maureen's terrified eyes darting from him to her husband. He realised that she was too scared to serve him, probably because Brancher had warned her not to.

She nervously shoved the dish down onto the bar in front

of Clinton and dashed away before he had a chance to thank her.

As he tucked into the meal, he heard Brancher hiss at Maureen, 'What did I tell you about serving his sort?'

'I had no choice, Brancher. Mrs Berry made me,' she answered quietly.

'I'll see you at home,' he snarled.

Clinton heard heavy footsteps stamp across the pub floorboards. Turning cautiously, he was relieved to see Brancher marching out of the door and felt that he could breathe easy again, but he felt sorry for Maureen. Her husband reminded Clinton of his tyrannical father and, once again, he was prompted to remember the suffering his mother had endured for years. Maybe that was why he felt compelled to reach out to Maureen.

'I don't t'ink your husband likes me,' he said, with a big smile.

Maureen stared back at him like a rabbit caught in car headlights. Her mouth opened and closed, but no words came out.

'I'm Clinton, from British Honduras. Nice to meet you, Maureen. It is all right to call you Maureen?'

She nodded, and gazed down.

'I'm a lumberjack by trade. The British government brought us over to fell trees in Scotland. And now I find myself in Battersea and starting work at the power station. London is a sweet, sweet place to live. And the people are friendly, mostly.'

Maureen looked up and gave him an awkward smile before scurrying away to the kitchen.

'What's got into her?' Mrs Berry asked, her eyes following

Maureen as she dashed off. 'I hope you haven't said anything to her that you shouldn't have, young man,' she warned, with her hands on her wide hips.

'No, Mrs Berry, I wouldn't be anything but polite.'

'I know, love, I'm only joking. Maureen's a bit shy, but she'll soon come out of her shell.'

More like she's terrified of her husband, Clinton thought.

'How's your corned-beef hash?'

'Delicious, t'ank you, Mrs Berry.'

'Good.'

Mrs Berry wandered off and Clinton enjoyed the rest of his meal. As he savoured each mouthful, he found that he couldn't stop thinking about Maureen. But not in a romantic way. That would be silly. After all, the woman was married. And, as he'd warned Alberto, romance could lead to trouble and they could end up in prison: Clinton wanted to avoid a jail sentence at all costs!

7

Maureen's feet were killing her. She'd been on them since early that morning and was glad to get home after her first day in the Battersea Tavern. And best of all, though tired, she was home in time to cook the dinner.

As she put her key in the front door, her stomach knotted and her heart hammered. She was dreading facing Brancher. When he'd stormed out of the pub earlier, he'd said, *I'll see you at home.* Maureen knew that his words had been a veiled threat, and now she'd have to face his accusations and a tirade of verbal abuse. Yet the thought of her grandparents overhearing anything worried her more than Brancher's inevitable vile words.

She slipped into the front room and closed the door quietly behind her. Her gran was dozing in the armchair but stirred and opened her eyes.

'Hello, pet. How did your first day go?'

'Great, thanks, Gran. Is Brancher home?'

'I don't know. I must have nodded off. Why are you whispering?'

'No reason.'

'What's the matter?'

'Nothing, Gran.'

'You look like you've got the weight of the world on your shoulders. Has someone upset you? One of Winnie's customers?'

'No, of course not,' Maureen answered quickly. But she couldn't tell her gran the truth; that she was anxious about Brancher shouting at her.

'I should hope not. And if any of them do, you make sure that you tell Winnie. She'll soon put them straight.'

'Yes, I know, thanks.'

'Put the kettle on, pet, there's a good girl.'

Maureen swallowed hard as she opened the front-room door and stepped into the passageway. As she walked towards the kitchen, her heart felt as though it might pound out of her chest. It was such a relief to find that Brancher wasn't in the kitchen, but then, Maureen thought sadly, it was only a matter of time before she had to face him.

She fished in her pocket for a packet of matches and after putting a full kettle on the gas stove, she tensed when she heard the front door open. But she soon relaxed when she heard her granddad's voice calling along the passageway.

'I hope that kettle is on?'

She walked over to the kitchen door and smiled warmly at him as he removed his flat cap and coat, throwing them both over the newel post.

'Yes, Granddad, and it'll soon boil.'

'How did you get on today?' he asked.

'Fine. I quite enjoyed it.'

He lowered his voice and asked quietly, 'How's your gran?'

'She seems fine. Why?'

'She's not said anything to you, then?'

'About what?'

'I dunno. Me?'

'You?'

'Yes. Has she mentioned my memory or anything?'

'Well … yes, she has, actually. She's worried that you're getting forgetful.'

'I'm just old, my brain ain't as sharp as it used to be.'

'I know, Granddad, and I told her that. But you know what a worryguts my gran is.'

'Yes, she is. I better go and say hello to the old gal.'

The kettle whistled, letting Maureen know that the water had boiled. As she waited for the tea to brew, her back stiffened when she heard the front door open again and her husband clumping along the passageway.

Maureen quickly closed the kitchen door behind her husband and then stirred the teapot, keeping her face turned away from Brancher. 'Hello. I've just made a fresh pot of tea,' she said nervously while still avoiding looking at him.

To her shock, she felt a strong grip on her arm and Brancher yanked her round to face him. 'Your first day at work and you couldn't help yourself, could you?' he hissed.

'What?' she asked, though she knew why Brancher was furious: she'd caused it. Once again, he was upset and it was her fault.

'You was told to have nothing to do with them darkies. And what happens? I come in and find you serving one of them. *My wife, serving* a coloured man! How do you think that makes me look, eh? Are you trying to make me look like an idiot?'

'N-n-no, Brancher. I didn't want to serve him, but Mrs Berry said I had to.'

'And if Mrs Berry told you to stick your head in the gas oven, would you?'

'No, but ... but, it's my job. If I don't do as I'm told, she'll sack me.'

Brancher stepped closer and pushed his face into hers. She could feel the end of his nose and his hot breath against her cheek. 'You tell Mrs Berry that you won't serve any coloured men. And if she sacks you, fine.'

'But we need the money, Brancher.'

'Yeah, well, we'll see about that. Just do as you're told, get it?'

'Yes, Brancher.'

'Make me something to eat,' he snapped.

'I'm just going to have a cuppa and then I'll get the dinner on.'

Maureen stifled a yelp when Brancher grabbed a handful of her hair and yanked her head back.

'You thick cow. I said, get me something to eat. NOW!'

A tear slipped from Maureen's eye and she winced in pain. 'Yes, Brancher,' she muttered, her voice shaky.

As he released the grip on her hair, she jumped, startled by the sudden wailing of the air-raid siren.

'Great, that's all we need,' Brancher moaned.

Maureen was grateful for the interruption and mumbled, 'I'll get my gran and granddad, we need to get in the shelter.'

'Yeah, you do that,' Brancher said as he stamped towards the door.

'Where are you going?' Maureen asked, alarmed.

'If you think I'm sitting cooped up in that rotten shelter with your grandparents for hours on end, you can think again.'

She didn't like the idea of him being in the shelter with them either, so she kept her mouth shut and watched Brancher march out of the house. Though she hoped he'd keep himself safe.

Her granddad came out of the front room as Maureen went to walk in. 'Where are you going?' she asked. He looked straight past her and headed for the front door. 'Granddad,' she called, but he ignored her.

'Give us a hand, pet,' her gran shouted, struggling to push herself out of the armchair.

As Maureen heaved her gran from the chair, she glanced through the net curtains and, to her dismay, she saw her granddad wander past the window.

'Where's your grandfather going?'

'I don't know, Gran, but I'm sure he'll be back any second,' she soothed.

'I don't like going in that Anderson without your grand-dad.'

'It's all right, I'll look after you.'

'I know you will, pet, but go and get the silly old bugger. Tell him to stop muckin' about.'

'Shall we just get under the kitchen table instead of going to the shelter and wait for Granddad there?'

'No, best not. Just go and find him.'

Maureen ran to the front door and then looked up and down the street. She could see people rushing around to take cover and then she spotted her granddad standing in the street. He was looking back and forth and appeared to be confused.

Maureen raced to him and grabbed his arm, gently pulling him back towards the house. 'Come on, Granddad, come back inside.'

'What? What's going on?'

'It's an air-raid warning. We have to take cover. Hurry, Granddad, look sharp.'

As the low hum of the approaching Royal Air Force planes came closer, her granddad allowed her to lead him home. The blank look in his eyes and his obvious disorientation was a grave concern to Maureen, but, right now, she had more pressing matters on her mind.

'I've found him,' she called to her gran, breathlessly, as she urged her granddad along the passageway and into the kitchen. 'Wait there,' she told him, 'I'll get Gran.'

'What on earth was he playing at?' her gran asked.

'I don't know, but come on, Gran, we need to hurry,' Maureen answered, ushering her through to the kitchen.

'All right, dear. Bring a flask of hot water. Gawd knows how long we will be in there. And you've got a packet of matches in your pocket, haven't you?'

'Yes, Gran, always.'

After quickly filling a flask, Maureen helped her grand-parents navigate through the kitchen and out into the back yard. When she yanked open the door to the shelter, she was pleasantly surprised to see that her gran had made it quite comfortable. But as the sound of the engines above became louder, nothing eased the fear that engulfed her, causing her to tremble uncontrollably.

Len sat silent, staring at the corrugated tin wall.

'You're shaking like a leaf,' her gran commented, lowering herself onto a camp bed with difficulty and eyeing Maureen.

'I know. I feel like I can't breathe.'

'Take a few long, deep breaths.'

Maureen sucked in the damp and musty air, then slowly breathed out through her mouth. She began to feel a little calmer, but then she heard the strange sound of a rocket directly overhead. 'They're right above us, Gran!' she cried.

'It's all right. It'll pass.'

Thankfully, her granddad seemed to be more like his old self.

'Bleedin' Hun. If I was a younger man—'

'Shush, Len, listen,' Renee snapped.

Maureen and her gran held their breath, their eyes looking upwards as they waited to hear if the rocket motor would cut out. They knew that if there was silence above them, the chances were that the V1 bomb was falling out of the sky and heading in their direction.

'I can't hear it!' Maureen exclaimed, terrified.

'Come here, pet,' her gran beckoned.

Maureen fell into her gran's open arms and held tightly to the woman. She squeezed her eyes shut, expecting to be blown to smithereens at any moment.

A devastating boom reached her ears, and she felt the vibration of the blast rattle the shelter. The bomb had landed, close by but not on them.

'Oh, Len! Oh my goodness, Len!' Renee cried, squeezing Maureen tighter.

'Calm down, woman, and stop panicking. We'll be all right, old gal. We're fine, ain't we?'

Maureen couldn't talk. Fear had rendered her momentarily frozen in time, like a statue.

Her gran sensed her fear and soothed, 'There, there, pet. You heard your granddad. Everything will be all right. We're all fine.'

Yes, they were, for now, but a bomb had landed on Battersea and it had only been sheer luck that it had missed them.

A thought flashed through her mind: had Brancher been killed? Maureen felt awful for momentarily wishing that he had and quickly chastised herself. She wanted him to be safe, of course she did. Guilt washed over her for thinking such a wicked thing. But he made her life a misery and she knew that she'd be happier without him. She also knew that she'd never have the courage to leave him. *Til death us do part.* Forever.

In the cellar of the Battersea Tavern, Winnie pulled Martha onto her lap just as the sound of a terrific explosion shook the building. *We shouldn't be here*, she thought, imagining being tucked up safely in a warm bed somewhere outside of London.

Carmen crossed herself, and cried, 'Jesus, that was close!'

'I didn't think that you were religious,' Winnie said, trying to keep her voice light.

'I'm not, but, at times like this, I'll take help from wherever it comes.'

'That was one of those V1 rockets, wasn't it?' Rachel asked.

'Yes, love, I think so,' Winnie answered. She was pleased to see that Rachel didn't appear too terrified. Though having Alberto sat with his strong arm over her shoulders was probably helping to keep her calm. Even Martha didn't seem to be worried. Winnie thought that maybe the girl was too young to understand that death had flown overhead and had only just missed them. She shuddered at the thought and her heart went out to the poor blighters who had just been hit.

It wasn't over yet. She could hear more pilotless bombs in the skies and any one of them could land on the pub. But Winnie refused to allow her fear to show. Instead, she smiled across to Carmen.

'You know the drill. Once we get the all-clear, it's all hands on deck. Rachel, you can get the urn on. I'll get some clean sheets and rip 'em up for bandages. Carmen, you can pop to the corner shop and buy all the sugar that you can get your hands on. I know that Mr Coggins keeps sugar back. I don't care what he's charging, insist on buying the lot.'

Tommy had come back to the pub to add the bolts to the back door and was halfway through the job when the air-raid siren had sounded so was now in the cellar too. 'Whoa, Winnie. That sounds to me that you're buying goods off the black market, which you know is illegal,' he said, wagging his finger at her.

'Behave yourself!' Winnie chastised. 'Gawd knows what's gone on out there. Folk will be injured and shocked, or worse. I'm offering a cup of sweet tea and a bit of sympathy to anyone who needs it. Are you going to arrest me for that?'

'No, Winnie, of course not. But I'll go and get the sugar from Mr Coggins. He won't try to rip *me* off,' Tommy smiled.

Winnie's voice softened. 'That's good of you, Tommy, thank you. And thanks ever so much for changing the locks on the back door too.'

'No problem. I haven't finished yet. There's still a bottom bolt to put on.'

'Let me know how much I owe you.'

'Nothing, Winnie.'

'Don't be daft. What about the cost of the locks?'

'I'm just happy to give you some peace of mind.'

'That's kind of you, Tommy, but I'd rather pay.'

'I won't hear of it. You can give me a pint or two instead.'

'Sounds like a good deal to me.'

Tommy looked over to Alberto, asking, 'You're new to Battersea?'

'Yes.'

'How are you getting on?'

'Fine, t'ank you. I start work at the power station on Monday.'

'You'll get on all right there. I know a few fellas who work at the station and speak well of the place. They arrange days out and all sorts. You've landed on your feet, laddie.'

'Alberto is from British Honduras,' Rachel told Tommy.

'Yes, I heard. I've got to say, young man, it was a brave thing that you did. To leave your home, your country and everything you know to come over to Scotland, well, I take my hat off to you. If you get any bother, you be sure to give me a shout.'

'T'ank you, Sergeant Bradbury.'

Winnie thought that Alberto was being unusually quiet. He normally had plenty to say and she wondered if fear of the V1 rockets was scaring the life out of him and he was trying to put on a brave face for Rachel's sake.

Another explosion shook the building. Winnie tensed and held in a gasp. She didn't want to worry Martha. Thoughts of Jan crossed her mind. She assumed that her daughter would be rushed off her feet at St Thomas' Hospital. It never ceased to amaze her how Jan carried on nursing through the thick of it. 'I expect my Jan is busy,' she said sadly, voicing her thoughts.

Rachel nodded, saying, 'Alberto is looking forward to meeting her on Sunday, aren't you?'

'Yes, t'ank you for the invite.'

'I'm doing a nice roast dinner. Why don't you come too, Tommy? The more, the merrier.'

'Thanks, Winnie, but I wouldn't want to impose.'

'I insist. Anyway, it'll be good for Alberto to have another fella around the table, otherwise the poor bloke will be sur-rounded by women.'

'Well, if you insist, I'd love to join you and it would be nice to meet Jan.'

Winnie turned to glance at Carmen, who gave her a raised-eyebrow, *funny* look.

'What?' Winnie mouthed to her.

Carmen discreetly flicked her head to Tommy and then winked at Winnie.

Oh my goodness! Winnie thought, suddenly worrying that she'd given Tommy the wrong impression. Yes, she was grate-ful for his help with changing the locks and she enjoyed his company, but that was as far as it went. She hoped that Tommy didn't think that her invite meant anything more than friendship. After all, thinking back, Brian had been con-vinced that the bloke held a torch for her. As far as Winnie was concerned, Tommy's attention and his compliments were flattering, but romance was not, and never would be, on the table. Brian had been enough to put her off men for life, but then she'd stupidly made a fool of herself over *Have it* Harry

Hampton, the local spiv and Carmen's husband. As it turned out, he had been just as awful as Brian.

Winnie thought that, when it came to men, she must be a very bad judge of character. She was better off without one; they only led to heartache.

8

Clinton dared to sneak a glance along the public shelter to where Brancher was huddled with two shady-looking characters, whispering and deep in conversation. Thankfully, Brancher hadn't noticed him sat in the corner at the opposite end of the narrow, concrete building. He quickly pulled his eyes away, hoping that he could evade the man's attention.

To him, the brick shelter offered no more safety than a house. If a bomb landed on it, chances were that all fifty or sixty people inside would be killed. It wasn't comfortable either; just hard, wooden benches running the length of the walls on each side. The place stank too.

Closing his eyes, Clinton's mind drifted to British Honduras and warm thoughts of his family. He missed his dear mother and sisters; it had been years since he'd seen them. But at least he knew that they were well and that the money he sent them would be helping to better their lives and to keep his sister alive. The girl had been diagnosed with a life-threatening disease and now relied on the money that he sent home to buy her medications. The doctor had said that she'd be plagued with the illness for the rest of her life.

It was a big responsibility on Clinton, but now that he had a steady job in the power station, he'd be able to send them money on a regular basis. His friend, Alberto, had no desire or reason to ever return to their country. In fact, it would be better for Alberto if he stayed away. But Clinton knew that one day, he'd go home, and it was a day that he was very much looking forward to.

The all-clear siren sounded, snapping Clinton from his thoughts. The wailing sound came as a great relief to his jangled nerves. It was bad enough that rockets were being launched on Battersea, but having to share an air-raid shelter with Brancher had left Clinton feeling nervously exhausted. He pushed himself against the wall, trying to look as small as possible, and finally relaxed when he saw Brancher and his two pals leave.

London had been flooded in daylight when Clinton had taken cover in the shelter, but when he came out, he emerged into darkness. The acrid taste of brick dust and concrete hung in the air. Fire engine and ambulance bells rang out. A sense of gloom shadowed Clinton. Battersea, his new home, had been hit hard and he dreaded to think of the devastation.

As he made his way back to the lodgings, he passed the Battersea Tavern and was surprised to find it open. He was even more surprised when he walked inside and found Alberto behind the bar.

'What are you doing?'

Alberto smiled widely. 'Helping out. Just washing up some teacups.'

Mrs Berry bustled past, stopping briefly to ask, 'Are you all right, love?'

'Yes, t'ank you, Mrs Berry. Is there anything I can do to help?'

'No, but thanks for asking. Get yourself a cuppa. I expect you're as shaken up as the rest of us.'

The door opened again and a short, skinny man rushed in, announcing, 'It was St John's Hill. The rocket blew up a couple of shops and some houses. It's bad ... really bad. The Jerries are gonna destroy Battersea. They're gonna flatten London!'

The pub fell silent until Mrs Berry said firmly, 'All right, Pete, that's enough of that sort of talk in my pub, thank you very much. Sit yourself down and Carmen will bring you a cuppa.'

An older man came to stand beside Clinton and offered a friendly smile. 'You must be Alberto's friend, Clinton?'

'Yes, that's right.'

'Pleased to meet you, laddie. I'm Sergeant Bradbury. As I told Alberto here, the pair of you are fine young men and did a brave service for Britain. If you get any problems, you be sure to let me know.'

Clinton's heart began to race. 'T'ank you, sir,' he said anxiously, his mouth feeling dry.

The policeman walked over to the urn and Clinton leaned over the bar. 'Are you mad?' he hissed at Alberto.

'What?'

'He's a policeman!'

'Yes, I know.'

'What are we going to do?'

'Not'ing. We just act like normal. Stop looking so worried, you'll raise suspicion.'

'I can't believe you! How can you be so blasé?'

'He has no reason to t'ink that we've done anyt'ing wrong. But he will if you carry on behaving like a scared rat.'

Clinton had heard enough. First, his friend had taken a girlfriend and now he was fraternising with the local policeman. So much for keeping their heads down! He turned on his heel and marched angrily from the pub. The way Alberto was going, Clinton felt sure that they'd both soon be thrown into prison. He shuddered at the thought, worried about what would become of his mother and sisters. If he wasn't in a position to send home money, his little sister might die.

Maureen was sat at the kitchen table nursing a cup of Camp coffee. Her stomach knotted when she heard the front door slam close. She knew that it was Brancher coming home. It was late, her grandparents were in bed, but her selfish husband had made no attempt to come into the house quietly.

'I just heard that the V1 landed on St John's Hill,' he said, dragging out a seat at the table.

'It was awful. The ground shook. I don't think that I've ever been so scared.'

'Yeah, these bombs ain't good news for Britain.'

'I don't like the way that you hear 'em coming and then that eerie silence until they land. I swear I was holding my breath for ages. Do you want a cup of coffee?'

'Yeah, go on then.'

Maureen went over to the kitchen side, pleased that Brancher seemed to be in an amenable mood for a pleasant change. She wouldn't ask him where he'd been and risk annoying him. As he always said, she *knew what buttons to press* to kick him off. And he was right; it was always her fault. She'd do or say something stupid that would annoy him, or she'd inadvertently make a comment to undermine him. She had to try her best to stop setting him off.

Brancher pulled off his boots and stretched his legs out, resting his feet on a seat. 'We'll be getting out of this dump soon,' he said, with a sniff.

Maureen spun around from the worktop to look at him, her brow furrowed. 'What do you mean?' she asked.

'You'll see.'

'I-I-I don't understand.'

'Never you mind. But don't get your feet too comfy under the table here. We'll have our own place soon enough.'

Maureen panicked inside. She didn't want to leave her grandparents' house and be alone with Brancher again. Thinking quickly, she blurted, 'But we can't afford a place on what I earn at the pub.'

'You won't be working there for much longer.'

'Have you found a job?' she asked tentatively.

'Something like that. But keep your mouth shut.'

'What job?'

'A one-off. But I don't want you telling anyone.'

Maureen wrung her hands nervously, her mind racing. *A one-off* could only mean one thing: Brancher was up to no good and he planned on robbing someone. It wouldn't be the first time that he'd broken the law. But at least this time, he wasn't involving her. She still cringed at the shame of looting bombed houses and wrecked shops. She had hated doing it, but Brancher had forced her. Tears pricked her eyes and she turned back to the kettle so that he wouldn't see her crying. She'd never forgive herself for tugging a gold wedding band from the finger of a dead woman. The memory still haunted her and disturbed her sleep. Stealing something so personal from a bomb victim had left Maureen detesting herself. If only she'd had the guts to say 'no' to Brancher.

'We'll move somewhere better. Clapham or Streatham.'

Another thought struck her.

'But what about my granddad?' she asked.

'What about him?'

'I don't think he's very well, Brancher. I'm worried about leaving my gran alone to cope with him.'

'I'm offering you a nice house in a nice borough and you're turning your nose up?'

'No, Brancher. I'm grateful, really I am, but my grand-parents are getting on and there's no one else to look after them.'

'It ain't your job to look after them. You're *my* wife. I'm your priority, not them!'

'Yes, I know, but they're old and they need me.'

'They managed fine before we moved in and they'll cope well enough when we move out. It ain't open for discussion. We're going and that's that.'

Maureen stirred the coffee cup, her mind turning. She didn't want to upset her husband or make him feel that he was second-best to her grandparents, but she couldn't stand the thought of leaving them. 'Perhaps we could move out but still stay in Battersea, for now, so that I can keep an eye on them?' she suggested, hoping that he'd agree to her compromise.

To her delight, Brancher shrugged. 'If that's what you want, I suppose so. But I ain't having you working in that pub for much longer.'

Placing the cup of coffee on the table in front of him, she gushed, 'Thank you, thank you so much.'

'Battersea ain't so bad. All me mates are here, well, those that ain't gone off fighting. I heard today that Freddie Waring got killed in battle. You remember Freddie?'

Maureen sat back at the table, nodding her head sadly. 'Yes, I remember him. His little sister was in my class at school. 'Ere, do you remember when you and Freddie chased me and his sister all the way to Nine Elms?'

'Cor, blimey, yeah. Freddie was doing his nut 'cos Lillian had pinched his bike. The pair of you rode off on it, so me and Freddie ran after you.'

'That's right.'

'And when we caught you, we let you off the hook ... for a kiss,' Brancher grinned.

'That was my first ever kiss,' Maureen recalled fondly.

'I'm glad I got to you before Freddie. He fancied you, but I warned him off.'

'I know. Lillian told me. She must be heartbroken. Do you think that I should visit her and offer my condolences?'

'No, I wouldn't. You don't want to get mixed up with them lot. I've heard that Lillian and her old man let their six kids go hungry while they throw booze down their necks.'

'Really? Poor Lillian! She was always so respectable.'

'No she weren't, she was a right tart.'

'No, not Lillian.'

'Yes she was! You don't know the half of it. Her old man put her on the game. And he ain't the father to half of them kids.'

'Blinkin' 'eck, I'm shocked to hear that.'

'Like I said, Maureen, you stay well away from her.'

'Yes, I will. But what a shame. Lillian used to be such a nice girl.'

'Well, she ain't nice no more and I don't want my wife associating with someone like her.'

Maureen chewed on her thumbnail as she thought about her friend from school. And she remembered the hurt expression on Freddie's face when she'd planted a kiss on Brancher's cheek. She'd been thirteen and her lips had never touched another man since. But she'd often secretly wished that she'd married Freddie instead of Brancher. Though back then, Brancher had been quite charming and a looker too. They hadn't married until many years after that first kiss and now she was left with just bittersweet memories and a life full of regret.

'Make me a bite to eat,' Brancher ordered.

'It's late, wouldn't you rather go to bed?'

'If I want to go to bed, I will. But, right now, I want something to eat. Or are you only serving up food to coloured men now, eh?' Brancher sneered.

Maureen tensed. She should have known better than to question her husband and now he was dragging up her mistake from earlier. In an instant, his good mood had been replaced with a contemptuous scowl on his face.

She hurried to the larder, her shoulders rounded, and took out what was left of the loaf of bread.

'I don't want a sandwich. Make me something hot.'

'But I don't want to wake my grandparents.'

'Sod 'em. So what if they wake up? It's not like they've got to get up for work or anything.'

Reluctant to argue with Brancher for fear of upsetting him, Maureen took the frying pan from out of the oven, asking, 'Spam and chips?'

'Yeah, that'll do.'

As she peeled spuds over the kitchen sink, she tensed when Brancher remarked, 'You're looking a bit skinny. You need to put on a few pounds. I like my women with a bit of meat on them.'

'It's hard to put on weight when there's food shortages and we're living on rations.'

'Have a plate of chips with me.'

'I'm not hungry.'

'A plate of chips won't hurt. Have some.'

Maureen quietly sighed. Her stomach was doing somersaults at the worrying thought of what Brancher's *job* was going to be. She couldn't face the thought of eating but would have to try to force some chips down, to keep him happy.

Half an hour later, Brancher smacked his lips together at the sight of the meal in front of him. Maureen peered down at her chips and slowly forked one into her mouth.

'That's it, gal, eat up,' he encouraged, his mouth full. 'You've got the appetite of a sparrow.'

She smiled feebly across the table.

He pointed his knife towards her plate. 'Come on, get 'em down you before they go cold.'

Maureen shoved another chip into her mouth and slowly chewed, but it felt like such an effort. 'I'm really not hungry,' she moaned.

'I told you, you need to plump yourself up a bit. I want to see that plate clean. In fact, you can eat these an' all.'

Brancher grabbed a handful of his chips and plonked them on her plate.

Maureen almost heaved at the food piled high. 'That's too many.'

'Stop complaining and just bloody eat what's in front of you. Christ, it's only a plate of chips!'

'But I've already had my tea.'

Without warning, Brancher jumped to his feet, sending his chair falling backwards. In two swift steps, he was towering over her and viciously grabbed a handful of her hair at the back of her head. Maureen tried not to cry out. She didn't want her grandparents to hear. 'I said, eat your bloody food,' he hissed.

Brancher snatched some chips from her plate and roughly pushed them in her face. He ground his hand over her mouth, chin and cheeks, smearing the warm, greasy potato over her skin, his force and strength hurting her.

As silent tears fell from her eyes, she tried to turn her face away, but he still had a firm grip of her hair.

'Are you going to shut up and eat them now?' he asked in a threatening manner, releasing her hair.

Maureen nodded, wiping her face. Her lip throbbed and she could taste blood in her mouth. The aggression that Brancher had used to ram the chips into her mouth had split her lip and she could feel that it was swelling.

'I've lost my appetite,' Brancher spat. 'You always ruin everything, you stupid, useless cow.'

She lowered her eyes as his feet clumped heavily across the kitchen and she jumped when he slammed the kitchen door behind him. The thud was sure to wake her grandparents. Concerned that her grandfather would come down to see what the noise was about, Maureen acted quickly. She dashed to the sink and splashed cold water on her face. Then she picked up Brancher's chair and hurriedly cleared away the mess of the squashed chips while dabbing at her cut lip with her hankie.

Thankfully, her grandparents must have slept through the commotion. But Maureen couldn't face going up to bed and lying beside her husband. Instead, she slipped into the front room and curled up on the sofa. Quiet sobs escaped her sore lips. She knew she only had herself to blame for Brancher's outburst. She should have just eaten the damn chips instead of making a fuss. After all, her husband only had her best interests at heart and it wasn't as if he was trying to poison her.

As Maureen dashed away her tears, she felt a new determination inside: she'd have to do better in future and she'd be a more compliant wife. Whatever it took, she'd make her husband happy.

9

Winnie chewed the end of her pencil as she sat at the kitchen table mulling over her shopping list. If she didn't write one, she knew that she'd return home without several important items. It was Friday, and she had a big roast to prepare for Sunday. It wouldn't do to miss things from her list.

Rachel came into the room looking pretty in a red and black floral summer dress. Winnie was pleased to see that the girl had made an effort with her appearance for her date with Alberto. He seemed to be a nice young man and was clearly making Rachel happy.

'Have you got a minute, Win?' Rachel asked, her voice hushed.

'Yes, love. I'm just writing out a shopping list so that I don't forget anything.'

Rachel chewed on her bottom lip, looking worried.

'What's wrong?' Winnie asked.

'It's Maureen. She's downstairs cleaning. I noticed that she's got a thick lip. When I asked her about it, she said that she fell up the stairs at home.'

'Hmm.'

'I'm not sure that I believe her. What do you think?'

'I don't know, love. I wouldn't have thought that Brancher was the sort of bloke to knock her about, but you never know what goes on behind closed doors.'

'She was right cagey about it. I'm sure that there's more to it.'

'You could be right. But if Brancher has given her a backhander, it's unlikely that she'll tell you the truth. Look at me and Brian: he used to hit me from here to kingdom come but I always covered for him and never told a soul. It's the shame of it. Poor Maureen will be too embarrassed to admit the truth.'

'Oh, Win, she's such a sweet little timid mouse. I hate to think of her being bullied by her husband.'

'I know, but what goes on between a husband and wife is none of our business.'

'Can't you speak to her? You've been through it. You understand.'

'I could, but I doubt it will change anything. Though I suppose it could be good for her to have someone to confide in.'

'Thanks, Win. I think it's best coming from you.'

'What time is Alberto calling for you?'

'Any minute now. Do I look all right?' Rachel asked and gave a twirl.

'You look beautiful. Where are you going?'

'Alberto has never seen Big Ben or Buckingham Palace, so I've suggested that we get a bus up to town. Martha will love it.'

'What a smashing idea! But don't be out for too long, will you?'

'Why?'

'I'd just feel better knowing that you are close to home if there's another air raid.'

'I hope there isn't, but we'll only be gone for a few hours.'

'Go on, you get off then, and I'll pop downstairs and have a discreet word with Maureen.'

Carmen came into the kitchen as Rachel breezed out. 'I caught the end of your conversation. What's wrong with Maureen?'

'It could be something or nothing. Rachel said that Maureen has a thick lip and reckons that she fell up the stairs.'

'And you think that Brancher has hit her?'

'I don't want to jump to any conclusions. I didn't think that Brancher was like that, but no one ever thought that Brian was knocking me about. I'll be very disappointed with him if he has hit her.'

'You and me both! I'll tear strips off him if he's hurt her.'

'Yes, me too. There's tea in the pot,' Winnie said, pushing herself to her feet. 'I'll be downstairs having a chat with Maureen if you need me.'

Winnie found Maureen sweeping down the stairs to the cellar.

'You all right, love?' she asked, keeping her voice light.

'Yes, thank you, Mrs Berry.'

Maureen had her head down; Winnie couldn't see her face. 'I'm going to have a nice cool drink. Care to join me?'

'Erm, I think I'd rather get on with my work if you don't mind, Mrs Berry?'

'Don't worry about that for now. You've been doing a grand job. Come and join me in the back kitchen.'

Winnie poured two long glasses of ginger beer and was

pleased to see Maureen edge into the room and sit at the table, but still the young woman kept her head lowered.

After Winnie placed the glasses on the table, she gently popped her finger under Maureen's chin and raised her face. Their eyes met and Winnie recognised the humiliated and frightened look in Maureen's eyes. Her heart went out to the poor girl. Looking at Maureen was like gazing at a past version of herself.

'Don't bother sticking up for him or lying to me ... Did Brancher do this?'

Maureen cast her eyes downwards and shook her head.

'My husband used to knock seven bells out of me. I used to try to cover my black eyes with a bit of make-up. I put up with it for years. He mellowed as he got older. Is that what you're going to do? Wait 'til Brancher gets old and calms down?'

'No ... I, erm ...'

'Listen, love. Whatever he's made you believe, this is *not* your fault. He's got no right to do this to you. Do you understand?'

'But ... but—'

'But, nothing. I don't blame you for not standing up for yourself. I never did. But I wish someone had sat me down, like I am now with you, and had told me that I wasn't to blame. See, every time that Brian hit me, he made me think that I'd done something wrong. And I stupidly believed him. I'd go out of my way to try to prevent a good hiding, but no matter what I did or didn't do, he'd always find an excuse to batter me and he always made me feel that I deserved it.'

Winnie could see the recognition in Maureen's eyes.

'Brancher does the same, doesn't he?'

Tears began to cascade from her eyes.

'It's all right, love. You've nothing to be ashamed of. You can talk openly to me. It won't be anything that I haven't been through myself. Does he buy you presents after and apologise, promising that it will never happen again ... until the next time?'

Maureen frantically shook her head. 'It's not like that, Mrs Berry, I swear. Brancher doesn't hit me.'

'Your swollen lip tells a different story.'

'He didn't hit me, honestly ... he, erm, he ... It was my fault. Brancher thinks that I'm too thin and he wanted me to eat. I shouldn't have moaned. I should have just eaten the chips.'

Winnie sighed. She could picture the scenario. 'He shoved them in your face?'

'Yes, but only because I said that I wasn't hungry. I made him lose his temper.'

'Oh, love, *you* didn't make him lose his temper. What he did is despicable and he's got no right to do that to you.'

'But like I said, he doesn't hit me. He gives me a shove now and then and is a bit rough sometimes, but I can put up with that. It's his ... his ...' Maureen's voice trailed off as juddering sobs wracked her body.

Winnie reached across the table and took the girl's hand in her own. 'What is it, love? What does he do?'

'It's his words,' she cried. 'He's so nasty to me. I try my best, really I do, but I never get it right.'

Winnie allowed Maureen to bawl her eyes out for a few minutes. Once she'd calmed down a little, she handed her a handkerchief. 'Now, young lady, you listen to me. You are not doing anything wrong. And no matter how hard you try,

Brancher will always find fault and give you a hard time. In my experience, the best way to stop him from hurting you is to confront him.'

Maureen stared wide-eyed at Winnie. 'I couldn't ... I wouldn't dare.'

'I know the thought of it is terrifying, but do you want to continue to live like this?'

'No, of course not, but I haven't got the guts to answer him back. And if I did, what if he *really* hurt me?'

Winnie could see that Maureen wasn't ready to stand up to her husband. She clasped her hands on the table as her mind turned, then offering, 'I'll speak to him.'

'No! Oh, gawd, Mrs Berry, please don't.'

'Don't panic. I'll have a quiet word with him. I'm sure that he'll listen to me.'

'He won't, Mrs Berry, and if he finds out that I've spoken to you, he'll be ten times worse!'

'All right, don't upset yourself. If you don't want me to say anything to him, I won't. But take some time to think about it, eh? If he knows that I know what he's been doing, it might make him think twice before hurting you again.'

'I understand what you're saying, and thank you. But I'd really rather that you didn't speak to him ... I'll do it. I'll tell him that I'm not putting up with it any longer.'

'That's right, love! Be brave. You can do it, Maureen, I know you can. But I'm telling you this: if I see any more cuts or bruises on you, I'll be pulling Brancher over the coals. He can't be left to get away it.'

'Thank you, Mrs Berry.'

'It's nearly opening time,' Winnie said, pushing herself to her feet. 'Listen, love, if ever you want to talk, I'm always here.'

After plastering on her welcoming smile, Winnie opened the doors of her pub, but inside she was in turmoil. She wanted to wring Brancher's neck but had to respect Maureen's wishes, though she strongly believed that a quiet warning in his ear was required. She'd say something to Brancher that wouldn't make him suspect that his wife had spoken about him. And she hoped that the young woman would find the courage to stand up for herself, though Winnie doubted it very much.

With nothing better to do that lunchtime, Clinton ambled into the Battersea Tavern, though he knew it was nearly closing time. Mrs Berry seemed busy with a rowdy crowd of ladies from the local factory, so he tried to catch Maureen's attention. After several attempts, he began to feel sure that she was deliberately ignoring him. He marched along the bar and, standing directly in front of her, he waved.

Maureen smiled, though she looked uneasy.

Clinton's eyes narrowed when he noticed that her lip was cut. He knew instantly that her husband had wounded her and his temper flared inside. After seeing his mother cowering from his father, he'd never understood how a man could be so cruel to a woman, especially a woman who should be loved and cherished.

Maureen glanced around, and Clinton guessed that she was looking to see if Brancher was in the pub. The last thing that he wanted to do was make her feel uncomfortable.

'What can I get you?' she asked.

'Mrs Berry will serve me, t'ank you,' he said, letting her off the hook.

Maureen gazed at him for a moment with gratitude in her large, brown eyes.

As she went to walk away, Clinton said quietly, 'He shouldn't do that to you. He's not a good man.'

Maureen's eyes flitted around nervously. And then she leaned over the bar towards him. 'He's *my* husband, and it's nothing to do with you,' she said, giving Clinton a reproachful look before scurrying away.

He should have expected that reaction. His mother had been the same. Clinton had struggled to accept his mother's defence of his father, but the woman had always stood up for him, just as Maureen was doing for Brancher. *Misplaced loyalty*, Clinton thought, shaking his head.

Mrs Berry bustled over, smiling as usual. 'Hello, love. I expect you're missing Alberto while him and Rachel are out sightseeing.'

'Actually, I've quite enjoyed the peace and quiet,' Clinton laughed. 'But I'll be pleased to start work on Monday. I've had a lot of hours to fill with just my thoughts.'

As Mrs Berry placed a half pint of ale on the counter, she said, 'Well, make the most of the peace and quiet as I should think that Alberto will be bringing Rachel home very soon.'

Clinton picked up the glass and gave a nod of his head to the friendly landlady. But his back stiffened when he realised that Sergeant Bradbury, in full uniform, was now standing beside him.

'Afternoon, lad. How do?' the old policeman asked.

'Good, t'ank you, sir.'

'Right you are. That's what I like to hear.'

Mrs Berry tutted, and said, 'Drinking on duty, Tommy, that's not like you.'

'I'm not here for a drink. I just popped in to make sure that there haven't been any more *incidents*.'

'No, nothing, thanks. We're all nice and secure since you put those new locks and bolts on the doors.'

The policeman lowered his voice and asked, 'What's happened to Maureen?'

'Oh, that … she's saying that she fell up the stairs,' Mrs Berry answered quietly, pursing her lips.

'Likely story. I've seen it many times before,' Tommy acknowledged.

'Yeah, well, I've had a word with her.'

'And I'll be having words with her husband.'

'I wouldn't, she doesn't want anyone to say anything to him about it.'

'It's not right, Winnie,' Tommy said, disapprovingly.

Clinton knew it was rude to eavesdrop on their conversation, though he couldn't help himself. But Mrs Berry and Sergeant Bradbury quickly changed the subject when Brancher walked into the pub.

Mrs Berry didn't offer the man her usual smile and scowled at him instead. Clinton could feel the tension in the atmosphere and gazed down into his drink. He'd done well to avoid trouble thus far and didn't want to get caught up in any now.

Brancher seemed oblivious to the contempt for him and said cheerily, 'Hello, Tommy. How are you?'

'It's Sergeant Bradbury to you, young man.'

'All right, keep your hair on.'

'And less of the lip or I'll whip you straight down to the station!'

'Pardon me for breathing,' Brancher mumbled.

'I hope you're keeping out of trouble. I'm watching you, Brancher Fanning.'

'Of course I am.'

From the corner of his eye, Clinton saw Mrs Berry lean forward towards Brancher. 'I don't want to see Maureen with any more cuts and bruises. *Falling up the stairs* ain't good for my business. You know what I'm getting at.'

'Flippin' 'eck, can't a bloke just have a quiet drink in his local without getting it in the neck from the pair of you. I've had enough of this... Maureen, get your coat, we're going home.'

Brancher's booming voice caused the pub to fall into silence. Clinton discreetly glanced over the top of his glass to see a very worried-looking Maureen darting out to the back. She soon returned with a coat over her arm and kept her eyes down as she came through the bar hatch.

Brancher walked out, appearing impatient.

'I'll see you next week, love,' Mrs Berry said to Maureen.

With the door behind Brancher closed, as Maureen passed Clinton, he touched her arm. 'Don't let him hurt you,' he said, tenderly.

For a brief moment, their eyes locked and Clinton could see her unshed tears. But then she snapped her head forward and hurried out after her husband.

'I shouldn't have said anything to him and hope I haven't made things worse for Maureen,' Mrs Berry said, shaking her head.

'I'll be keeping my eyes on him, Winnie, don't you worry. If he steps out of line, I'll be there waiting.'

Clinton took some hope from the policeman's words and hoped that Brancher would do something that would lead to his arrest, though he prayed that Maureen wouldn't get hurt. He liked Battersea, and he enjoyed being in the Battersea Tavern. The place would be so much better if Brancher wasn't around. And Maureen would be a lot safer too.

On the bus back to Battersea, Rachel's arm was going numb from holding Martha on her lap. Her daughter was sound asleep and exhausted after their day out in London to see the sights. Alberto had been fascinated with the grand buildings and architecture, though they had both been filled with poignant feelings. It had been sad and quite distressing to see the damage that Hitler's bombs had caused. So much history had been destroyed and many lives lost.

'It's nice to get back to Battersea,' Rachel mused.

'Didn't you enjoy being in central London?' Alberto asked.

'Yes, it was smashing. I just feel more at home in Battersea. I know we still get glared at and I've heard the awful whispers behind our backs, but it doesn't bother me here.'

'But it did bother you today?'

'Yes, I suppose it did. It's silly really, but it feels different when it's strangers that are judging me. Here, in Battersea, I don't know *everyone*, but it feels like we're all cut from the same cloth.'

'It's good to have a place to call home.'

'This is your home too now. I wasn't brought up in Battersea either, but I consider it home.'

'But I'll never be *cut from the same cloth*. You only have to look at the colour of my skin to see that.'

'Nonetheless, Battersea has made you feel welcome enough, hasn't it?'

'Yes, pretty much.'

'There you go, see. That's what people are like in Battersea and …' Rachel's words trailed off as a familiar face set her heart racing and her jaw dropping.

As the bus trundled towards Clapham Junction, she turned in her seat as much as she could, straining her neck to look out of the window at the man walking on the pavement.

'Oh, no,' she muttered.

'What is it?' Alberto asked.

'Winnie was right. He's back.'

'Who?'

'David. David Berry. Winnie's son … Martha's father.'

Rachel had divulged very few details about David to Alberto. She hadn't mentioned that he'd abused her when she'd been unconscious in a drunken stupor and that was how Martha had been conceived. Things like that were best left unsaid. It wasn't the done thing for a woman to complain of an assault, and even if she did, she'd likely get blamed. But seeing David swaggering brazenly down the street had caused a flood of uncomfortable memories to flood back. She fought hard to hold back her emotions, especially as Martha was curled up on her lap. But the thought of David being back in Battersea sent a shudder down her spine and tears pricked her eyes. *Will I ever be free from him?* she thought, angrily.

'Will he want to see Martha?' Alberto asked.

Rachel kissed the top of her daughter's soft, blonde hair, the same colour as her own, and then lowering her voice, she whispered, 'I won't allow him to see her, not ever. And I'd rather not talk about him.'

Alberto discreetly held her hand for the rest of the journey home and then carried Martha from the bus stop to the pub.

When they went in through the back door, Carmen was in the passageway.

'Is Winnie upstairs?' Rachel asked urgently.

'Yes, putting her feet up in the front room. Are you all right? You look like you've seen a ghost.'

'I have. Let me get Martha to bed.'

Alberto handed over the child, who only lightly stirred. 'I'll see you tomorrow,' he said.

Rachel was grateful that he seemed to sense her need for him to leave. 'Yes, and thank you for today.'

Upstairs, once her daughter was tucked up in bed, Rachel went through to the front room to be greeted by Winnie and Carmen. The women looked as though they were waiting anxiously for her news, but then Winnie blurted, 'You've seen him, haven't you? You've seen David?'

Rachel nodded and gulped. It was clear that the news was no surprise to Winnie, but the woman still looked horrified.

'I knew it! I bleedin' knew it! I said, didn't I? I said it was him who broke in the other night. Honestly, that good-for-nothing pig! He's back here for money, but he won't be getting a penny out of me.'

Carmen jumped up from the sofa and rushed to Rachel's side. Placing an arm over her shoulders, she soothed, 'It's all right. Come and sit down. There's a cuppa on the table for you. It must have been an awful shock for you.'

'Gawd, I'm sorry, love,' Winnie said. 'There's me ranting on without a thought for how you must be feeling.'

'Don't be daft, Win. You've every right to rant. But yes, it was a terrible shock. Do you think he will want to see Martha?'

'I doubt it. He's never bothered about the girl before now.

Anyway, so what if he does? He can go and take a running jump!' Winnie said firmly, rolling up her dress sleeves as if she meant business. 'He'll have to get past me first. I won't have him turning up in my granddaughter's life and upsetting the apple cart.'

'Thanks, Win.'

'I'll let Tommy Bradbury know that you've seen him. I know he's my son, but I hope the police catch up with him. He can rot in gaol for all I care.'

Rachel sipped her tea, feeling calmer now that she had the reassuring support of Winnie and Carmen. And she knew that her mother, Hilda, was a force to be reckoned with too. If David had any intention of wanting to see his daughter, he'd have to fight his way through a barrier of strong women. But knowing David to be a coward, she doubted that he'd even try.

10

On Saturday morning, Maureen sat at the kitchen table and yawned, stretching her arms over her head. Brancher had gone mad when they'd left the pub the day before, but she'd managed to convince him that she hadn't spoken to Winnie about her cut lip. She'd said that Winnie's husband had knocked her about, so the woman had jumped to the wrong conclusion.

'You must be glad that you don't work at weekends,' her gran said.

Snapping back to the present, Maureen replied, 'I am. I don't think that I got a wink of sleep in the shelter last night. I was worried about Brancher. I wish he'd come in the shelter with us.'

'You and me both, I'm shattered too. I couldn't give two hoots about your husband, but your granddad was snoring his head off which kept me up.'

'Where is he?'

'Gone to get his paper.'

Maureen regretted mentioning Brancher but thankfully, her gran didn't ask where he was. If she had, Maureen wouldn't know what to tell her. She felt foolish for not knowing her husband's whereabouts. He'd been out all night, though Maureen didn't suspect that he was with another woman. In some ways, she wished that he were, but she had a feeling that he was doing the *job* that he had mentioned.

'Right, we've got the house to ourselves for ten minutes... are you going to tell me the truth about what really happened to your lip?'

Maureen had believed that her injury had gone unnoticed by her gran, so the direct question came as a shock. She stared at her gran, with eyes stretching wide, her mind racing as she tried to think of something to say.

'I know you, Maureen, I brought you up. You can't hide things from me.'

Maureen looked down at her fidgeting hands on her lap.

'This isn't the first time that he's hurt you, is it?'

'It was an accident, Gran. He didn't mean to do it.'

'Well, in all the years that I've been married to your grand-father, he's never once *accidently* given me a thick lip. I put up with a lot of things from Brancher. He's loud, messy, selfish, lazy and rude, but I won't tolerate him hurting you, especially in my house.'

'He really didn't mean it, Gran. Brancher isn't like that. He's got a bit of a temper on him, but he doesn't hit me.'

'I can't say that I'm surprised that you're covering for him, but I'll be watching him like a bloomin' hawk from now on. Cor, if your brother were here, he'd soon put Brancher in line.'

Maureen smiled at the thought of Stephen. 'He's always stuck up for me.'

'He has, he's a good boy. He takes after your granddad. Your mother would have been very proud of him.'

'From what I've heard, our boys are pushing the Nazis back through France. I hope that means that the war will end soon and Stephen can come home.'

'Me too, pet, me too. But Stephen is fighting the Japs on the other side of the world, not the Germans in Europe.'

'At least he's driving a tank, Gran. I feel a bit better thinking that he's safe in that big machine.'

'Yes, me too. So, what have you got planned for the weekend?'

'Well, I'm going shopping soon and I thought I'd get us something nice for tea.'

'You don't want to be spending your day off shopping and cooking.'

'I do. I like cooking.'

'You ought to be out in the park or something in this nice weather. Or haven't you got any friends that you could meet up with?'

Maureen shook her head. Brancher didn't like any of her friends so she rarely saw them nowadays. 'I've lost touch with them. But really, Gran, I'm happy doing a bit of shopping and cooking. It's nice to be at home spending some time with you.'

'If you say so. Take a few bob out of my purse and treat yourself to a new pair of shoes. You can't keep wearing those scruffy things, not now that you're working in the pub.'

'Are you sure?' Maureen asked. She looked down at her tatty shoes, grateful for her gran's offer. Knowing that Brancher would demand her wages, she knew that a new pair of shoes wouldn't be forthcoming from him.

'Yes, I'm sure,' her Gran answered. 'But from what I've heard, there won't be many styles in the shops for you to choose from. Anyhow, if you're going shopping, you'd better give me a hand into the front room. Me legs are playing up today and I'm shattered, so I'll have a doze in my armchair while you're out.'

With her gran leaning heavily on her arm, Maureen pushed open the front room door to be met by a blast of heat.

Her gran tutted. 'The silly old bugger has lit the fire. I told you, he's not right, Maureen. It's mid-June, what on earth was he thinking? Open the windows, pet, it's like an oven in here.'

'Shall I get some water to put out the fire?'

'No, it's fine. It'll burn itself out soon enough.'

Maureen made sure that her gran was comfortable before heading out. As she made her way to the shops, her mind turned with worrying thoughts about her granddad and then flitted to fears about what Brancher was up to. The stress was giving her a headache. But as she drew closer to the high street, her heart dropped when she saw where a V1 bomb had landed. Two shops had been reduced to rubble and what appeared to be a van was still smouldering. She stood and gazed at the devastating scene, hoping that no one had been killed.

A woman carrying a full shopping basket passed Maureen. 'It's business as usual,' she said. 'The rest of the shops are open.'

'Thanks,' Maureen replied, but she couldn't face walking along the high street now, not knowing that dead bodies might have been pulled from the debris.

She turned around and decided to shop at the Northcote Road market instead. It would take her a while to get there, but she wasn't in any rush. And as Brancher wasn't around, she didn't have to answer to him about her movements, for a change. In fact, she felt somewhat free and intended to make the most of it.

Len ambled home with his newspaper tucked under his arm. He had a niggling feeling that he was supposed to do something today, but for the life of him, he couldn't remember what it was.

Indoors, he found his wife sat in the front room but wondered why she had the coals burning in the summer. 'What have you got that on for? You're not cold, are you?' he asked, sitting beside the hearth opposite her.

'No, I'm bloomin' roasting! I didn't light it; you must have done.'

Len was about to protest that it wasn't him, but he couldn't be sure so decided to keep quiet and read his paper instead. He scanned the pages, looking for something that might interest Renee. He knew that his wife wouldn't want to hear about troop movements or torpedoed ships. When an article about Princess Elizabeth caught his eye, he read it aloud. Len prided himself on his accomplished reading skills, especially as most of his mates could only just about sign their names. And Renee always said that she enjoyed him reading to her. But when he'd finished the article and looked over the top of the newspaper, his wife's eyes were closed and he could tell by her heavy, rhythmic breathing that she was in a deep sleep.

He rolled his eyes and turned to the back of the paper. But as he studied the small black print, the letters suddenly meant nothing to him and became a blur. Len squinted and pulled the newspaper closer. When he still couldn't fathom the words, he threw the paper angrily to one side and stood up. There was something he had to do. What was it?

Feeling frustrated, he marched out of the room and through the front door. And like a light bulb switching on, he remembered: Brancher. He had to confront his grandson-in-law and get to the bottom of why Maureen had a swollen lip. He wondered how he could have forgotten something that was so important.

On a mission now and determined to remember, Len assumed that Brancher would most likely be in the pub. He felt sick to the pit of his stomach at the thought of that man hurting his granddaughter and made a beeline for the Battersea Tavern to have it out with him. Granted, the man was nearly half a century his junior, but Len had once been a boxer and he believed that he was still nimble on his feet and could throw a good punch. At this moment in time, nothing would give him greater pleasure than putting Brancher on his sorry backside.

Len barged into the pub and looked around, but there was no sign of Brancher.

'Hello, love, are you all right?' Winnie asked.

'Yes, fine. Has Brancher been in?'

'Not today. If I see him, shall I tell him that you're looking for him?'

'Yeah, you do that.'

'Are you sure that you're all right, Len?'

'I will be once I get my hands on that git.'

'Why? What's he done?'

'Don't tell me that you didn't notice Maureen's face?'

'I did, and I spoke to her about it. She won't thank you for interfering.'

'I won't stand back and let Brancher lay another finger on my Maureen. If you see him, send him home to me.'

Len didn't wait for Winnie to reply. He spun around and headed back home, trying hard to keep his focus.

As he turned the corner onto his street, he stopped suddenly and stared in disbelief. Thick, black smoke billowed out of the windows of his house and he could see orange flames licking the window frames.

'Renee!' he called in panic.

Len ran towards the house, praying that his wife had been rescued from the fire. Guilt washed over him as he remembered throwing the newspaper to the floor. Had it landed near the fire? Had he set his own house alight and, God forbid, killed his dear Renee?

A crowd had gathered outside and someone told him that they had called the fire brigade.

'Renee... My Renee...'

Pushing through the throng towards the house, Len felt strong arms pulling him back from the intense heat.

'Ger off me! I have to get Renee!'

'You can't go in there, Len, it's too late,' his neighbour said.

'No! Get your hands off me!'

'Len, just wait for the fire brigade. The fire is too strong. You can't get in the house. We've tried, mate, we all really tried. I'm sorry... She's gone.'

As Len's neighbour released the grip on his arm, over the roar of the fire, Len heard the bell of the fire engines approaching. He held his arm protectively over his face as he stared dumbstruck at the burning house. Renee, his beloved Renee, was dead.

'I can't live without her,' he mumbled.

Almost mechanically, Len walked purposefully towards the front door, ignoring the shouts and screams from behind.

'Len … come back … what are you doing?'

As he walked through the burning door and into the choking blackness inside the house, he could feel his skin blistering in the searing heat and his lungs aching for air. He knew that he was never coming out again. He would die, beside his wife, the woman with whom he'd shared most of his life.

'I'm coming, my love … I'm coming,' he said, coughing and his eyes stinging.

Len's shirt and trousers were alight as he stumbled in agony into the front room. And there, beside the charred and scorched remains of Renee, Len took his final, suffocating breath.

Maureen was pleased with her purchases, but as she trudged home, she wished that she hadn't bought so much. Her arms ached with the weight of her shopping bags and her feet were sore too. But she smiled at the thought of her grandparents' faces when she presented them with a fancy meal tonight, though, granted, it would only be a tasty stew.

She heard footsteps catching up from behind and was then horrified to find Clinton walking in step with her.

'Hello, Maureen. You look like you're struggling there. Let me take your bags for you.'

'Er, no, I'm managing fine, thank you,' she lied.

'We're heading the same way. Please, allow me to help you.'

'I said, I'm fine, thank you,' Maureen answered curtly. She could feel her heart pounding. If Brancher saw her walking with Clinton, he'd be outraged!

'You seem to have made your rations go a long way,' Clinton said light-heartedly, pointing at her bags.

'It's mostly veg and a bit of fruit.'

'Ah, I miss the fruits from my homeland. Guavas, mangoes, watermelons, papaya ... my mouth is watering just thinking about them.'

'I've never heard of them. I've just got plain old apples, but I'd kill for a banana. We ain't seen bananas in the shops since the war started.'

'Your bananas probably came from my home. Big steamships used to take them from the plantations.'

'To tell you the truth, I've never really given much thought to where my bananas came from,' she said with a smile, but then remembered who she was talking to and the trouble it could land her in. 'I'm sorry, Clinton, I don't mean to be rude, but I really must get on.'

'I understand. Your husband wouldn't be happy to see you in the street with me.'

Maureen didn't answer but gave him a sideways glance and a weak smile.

'If you're sure you won't let me carry your shopping?'

'I'm sure, thank you. Anyway, I'm nearly home now.'

'Do you live near the Battersea Tavern?' Clinton asked, looking concerned.

'Yes, why?'

'Look,' he answered, pointing to dark-grey smoke rising through the sky over the rooftops.

'Blimey, I wonder what's happened. I didn't hear an air-raid siren.'

'No, neither did I.'

Maureen peered at the smoke, trying to gauge where it was

coming from. 'That looks awfully close to my house. Here, take these,' she said urgently, handing her shopping bags to Clinton. 'Hurry.'

She began to think the worst and fear snaked through Maureen's veins as she ran towards home. When they dashed around the corner and onto her street, Maureen screamed when she saw the fire engine and ambulance outside her grandparents' smouldering home. Oblivious to Clinton running beside her, she charged towards the house.

When the crowd outside saw her coming, she was stopped and someone took a firm grip of her shoulders.

'I'm sorry, Maureen. There was nothing that we could do for your gran and we tried to stop Len, but...'

'W-what?' Maureen asked, unable to absorb what she was being told.

'They're both dead. I'm so sorry.'

'No ... no ... they can't be,' she wailed.

'We did everything we could, but the fire had a hold before we realised that the house was alight. By then, it was too late. We couldn't get in. We tried, Maureen, we just couldn't get past the heat.'

'My granddad?'

'He ... he, erm, he wouldn't listen. I didn't know what he was going to do. If I'd known, I would have stopped him.'

'What do you mean?'

'Your granddad ... Len ... he, er, erm ... he went into the house.'

'When it was on fire?'

'Yeah. He wouldn't listen. I told him not to.'

Maureen's legs felt weak and buckled under her. She

132

dropped to the ground, but several people pulled her back to her feet.

'They're both dead?' she mumbled, peering at the sea of faces around her.

'Yes, I'm sorry, they're both dead.'

Maureen's chest felt tight and bile burned the back of her throat.

'Once the fire brigade give us the thumbs up, we'll go in and see if there's anything we can salvage from the house for you. But there's nothing that you can do here. Have you got somewhere you can go ... for now?'

Maureen shook her head. She feared that if she opened her mouth, vomit would spew out.

'I'll take her to the Battersea Tavern,' Clinton suggested.

'That's a good idea. You'll be all right there, Maureen. And if we see Brancher, we'll tell him where to find you.'

Maureen nodded, but she wasn't really sure what she was agreeing to. Her mind could only think of one thing: her grandparents were dead. 'I've bought them a nice supper for this evening,' she mumbled.

'Come on, Maureen,' Clinton urged. He placed his hand gently on her elbow and led her away from the burned-out house.

'I can't believe it ... I can't believe that they're really dead,' Maureen uttered, shaking her head.

As they slowly walked towards the pub, Maureen began to shake. She trembled from head to toe, even her teeth chattered.

Clinton rushed her through the pub door, calling out to Mrs Berry. 'She's in shock.'

Whatever happened next was nothing but a blur to

Maureen. She was vaguely aware of collapsing, being carried, lying on a couch, sipping brandy, blankets on her... Was it real? Was she in a terrible nightmare or had she just seen her grandparents' house on fire and heard that they were both killed? She couldn't be sure of anything and didn't trust her own mind. But she hoped that if this was all a horrid dream, she'd wake up in a minute and everything would be as it should.

Hours later, Winnie was in the kitchen but could hear Maureen's sobs from the front room. As she searched through her purse for some coins, she turned to Carmen, shaking her head. 'I don't know what to do with her, she's hysterical. I'm going to the telephone box to call the doctor. Perhaps he can give her something to calm her down.'

'Where's her husband? That's what I'd like to know! From what I can get out of her, she ain't seen him since yesterday.'

'I don't think Brancher would be much use at the moment.'

'Maybe not, but he's all she's got left now.'

'The poor girl. Stay with her, Carmen, I'll be as quick as I can.'

Winnie hurried down the stairs and out of the back door. As she made her way to the telephone box, she had to pass the street where Len and Renee had lived. There were still a lot of people on the street, gaping and gossiping about the tragedy. Winnie took a moment to look at the burned-out house and suppressed the urge to cry. Len had been one of her regular customers since she'd first opened the doors of the Battersea Tavern a quarter of a century ago. She'd miss the miserable old bugger, and though she hadn't seen as much of Renee lately, it still hurt to think of her gone. And to have both their lives ended in such a dreadful manner didn't bear thinking about.

After speaking to the doctor, Winnie rushed back to the pub. As she climbed the stairs to the front room, she could hear that Carmen hadn't been successful in calming Maureen. She hoped the doctor would arrive soon with some sort of magic pill.

Winnie pushed open the door and decided to try a firmer approach with Maureen. She didn't want to sound hard or uncaring, but if the woman continued in this state, she'd make herself ill.

'Right, listen to me, Maureen...' she ordered, firmly.

'Why...Why would my granddad go into the house? He must have known that it would kill him...'

'Maureen,' Winnie snapped. 'Listen, love—'

'Do you think they felt any pain? Oh, God, I can't stand the thought of my grandparents being burnt to death. Blimey, they're dead, they're both dead! I won't have them buried in cardboard coffins. You've seen them, haven't you? All the people who were buried in cardboard coffins. Loads of them, I saw them. Cardboard coffins for the dead. Hitler's bombs. Too many dead. Cardboard coffins. I can't have that for my gran and granddad.'

'Maureen!' Winnie shouted over Maureen's ramblings.

At last, she was quiet and looked up at Winnie with red, swollen eyes.

'You're not doing yourself any favours, love. Neither Len nor Renee would want to see you like this, would they?'

Maureen dropped her head into her hands, her shoulders jerking as she wept uncontrollably.

Carmen whispered in Winnie's ear, 'Is the doctor coming?'

'Yes.'

'Good. She won't listen to reason. Best leave her alone for a while and let the doctor sort her out. I think we're just making matters worse.'

Winnie eased Maureen back on the sofa and put a blanket over her legs. 'Lay down and have a rest,' she said softly. 'Me and Carmen will be in the kitchen if you need anything.'

As Carmen put the kettle on, Winnie heard a hammering at the pub door.

'I hope that's the doctor,' she said.

Downstairs, she answered the door to find Tommy on the step, holding his helmet under his arm.

'I've just heard, Winnie. Someone said that Maureen is here.'

'Yes, she is. Do you want to come in?'

'I realise that it's a difficult time for her, but I need to ask her a few questions.'

'You won't get any sense out of her. I've just had to call for the doctor. The poor girl is in such a state. I'm afraid your questions will have to wait. But you're welcome to come in for a cuppa?'

'I wouldn't say no, thanks, Winnie.'

Upstairs, Carmen's eyebrows raised at the sight of seeing Tommy following Winnie into the kitchen.

' 'Ark at her,' Tommy said, flicking his head towards the front-room door which was pulled to. 'No wonder you've called for the doctor.'

'She's been like it for hours now. We were hoping that she'd cry herself to sleep. You haven't seen Brancher, have you?' Carmen asked.

'No. I take it he doesn't know yet?'

'We don't think so.'

'Fat lot of good that he'd be,' Winnie added. 'Sit yourself down, love, there's fresh tea in the pot.'

'I'll leave you two to it. See you, Tommy,' Carmen said, slipping out of the kitchen with a smirk.

'Any idea how the fire started?' Winnie asked.

'They're not sure, but there are several accounts of smoke being seen coming from the chimney this morning.'

'In June?'

'Yes, seems odd.'

Winnie thought of poor Len. Maybe in his confusion, he'd got the coals burning.

'Will Maureen be staying with you for now?'

'I don't know, Tommy. If she's got nowhere else to go, then I suppose she'll have to. I won't see her on the streets.'

'And Brancher?'

'Well, he is her husband, so I won't have much choice.' Winnie wasn't keen on having Brancher under her roof, but at least she'd be able to keep an eye on him and ensure that he wasn't hitting poor Maureen.

'Changing the subject,' Tommy said, 'there's been no sightings of your David. Every officer from the station is keeping an eye out. Is Rachel *sure* that she saw him?'

'Yes, she's sure, but maybe he's buggered off again. He didn't find any money here so there wouldn't be much point in him staying in Battersea.'

'Well, just in case he's still around, I'll make sure that my colleagues keep looking. There was a violent robbery last night by masked men. The distillery was turned over. The nightwatchman and a fire warden were injured by the perpetrators. Do you think that David could have been involved?'

'I don't know, Tommy. I wouldn't like to think so, but I wouldn't put anything past him. Are the injured fellas all right?'

'The watchman was pretty badly beaten, but the fire warden escaped with just a few cuts and bruises. The gang that did the job are a nasty bunch and dangerous. Make sure you keep your doors bolted at night.'

Carmen popped her head around the door. 'The doctor is here,' she said.

'Excuse me, Tommy. Help yourself to another cuppa.'

Carmen raised her hand, saying, 'It's all right. I'll see to him. You stay there.'

Winnie was grateful for Carmen's help. Though she felt sorry for Maureen, she found it difficult to witness so much grief and pain.

'This is the first time I've been upstairs. You've got plenty of room, it's nice and spacious,' Tommy commented.

'Yes, the flat is a fair size. Good job an' all if I'm going to be putting up Maureen and Brancher for a while.'

'It's going to be awkward for you tomorrow with everyone coming for Sunday dinner. Are you going to cancel?'

'No, I don't think so. I haven't seen my Jan for weeks. I'm sure I'll manage.'

'I could come early and help, if you like?'

'That's kind of you, Tommy, thank you, but that won't be necessary. Carmen and Rachel will be here. Anyway, you're a guest, I couldn't have you mucking in.'

Three loud thuds on the door downstairs startled Winnie.

'Who could that be?' she thought aloud, pushing herself to her feet.

'I'd best get going, I'm on duty. Thanks for the tea. I'll see you tomorrow.'

Tommy followed Winnie down the stairs. As she approached the door, the person on the other side knocked loudly again.

'I think it might be Brancher,' she said, suddenly feeling tense.

'Let me deal with him,' Tommy offered.

Winnie nodded and stepped aside. When Tommy opened the door, Brancher burst through.

'Where is she? Maureen, is she here?' Brancher asked frantically.

'Yes, son, she's upstairs. The doctor is with her.'

'Doctor? Is she hurt?'

'No, she's not hurt, but she's very distraught.'

Brancher pushed past Tommy, yelling, 'Maureen!' as he ran towards the bar.

'Oi, just slow down. You can't go barging in and upsetting her,' Tommy said, chasing behind him.

Brancher turned and spat, 'She's *my* wife. Don't tell me what I can and can't do!'

Winnie hurriedly followed Brancher and Tommy up the stairs. Carmen was waiting at the top, the doctor behind her. She held her hands in front of her to try to stop Brancher. 'She's resting. The doctor has sedated her.'

'I want to see my wife!' he barked.

'You can, but you need to calm down.'

'What is it with you lot? I just want to see Maureen. Move out of my way!'

Carmen, with pursed lips, stepped aside. The doctor appeared most uncomfortable and made a hasty exit. Brancher flew into the front room with the others in his wake.

Winnie was pleased to see that Maureen was quiet now, but she looked only half with it.

'Maureen … Maureen … I'm here,' Brancher said.

His gentleness surprised Winnie.

Maureen didn't respond.

Brancher pulled her up and placed his shoulder under her arm, semi-carrying her off the sofa.

'What are you doing?' Tommy asked.

'I'm taking my wife.'

'Whoa, slow down, son. She's in no fit state to go anywhere. And where are you thinking of taking her?'

'I dunno. We'll find somewhere.'

'Well, I think you should leave her where she is, for now. Mrs Berry has already agreed that Maureen can stay here tonight. She's had a traumatic shock and needs to rest.'

'I'll do what I see fit with my wife. Either help me get her down the stairs or move out of my way,' Brancher argued.

Winnie was shocked at the lack of respect that Brancher was showing Tommy, especially as the man was in his policeman's uniform. 'Sergeant Bradbury is right, Brancher. You shouldn't be dragging Maureen around. She'll be better off left on my sofa.'

Ignoring their advice, Brancher hauled Maureen from the room. The woman could hardly put one foot in front of the other and was clearly woozy from the drugs that the doctor had administered.

Seeing how determined Brancher was and knowing that there was little that the law could do to stop him, Winnie nudged Tommy and whispered, 'Give him a hand down the stairs before he has an accident with her.'

Maureen's shopping bags were by the door, which she must

have seen. Her head lulled to one side as she mumbled, 'My shopping … cooking a special dinner for my gran and—'

'It's all right, love. I'll look after your shopping for you,' Winnie assured. Then she quietly explained to Brancher, 'When Clinton brought Maureen here, he dropped her bags off too.'

Brancher's darkened eyes stretched wide and Winnie was sure that she saw him snarling. 'Clinton brought my wife here?'

'Yes, that's right and you should thank him for looking after her.'

Without saying another word but with an angry scowl, Brancher dragged Maureen out of the pub.

'I'll be needing to ask Maureen a few questions, so I want to know her whereabouts,' Tommy demanded.

Brancher didn't bother to look back but shouted, 'I'll be in touch.'

'Make sure you are.'

Winnie stood at the door and watched sadly as Brancher lugged his semi-conscious wife along the street. She'd never thought badly of him until she'd seen Maureen's fat lip. But now she could see that he was very much like her own husband had been: possessive and unreasonable. It had taken Winnie far too long to stand up to Brian, but she had eventually and had been happier for it. Now with Len and Renee gone, Winnie knew that Maureen would become even more reliant on her husband and she hoped that the woman wouldn't become his punchbag.

II

Martha was playing happily with Cake, rolling a ball for him across the kitchen floor, as Rachel stood at the sink and peeled potatoes in preparation for today's big Sunday lunch. She loved to hear her daughter laughing and she couldn't help but smile at the sound of Martha's giggles. But her pleasure was marred by the worrisome thought of David being in Battersea.

'Thanks for doing that, love,' Winnie said as she came into the kitchen.

'No bother. I would have done the veg too, but Carmen beat me to it.'

'You've got to be quick off the mark to get ahead of Carmen. I don't think she went to bed after last night's bombings. I'm pretty sure that she was out here at the crack of a sparrow's fart, getting things ready.'

'Where is she now?'

Winnie sighed before answering, 'She's gone to see if she can find Maureen and Brancher. She's worried sick about Maureen, but it'll be like looking for a needle in a haystack.'

Rachel dried her hands on her pinny and sat at the table

142

with Winnie. She glanced around at Martha; the girl was growing up fast and she didn't want her to hear their conversation. 'Martha, take Cake into the bedroom with you and put your shoes and socks on. We'll take him for a walk,' she instructed.

She waited until Martha was out of earshot and then continued her chat with Winnie.

'I can't believe that we're never going to see Len again. I don't understand, Win, why did he walk into the fire?'

'Who knows, love, but Len wasn't well.'

'What was wrong with him?'

'His mind was going and he knew it was. Maybe he couldn't face life without Renee. It's so sad.'

'And what about their funerals? Maureen will have to arrange things, but I don't know if she'll be strong enough.'

'Carmen will help, well, she will if she can find her.'

'Have they worked out how the fire started?'

'No, not really. There's speculation that Len lit a fire in the hearth that somehow spread. But I don't suppose we'll ever really know.'

'What an awful way to go,' Rachel said, shuddering at the thought of burning to death.

'I can't think of anything worse,' Winnie replied, her eyes filling with tears.

'I'm sorry, Win, I shouldn't have said anything.'

'Don't be daft, love. You only said exactly what we're all thinking. It's harrowing to think of Len and Renee's last moments. I can understand why Maureen got herself in such a state. But, call me selfish, I won't allow us to dwell on it today. I don't want my lunch spoiled by sadness.'

'No, you're right, Win. It's been a while since Jan has had time to visit. Let's make it a happy day!'

'That's the spirit. Now, take the pup for a walk and I'll finish off peeling the spuds.'

Rachel stood up and gave Winnie a kiss on her cheek. The woman always had a knack of lifting the mood.

Outside, Rachel had Martha's hand in her own and Cake's lead in the other. The streets were typically quiet for a Sunday morning. She tried to relax, but the fear of coming face to face with David was never far from her mind. As she turned a corner, she was pleased to see her mother walking towards her.

'Nanna,' Martha squealed, yanking her hand free of Rachel's before skipping towards Hilda.

'Hello, Mum,' said Rachel. 'Are you on the way to the pub?'

'Hello, darling, and yes, I thought I'd turn up early to see if you all need a hand.'

'Thanks, Mum. We'll walk back with you.'

As they strolled along the road, Hilda asked, 'So, how are things going with Alberto?'

Rachel could feel her cheeks flushing and a wide smile spread across her face. 'Really good. I like him a lot and so does Martha.'

'Aw, that's smashing to hear.'

'He starts work at the power station tomorrow.'

'That's good news. But it means that you'll be seeing less of him.'

'Yes, I know, but we'll have some weekends and most evenings.'

'I heard about the fire,' Hilda whispered. 'Terrible!'

'You can say that again! Winnie said that Maureen was inconsolable. She had to call the doctor to her.'

'I can't say that I'm surprised. Has anyone got word to Stephen?'

'Oh, blimey, I hadn't thought of that! I don't suppose that Maureen's thought about telling her brother. Mind you, with him fighting oversees, it's probably best that he doesn't know.'

'Hmm, maybe. But I think he'll be upset if he comes home to find that his grandparents are dead and no one told him.'

'You should mention it to Carmen, Mum. She's taken Maureen under her wing... if she can find her.'

'What do you mean?'

'Brancher has taken her, but no one knows where.'

'Great. I should imagine that he's about as much use as a chocolate fireguard. 'Ere, talk of the devil, isn't that him?' Hilda said, pointing to a man further along the street.

'Yes, I think it is,' Rachel answered, though it was difficult to tell.

'Look at him... he's pulled his flat cap right down low over his face. He's up to no good, I can tell.'

'Shall we follow him?' Rachel suggested.

'I will, but I want you and Martha to go home.'

'All right, but be careful,' Rachel answered. Martha was skipping just in front of them. She called the girl to her and took her hand. 'You'll see Nanna soon. She just has to run an errand and then she'll come to see us,' she explained as she gently pulled Martha along the street.

Back at the Battersea Tavern, Winnie was opening the pub for the late-morning and lunchtime trade. Rachel sent Martha upstairs with Cake and then dashed into the bar.

'We've just seen Brancher,' she announced to Winnie. 'Mum is following him. He looked right shady. Mum thought that he was up to no good.'

'Oh blimey, I hope she doesn't land herself in any bother.'

'She said that she'll be careful. What do you think he's up to?'

'I've no idea, but if he's out and about, that must mean that Maureen is by herself. Gawd, I hope the woman is all right.'

'Brancher might have been on his way home and Mum will find out where they are staying.'

'Hope so, love, hope so,' Winnie replied, sadly.

Rachel noticed that Winnie was gazing at the door with a distant look in her eyes.

'Are you all right, Win?' she asked.

'Yes, love. Just thinking about Len. That door would normally open about now and he'd breeze in, looking like he was chewing a wasp. I'm going to miss his miserable face.'

'Do you want me to take his tankard away and give it a polish? Perhaps Maureen would like it? Everything in their house is cinders now. Len's tankard might be the only thing she has to remember him by.'

'That's a lovely idea. You're such a thoughtful girl.'

Rachel gave Winnie a warm smile before taking the tankard upstairs. Sitting at the kitchen table with a soft cloth and a can of Bluebell polish, she gently rubbed the metal but couldn't stop her mind from turning. She could feel her stomach knotting with worry about her mum following Brancher. Worse, her nerves were still jangling since she'd caught sight of David in Battersea. She could only hope that it was the last that she'd see of him.

★

Maureen's heavy eyelids slowly opened and she found herself looking at a ceiling that she didn't recognise. Wondering where she was, she pushed herself up and gazed around the room. Her mind felt hazy and she squinted with confusion as she tried to work out whose bed she was laid on.

Bright sunlight streamed through the window. Maureen eased her legs over the edge of the bed and went to walk over to the window to look outside, hoping that it would give her a clue to her whereabouts. But feeling dizzy, she sat back down and drew in a long breath. Where was she? And how did she get here?

As she searched her mind for the answers, the traumatic events of the day before rushed back into her head. Her grandparents were dead, killed in a devastating house fire! But had she dreamed it? Was she dreaming now? Feeling groggy, Maureen couldn't be sure of anything.

She spotted a glass of water on the small table beside the bed and quickly glugged it down. Her head cleared a little and she looked around the room again. A double bed, a large oak wardrobe, a set of mismatched drawers, the pale, yellow-flowered wallpaper, she didn't recognise any of it. But she saw something familiar on a wooden stool in the corner.

Standing unsteadily on her feet again, she walked to the stool and picked up a shirt and instantly recognised it: Brancher's shirt. This gave her some relief. And when she peered through the window, she could see the railway lines of Clapham Junction train station. Again, more relief flowed over her as she realised that she was still in Battersea.

But the memory that suddenly hit her next knocked her off her feet. Maureen crumpled onto the floor as grief engulfed her and she realised that what had happened yesterday hadn't been a dream. The fire had been very real and now her grandparents were dead. Tears flowed unchecked down her face. She needed comfort and wanted Brancher. But where was he?

Eventually, Maureen swallowed the knot of agony in her throat and fought to stop crying. She dashed the tears from her face and now, somewhat composed, she clung onto the windowsill, pulling herself back onto her feet. She thought that Brancher must be somewhere else in the house and went in search of him. But when she pulled on the bedroom door, she was astonished to find that it wouldn't open. She banged on the door with her fists and called out Brancher's name, shaking the door and wriggling the doorknob until panic began setting in.

'Brancher … Let me out …' she shouted, desperately.

She placed her ear to the door and listened for any sounds. When she heard nothing, she knew it was useless to continue to shout for her husband. But she couldn't understand why he had locked her in the room.

She went back to the window and looked down onto the street. If she could catch someone's attention, maybe they could get in and release her. But Maureen quickly dismissed that thought. Brancher would be furious if she defied him and he must have had a good reason for keeping her locked up. She'd just have to be patient and wait for him to return.

With nothing but her thoughts to occupy her, Maureen curled up on the bed and cried again for her grandparents. She must have drifted back off to sleep, because the next thing she became aware of was the sound of heavy footsteps coming up the stairs and towards the bedroom door. She knew that it was Brancher and quickly sat up, smoothing down her tangled hair.

The lock turned and Brancher came in, but Maureen's heart dropped at the sight of his angry face. 'Hello,' she said, croakily.

'You're awake then.'

'Yes. Where are we?'

'Maysoule Road. I've rented us this house, for now.'

'Can we afford it?'

'Course we can. I didn't pay for it with fresh air.'

Maureen thought that it would be best to remain quiet and not ask Brancher any more questions. He'd obviously gone through with the *job* that he'd mentioned. She was grateful that he hadn't been caught and imprisoned. After all, for all Brancher's faults, he was her whole world now and she couldn't bear to think of life alone and without him. Though she tried not to cry again, tears slipped down her cheeks. She looked at Brancher longingly, desperate for him to wrap his arms around her. Instead, she was met with his accusing eyes.

'Pull yourself together,' he spat, 'and consider yourself lucky that I brought you here. After what I've heard about you, I should have left you to rot at the Battersea Tavern.'

Maureen's eyebrows knitted together as she tried to fathom what she'd done wrong.

'Don't look at me like you don't know what I'm talking about, you dirty cow.'

'W-what?'

'I knew you'd play all sweet and innocent. That's about the only thing you're good at.'

'I'm really sorry, Brancher, but I don't know what I've done to upset you.'

Brancher stomped across the room and he leaned in towards Maureen. She pulled back, afraid that he was going to hurt her.

His finger jabbed at her shoulder as he growled, 'You was with that coloured man!'

Maureen furiously shook her head. 'No, no, no, Brancher, I wasn't,' she cried, her pulse racing with fear.

'Don't bloody lie to me! Mrs Berry told me that he brought you and your shopping bags to her pub. Still going to try to deny it, are you?'

'But ... but it wasn't like that. The house, the fire ... my grandparents ...' Maureen's voice trailed off as she began sobbing.

'You're on your last warning, woman. If you make a fool out of me again, you'll be sorry.'

Maureen's head was lowered, she didn't see Brancher leave the room but she heard the door slam close and the lock turning. She threw herself back down on the bed and curled herself into a ball as her heart broke. The pillow soon became sodden with her tears as she questioned how she could have been so stupid. She'd known it had been risky when Clinton had walked beside her, but she could never have anticipated turning onto the street to find her grandparents' house ablaze. From the moment of that horrific discovery, her recollections were a blur.

'What does it matter?' she asked aloud. Clinton may have walked her to the Battersea Tavern, and yes, she'd been wrong to allow it, but all that paled into insignificance in the wake of her grandparents' deaths. If only Brancher would see it that way too.

★

Winnie kept her eyes on the door, anxiously waiting for Hilda to arrive. After discovering from Maureen that Brancher wasn't the nice young man that Winnie had once thought, and seeing how he'd dragged Maureen out of the pub, Winnie was quite wary of him now. She knew his sort, a wolf in sheep's clothing. Brian had been the same. And Carmen's son, Errol, he was another bloke to be cautious of. At least she could say with confidence that though her own son, David, was a bad 'un, he never resorted to using his fists on women. Though what he'd done to Rachel was despicable and unforgivable.

Finally, the door opened and Hilda came in. The woman looked quite red-faced and gasped to regain her breath.

'I know where Brancher is,' she said. 'I followed him. He went into a house on Maysoule Road.'

'Well done, love. Did he see you?'

'No, I don't think so.'

'Good. Carmen will be back soon. She'll want to know.'

'I don't think that Carmen should knock on Brancher's door alone.'

'Me neither. I'll go with her. Until then, I expect you're gasping for a cuppa. Rachel's upstairs, so go on up. I'll be joining you as soon as Carmen returns to take over behind the bar.'

A steady stream of customers flowed through the doors. Each one of them mentioned the fire and said how sorry they were to hear about Len. The old boy never spoke much and always had a dismal face, but it was clear that he'd been well thought of.

Winnie was pleased when Carmen returned as she knew that the information Hilda had gleaned would put a smile on her face. 'Hello, love.'

'I couldn't find her anywhere. I asked around, but no one knows where Brancher has taken Maureen.'

'It's all right. Hilda saw him earlier and followed him. He went into a house on Maysoule Road.'

Carmen's dark eyes widened and she smiled. 'Thank Gawd for that. I was getting really worried. What door number, do you know?'

'No, but Hilda will. It'll have to wait for now though. I don't want you going round there by yourself, so I'll come with you. But there's no time at the moment. Jan will be here soon and I've got a big dinner to sort out. I need you behind the bar.'

'Yes, of course. But I'd like us to go round there sooner rather than later. This evening?'

Winnie nodded in agreement as Carmen came behind the bar and at the same time Tommy walked into the pub. She noticed that he looked very dapper, even wearing a tie. It was nice to see that he'd made an effort for her special lunch.

'Hello, ladies. I'm not too early, am I?'

Winnie and Carmen exchanged a look, both thinking the same thing about the visit to Brancher's house. It was Winnie who replied, 'No, you're not too early. Do you still need to ask Maureen some questions?'

'Yes.'

'Well, we know where she is and we're popping round there later. Do you want to come with us?'

'Too right, I do.'

Carmen went to the far end of the bar to serve two young men in khaki army uniforms.

Tommy leaned one elbow on the bar and said quietly to

Winnie, 'Between you and me, I'd like to ask Brancher a few questions too.'

'What about?'

'Where he was on Friday night.'

'The night of the robbery at the distillery?'

'Exactly.'

'Bloomin' 'eck, Tommy, you don't think that he had anything to do with it, do you?'

'I hope not, Winnie. Maureen could do without Brancher being behind bars right now. Anyway, keep that to yourself,' he whispered, tapping the side of his nose.

'I will, love. Come on, let's go upstairs.'

'That's the best offer I've had in a while,' Tommy chuckled.

'And that's the only offer you'll get from me. Behave yourself,' Winnie retorted with a smile and then she called down the bar to Carmen, 'I'm going up. Shout if you need me.'

Upstairs, Hilda had extended the table and had laid out the plates and cutlery. Rachel had been keeping an eye on the cooking. And Martha was sat on the kitchen floor with a colouring book and three very worn-down crayons. Cake, who would usually greet visitors by jumping up and down with excitement and peeing on the floor, was curled up asleep beside Martha.

The delicious aroma of the roasting chicken twitched Winnie's nostrils. It wasn't a big bird to share between her guests. They'd only get a couple of slices of meat each, but Winnie had made up for that with the large amount of vegetables on offer.

Rachel turned from the stove, her face pink and glowing from the steam coming from the saucepans. 'Hello, Sergeant

Bradbury,' she said, wiping her forearm across her brow. 'Dinner won't be long.'

Hilda pulled out a seat at the table. 'Please, sit down. What can I get you to drink?' she asked.

'Blimey, a fella could get used to all this attention from you lovely ladies. I'll have a cold drink if there's one going?'

'I'll have one an' all,' Winnie added as she walked over to the stove to see how Rachel was managing. 'Thanks, love, it all looks good. Alberto will be here soon. Go and tidy yourself up, I'll take over here now.'

Rachel called to Martha, who showed off her drawing as she passed Tommy. As they left the kitchen, Jan came in and stood just inside the doorway looking uneasy, as she always did in a room full of people.

'Oh, Jan, you're here!' Winnie exclaimed and rushed towards her. 'Let me look at you,' she said, holding her adopted daughter by the shoulders and eyeing her up and down. 'You look smashing, love, but you've lost a bit of weight. Are they feeding you properly at that hospital?'

Jan smiled warmly. 'Hello, Mum. Yes, I'm eating well enough,' she said and kissed Winnie on the cheek.

'Give us a cuddle,' Winnie gushed. 'It feels like it's been ages since I've seen you.' As she held her daughter in her arms, she could feel Jan's bones and thought that the young woman felt and looked far too thin. Pulling away, she said, 'I hope you've got an appetite. As usual, I've cooked enough to feed the five thousand. Sit down, love, up there next to me, and Hilda will pour you a drink. How was your journey from Westminster?'

Jan sat down, glancing at Tommy. 'It was fine. I won't be able to stay as long as I'd have liked to.'

'It's all right, love, I understand. I suspect that this latest Nazi onslaught is keeping you busy. Those rockets are a blinkin' disgrace!'

Tommy cleared his throat, before saying, 'Your mum tells me that you're a nurse. She's ever so proud of you and rightly so.'

Jan looked bewildered and smiled politely.

'Sorry, love, I should have introduced you. This is Sergeant Bradbury, a very old friend of mine.'

'Pleased to meet you, Sergeant Bradbury.'

'Please, call me Tommy.'

Then Winnie added, 'And Alberto will be joining us. He's Rachel's fella. Such a nice chap, from British Honduras, you know.'

'British Honduras … where's that?'

'South America. I'll leave it to him to tell his story. It's fascinating.'

A while later, once dinner had been served, Winnie glanced around the table at the happy faces and smiled as they chatted easily. Nothing warmed her heart more than having her dearest loved ones together, especially Jan. And for the last couple of hours, she'd forgotten her worries about David being back and her sadness over Len and Renee's death.

When they'd filled their bellies and after everyone had thanked Winnie and complimented her dinner, she began clearing away the plates. Jan jumped up to help, but Winnie gently ordered, 'Sit down, love, relax. You don't get much time off and I'm not having you doing dishes.'

Jan placed a staying hand on Winnie's arm. 'Actually, Mum, can I have a quiet word … in private?' she whispered.

Winnie placed the plates on the kitchen side and wiped her hands on a towel. 'Of course,' she said, 'Let's go through to the front room.'

After closing the door behind her, she sat beside Jan on the sofa.

'What's wrong, love?' she asked, her heart pounding with worry.

'Nothing, really, I suppose. It's Terry ... in his last letter to me, he talked about us starting a family when he gets home.'

Winnie clasped her hands together in delight and beamed. 'Oh, that's wonderful ... isn't it?'

'I'm not sure. I'm worried that I won't be a good mum.'

'Why on earth would you think something as daft as that?'

Jan's eyes began to well. 'I'm worried that I'll be like my *real* mum.'

'Oh, love, you're *nothing* like her. The woman had a screw loose. She wasn't well. She'd never have kept you a prisoner in your room if she'd been of sound mind. And all that religious fanatical stuff, it was her illness that made her like it.'

'But what if I'm the same as her? As far as I know, my mother wasn't always mad. It crept up on her – either that or she hid it well at first. And I don't think my mother ever thought that there was anything wrong with her. What if I'm mad and I don't know it? Or what if I start going mad?'

'You're not, and you won't,' Winnie assured adamantly. 'Listen to me. You. Are. Not. Mad. If you were, don't you think that I'd be the first to tell you, eh? I'd want you to get treatment, but even if you did get poorly, you'd have a lot of support around you. Your mum didn't have anyone. She battled on alone and her illness got worse and worse. Whereas you have me, Rachel, Hilda and Terry.'

'I never thought of that, thanks Mum, that's put my mind at ease.'

'Good. Oh, love, and as for Terry wanting to start a family, I can't wait to be a nanny again.'

'Let's hope this war ends soon and Terry gets home safely.'

'I'll second that.'

The door flew open and Martha came skipping in with Cake beside her. 'Aunty Jan … Aunty Jan … me and Mummy are taking Cake for a walk. Will you come with us … pwease, pwease?'

Jan held her hand out to the girl. 'Pull me up then,' she smiled.

When Martha tried to heave Jan off the sofa, Jan playfully yanked the girl towards her and tickled her ribs. Martha chuckled and squirmed.

'Give me a kiss and I'll let you go,' Jan teased.

Martha threw her arms around Jan's neck and kissed her cheek. 'I wish I could see you every day,' she said sweetly.

'Me too, darling. I've missed you and you've grown so much since I last saw you.'

Winnie gave Jan a gentle nudge. 'See, told you … You'll be a smashing mum,' she smiled.

Her heart filled with joy and she was bursting with pride. But it was such a shame that she couldn't feel this same way for David, her own flesh and blood. She blamed herself for his failings. She'd spoiled the boy, catered to his every whim and had refused to see his faults. Motherhood didn't come with instructions and she'd made mistakes. Winnie watched as Jan walked out of the room holding Martha's hand. She had no doubts that, once a mother, her daughter would make mistakes too. But she also knew that Jan would be the best mum that a mum could be.

Then another thought struck her, one that made her smile; she could picture her grandchildren playing in a large garden, open fields all around them and fresh, clean air.

Don't be daft, Winnie told herself, *daydreams, that's all it is, just daft daydreams.*

12

Clinton was glad that he hadn't been invited to Winnie's big lunch. He wouldn't have felt comfortable sharing a gravy jug with a policeman. And he still couldn't believe how unconcerned Alberto was about the situation.

With his long legs stretched out in front of him on the bed and his head propped up on a pillow, Clinton read the same page of his book for a third time. The words still weren't going in because his mind was elsewhere. He slammed the book closed and threw his legs over the side of the bed. He shouldn't have to worry about Alberto shooting his mouth off. They'd made an agreement before they'd left Scotland: what they'd done would *always* remain strictly between them. Yet Clinton had a terrible sinking feeling that his dear friend would say something that would drop them both in it.

His shoulders tense with worry, he grabbed his jacket and marched out of the house. He hoped that some fresh air and the sun on his face would help him to relax. Ambling down the street aimlessly, he tried to clear his head.

★

Clinton had been walking for about half an hour. The sun was beginning to set, casting a warm orange hue over the grey, lacklustre streets. His stomach grumbled, reminding him that it was well past teatime. He was about to turn back and head for home when a muffled groaning sound caught his attention.

His eyes quickly searched for where the noise had come from, and then he heard another cry of pain. Straining his neck to look up an alley and past a couple of dustbins, Clinton was horrified when he saw three men towering over a man on the ground. The men were putting the boot in, kicking the poor fella hard in his head and ribs.

Clinton stood wide-eyed in disbelief. His instincts told him to rush in and help the man who was being beaten. But his head warned him not to. He knew it would be foolhardy to intervene and, if he did, he'd likely end up getting attacked too.

The man who was doing most of the kicking had his back to Clinton, but he suddenly turned around. Clinton baulked when he saw that it was Brancher. For a brief moment, their eyes locked and Clinton knew that Brancher had recognised him. The man scowled at him; his bloodied fists clenched. Now Clinton's instincts told him to run!

He sped along the street, his heart pounding hard and fast. When he glanced back over his shoulder, he was relieved to see that Brancher wasn't in pursuit. He'd saved himself from a good hiding, for now. But he'd witnessed what Brancher had done to that poor man on the ground and he feared that Brancher would use every method of intimidation and violence to ensure Clinton's silence.

★

The sun had gone down by the time that Maureen heard her husband return home. *Thank gawd*, she thought, desperate to use the toilet and refusing to sit on the bucket that had been left in the room. She sat on the edge of the bed, her fingers discreetly crossed, praying that he would be in a good mood. As she anxiously waited for him to unlock the door, she listened to the sound of his booted feet coming up the stairs. He didn't seem to be stomping. She hoped that this was a good indication of how he was feeling.

Brancher unlocked the door and pushed it open. Maureen studied his face, comforted when she saw that he was smiling.

'I'm starving. Make us some dinner.'

She jumped to do his bidding, but as she went to pass him in the doorway, he blocked her path. She tensed, expecting the worse, but to her astonishment, Brancher wrapped his arms around her and pulled her towards him. Being held so tightly and close to him made Maureen feel safe and she found herself crying into his chest.

'Come on, sweetheart, pull yourself together. Every time I look at you, you're bawling your eyes out and it ain't a pretty sight.'

'I know, I'm sorry,' she sniffed.

Brancher stepped back and looked down at her. As she fought to compose herself, she saw a rare glimpse of tenderness in his eyes.

'Please don't lock me in the room no more. I promise I won't mess up again.'

'Can I trust you, Maureen?'

'Yes, you can.'

'All right, but you'd better not let me down or show me

up again, so that means that you're to stay away from those darkies.'

As they made their way down the stairs, Maureen gazed around, impressed with the standard of her new home but sad at the thought of how Brancher had paid for it. 'Have you got any shopping in?' she asked.

'Eh? Oh, bugger, no, not a lot. But I'm sure you'll be able to rustle up something.'

'I'll do my best, but I'll have to go shopping tomorrow. Erm, where's the loo?'

'In the back yard. We ain't got to share it either,' Brancher answered proudly.

After darting outside and into the privy, Maureen checked for any spiders before sitting on the toilet. She hurried to do her business, acutely aware that Brancher was waiting for his dinner.

Back in the kitchen, Brancher threw her a wink and fished in his trouser pocket. He then handed her a couple of pound notes, saying, 'You've only got the clothes you're standing in, so you'd best get yourself some new stuff. It might cheer you up a bit.'

Maureen accepted the cash with stunned reluctance. She knew that it was stolen money. 'Thank you,' she said and then, seeing as Brancher was in a good mood, she added, 'I need to arrange the funerals for my gran and granddad.'

Brancher's eyes darkened and he frowned. 'I ain't paying a penny for them to be buried.'

'You don't have to,' Maureen retorted quickly. 'They had insurance policies which should cover the costs.'

'Make sure it does 'cos I don't see why I should have to cough up to put them in the ground.'

She quickly turned her back to Brancher to look in the larder but also to hide the tears that were stinging her eyes again. He could be so thoughtless! The way he'd spoken coldly about putting her grandparents in the ground had hurt her. But, as usual, she kept quiet and wouldn't risk saying anything that might rile him.

In the larder, she found a few basic provisions that would just about stretch to something resembling a meal; potatoes that were nearly sprouting and a tin of corned mutton. She wondered why Brancher had bought the mutton as it was a food that he always complained about. She searched through the cupboards and found a battered old saucepan, a blunt chopping knife and few other useful items, but there was a lot lacking. 'I'm going to have to write a list of things that we will need.'

'You shouldn't want much; the house is furnished. What are you saying? You need more money?'

Maureen nodded, biting on her bottom lip and hoping that Brancher wouldn't explode with anger. She was grateful when he reached into his pocket again and laid a few more notes on the table. But as he put the money down, she noticed that his knuckles were swollen and bleeding.

'Brancher, your hands!' she said, rushing towards him.

'You should see the other fella's face,' he boasted.

Maureen didn't ask any questions. She'd rather not know. The idea of the violence that her husband had inflicted on *the other fella* turned her stomach. She felt sickened at the dreadful thought that it may have been Clinton on the receiving end of Brancher's fists. Christ, she hoped it wasn't! Especially as the man hadn't done anything wrong and had only helped her when she'd needed it.

Once the potatoes were simmering on the stove, Maureen went to sit at the small kitchen table.

'Don't you want to have a look around your new house?' Brancher asked.

'Yes, of course,' she answered, though she wasn't really bothered.

In the front room, Maureen quite liked the burgundy colour scheme. The sofa looked like it had seen better days and the net curtains and windows needed a good clean.

Brancher followed her in and asked, 'What do you reckon? All right, ain't it?'

'Yes, it's lovely,' she answered, but in truth, it didn't feel like home.

'We'll be stopping here for three months and then we can think about moving out of Battersea. There's no point in staying here now that we don't have to.'

Again, his words jabbed at her heart. He hadn't said *now that your grandparents are dead*, but that is what he'd meant. Anyway, Maureen was past caring about where they lived. She was more concerned about where the money had come from to pay the rent on the house. And considering how generous Brancher was being with his cash, it led her to believe that the *job* that he'd done must have been a big one.

'There's a shed in the yard, but I don't want you going in there. Is that clear?'

She nodded. Maureen had no desire to go into his shed, and she could guess that he had stashed stolen items in there. Her jaw clenched. She hated harbouring robbed things. If the police caught up with him, she could end up in trouble with the law too. 'I'd better see to our dinner,' she said, lowering her eyes so that he wouldn't see her disappointment.

Brancher grabbed her arm but not in a rough or threatening way. 'I know I've not been good to you lately, but I've been under a lot of pressure. Things are gonna change. It's just you and me now, and I'm going to be better. Just make sure that you're a good girl, eh?'

Maureen swallowed hard and forced a smile. She'd heard similar words from Brancher so many times before. She didn't doubt that he'd *be better*, but she knew it wouldn't last: it never did.

Winnie was pleased to finally be on Maysoule Road. It had been quite a trek from the pub and her feet were aching. She was grateful that Tommy was carrying Maureen's shopping bags. Despite feeling weary, she'd had a good laugh with him and Carmen en route. And though she'd been sad to say goodbye to Jan, she'd had a smashing time with her too. She hoped that Brancher wasn't about to spoil the end of what had been a very nice day.

As they walked along the road, Carmen fell quiet and Winnie asked, 'Are you all right?'

'Yes, just thinking ... How has Brancher managed to pay to rent them a house?'

'That's a very good question,' Tommy commented.

'He wasn't working and Maureen couldn't afford it on the wages I pay her,' Winnie added. In her mind, it was beginning to look more and more likely that Brancher had been involved in the distillery robbery. But she wouldn't make accusations without proof and it was down to Tommy to get to the truth.

'This is it,' Carmen said, stopping outside of a neat Victorian terraced house with a small, walled front garden.

Many houses in the area had been bombed and flattened, and many more had fallen into ruin due to poverty, but this row of housing appeared to be well kept. Again, Winnie wondered how Brancher could afford to pay for a house, particularly of this standard.

Tommy, flanked by Winnie and Carmen, cleared his throat and stepped forward to knock on the door. When Brancher opened it, he rolled his eyes at the sight of them on his doorstep. 'What?' he spat.

'Evening, Brancher,' Tommy said, his tone rather stern. 'We've brought Maureen's shopping. Can we come in? The ladies here would like to see Maureen and I have a few questions for you.'

'No, you can't come in. We're just about to sit down to eat our tea. Give those bags here.'

'I won't keep you long,' Tommy said, handing over the shopping.

'I told you, N.O. No.'

'Would you rather I took you down to the station for questioning?'

'About what?'

Tommy cleared his throat again. 'Where were you on Friday night?'

Brancher huffed, clearly irritated. 'I was with my mates, we were playing cards.'

'Can anyone verify that?'

'Ask Gus. He'll tell you. We were at his sister's house. Me, Gus, Jacko and his brother-in-law, Kipper.'

'I see. Well, I will be checking with them, so if there's anything different that you'd like to add, now would be a good time.'

'I hope you ain't trying to stitch me up for something, Tommy?'

'It's Sergeant Bradbury, and I'm investigating a serious robbery.'

'Huh, robbery … you should be asking them darkies about it. Now, have you finished?'

'Not quite. You're renting this property?'

'That's right.'

'Did you pay your rent in cash in advance?'

'So what if I did?'

'Where did the money come from, Brancher? Because we all know that you were skint.'

Brancher leaned forward and growled, 'None of your business. Now clear off and let me eat me dinner in peace.'

Brancher went to slam the door closed as Carmen called, 'Wait! I'd like a quick word with Maureen.'

He called over his shoulder to his wife, sounding impatient, and then Maureen appeared. She stood behind her husband, looking scared.

'Hello, Maureen. Sorry to intrude,' Carmen said sweetly. 'We just wanted to see how you are?'

'I'm fine, thank you.'

Brancher spoke again. 'Right, you've heard her, she's fine,' he snapped.

Before he could close the door in their faces, Carmen quickly asked, 'Would you like me to help you to arrange Len and Renee's funerals?'

'Er – Er … erm …' Maureen stuttered.

'No, she wouldn't,' Brancher answered bluntly.

'Are you sure? It's no bother. I'd be happy to help.'

Brancher glanced behind at his wife, who had cast her eyes downward. 'If she accepts your help, will you lot bugger off?'

'Yes, of course.'

'Fine. Maureen will come to the pub tomorrow.'

'Great, thanks. See you tomorrow, Maureen,' Carmen said, but Brancher had already slammed the door shut.

Winnie shook her head in disbelief at how rude Brancher had been. And now she felt sure that he'd been involved with the robbery, though it appeared that he'd been clever enough to arrange an alibi. She'd been pleased to see that Maureen was up and about and no longer hysterical and was relieved to know that she'd be visiting the pub tomorrow. Yet something felt wrong. Winnie couldn't put her finger on it, but Maureen had looked very scared. Perhaps the woman knew something about Brancher's role in the robbery and she was worried about Tommy visiting the house. Or worse, maybe Brancher had been bullying and abusing her again. Either way, Winnie planned on having a good talk with Maureen tomorrow. It was the least that she could do for Len in his memory.

13

On Monday morning, Clinton was already awake when he heard the ringing of Alberto's alarm clock.

Alberto groaned loudly and reached his hand out from under the bedcovers to stop the noise. 'Man, I was having such a nice dream about Rachel.'

'No time for that. It's good to wake up knowing that we are starting work today,' Clinton replied cheerily. But his breezy comment masked his unrest. He'd hardly slept, and not solely because of the midnight air raid.

Once they'd heard the all-clear and had returned from the public shelter, Clinton had wearily climbed back into bed. But he'd spent hours tossing and turning with images running through his mind of Brancher beating up the man in the alley. Clinton hadn't told Alberto what he'd seen, nor had he voiced his fear about Brancher coming after him. And with every thought of Brancher, another of Maureen came too. He worried about the woman and hoped that she was coping with the horrendous death of her grandparents.

But something else concerned him: the way his pulse quickened when pictures of her flashed in his head and the unsettling desire he felt to hold her. He'd told himself to forget her. After all, she was a married woman, wedded to his enemy. And even is she was free to court him, he couldn't possibly involve himself with a woman, especially after he'd been upset with Alberto for taking a girlfriend. Yet no matter how hard he tried, he couldn't push away thoughts of Maureen, and neither could he shake the memory of Brancher's sinister face.

'I completely forgot that I'm supposed to be visiting Cheryl today,' Carmen moaned.

Winnie pushed her breakfast plate to one side and rested her elbows on the kitchen table, saying thoughtfully, 'You should go, love. You don't want to give your girl any more reason to be upset with you. I can deal with Maureen.'

'Are you sure?'

'Yes, of course. It's important that you spend time with your daughter. And I wanted to have a chat with Maureen, so it makes no odds if you're not here.'

'Thanks, Win. You're right, I should go. Cheryl is still frosty with me since that last falling out I had with her gran. Honestly, I try to bite my tongue with that woman, but I'm sure she keeps picking fights with me, knowing that Cheryl will take her side. Mind you, she's Harry's mother, so it's nothing more than I expect.'

'I don't think that Edie will ever like you, no matter how hard you try with her.'

'I think you're right. She hasn't liked me since the day I married her son. But I make the effort with her for Cheryl's sake. Sometimes I feel that I'm wasting my time. Let's face it, me and Cheryl have never been close and we never will be. We don't have a special mother-and-daughter relationship like you have with Jan.'

'You were there for her after she nearly died in Balham Underground station and she knows that you'll be there for her whenever she needs you. That's what counts.'

'I suppose so and I've only got myself to blame. Oh well, I'd best get off. Good luck with Maureen. We can start arranging her grandparents' funeral tomorrow. See you later, Win.'

'Yes, love, cheerio, and say hello to Cheryl from me.'

Winnie enjoyed a few minutes' peace and quiet before Martha and Cake came tearing into the kitchen.

'Nanna Hilda is taking me and Cake to the park today,' her granddaughter announced with gusto.

Hilda followed in next. 'Morning, Win.'

'Morning, love. I didn't hear you knocking downstairs.'

'Rachel let me in. Any tea in the pot?'

'Can a duck swim?'

Hilda smiled and poured herself a cup. She sat at the table opposite Winnie and sighed deeply.

'Everything all right?' Winnie asked, her brow creasing.

'Yes, fine,' Hilda answered, but then whispered, 'I saw some terrible sights last night.'

Winnie glanced around to Martha. 'Take Cake and go and get some pennies from the pot on my dressing table. You can spend them when you're out with your Nanna Hilda today.'

Martha leapt into the air with joy. 'Fank you,' she yelled excitedly as she ran off.

'The doodlebug?' Winnie asked Hilda, stating the nickname of the V1 rockets that she'd heard from her customers.

'Yes. A mother and her three kids. We could hear the young boy crying for his mum for over an hour before they found him. But by the time he was dug out, he was dead. The poor love must have been in pain and so scared, buried in the dark, wanting his mum. It really got to me. And do you know the first thing that I thought of? Whisky. I really wanted a whisky.'

'Don't beat yourself up, love. Witnessing something so horrid like that would be enough to drive anyone to the bottle. But you didn't have a drink, did you?'

'No, though I was sorely tempted.'

'You did well. You've stayed on the wagon for ages now. Keep it up. We can't have you going back to your old ways.'

'Don't worry, I won't. I promised Rachel that I'd stay sober and I have. But it's hard sometimes, Win. The urge to drink is never going to go away, is it?'

'I don't know, love, I doubt it. You might have to fight it your whole life, but you've proved that you can do it. And you're a much better person for it.'

'I know. I don't know how you all put up with me for so long when I was a drunk.'

'It weren't always easy, but we love you.'

'Where's Martha?' Rachel asked as she came into the kitchen and looked around.

'In my room squirreling away all my pennies,' Winnie replied.

'What?'

'I told her to help herself.'

'You spoil her.'

'I know, but I'm allowed to. Are you going to the park with your mum?'

'No. I thought I'd help out behind the bar today so that you and Carmen can have some time with Maureen.'

'Oh, you're a good girl, thanks, love. And as it happens, I could do with your help today. Carmen has gone to visit Cheryl.'

A couple of hours later, Winnie popped to the grocer's, leaving Rachel to keep an eye out for Maureen. As usual, Mr Coggins enquired after Carmen, to which Winnie curtly told him that she was well.

When she returned to the pub, she was disappointed to find that Maureen hadn't turned up. And by closing time, there was still no sign of her.

'Maybe she's too upset to face venturing out today,' Rachel suggested.

'Could be, but it's not like Maureen to say that she will do something and then not do it.'

'But wasn't it Brancher who said that Maureen would visit today?'

'Hmm, yes, but even so, I'm surprised that she hasn't come.'

'Are you going to go round to see her?'

'Carmen will insist.'

They hadn't noticed that Carmen had come in through the back door. 'I will insist on what?' she asked, sounding breathless.

'Oh, hello. We were just saying that Maureen hasn't been in today so we'll have to go and see her again.'

'Yes, we will, but forget that for a minute … listen to this …'

'Are you all right, love? You're out of breath.'

'Yes, I know, Win. I rushed back here 'cos I've got

173

something to tell you … You won't believe who I bumped into on my way home?'

'Give us a clue,' Winnie asked, intrigued.

'I'll tell you who … Stephanie Reynolds, my Errol's ex-girlfriend, and very chatty she was too!'

'Oh yeah, what did she have to say for herself?' Winnie asked.

'Well, good news … David has left Battersea.'

Winnie and Rachel stared at Carmen, both silent for a moment as they digested the information.

'Are you sure?' Winnie finally questioned.

'Yes, very sure. Stephanie said that she'd run into David at the train station this morning. She said that he was in a bad way, beaten up black and blue. Apparently, he'd fallen out with some blokes that he'd been working with and it was best for him to get out of the area.'

Winnie gasped and her hand flew over her mouth. She didn't like the idea of her son being hurt, but she had to admit to herself that a huge weight felt as though it had lifted from her shoulders. 'What blokes? And what work was he doing?'

'I don't know, Win. Stephanie said that she'd asked him but he wouldn't say. She had the feeling that he'd been involved in something shady. He never said where he was going neither. But I thought you'd both be pleased to hear that he's gone.'

'Too right!' Rachel said. 'And I hope he stays away for good now.'

Winnie nodded in agreement but felt her insides clench as she pictured David's battered face. For all his faults and the pain he'd caused, she still felt her natural motherly instinct to protect him. 'Yep, good riddance to bad rubbish,' she said, dusting off her hands, though, in truth, she'd liked to have known where he'd gone and hoped that he was all right.

'I'll put the kettle on,' Rachel offered. 'You look like you could do with a cuppa, Carmen.'

'We always seem to be drinking tea, but it's a lovely idea, thanks. And then I think we should get round to Maureen's.'

'I reckon we'd be better off going in the morning,' Winnie suggested. 'There'd be more chance of Brancher being out.'

'Yes, you're probably right.'

Winnie heard a light tapping on the back door and knew that it would be Hilda returning from the park with Martha and Cake. They'd been gone for hours; Winnie had expected them to have returned a while ago.

'She's worn out,' Hilda said, nodding down at a very sleeping-looking Martha.

Cake appeared equally exhausted too as he followed Rachel, who was now carrying Martha up the stairs.

'We've had a wonderful day,' Hilda told Winnie and Carmen. 'It was just what I needed to take me mind off this bleedin' war and those flippin' bombs. But I could do with a cuppa.'

'Come on, sit down. You look done in,' Winnie smiled. 'I've got some spuds and cabbage from yesterday. Let's have a bit of bubble and squeak and a nice cuppa to wash it down.'

'See, tea again,' Carmen said.

'It's the best there is for a pick-me-up,' Hilda replied.

As Winnie fried the leftovers, Hilda poured her tea from the cup and into the saucer before quietly slurping it and then exhaling a loud, 'Ahh.'

'She's gone out like a light,' Rachel said, joining her mother and Carmen at the kitchen table.

Winnie served up the meal and they all tucked in. 'How's Cheryl?' she asked.

Carmen placed her fork on the table and shook her head. 'She's well and sends her love to everyone. But everything is *Edie this* and *Edie that*. Don't get me wrong, I'm pleased that she's got a good relationship with her gran ... but I can't help being a bit jealous.'

'I was the same when Jan was always with my mum,' Rachel said, smiling across the table at Hilda. 'But just because they were together a lot, it didn't mean that Mum loved me any less.'

Hilda smiled back. 'That's right, darling.'

'I know, and I suppose I should count myself lucky that Cheryl gave me another chance to be in her life. The way I behaved, I didn't deserve it,' Carmen lamented. 'Gawd, I was awful. So cold ... I was more concerned about my husband's disgusting secrets than I was about my kids. Oh well, I can't change the past and I'm glad for what I have now.'

'Talking of kids, you ain't heard ...' Winnie said to Hilda, 'Carmen bumped into Stephanie Reynolds and found out that David has left Battersea.'

'That's good news! Did she mention Errol?'

Carmen chewed her food and swallowed it down before answering, 'Only to say that she hadn't seen or heard anything from him.'

Winnie grinned and all eyes fell on her. 'What?' she asked, glancing from one woman to the other.

'I know you're pleased that David has buggered off again, but what's with the soppy smile?' Hilda asked.

Unable to contain herself any longer, Winnie blurted, 'Well, still talking of kids … Jan and Terry are going to start a family as soon as he gets home.'

'Oh, Win, that's wonderful,' Carmen chirped.

'Yes, but don't mention it in front of her. She doesn't want me telling anyone yet. But I'm fit to burst and couldn't keep it to meself!'

Rachel reached across and held Winnie's hand. 'Martha will love having a baby cousin to play with,' she said, then adding, 'Our family is getting bigger.'

Hilda raised her eyebrows. 'I hope you're not thinking of expanding!' she warned Rachel.

'No, not yet!'

'*Yet*? So, you've thought about it?'

Rachel's cheeks pinked up as she answered, 'No … not really … but I can't say that I haven't had silly daydreams about it. I really like Alberto and I'm sure he likes me too. But it's far too soon. Though *Rachel King* does have a nice ring to it.'

'Slow down, girl,' Hilda cautioned. 'You've only known him two minutes.'

'I know, I know … but a girl can dream.'

'Nothing wrong with dreams, especially ones that might come true,' Winnie said, thinking of her dream of a new life outside of London.

'You're right, Win, there's nothing wrong with dreams, but I don't want Rachel rushing into something and getting her heart broken,' Hilda warned.

'Don't worry,' Rachel assured, 'I've got my head screwed on.'

'Anyway, it's nice to have a bit of romance in the air,' Winnie said.

Carmen looked at Winnie and laughed.

'What's so funny?'

'You ... romance ... you can't see what's right under your nose,' Carmen answered.

'What's she going on about?' Winnie asked Hilda, who was also chuckling.

'I think she's talking about Tommy Bradbury.'

'What?' Winnie spluttered.

'Come on, Win, don't tell me there's nothing going on,' Carmen challenged jovially.

'I don't know what you're talking about!'

'Leave off, Win, it's as clear as day,' Hilda laughed.

'What is?'

'He fancies you!' Carmen said. 'And, well, it looks like a two-way thing.'

'You think that I fancy Tommy?'

'You do.'

'I bloody well don't! Is that what you all think?'

'Yeah,' Hilda said.

'I've been waiting for you to tell us that you're getting engaged,' Rachel added.

'See, told you,' Carmen chortled.

'For gawd's sake, I've never heard anything so ridiculous! Why on earth would you all think that?'

'You're always flirting with each other,' Carmen answered.

'We are not! He might flirt with me, but I certainly don't flirt back!'

Hilda nodded her head. 'You do, Win. But it's nothing to be ashamed of. Tommy is a lovely fella.'

'Will you lot pack it in? There is nothing going on with Tommy Bradbury and there never will be.'

'If you say so,' Carmen sniggered.

'Yes, I do,' Winnie said, resolutely. But it got her thinking. Had she been flirtatious? She didn't think so. She'd thought they just enjoyed a bit of friendly banter together. It hadn't crossed her mind that it could be seen as anything else.

'Why hasn't he got a wife?' Rachel asked. 'I mean, he's a nice man, you would have thought that a woman would have snapped him up by now.'

Winnie thought back to years ago, recalling a tale she'd heard about Tommy from before she'd known him. 'I believe that he was engaged to be married but his wife-to-be died a week before the wedding. I don't think he got over it and then he threw himself into his work.'

'That's sad, but he seems to be over it now and ready for romance again,' Carmen quipped.

'Maybe so, but not with me,' Winnie replied steadfastly.

She worried that she'd given Tommy the wrong impression and had been unwittingly leading him on. If that were the case, she'd have to nip it in the bud before he got the wrong idea about their friendship.

Maureen had been relieved that she hadn't had to go out shopping and was grateful that Sergeant Bradbury, Mrs Hampton and Mrs Berry had brought her groceries to the house yesterday evening. She'd used most of her ration coupons on purchasing the food for the special meal that she'd intended to cook her grandparents. When she'd placed the food in the new larder, her heart had been heavy, but once again she'd forced herself to hold in her grief in front of Brancher.

She sat at the kitchen table and wrung her hands as she peered at the money that Brancher had left for her. He'd wonder why she hadn't taken it and spent it on the things that were needed for the house and new clothes. But the money felt tainted.

The front door opened and Maureen nervously sprang to her feet. Brancher had been out all day, he'd be hungry and expecting his dinner. The kitchen was filled with the aroma of a stew slowly cooking in the oven – the stew that was meant for her gran and granddad.

'Something smells good,' he said, as he came in. Then, sitting at the kitchen table, he pulled off his boots. 'What's that money still doing there?' he asked.

'I – erm – I'll get what I need tomorrow. I've been busy cleaning all day, you know, making the place our own,' she lied. She had been cleaning all day, but, in truth, Maureen hadn't been able to face going out.

'Didn't you go and see Mrs Hampton and Mrs Berry?'

'No. I'll see them tomorrow.'

'Make sure you do. I don't want those nosey parkers at my door again, especially seeing as it was Mrs Berry's son that I kicked the shit out of yesterday.'

'Oh my goodness, why?' Maureen asked, but instantly regretted firing a question at him.

'You don't need to know. But the profits from the job are going three ways now, not four, and that means we're pretty well off! How do you like that, eh? Your old man ain't short of a bob or two,' he boasted.

'That's great,' Maureen answered, forcing a smile, somewhat

calmed to discover that it hadn't been Clinton who'd been the cause of Brancher's bloodied knuckles.

'Yeah, that's right, Maureen, it is great! So you make sure you get yourself some new clobber. I can't have you walking about like a pauper's wife.'

'I will, Brancher,' Maureen assured. She'd washed out her clothes at the sink today and they were still a bit damp, but it was nice to get rid of the smell of smoke that had lingered in the fibres since the fire. It had been a constant reminder. Not that she needed reminding. There was hardly a minute throughout the day when she hadn't thought about her gran and granddad.

Dinner finished, Brancher had shown his appreciation for the stew by slapping her backside and telling her that she'd knocked up a tasty meal. Maureen knew that this was his way of trying to be better, as he had promised, and she appreciated the effort that he was making.

In bed that night, after she'd reluctantly submitted to his conjugal rights, Brancher draped a loose arm across her stomach as he snored in her ear. Maureen laid in the darkness feeling empty and resentment began to gnaw at her insides. She'd hated every moment of having Brancher on top of her, pounding her body as he'd grunted with pleasure. She didn't enjoy sex with him at the best of times, and now, wrapped in her grief, it had been the last thing that she'd wanted. She tried to reason that it was Brancher's way of showing that he cared or maybe he'd been trying to offer her comfort. But deep in her heart, she knew the act had been selfish on his part, Brancher only thinking about his own needs.

She closed her eyes in a bid to stop tears from falling. She needed a friend, but Brancher had put paid to that. Emotionally exhausted, with her husband beside her, as she tried to sleep, Maureen had never felt so alone.

14

On Tuesday morning, Winnie gave Martha a big cuddle and then ruffled her granddaughter's soft, blonde hair. 'You be a good girl for Mummy today,' she gently warned.

'I will, Nanny.'

Rachel had a packed lunch prepared and looked ready to leave. She was taking Martha for a rare trip to the lido in King George's Park. The open-air pool had been opened a year before the war had started, but swimming had never been something that Winnie would consider doing. In fact, she was sure she'd sink like a brick. She waved Rachel off, saying, 'See you later, love. Have a nice day.'

Once they'd left, Winnie turned to Carmen, her face serious and lips tight.

'I think we should wait and see if Maureen comes in today. If we go marching round to her house and Brancher is there, it will be a waste of time. Maureen clams up in front of him and watches what she says.'

'You're right, Win, I was thinking the same. But if she doesn't come in today, we'll have to go to her.'

★

The morning passed quickly and Winnie was beginning to lose hope of seeing Maureen. But then she walked in, her puffy eyes looking nervously around.

'Hello, love,' Winnie said, keeping her voice light and her smile wide.

'Hello, Mrs Berry. I'm sorry that I didn't come yesterday …'

'Not to worry, you're here now. Come on upstairs, I could do with a break and I expect you could do with putting your feet up an' all. It's quite a walk from your house to here.'

Winnie noticed that Maureen was still in the same clothes as she had been on the day of the fire. They appeared clean and fresh, but the woman obviously had nothing else to wear.

As they trudged up the stairs leaving Carmen to run the pub, Winnie said, 'Carmen will sort out a few dresses for you. There's no point in me offering you any of mine, they'd drown you.'

'Er, no, it's fine thank you, Mrs Berry. I'm going to buy myself some clothes. I've just not felt up to it.'

'Are you sure? You're going to need new undergarments and everything. It'll cost you a pretty packet to kit yourself out, even from the second-hand shops.'

'Yes, I know, but I've always been good at making my money go a long way. I'll manage. I'm quite good with a needle and thread too. If I can get my hands on any material, I'll be able to make myself some clothes.'

In the kitchen, as Maureen seated herself at the table, Winnie's mind raced: new house, new clothes, where was all this money coming from? It had to be from the robbery. She put a kettle of water on the stove and then sat opposite Maureen. 'Are you hungry?' she asked. 'I could knock you up a sandwich.'

'No, thanks. I haven't got much of an appetite since ... you know.'

'I don't suppose you have, love, but you must eat to keep your strength up. Are you sure I can't tempt you with something?'

'No, really, thank you.'

'All right, but promise me you'll take care of yourself.'

'I will.'

'Good. How's Brancher been with you?'

'He's making an effort to be nice.'

'I hope he keeps it up! Now, Carmen is going to come up shortly and talk to you about Len and Renee's funerals. It's not going to be easy for you, but it needs sorting.'

'I know. And I really appreciate the help. I don't think that I could manage it by myself.'

'It's not a problem, love. Anything – and I mean, *anything* – you need, you only have to ask.'

The kettle boiled and Winnie placed a cup of tea in front of Maureen.

'Drink up, while it's nice and hot,' she said, sitting down again at the table. 'Like I said, Carmen will be up soon, but I wanted to have a chat with you first. You trust me, don't you?'

'Yes, of course I do.'

'I'm going to be direct with you, Maureen, and it's only because I care about you, do you understand?'

Maureen nodded but looked unsure.

'Sergeant Bradbury is investigating a robbery at the distillery which he suspects that Brancher is involved in. And knowing Sergeant Bradbury, he won't let it rest until he gets to the bottom of it.'

Maureen lowered her eyes and Winnie saw her swallow hard.

'You've got a nice new house, you're getting new clothes… you can see how it looks, can't you? I mean, it doesn't take a genius to put two and two together.'

Maureen kept her eyes down but had started chewing her fingernails.

'I think we both know the truth, don't we?'

Maureen slowly lifted her head to meet Winnie's eyes, tears streaming down her face. 'I didn't want nothing to do with it, I swear. I *hate* having to spend the money he's given me and I *hate* that house 'cos I know that Brancher has paid for it with stolen money.'

'It's all right, love, it's not your fault. But I'm convinced that Brancher's crime is going to catch up with him and I don't want you getting in trouble too. Is there anything in the house that could incriminate you?'

'What do you mean?'

'Stolen goods. If the police search the place and find anything from the robbery under your roof, then you could end up on the wrong side of the law too.'

Maureen gasped. 'But I had nothing to do with it!'

'It's not me that needs convincing, love, but a judge will. So, is there *anything* that could land you in it?'

Maureen thought for a moment and then blurted, 'Oh, gawd, the shed! He told me not to go in it.'

Winnie slumped back in her seat. Just as she'd suspected, she'd guessed that there would be evidence somewhere and it wouldn't be long before Tommy found it. 'You've got two choices… Either get rid of whatever is in the shed or come clean to Sergeant Bradbury.'

'I couldn't speak to the police! Brancher would go mad if he found out.'

'Then you'll have to persuade him to move the stuff out, sharpish too.'

'But what if he won't?'

'He *has* to, Maureen, unless you both want to end up behind bars.'

Winnie plucked a clean handkerchief from up her sleeve and passed it to Maureen.

Once she'd blown her nose and dried her tears, Maureen spoke quietly, her voice shaky, 'I think that David, your David, was involved too.'

This didn't come as a huge surprise to Winnie. 'Did Brancher and his mates beat David up?'

'Yes, I think so, and cut him out of the deal. I'm so sorry, Mrs Berry.'

'No need for apologies, it's not your fault. And, to be honest, David deserved everything he got. Right, you know what you've got to do ... get Brancher to move the stolen goods, all right?'

'Thanks for the warning, Mrs Berry.'

'Yes, well, it's for your sake, not Brancher's.'

Maureen smiled weakly and blew her nose again.

'Pour yourself another cuppa,' Winnie said. 'I'll go down and tell Carmen to come up.'

As Winnie trudged downstairs, the sound of a commotion from the pub reached her ears. She picked up her pace, wondering what was going on. When she walked through to the bar, amid the noise of raucous laughter, her customers were all peering across to the far corner. Winnie strained her neck for a better look. She saw Carmen waving a broom over

Mr Coggins. The man looked terrified and was protectively covering his head with his arm as he tried to fend off Carmen with his other hand.

Winnie dashed around the bar and towards the warring pair. 'What on earth are you doing?' she yelled.

Carmen briefly took her blazing eyes off the cornered grocer to look at Winnie. 'Him, the filthy so-and-so, he tried it on with me.'

'What?'

'That's right. I went down to the cellar to change a barrel. Next thing I know, he's got his dirty paws all over me.'

'Mr Coggins!' Winnie admonished.

'I tell you, Win, if I weren't a lady, I'd shove this broom right up his—'

'Yes, Carmen,' Winnie interrupted, 'and no one would blame you. But I think that Mr Coggins has learned his lesson.'

Carmen lowered the broom and stepped aside. 'Go on, you 'orrible git, get out! I've a good mind to tell Mrs Coggins what you did!'

Mr Coggins, red-faced with embarrassment, scampered past Carmen uttering an apology.

Carmen chased him out of the door with the broom, barking, 'Go on, bugger off and don't come back.' When she turned back around to face the pub, Winnie's customers gave her a round of applause.

'Well, you showed him,' Winnie remarked.

Carmen smoothed down her dress and patted her hair. 'I did. Sorry about that. Shall I go upstairs and see Maureen now?'

'Yes, love, and tell her what you did with the broom to Mr Coggins. It might make her smile.'

As the pub quietened down, the door opened and Tommy came in. Winnie noticed that he was in uniform, which probably meant that he was on official business. She plastered on a welcoming smile, but she was worried about Maureen upstairs.

'Good afternoon, Winnie. Is Carmen here?'

'Hello, Tommy. She's busy at the moment. Anything I can help you with?'

'I've had a complaint from Mr Coggins. I just passed him in the street and he was quite vocal about being attacked by Carmen. In his words, *the woman is a flippin' nutter and needs locking up.* Would you care to explain to me why Mr Coggins is so upset and brandishing a bruised arm?'

'I'll happily explain to you and it's him who needs locking up, the pervert! He sneaked down to the cellar behind Carmen and made himself a nuisance. His advances weren't welcome, so Carmen chased him off with the broom.'

'I see. He never said anything about going down to the cellar.'

'Well, he wouldn't, would he? You tell him to stay out of my pub and I shall be registering my ration book elsewhere,' Winnie snapped.

'All right, don't shoot the messenger.'

'Sorry, Tommy, I'm just annoyed that he had the cheek to complain about Carmen. Can I get you a drink whilst you're here?'

'No thanks, I'm on duty. But I'll pop back this evening.'

'Okey-dokey, see you later.'

'Yes, you will, and I shall look forward to it,' Tommy said, raising his eyebrows and grinning.

Winnie recognised that look; he was flirting with her. And after Carmen, Rachel and Hilda teasing her about it, she kept her smile tight and quick. It wouldn't do to allow Tommy to think that there was any chance of a relationship between them. They were friends, and friends only.

After work had finished for the day, on their way home from the power station, Clinton kept his guard up and his eyes peeled for Brancher. He'd felt relaxed in the boiler room, safe in the knowledge that Brancher couldn't get to him. But now, on the streets, as a wave of men on bicycles passed him, he couldn't help fearing that the man would appear, ready to attack him.

Alberto, oblivious to Clinton's worries, boasted, 'I'm going home to get washed up quickly and then I'm seeing Rachel. The girl is missing her Alberto.'

Clinton didn't respond.

'Hey, are you all right?' Alberto asked.

'Yes, just tired. It's long hours and hot in that boiler room.'

'Not as hot as the sun at home. Ahh, t'ink of it, Clinton, do you remember the warmth of home?'

'Every day, my friend, every day,' Clinton lamented. He missed home, and his mother and sisters. But if he returned to British Honduras now, he'd never be able to earn enough money to pay for the medicine that his sister desperately needed. He was trapped in Britain, under a weak sun in a grey sky, with bland food and dirty streets. At least most of the people were friendly – well, all but one.

When they reached the boarding house, Clinton carried on walking.

'Hey, where are you going?' Alberto asked.

'To the river. I want to see the water.'

'Why do you want to see the filthy Thames?'

'I just do,' Clinton replied as he mooched off. Going indoors would be the sensible and safest thing to do, but he felt drawn to the river. There was something about the flowing water that had a calming effect on his soul. He liked to sit beside it and allow his mind to drift to his home on the other side of the world.

Clinton wasn't sure for how long he'd been at the river's edge, but the sun had almost set. He stood up and brushed himself down, sighing deeply as he turned to head back to the lodgings. A few hours of quiet contemplation had calmed his nerves and left him feeling mellow. But the sudden wailing shriek of the air-raid warning siren filled him with dread and his body tensed.

Clinton scrambled up the shoreline, over pebbles and muddy sand, and ran up the moss-covered slippery steps. Back on the streets, he frantically looked around. The nearest public shelter that he knew of was quite some distance away and he could already hear the chilling drone of the Nazi rockets approaching.

He ran along the quiet street, hoping to bump into a warden who could direct him to safety. But there was no one to be seen.

Clinton looked skyward. Glimmers of light flashed through the darkening sky: anti-aircraft gunfire. The rockets were close, almost overhead. Panic snaked through his veins and his heart hammered as he fled for cover. It was fine all the while that he could hear the rockets' engines. But then it went quiet. Clinton stopped running and stood motionless, gripped in terror, hardly breathing as he waited for the rocket to fall out of the sky.

A sudden whoosh, a strong blast of air, a deafening explosion. He felt his body lift off the ground as he was thrown backwards, landing heavily against a wall. Flying debris blasted his shocked body. Pain tore up his arm. The air was thick with dust, rendering him unable to see anything, but he could feel heat from a roaring fire close by. There were no screams. No cries for help. Just the sound of flames crackling, the growl of the inferno and the sound of tumbling bricks.

Clinton wiped his eyes, trying to clear away the dirt. He looked around frantically. The street that he'd just ran along had gone. At least eight houses were now nothing but rubble. A red hot glow seemed to be coming out of the ground where the homes had once stood. He tried to get to his feet, but when he pushed himself up, he screamed out in agony and collapsed back to the ground. He realised that his arm was broken, but he was alive. By some miracle, he'd survived by the skin of his teeth. 'T'ank you, God,' he cried.

As Clinton rested his head on the wall and closed his eyes to calm himself, he heard the sound of bells approaching. The street became a hive of activity as firemen fought to control the fires. Men wearing warden's armbands came to search for anyone who may be trapped under the bombed houses. Clinton wanted to help but he couldn't. Instead, he cradled his throbbing arm, the pain was intense, reminding him that he was lucky to be alive.

'You all right there, son?' a kindly old man asked.

'Yes, sir, I t'ink so. I had a lucky escape.'

'You don't look that lucky to me. Hang on, I'll go and fetch some help.'

'No, it's fine, please, let them find the people who need help more than me.'

The old man, his back crooked, sucked in a big breath, shaking his head. 'They won't find no one in there who needs help, son. They'll all be goners. You sit tight, I'll get an ambulance.'

'No, I don't need an ambulance.'

'You do, son, trust me, you do.'

Clinton frowned. He only had a broken arm and didn't think that it required an ambulance. But then he became aware of something dripping down the side of his face. He reached up and felt the sticky liquid. When he looked at his hand, he realised that it was blood, and there was lots of it.

The old man had hobbled off. Clinton could see him through the smoke, approaching a waiting ambulance. He pointed towards Clinton and then two shadowy figures were rushing towards him. Clinton squinted his eyes, trying to focus, but his vision was becoming blurry and his head felt light.

'Please don't let me die, God,' he prayed, as he felt as though his life was ebbing away. Thinking of his family who needed him, he mumbled, 'Please, Lord, don't take me,' and then his world slowly faded into darkness.

15

The next evening, Rachel turned away from the front room window and glanced at the clock on the mantle again. Alberto had said that he'd call for her at seven o'clock, but it was now twenty to eight and there was no sign of him coming down the street.

'Relax, he'll get here when he gets here,' Winnie said. 'I'm sure he has a very good reason for being late.'

'I suppose so,' Rachel sighed and slumped onto the sofa. 'Thanks for watching Martha for me. This is two nights running now that you've kept an eye on Martha so that I can go out with Alberto, I'm ever so grateful.'

'It's not a problem, love. Wednesday evenings are usually quiet. I'm sure Carmen can manage by herself downstairs. And we couldn't expect Hilda to miss her fire-watching duties. Anyway, Martha is no bother, she sleeps like an angel.'

Rachel went back to the window and looked expectantly along the street. Her pulse quickened and her stomach flipped when she saw Alberto. 'He's here.'

'I told you he would be. Off you go, have a nice evening

and don't worry about Martha. She's out for the count and won't even notice that you're gone.'

Rachel hurried from the window, checked her reflection in the mirror and then gave Winnie a quick peck on the cheek. 'Thanks, Win. I won't be late.'

She dashed through the bar and out onto the street, just as Alberto was about to walk into the pub. She almost bumped into him, but when she saw the disconcerted look on his face, her racing heart sank.

'Hello. Is everything all right?' she asked.

'I'm sorry I'm late.'

'What's wrong?'

'Let's go inside.'

Rachel nodded and went back into the pub, with Alberto in her wake.

'I thought you two were off somewhere nice tonight. Had a change of plans?' Carmen asked from behind the bar.

Rachel looked at Alberto for an answer.

He scratched his head and then rubbed his fingers on his brow as he explained, 'Clinton was hurt last night. He got caught up in an explosion.'

'Good grief! Is he all right?' Rachel asked, dreading what she might hear next.

'Yes, he's badly shaken, a few cuts and bruises, a nasty gash on his head and a broken arm. But the doctors said that he's lucky to be alive.'

'The poor fella, give him my best,' Carmen said before going off to serve a customer.

Alberto sat on a bar stool and beckoned for Rachel to do the same. 'I had to help him settle down. He'll get used to his arm being in plaster, but he feels pretty useless at the moment. That's why I was late.'

'Don't worry. I'm just relieved to know that Clinton wasn't seriously hurt or worse.'

'He's lost his job because of it.'

'Oh no!'

Alberto looked down at the floor and then took Rachel's hand in his. 'I'm sorry, but it means I won't be able to afford to take you out. I've promised Clinton half my wages because he needs money to send home to his family. And I won't be able to see as much of you, not until he can look after himself better. I hope you understand.'

Rachel smiled warmly at her man. She admired his loyalty. 'You're a lovely bloke, Alberto, and of course I understand. Clinton is lucky to have such a good friend.'

'T'ank you. He'd do the same for me.'

'I'm sure he would. Can you stay and have a drink with me?'

'Yes, maybe even two. You're much better company than Clinton,' he laughed.

Rachel enjoyed an hour with Alberto. He told her about the power station and she told him about her adventures to the park with Martha and Cake. But, all too soon, he said he'd better go back and check on Clinton.

'I'll walk with you to the end of the road,' she offered, hoping to receive a goodnight kiss away from the prying eyes in the pub.

They strolled hand in hand along the street. It wasn't much of a date, but with a cool breeze in the summer air and a clear night, full moon and sky full of stars, Rachel thought it was quite romantic.

On the corner of the street, Alberto stopped and gently pulled her into the shadows. He cupped her face in his large hands and gazed down into her eyes. 'I t'ink the world of you, Rachel,' he said huskily.

Before Rachel could tell him that she felt the same, his lips were on hers and his tongue explored her mouth as he passionately kissed her. She could feel her body trembling and responding to his touch. His kiss became deeper and she found herself losing control. Quickly pulling away, she gasped, 'Wow ... But no.'

Alberto shrugged. 'One day, my queen, one day soon ... Alberto will have the delights of his queen.'

Rachel was on the verge of saying that *one day* wouldn't be until she had a ring on her finger. But she didn't want to scare him away with talk of marriage yet. Instead, she stood on the tip of her toes and kissed his cheek. 'One day, my king,' she smiled, 'one day.' There was no doubt in her mind; Alberto King had won her heart and *one day*, soon she hoped, she would, indeed, be his queen and have a wedding ring to prove it.

Clinton tried to make himself comfortable on his bed, but his arm ached and his head was throbbing. To make matters worse, whenever he did manage to nod off, he woke with a start, reliving the sound of a terrific explosion ringing in his ears, along with the sensation of being hurled through the air.

He was pleased when Alberto came home and was keen to hear news from the power station. He assumed that it was unlikely that he'd still have a job, but until he knew for sure, he held on to hope.

'You're late, man. I t'ought you'd be home hours ago,' he said, easing himself up.

'Yes, sorry. I had to see Rachel.'

'Why didn't you come home first?'

'I was busy with another beautiful lady. Ah, Clinton, I tell you, the good Lord has sent me an angel from heaven to behold.'

'What are you talking about, man?'

'Mr Caymen's daughter, Rita. She is the most glorious woman I've ever seen.'

'Oh, no, Alberto, stay away from her! You can't get mixed up with our supervisor's daughter.'

'Not our supervisor... *my* supervisor.'

Clinton drew in a long breath of disappointment. It was just as he'd already guessed; he'd lost his job.

'I'm sorry, I tried to talk Mr Caymen round, but he can't hold your position open.'

'I understand, but t'anks for trying. I don't know what I'm going to do now... you know how much my sister relies on me for the money for her medicine.'

'Don't worry, my friend, I'll make sure she gets it.'

'How?' Clinton snapped.

'*I'll* send her the money.'

Stunned by the generous offer from his friend, Clinton asked, 'You'd do that for me?'

'Yes, of course I would. But listen... if Rachel says anyt'ing, you must let her believe that I'm sharing *half* my wages with you.'

'Why?'

'Because that's what I told her.'

Clinton's eyes narrowed as he surveyed his friend's face.

'Why did you tell her that? And don't tell me that you said it to make yourself look good. What's the truth, Alberto?'

'I can't take out two women on my wage,' Alberto shrugged.

'No, no, no… please don't tell me that you're t'inking of taking out Mr Caymen's daughter too?'

Alberto smiled wryly, 'The women love Alberto King; I couldn't disappoint her.'

Clinton looked down at the floor, his temper raging. 'How could you do this to Rachel? You said that you like her!'

'I didn't lie. I do like her.'

'So, why would you treat her like this?'

'Oh, Clinton, calm down, man. I'm Alberto King. Henry the eighth had six wives. It's what kings do.'

'You're not royalty! What is wrong with you?'

Alberto threw Clinton a scowl. 'There's not'ing wrong with me, man, so jump down off your righteous horse. I'm just having a bit of fun, that's all.'

'I hope Rachel sees it that way.'

'Rachel never needs to know.'

Clinton couldn't look at his friend any longer and snatched his book from the bedside table, burying his nose in the pages. It was bad enough that Alberto was cheating on Rachel, but his friend had roped him into his lies too. Clinton's jaw clenched with frustration. Alberto had him over a barrel. He'd have to keep quiet and go along with the deceit or else Alberto could retract the offer to pay for his sister's medicine. It seemed that Clinton was going to be a part of Alberto's web of lies whether he liked it or not.

16

Maureen tramped along the street, laden with bags of second-hand clothes, and with Carmen walking beside her. The woman had been a godsend. Maureen was grateful for her help and wasn't sure how she would have coped without her. She'd found it a strain in the undertakers and had been relieved when Carmen had taken charge. And after, in the shops, Carmen had haggled for some bargain prices, which meant that Maureen's clothes ration coupons and money had stretched further. And thank goodness for the extra coupons that Mrs Berry had given her.

'You're coming into the pub to say hello to Winnie, aren't you?' Carmen asked.

'Oh, erm, I'm not sure. I really ought to think about getting home.'

'Come on, just a quick visit. It's a long way to your house from here. Have a rest, your feet must be killing you, I know mine are.'

'Yes, they are, my arms too. But I can't stop for long,' Maureen replied, keen to get back home. She hadn't yet spoken to Brancher about what might be hidden in their shed, and it was causing her a great deal of worry.

Maureen followed Carmen into the Battersea Tavern, pleased to see that it was quiet, which meant that she wouldn't be bombarded with sentiments of condolences.

'Hello, love, looks like you've bought half of Clapham Junction,' Mrs Berry smiled from behind the bar.

'I've only bought what I need. I haven't been wasteful and it wasn't easy to find anything affordable except for utility clothing.'

'I'm sure, I'm only kidding with you. Sit yourself down. What would you like to drink?'

'Just a glass of water, please, Mrs Berry.'

'I'm putting the kettle on upstairs. Do you want to come up for a cuppa?' Carmen asked.

'No, thank you, just water is fine,' Maureen answered, knowing that waiting for the kettle to boil and having a cup of tea would mean she'd be in the pub for longer than she wanted.

Maureen sat at a table nearest to the bar and was pleased to place her bags on the floor. Mrs Berry waddled over, her wide hips swinging from side to side, and with a tall glass of water in her hand.

'Here you are, love. And it's about time you started calling me Winnie,' she said, and then whispered, 'Have you told Brancher to clear out the shed?'

'No, not yet. He didn't get home until really late and he wasn't in the best of moods this morning. I'm going to speak to him today.'

'All right, make sure you do.'

As Winnie was speaking, Maureen looked past her and saw

Clinton come into the pub. He glanced around and, when he saw her at the table, he walked over. Maureen quickly lowered her eyes.

'Hello, Mrs Berry, Maureen,' he greeted.

Winnie turned around to speak to him, exclaiming, 'Oh, Clinton, look at the sorry state of you! Alberto told Rachel about what happened. I'm glad to see that you're just about in one piece. How's your arm feeling?'

'Sore.'

'I should think it is,' Winnie said, and then turning back to Maureen, she asked, 'Did you know about Clinton getting hurt in an explosion? If he'd been a few more feet up the road, he would have been killed!'

'Yes, Carmen told me.'

Winnie began to walk away, saying to Clinton, 'Sit down, keep Maureen company and I'll get you a drink.'

Maureen's head snapped up and she met Clinton's eyes. He looked uncomfortable and she wondered if he could sense her panic.

'Do you mind?' he asked, pointing to a seat adjacent to hers.

She shook her head. She didn't mind at all, but Brancher would.

'How are you?' Clinton enquired as he sat down.

'Oh, you know, all right,' she said with a sigh. 'Carmen took me to make the arrangements today for my grand-parents' funerals. It wasn't easy, but it had to be done.'

'I'm so sorry, Maureen. Is there anyt'ing I can do?'

'No, thank you. And thank you for bringing me here that day.'

Maureen's mouth felt incredibly dry and her heart raced.

She picked up the water and slowly sipped it, briefly looking over the top of the glass, meeting Clinton's eyes again. He held her gaze, but she quickly looked away as her stomach jumped.

Winnie plonked a drink on the table for Clinton and then she bustled off again.

Maureen wanted to fill the silence between herself and Clinton but couldn't think of anything to say. Her nerves were jangling, fearing that Brancher would walk in. She knew she should get up and leave, yet she found that she *wanted* to sit with Clinton. It had been a long time since Maureen had done anything that she wanted to do, especially something so daring.

Clinton broke the awkward silence, asking, 'Will you be coming back to work here?'

'No, I don't think so. My husband doesn't like me working at the pub.'

'That's a shame. It was nice seeing you behind the bar. You're much prettier than Mrs Berry and Mrs Hampton, but don't tell them that I said that.'

Maureen shot him a look and saw that he was smiling at her, a friendly, genuine smile that touched her heart. For the first time since the death of her grandparents, she smiled too.

'I'd better get going,' she said with reluctance.

'You have a lot of bags there. Would you like me to help you home with them?'

'Thank you, that's kind, but I don't think you'd be much help … I mean, with your arm in a cast.'

'I've still got one perfectly good arm and could take at least some of your bags.'

'I'll manage.'

Seeing Clinton's dejected expression, Maureen felt compelled to be open and honest with him.

'It wouldn't be good if my husband saw us together.'

'Wouldn't be good for who? Me? Because if that's the case, I'm not worried.'

'It wouldn't be good for *either* of us,' she answered, feeling ashamed.

'Your husband is not a good man, Maureen.'

Again, she sighed. 'I know. But he's my husband and he's all I've got.' Acutely aware of her loneliness, tears began to pool in Maureen's eyes. She sniffed, and fished in her pocket for a handkerchief. Dabbing at her eyes, she said sadly, 'Take no notice of me, I'm a silly mare. It's just been a very upsetting time. I really do have to go.'

Maureen stood up to leave, but, reaching down for her shopping bags, she felt Clinton's hand over hers. A jolt shot through her body. She wasn't sure if it was the shock of him touching her or the thrill of it.

'Let me take you somewhere to take your mind off t'ings,' he offered.

Maureen snatched her hand away and, feeling flustered, answered, 'No, I don't think that it would be a good idea.'

'I had a brush with death the other night and it's made me realise how short life is: too short to be unhappy. I just want to take you away from here for one day, that's all. You never know, you might enjoy yourself,' he teased.

'I couldn't! What if Brancher found out?'

'He won't, I promise you.'

Maureen shook her head, but she was tempted to agree.

'If you change your mind, I'll be at the train station to-morrow at ten. I'll wait for you.'

She gazed wide-eyed at him for a moment before gathering her bags and rushing out of the pub. Her heart was pounding and her mind raced. She would have liked to have accepted Clinton's offer, but the thought of Brancher finding out terrified her. She knew that if he even got a sniff that she'd spoken to Clinton, her husband would make sure that her life wasn't worth living.

Winnie was peeved that because Mr Coggins couldn't keep his hands to himself, it meant that she had to traipse an extra half a mile to the next grocery shop. But, she supposed, at least it was nice weather and she could do with the fresh air, though the air in Battersea felt far from fresh. She imagined breathing in the clean air of the countryside or the salty breezes beside the sea. She thought that it had to smell nicer than the pollution of London.

'Silly woman,' she muttered to herself, realising that she'd forgotten to bring her shopping list.

'Hello, Winnie, where are you off to?'

Winnie turned to see Tommy on his bicycle. He climbed off it and pushed it along beside her.

'Hello, Tommy, just on my way to the shop for a few bits and pieces. I shan't be using Mr Coggins' store again.'

Tommy rolled his eyes. 'If you get any more problems from him, you be sure to come to me ... though I must say, I quite liked hearing about how Carmen dealt with him.'

Winnie chuckled, 'You should have seen the look on his face, it was a picture.'

'I can imagine. Carmen brandishing a broom and threatening to shove it where the sun don't shine is enough to put the fear of God into any man.'

'Well, us ladies won't tolerate any sort of nonsense in my pub.'

'I admire you, Winnie. It can't be easy without a man about the place.'

'Huh, it's a lot easier without having to answer to a man, waste of space that most of them are, no offence.'

'None taken. But we're not all like Brian and David.'

'I know, sorry, love, but my husband left me with a bitter taste in my mouth and David turned out just like him. I'm better off without them.'

'Does that mean that you won't entertain the idea of coming to my niece's school play tonight?'

'Eh?'

'My youngest sister ... her girl has a starring role in a performance at Tennyson Street School this evening. I've got two tickets and was hoping that you'd accompany me?'

Winnie baulked. She felt put on the spot and wracked her brains to think of the right words to say to let Tommy down gently.

'Go on, Winnie, say you'll come,' he urged. 'It's going to be a full house and I don't want the only empty seat to be next to me. There'll be refreshments afterwards and I'd feel a right chump standing with a glass of squash all by meself.'

'Don't be daft, Tommy. You'll know loads of people there.'

'Yes, and they'll all be feeling sorry for me. I'm fed up with going to places alone. It would be nice to have a friend with me, for a change. Go on, say you'll accompany me?'

'Oh, all right, I suppose so,' Winnie answered. He'd put her in a position where she found it difficult to refuse him.

'Smashing! I'll pick you up at six, bombs allowing, God forbid.'

'By the way, before you shoot off, have you got any further with the distillery investigation?'

Tommy sucked in a sharp breath. 'Nope. I'm sure that Brancher has got something to do with it, but him and his mates are covering for each other. I bumped into Maureen earlier. She was loaded with shopping bags, which I reckon must have been purchased with stolen money. I just can't prove it.'

'I gave her my clothes coupons. You do realise that even if you prove that Brancher was behind the robbery, Maureen wouldn't have had anything to do with it.'

'Hmm, I'm not so sure. She's quick enough to spend the proceeds. She *must* know something about it, but she won't rat on her husband. But, in my book, keeping quiet about what she knows makes her just as guilty as him.'

'You shouldn't be so quick to judge her. You've seen for yourself what Brancher is like. Even if she does know what her husband has been up to, she'll be too scared to speak out against him. He rules her and none too kindly.'

'Sorry, Winnie, I agree with you in part, but the law is the law, plain and simple.'

'What are you going to do? Will you search their house?'

'No point. Brancher wouldn't be stupid enough to have incriminating evidence at home. But I'll be watching him. I'll have him, one of these days, I'll have him.'

Tommy was wrong, there was evidence in Maureen's home; it was in the shed. She was pleased to know that he wasn't going to conduct a search. At least that would keep Maureen out of the frame. But even so, with Tommy breathing down Brancher's neck, it meant that Maureen was skating on thin ice too. The poor, timid woman could do without having to deal with the police!

17

'I don't like to ask, but is there any chance one of you could watch Martha again tonight?' Rachel asked Winnie and Carmen.

Winnie had just tucked into her breakfast and had her mouth full. It was Carmen who answered, 'I'd be happy to, but I might be needed behind the bar if Winnie has plans to go out with her *fella* again.'

'Pack it in, he's not my fella,' Winnie protested, covering her mouth with her hand.

'Does he know that?'

'We're just friends.'

'I heard the pair of you come home last night, laughing and joking. If you ask me, it sounded a lot more than friends.'

'I didn't ask you, so button it.'

Rachel smiled and butted in, 'Erm, excuse me … can either of you babysit Martha tonight, please?'

'Oh, yes, sorry, love. Carmen can, she could do with a night off. I assume you'll be seeing Alberto again?'

'Yes,' Rachel answered. 'I know I said I'd take things slowly, but I'm really falling for him.'

'We can tell,' Carmen said. 'But it's nice to see you looking so happy.'

'Thanks. He does make me happy. So, what about you, Win?'

'What about me?'

'You and Tommy.'

'I don't know how many times I've got to repeat myself… me and Tommy are just friends.'

Rachel and Carmen exchanged a smiling glance. It seemed that Carmen enjoyed teasing Winnie as much as she did.

'Did your *friend* give you a kiss goodnight?' Carmen asked.

'No, he bleedin' didn't, because *friends* don't kiss goodnight.'

'Did he hold your hand when he walked you home?' Rachel quizzed.

'No, of course not.'

Rachel felt a gentle nudge and then Carmen asked Winnie, 'Have you got your dancing shoes ready?'

'What for?'

'For when Tommy takes you to a dance … I mean, that's what sweethearts do, isn't it? They go dancing together.'

'Right, that's enough, the pair of you!' Winnie blurted, going red in the face.

Rachel and Carmen laughed heartily.

'She's so easy to wind up,' Carmen chuckled.

'We're only playing, Win,' Rachel added.

'I know, but it's a bit of a raw nerve. I'm really worried that I'm letting Tommy think that we're more than just friends,' Winnie sighed.

'You like him, don't you?' Carmen asked.

'Yes, but not in *that* way.'

'Win, at our age, surely just liking him is enough? There's a lot to be said for companionship.'

'What would I want companionship with a bloke for? I've got you and Rachel here.'

'Yeah, but that's not the same as having someone beside you to fall asleep with and wake up to in the mornings,' Rachel argued.

'Sod that, thank you very much! I'm quite content in my single bed by myself. I had years of having to put up with Brian's snoring and him breaking wind all night. I swear he used to save up all his wind during the day just so that he could make the bedroom stink when I went to bed. I'm not going through that again.'

Again, Rachel and Carmen laughed.

'It's not funny. That man's guts were rotten. Churchill could have gassed the Jerries with it! They would have been begging to surrender if they'd encountered the stench that came from Brian's backside.'

Rachel laughed so hard that her ribs ached. Dear Winnie was blessed with a special way with words, the woman was so amusing but didn't know it, which made her even funnier. She thought the world of Winnie and having realised how happy Alberto had made her, Rachel decided that she'd like to see Winnie happy too. After all, Winnie was capable of giving love. It had only been two or three years ago when she'd developed feelings for Carmen's husband. But as it had turned out, Harry had been a dreadful man. Rachel thought that the experience had possibly left Winnie closed down to finding herself a fella. She thought it was such a shame, as Tommy seemed like a nice bloke and he clearly had feelings for Winnie. A thought struck her: she'd have a discreet word with him. Explain to Tommy that Winnie needed patience and to persevere with her and to not give up. Rachel was convinced that, given time, Winnie would come to realise that she had a future with Tommy.

'Are you daydreaming about Alberto again?' Carmen asked.

'Eh? Er, no ... I'd better take Cake for his walk,' Rachel answered.

Once outside, Martha asked if she could hold Cake's lead and Rachel told her she could but only if she held her hand too. She spotted Clinton ahead and called out to him. When he turned around and saw her, Rachel wondered why he appeared uneasy. He waited for her to catch up with him, but he was shifting from one leg to the other.

'Good morning. You're looking very dandy today. Are you going somewhere?' she asked.

'Hello. No, nowhere special,' he answered, avoiding her eyes.

Rachel could tell that he wasn't telling her the truth, but she didn't think that Clinton's activities were any of her business. Instead, she asked, 'Any idea where Alberto plans on taking me this evening? He's told me it's a surprise, but I'm dying to know.'

'Er, no, sorry, no idea.'

Again, she got the feeling that he was being cagey. 'How's your arm?' she asked.

'Not too bad, t'ank you.'

'I hope Alberto is taking good care of you. And listen, don't worry about me. I know that he has to look after you, so I'm quite happy with any snatched moments I get with him and I promise I won't take up too much of his time tonight. You just concentrate on getting better.'

'Oh, er, t'ank you. I have to go. See you soon.'

Clinton hurried away, leaving Rachel feeling fobbed off. There was something not quite right, but she couldn't put her finger on it. Before she could give it any more thought, Martha began yanking her along the street and started chattering about holding her breath underwater at the lido.

Clinton had felt awful about rushing away from Rachel and for not being very forthcoming with his conversation. But he couldn't look her in the eye and blatantly lie to cover up Alberto's dishonesty. He cursed his friend under his breath and wished that Alberto wasn't such a womaniser, especially as this wasn't the first time. However, he wouldn't dwell on it and allow it to bother him now; he had more important things on his mind. It was half-past nine and he was hoping that there was a slim chance that Maureen would turn up at the train station.

He made his way to Clapham Junction, his nerves fraught, though he didn't know why he felt so nervous as he doubted that Maureen would meet him. But it wasn't only the thought of Maureen that had him feeling tense; he was worried about Brancher too. Granted, it was unlikely that the man would have any knowledge of Clinton's plans for today, but he was still convinced that Brancher was vying for his blood.

Clinton arrived at the entrance to the train station amidst a throng of travellers going about their business. He stood outside and shoved his hand into his pocket, jangling the few coins he had. There was enough to purchase two return train tickets to Wimbledon and he hoped that his money would fund a couple of cups of tea and a cake too. He glanced at the flower stall and wished that he could afford to buy Maureen a bunch of fragrant freesias. But with no work, no income and little money left, such treats were out of the question.

Clinton glanced behind to look inside the ticket hall, where he could see a large clock on the wall. He checked the time: two minutes to ten. He was sure that Maureen wouldn't come. He heard the long, shrill sound of a guard's whistle from one of the platforms and then the grinding, roaring, chugging of the train as it pulled out of the station. He glanced behind again. Three minutes past ten. Maureen definitely wasn't coming.

Another train, people running into the station, crowds of folk coming out. He checked over his shoulder again. Nine minutes past ten. Hope of Maureen turning up had long since faded.

More trains, more people, twenty-five minutes past ten. Clinton was disappointed but not surprised. He'd been a fool in allowing himself to imagine spending his day with Maureen.

One last look over his shoulder. Twenty to eleven. He reasoned that it was time to give up and go home. But as he went to walk away, he spotted a familiar figure coming towards him. 'I don't believe it,' he muttered, a wide smile now on his face. 'I t'ought you wasn't coming,' he said, looking down into Maureen's dewy eyes.

'I nearly didn't,' she replied, timidly.

Clinton took her hand and led her through to the ticket hall. He could feel that her palm was clammy and he could see the tautness of her jaw. He hoped that she'd relax once that they were on the train. The sooner they were out of Battersea, the better.

★

214

Later that day, Maureen peered out of the window as the steam train trundled back towards Clapham Junction. She still couldn't believe that she'd plucked up the courage to secretly meet Clinton, but she was pleased that she had. Getting out of Battersea and from under the shadow of Brancher had given her a sense of freedom. She'd had a smashing few hours with Clinton and hadn't wanted their time together to come to an end. They'd talked easily and Maureen had found herself opening up, telling him about how unhappy she was with Brancher and how trapped and alone she felt. She'd been able to forget her grief for a while as she'd listened to Clinton's tales of home, a place she'd never heard of. He had described the forests and the beaches so vividly that she could imagine the beauty and feel the warmth.

The conductor passed through the train, shouting, 'Next stop Clapham Junction.'

Maureen instantly tensed. She dreaded going back home and her heart hammered at the thought of seeing Brancher. What if he'd found out about her little escapade with Clinton?

Clinton, sitting opposite her, leaned forward, and said softly, 'It's been lovely to see you smile today.'

Maureen couldn't answer. She sat rigid, suddenly overcome with fear. How could she have been so stupid and allowed herself to have been so irresponsible? All the wonderful feelings of the day faded. It wasn't just herself that she worried for, but Clinton too. Brancher would kill him!

'Maureen … are you all right?' Clinton asked, his gentle voice full of concern and so different from her husband's.

She shook her head.

'What's wrong?'

'I've made a terrible mistake ... I shouldn't be with you ... what if Brancher finds out?'

'I don't see how. I won't tell anyone about today, and neither will you. See, safe as houses.'

'Yeah, well, even houses ain't safe, not with Hitler's bombs landing on them!'

'Stop worrying, Maureen. Your husband is never going to know.'

'I wish I could be sure.'

'You can be. Stop worrying.'

Maureen nodded and peered back through the window as the train slowed, approaching the platform. Another worrying thought caused her to panic again. How would she explain the smell of soot from the steam train in her hair? It wasn't bath day until Sunday ... she couldn't drag the tin bath into the living room before then, Brancher would ask her why.

She drew in a long, deep breath and tried to calm her thoughts. Realistically, Clinton was right and Brancher would never discover that she'd been out *cavorting* on Wimbledon common. And the chances were, he wouldn't even be home when she got back. Now that Brancher had money in his pockets, he was out every night, rolling home late, stinking of booze and falling around drunk.

'Are you feeling better?' Clinton asked.

'Yes, I think so. But we shouldn't leave the train station together.'

'Fine. You go first. I'll wait ten minutes.'

'Thank you ... and thank you for a really special day.'

'Perhaps we can do it again sometime?'

'Oh, I don't think so. It's too much of a risk.'

'Not if we're careful.'

'I'm not sure, Clinton. I reckon I was pretty brave coming today, but now I'm back in Battersea, me bottle has gone.'

The train brakes screeched as it pulled up at the platform. Clinton reached out for Maureen's hand and gently kissed the back of it. 'I'll be outside the station again on Monday morning at ten. I really hope to see you.'

Maureen rose to her feet, hesitant to leave him, but she knew she had to. Fighting back tears, she smiled at Clinton, uttering, 'Goodbye.' He'd been a friend when she'd so desperately needed one, but as far as she was concerned, this would be their final farewell.

18

The next day, Rachel stamped through to the kitchen and sat down heavily on a seat at the table.

Winnie, with raised eyebrows, looked at Rachel and saw that she was pouting miserably. 'I take it you're still fed up that Alberto didn't show up last night?'

'Yes, I am. No word or explanation. I know he's helping Clinton, but surely he could have popped round for half an hour or something.'

'There's no point in getting annoyed with him until you know the full story.'

'I know the story; he was supposed to turn up at seven and surprise me. Instead, I spent the evening pacing back and forth to the window, waiting like a fool, only to be stood up. There, that's the full story!'

'I'm sure that he'll have a perfectly acceptable explanation. Now, young lady, put a smile on that pretty face of yours before you turn my milk sour.'

Carmen came into the kitchen, tutting. 'Has she still got the hump with Alberto?'

'Yes, *she* has,' Rachel answered.

'Well, Alberto seems a decent chap. I don't suppose that he let you down on purpose.'

'See, me and Carmen think the same,' Winnie said. 'Why don't you try cheering up, eh, love? He'll probably come round tonight and be full of apologies.'

Rachel shrugged, half-heartedly smiling. 'He'd better have a good reason.'

Winnie felt sure that he would and then Rachel would be back to her usual good spirits.

In her own home, Maureen sat at the kitchen table, chewing her thumbnail as she stared at the pot of tea. She listened carefully for sounds of movement upstairs. Brancher was still sleeping. Again, he hadn't come home until late and when he'd climbed into the bed, Maureen had pretended to be asleep. It was easier that way. She could avoid a confrontation or having to lay on her back for him. He'd stank of booze and had given her a couple of shakes, but she'd kept her eyes firmly squeezed shut, relieved when he'd given up and was soon asleep.

The floorboards creaked. He was up. Maureen breathed deeply and clenched and unclenched her fists in a bid to stop her hands from shaking. Still anxious about Brancher questioning her whereabouts yesterday, she'd concocted a story about undertakers and shopping.

Stop worrying, she told herself, Clinton's words ringing in her ears. After all, since Brancher had come into money, he'd hardly asked after her movements and seemed disinterested.

His heavy footsteps plodded down the stairs and he came into the kitchen, wearing just his underwear, running a hand through his dark hair and scratching his man parts with the other.

'Cor, my mouth feels like I've been licking a dog's arse. Make us a cuppa.'

Maureen jumped to his bidding, asking, 'Would you like me to do you some breakfast?'

'Yeah, go on then, but none of that Macon crap.'

As two thin slices of real bacon fried in the sizzling lard, Maureen had a pressing subject on her mind and ventured another question. 'Brancher... you know you said that I'm not to go into the shed... is that because you have stuff in there from the job you did?'

'Yes, so keep out,' he snapped.

'I will, but... erm... what if the police search the place?'

'The Old Bill, search here... why would they?'

'Well, I don't know, but if Sergeant Bradbury suspects that you're involved, he might get our place turned over.'

Maureen placed a bacon sandwich on the table in front of Brancher. He drummed his fingers, his eyes narrowing. 'Has someone said something to you?' he asked accusingly.

'No, no ... not really,' she blustered.

'What do you mean, *not really*? Who the flamin' hell have you been talking to?'

'No one... honest... I just heard Mrs Berry and Sergeant Bradbury discussing the robbery at the distillery.'

'And what did they say?'

'Not much... just that he was going to get to the bottom of it. It made me think about the shed and how it would probably be best to make sure that there's nothing in it that could link you to the crime.'

Brancher threw his sandwich onto the plate and leaned

back in his seat, slowly laughing. 'Don't you worry, treacle, the silly old codger won't find nuffink here, but you, my clever girl, have given me a bloody brilliant idea!'

Maureen, flummoxed, sat opposite her husband. 'Really?' she asked.

'Yep, really. You ain't quite as stupid as you make out.'

Seeing as he was in a good mood, she dared to ask, 'What's your brilliant idea?'

'Nothing you need to know about. I'll be out all day and I want you out of the house too. I suggest you go and see Mrs Berry again and, while you're there, see what you can find out about how much Tommy Bradbury knows.' His voice was light, but then he growled, 'All you have to do is keep your cakehole shut about the shed. Got it?'

Maureen nodded and chewed on her thumbnail again. It was a relief to know that, whatever he was up to, at least the shed would be cleared out. And best of all, he hadn't questioned her movements yesterday. She'd got away with meeting Clinton, but, although she'd had a wonderful day, she'd never risk it again.

Clinton sat at the bar in the Battersea Tavern, bored and with only a couple of coins in his pocket. He couldn't really afford to waste money in the pub, but he made his half a pint of ale last for a long time.

Rachel's mother, Hilda, came in and stood at the bar beside him. 'Hello, Clinton. Feeling any better?' she asked, indicating to his broken arm.

'Not bad, t'ank you. But I miss being at work.'

'Hmm, it can't be easy for you. If you're looking for something to do, we could always use more people on the fire-watching rota, though, as it's voluntary work you don't get paid.'

Clinton's interest piqued. Being out of work had left him feeling useless and he'd like to help his new-found community in any way he could. 'Where do I sign up?' he asked.

'Great, I'll take you to see my supervisor. I must warn you though, the role has its risks and it's not for the faint-hearted, especially if you don't like heights. I was on the roof of a factory the other night and I don't mind admitting that my legs were like jelly.'

'I understand. I'm happy to do whatever I can.'

'Good man. Mind you, to be honest, now that we aren't getting thousands of incendiaries dropping on us, there's not so many fires to look out for. But you never know when Adolf is going to send the Luftwaffe over again, so it's best not to let our guard down.'

Winnie came along the bar and was clearly pleased to see Hilda. 'Hello, love. Rachel is upstairs with Martha, go on up.'

'Will you still be here in an hour?' Hilda asked Clinton, then turning to Winnie, she explained, 'I'm taking Clinton to sign up for the fire-watching rota.'

Clinton looked at the few mouthfuls of ale left in his glass and didn't really want to spend the last of his money on another. But he knew that his drink wouldn't last him anywhere near an hour.

Thankfully, Winnie picked up his glass. 'Good for you, Clinton,' she said. 'That deserves a refill on the house.'

'T'ank you, Mrs Berry, and yes, I'll be here in an hour,' he told Hilda.

The prospect of volunteering had lifted his spirits and he

liked the idea of doing something worthwhile. And then the sight of Maureen walking into the pub added to his delight.

She looked as nervous and as timid as always as she offered him a shy smile. Clinton jumped down from the bar stool, but Maureen stood further along the bar away from him. He knew why: she was scared of her husband seeing them together. Respecting her wishes, Clinton kept his distance, but he felt compelled to communicate with her in some way. After asking Mrs Berry for a pencil and piece of paper, he scribbled her a short note.

Seeing you has made my day! Since our time on Wimbledon common, you're all I've thought about x

He folded the paper four times and then asked Mrs Berry to pass it to Maureen. The woman didn't ask him what it was about or why he couldn't give the note to Maureen himself; she was too busy serving customers to stop and ask questions.

Clinton watched Maureen unfold the paper and read the note. She briefly looked over to him, wide-eyed, and then squirrelled the paper away in the pocket of her cardigan. He'd hoped that she might respond and send him a message back, but he wasn't surprised when she didn't. Maureen would think that it was far too much of a risk and would be worried about what Mrs Berry would think of it. At least he'd let her know that she was on his mind and he hoped that she'd be brave enough to turn up at the train station on Monday.

19

Just after seven o'clock in the morning, Moaning Minnie sprang into life, signalling the all-clear. The rise and fall of the wailing siren had made Cake bark incessantly. Winnie would have been content to have stayed down in the cellar, dreading facing what she would meet upstairs. She knew that death had visited Battersea in the night and it was on her doorstep.

Winnie yawned and looked over to Rachel. The girl looked sheet-white and had Martha huddled on her lap. 'You all right, love?' she asked.

Rachel nodded her head, but Martha began whimpering again.

Carmen leaned towards Winnie and whispered, 'I think it's going to be bad, Win. That doodlebug landed pretty bloody close. When the whole place shook, I thought the roof was going to come down on top of us.'

'I know. I reckon we are lucky to escape unharmed. Come on, we can't hide down here forever. We need to go upstairs to check for damage, and then see what help might be needed. Carmen, get the urn turned on, love,' Winnie urged, and then she called across to Rachel. 'See if you can settle

Martha down in her bed and then I'll need you in the pub, all hands on deck.'

The women jumped into action and the sudden commotion distracted Cake, who finally quietened down. Winnie noticed that Martha was clinging to Rachel like a limpet to a rock. It wasn't safe for the girl to be in Battersea, but she doubted very much that she'd be able to convince Rachel to send her away to the countryside. Perhaps if they *all* moved away, Rachel might agree to that. But with fire engine bells ringing outside, Winnie knew that there was no time to ponder that now.

She pushed open the cellar door and was immediately hit by the acrid smell of burning. A haze of dust hung in the air, caught in the early-morning sunlight streaming through the windows. Winnie's brain couldn't fathom the sight at first. How was her pub so illuminated when she had heavy blackout curtains at the windows?

'Bloody hell!' Carmen exclaimed. 'The windows have been blown out and look at the state of the curtains! Oh my goodness, there's alcohol all over the floor ... all the bottles are smashed!'

Winnie gulped and stared in disbelief at the devastation around her as her mind was still trying to comprehend what had happened.

'Nanny ... Nanny ...' Martha cried, 'Who smashed up evweything?'

Winnie spun around to see Rachel holding the girl in her arms. 'It's all right, love,' she soothed, 'Just one of those silly bombs landed near us. We'll have the place shipshape again in a jiffy. Go upstairs with Mummy and get some sleep and then you can go to the park later.'

Martha nodded, so tired that her head was drooping as Rachel carried her away.

'I don't know where to start,' Winnie mumbled to Carmen.

'A broom, a dustpan and brush. We can't let anyone in until we've cleared away all the broken glass.'

Winnie drew in a deep breath and gathered her thoughts. She wouldn't allow herself to brood over the damage to her pub. They were alive, that's what mattered, and there were people outside who needed her. 'Yes, you're right,' she said firmly. 'You start behind the bar and I'll see to the windows.'

As Winnie began sweeping shards of glass, she heard Hilda's voice call through the broken window. 'Need a hand?'

'Oh, yes please, love. Hang on, I'll unlock the door.'

Hilda came in, her shoes crunching on the shattered glass underfoot. 'My heart's going thirteen to the dozen, Win. I thought you'd been hit... I've never been so scared in all me life!'

'It was close.'

'Not 'alf! Have you seen outside?'

'No and, to be honest, I don't know if I can bring meself to look.'

'I'll warn you, Win, it's a devastating sight. The grocery shop has gone and so have at least five houses.'

Carmen, behind the bar, leaned on her broom, asking, 'The grocery shop, you say?'

'Yeah, nothing but a pile of rubble.'

'What about Mr and Mrs Coggins? Are they all right?'

'I don't know. Their Anderson is buried under a load of bricks and debris. There's a group of people digging them out. I hope they were in their shelter 'cos they wouldn't have stood a bleedin' chance if they weren't.'

Winnie licked her dry lips and asked tentatively, 'Has anyone been killed?'

'Yes, I'm sorry to say that Mrs Palmer and her sister are both dead. Everyone knows that they never used their shelter and always got under their beds. There's nothing left of their house, Win, nothing. I doubt that they'll even find their bodies. Thank goodness that Mrs Palmer had her kids evacuated, though the poor mites are orphans now.'

'Good grief, it's heartbreaking. First, the kiddies lose their father at sea thanks to Hitler and his bloody U-boats, and now this!' she said sadly as anger towards the Germans festered inside. 'It ain't fair! The children deserve better. They didn't ask for this! None of us asked for this!' she shouted.

'Win, take a deep breath,' Hilda urged.

Winnie had allowed her anger to spill over and had to stop herself from crying with pent-up emotion. They'd survived the Blitz and then the mini Blitz, but these blasted rockets were too much, especially when they were landing on her street and killing her neighbours. 'I'm sorry,' she said, choking back a sob. 'It's just the shock talking.'

'Go and have some breakfast, Win, I'll clean up here,' Hilda offered, taking the broom from her.

'No, thanks. I'm all right. Let's get on with it together. Many hands make light work.'

After an hour, the pub began to resemble normality again and Carmen got the urn going as Piano Pete bordered up the windows. Pete, his roll-up stuck on his bottom lip, was one of Winnie's regulars and always livened up her pub by playing skilfully on her old piano. But, for once, the man wasn't offering to tinkle on the ivories.

Winnie knew that it would take a lot more than a jolly singalong to lift the gloomy mood of the street's residents. But she was eager to open her doors. After instructing Rachel to make sandwiches, Hilda prepared glasses of squash for the children, and Winnie opened up.

Tommy was first in, looking grave. 'Hello, Winnie, can I have a word?' he asked.

She pulled him to one side. 'What is it?'

'I thought I should let you know that Clinton and Alberto are at the station. I had to pull them in after a tip-off to the police station yesterday.'

'A tip-off about what?'

'The robbery at the distillery. The anonymous caller said that we'd find evidence in their lodgings, so I conducted a search and, well, what we found is pretty damning.'

Winnie shook her head in disbelief. 'I don't believe it, Tommy, not Clinton and Alberto. They're smashing lads, surely there's been a mistake?'

'I find it hard to believe too, but the evidence speaks for itself. Anyway, I can't stop, but I thought you'd want to let Rachel know.'

Winnie's mind raced. She *knew* who was responsible for the robbery and it wasn't Clinton or Alberto. Somehow, Brancher was behind this, but she couldn't prove it. 'It wasn't them, Tommy,' she protested. 'You and me both know who should be locked up and it's not those two young men.'

'Like I said, I think the same as you, but there's not much that I can do about it unless they can explain how the night-watchman's keys came to be in their room, along with four large bottles of gin and a wad of notes.'

'Oh no, it's not looking good for them, is it?'

'No, it's not. If a judge finds them guilty of robbery with violence, they'll both be spending a long time behind bars. Sorry, I must dash. I'll be back later once my shift is finished.'

Winnie stood and watched Tommy leave, her mind whirling.

'You look upset, Win. What did Tommy want?' Carmen asked.

'Clinton and Alberto have been arrested for the distillery robbery. I need to go upstairs and talk to Rachel. You'll be all right down here?'

'Yes, of course. Hilda is here to give me a hand. Oh, gawd, poor Rachel. She's going to be ever so upset.'

Yes, Rachel would be upset and Winnie wasn't looking forward to telling her about Alberto. *There must be something that I can do*, she thought, as she trudged wearily up the stairs. But there was only one person who might stand a chance of convincing the police that they had the wrong men: Maureen. Though Winnie doubted that she'd be able to persuade the woman to do the right thing and tell on her husband.

The walls of the police cell felt as though they were closing in on Clinton. He sat on a hard, wooden bench, rocking back and forward as he tried to figure out how they could get out of this shocking situation. Granted, he and Alberto hadn't been saints in the past, but he knew they were innocent of the accused crime and neither of them would ever hurt anyone.

Heavy boots thudded along the corridor towards his cell and then he heard the sound of keys jangling as the lock turned. A uniformed copper stood in the doorway, flanked by a large man in a suit and tie. 'With us,' the copper said in a none too friendly tone.

The copper roughly gripped Clinton's good arm and led him into a grey, windowless room. Filing cabinets lined one wall and three hard, uncomfortable-looking chairs were placed around a table.

'Sit,' the policeman ordered, pushing Clinton into one of the chairs.

Thanks to his broken arm, he'd avoided having to be handcuffed, but he hadn't been treated with kid gloves and wore the bruises under his ribs to prove it.

The man in the suit sat opposite and drew on a cigarette as he thumbed through several sheets of paper. It felt like they were sat in silence for a long time, the suited man looking over the papers at Clinton every now and then, shaking his head with a look of disgust written across his face.

'Well, well, well,' he finally said, stubbing out his cigarette. 'You and your mate are up to your necks in it. You'll be going down for a good few years for this. See, it's not just the robbery. Us coppers don't like it when one of our own gets hurt. The nightwatchman that you kicked the shit out of used to be a bobby here at this station.'

Clinton wanted to protest his innocence. He had no idea how the items found in their room had got there and could only assume that either the police were stitching them up for a crime that they hadn't committed or someone else was. He had a pretty good idea who that someone else might be, but he had no way of proving it.

'So, what have you got to say for yourself?' the suited officer asked.

Clinton swallowed hard. Feeling that he had no other

choice, he knew what he had to do. 'I did it, sir, but Alberto had not'ing to do with it.'

'If you're telling me that Mr King didn't carry out the robbery with you, someone else must have helped you?'

'No, sir. I did it by myself.'

'That's not true, is it? The nightwatchman said that at least three men jumped him. So, I'll ask you one more time and if you're not honest with me, PC Benson will help you to remember the truth.'

Clinton glanced sideways at PC Benson towering over him. He'd already felt the power of the man's fists and didn't want another beating. But he had to keep Alberto from going to prison. Clinton knew he couldn't work, not with a broken arm, but Alberto could and he hoped his friend would ensure that his sister in British Honduras would continue to get the money that she needed for her medicine. He quickly thought of something plausible to say. 'It was two of my friends from Scotland. Willy MacDonald and Douglas Murray.'

The man looked sceptical but scribbled down the names. Ones that Clinton had concocted, a couple of very common Scottish names. The police would have a hard time searching for them: it would be like trying to find two needles in a haystack.

'Right,' the suited man asked, 'and where can we find your *friends*?'

'I don't know. They took their cut of the money and went back to Scotland.'

'Where in Scotland?'

'I don't know where they live, but somewhere in Edinburgh, I t'ink.'

'Edinburgh is a big place; you'll have to think harder.'

Clinton was thinking harder, spinning out his lie. 'Willy's brother, Robbie MacDonald, I know he works on the Leith docks. I t'ink Douglas is a miner, if that helps.'

'No, it doesn't. It doesn't help at all.'

'I'm sorry, I'm telling you everyt'ing I know.'

'And you're still standing by the fact that Alberto King had nothing whatsoever to do with the robbery?'

'Yes, sir, that's right, sir. Alberto is an honest man; he works hard at Battersea Power Station. He had not'ing to do with it. It was me. All me. I planned it. I did it. I robbed the distillery and I attacked the nightwatchman. Please … write that down … write down my confession … I did it … write it down,' he pleaded, pointing to a piece of paper. Clinton was becoming frantic, verging on hysterical. He had to make the police believe that it was him and not Alberto. If he didn't and Alberto was sent to prison too, Clinton feared that his sister would die.

The suited officer looked at the uniformed copper and shrugged. 'Take him back down to the cells.'

'Please, sir, you *have* to write down my confession. Hands up, I did it. I'm guilty … guilty … guilty!'

As Clinton was roughly led away, the suited man called, 'You'd better get used to being locked up, 'cos prison is going to be your new home for a very long time to come.'

20

'I have to go and see him!' Rachel insisted. She knew in her heart that Alberto was innocent and the police had the wrong man.

'I'll doubt they'll let you see him, love. He's been arrested for a very serious crime,' Winnie tried to reason.

But Rachel wasn't listening. She was thinking of what she could take to the police station that might be of some use to Alberto in the cells. 'Can I leave Martha here?'

'Yes, of course you can. But I think you'll be wasting your time.'

Rachel threw a quick, 'Thanks,' to Winnie and hurried through to her bedroom. Martha was sleeping soundly after being up for most of the night in the cellar. Rachel quickly changed into some fresh clothes, ran a brush through her hair and grabbed a spare blanket. Then, in the kitchen, she made a sandwich, took an apple from the fruit bowl and a bottle of lemonade from the larder. It wasn't much, but she hoped the police would allow her to give them to Alberto.

After dashing through the pub and out onto the street, Rachel gasped, taken aback at what she saw. The street was almost unrecognisable! The pub still stood tall and proud, but just two houses down, the rest of the buildings were gone. Homes and their local shop flattened, nothing but piles of rubble. Firemen and volunteers were moving the debris brick by brick, their faces masked in dust.

Rachel hurried past, trying her best to push away any thoughts of her neighbours trapped in the wreckage. She dashed away a tear and picked up her pace. Alberto *needed* her; he didn't have anyone else in the world who could help him.

Arriving at the police station, she marched inside, determined that she'd see Alberto and wouldn't accept 'no' for an answer. She stood behind a woman at the enquiry desk, tapping her foot impatiently.

The woman with deep auburn, immaculately waved hair wore a jacket nipped in at the waist which accentuated her slim figure. Her stocking lines up the back of her leg were perfectly straight and Rachel could tell that they weren't drawn on with a pen. The woman had *real* nylons, something that Rachel hadn't been able to buy for years. Whoever the woman was she seemed very glamourous and looked out of place at the police station.

The woman's clipped voice reached Rachel's ears. 'I shan't leave until you allow me to see him. Is that clear, officer?'

'Yes, miss, as water, but I've already told you, Mr King isn't allowed visitors.'

'I demand to see Alberto King this instance! Or I shall be having words with my member of parliament.'

Rachel couldn't understand why this woman would want to see Alberto, unless she was representing him as his solicitor, but that was unlikely as solicitors were always men. She tapped the woman on the shoulder, saying, 'Excuse me.'

When the woman turned around, Rachel was struck by how young she was and how very pretty, wearing bright red lipstick and green eyeshadow.

'What?' the woman demanded.

'Erm, why do you want to see Alberto?'

'That's none of your business.'

'It *is* my business ... I'm his girlfriend.'

The woman frowned and looked at the blanket bundled in Rachel's arms and the brown paper wrapped sandwich in her hand. 'That's preposterous,' she said, eyeing Rachel up and down. 'You can't be his girlfriend ... I am.'

'W-what?' Rachel stuttered.

'You heard me. So if you're trying to dig for a story for the local rag or any other such contemptible newspaper, then I suggest you get on your merry way.'

Rachel shook her head, her mind in a spin. 'Alberto King ... you're Alberto King's girlfriend?' she asked.

'Yes, though I don't see what that has to do with you,' the woman sniffed haughtily.

'You can't be ... I told you, I'm his girlfriend.'

Again, the woman eyed Rachel up and down. 'I don't think so.'

Before Rachel could protest further, a door opened and Alberto came through it looking very tired, followed by a policeman. His eyes, popping like they were on stalks, looked from the glamourous woman and then to Rachel.

'Alberto,' the woman gushed, 'are they releasing you?'

Alberto swallowed hard and nodded.

The woman rushed towards him, her arms outstretched.

Rachel stood open-mouthed watching the scene in shock and disbelief. As Alberto embraced the woman, he looked over her shoulder at Rachel and mouthed, 'Sorry.'

Rachel's fuse blew. She marched across the room, grabbed the woman roughly by the arm and dragged her off Alberto.

'What do you think you're doing?' the woman snapped, looking most indignant.

'Tell her, Alberto, or I will.'

Alberto held out his hands and shrugged. 'Ladies ... ladies ... please, let's not make a scene in the police station.'

Rachel could feel her face flashing red with anger. She looked at the woman and spat her words out with venom. 'He's been seeing the both of us. He's a liar and a cheat!'

The woman sighed and turned to Alberto, asking, 'Who is this ridiculous woman?'

'She's not'ing, my darling, not'ing for you to worry about.'

'Me ... *ridiculous*?' Rachel repeated the woman's word, fuming. She pulled her arm back and then swung it round, slapping the woman hard across her cheek.

The woman yelped and held her inflamed face.

But Rachel didn't stop there. 'I'm nothing, am I?' she yelled at Alberto, clenching her fist and swinging a punch, catching him square on the chin.

Alberto didn't bat an eyelid, but the force of the blow had hurt Rachel's knuckles.

Moments later, she felt strong hands yanking her arms behind her back and heard a familiar voice in her ear. 'Now, now, that's enough of that, young lady.'

Tommy had a firm grip of her.

Rachel glanced at the copper standing behind Alberto. He was smirking, obviously enjoying the show. And then she saw that the one behind the desk looked like Stan Laurel, scratching his head with a dumbfounded expression.

'She struck me!' the woman screeched. 'I want her arrested!'

'It's him who wants arresting, the two-timing git!' Rachel shouted back, nodding her head towards Alberto.

Tommy still had a firm hold on her. If he hadn't, Rachel would have flown at Alberto and scratched his eyes out.

Tommy spoke calmly. 'Alberto, laddie, you've been leading these two ladies a right merry dance. I think you've got a bit of explaining to do.'

'Yeah, go on Alberto,' Rachel hissed, 'Explain yourself.'

Alberto looked sheepish and hung his head.

The other woman seemed to put two and two together. Rage, humiliation, embarrassment, Rachel wasn't sure what it was that she saw in the woman's eyes, but the glamorous woman glared at Alberto and asked, 'Have you been seeing *her* behind my back?'

Rachel answered for him. 'Yes, he has. He's been playing us both.'

'Is this true?' the woman pressed Alberto for an answer.

His silence spoke volumes.

After throwing him a look of contempt, the woman spun on her high heels and click-clacked out of the station.

Tommy released his hold on Rachel. 'Come on, I'll walk you home,' he said softly.

Rachel looked at Alberto and fought to hold back tears. 'I trusted you,' she said and turned to walk away with Tommy.

'Wait, Rachel, it's not what you t'ink,' Alberto began to implore.

'Best to ignore him,' Tommy advised.

Rachel agreed. She was worried that if she looked back at Alberto or opened her mouth, her broken heart would show.

As Tommy escorted her to the Battersea Tavern, he offered sentiments: 'He's not worth it,' 'You can do better,' 'It's his loss.'

Tommy's words didn't help to make Rachel feel any better. She'd let her guard down and allowed a man into her heart, only to be betrayed, again, and it hurt. Her ex-fiancé, Jimmy, the man she'd loved but who'd broken her heart by sleeping with her sister on the night before their wedding, had almost ruined Rachel's life. She'd come to Battersea to escape her pain and then she'd fallen for Arnold, another man who'd let her down. Then David, well, he'd used her against her will. After that, she'd kept her guard up, but Alberto had penetrated her barriers, and she'd stupidly lowered them. Now she wished that she'd never allowed him in.

As they drew closer to the pub, a tear slipped down her cheek and Rachel knew that she needed Winnie's comforting arms.

Brancher had left the house early and Maureen suspected that he'd be out again until late that night. With her grand-parents' funeral looming, she decided to visit the Battersea Tavern to discuss the catering with Winnie. She didn't have much money left and was reluctant to ask Brancher for more, especially as her gran would have been really annoyed at the idea of refreshments being served at her funeral that were paid for with stolen money.

By the time she'd trekked to the other side of Battersea, Maureen could feel sweat running down the back of her neck and her hair was stuck to her damp forehead. It was turning out to be a hot summer. *Clinton will be pleased with all this sunshine*, she thought with a smile. But her smile soon vanished as she approached the Battersea Tavern.

Maureen stood aghast, staring in horror at the destruction. The street looked so different to how it had yesterday. But it was a relief to see that the pub appeared unscathed, other than boarded-over windows. A shiver ran down Maureen's spine at the thought of dead bodies buried under the rubble. Weary-looking rescue teams were working hard and as Maureen drew closer, she heard a loud cheer.

'We've got 'em,' a fella shouted.

'They're alive,' called another.

A woman in a wrap-around apron and a turban-style scarf on her head took a hankie away from her mouth and cried, 'Thank gawd for that.'

'What's happened?' Maureen asked.

'Mr and Mrs Coggins from the grocery shop were missing and their Anderson got buried under a chimney stack. No one was sure if they were inside the shelter, but they were and they've been dug out alive.'

Maureen smiled at the good news and carried on to the pub. It was dark inside on account of the pallet wood at the windows, but Winnie had oil lamps and candles burning. Maureen assumed the electricity supply had been affected by the bomb.

The pub was full of local customers, some looking dazed, others slightly injured, many drinking weak tea and kids running around tables. She saw Winnie behind the bar. She looked very busy, so Maureen turned to leave, thinking she'd try again later. As she was about to walk out, Carmen appeared in front of her.

'Hello, Maureen. Either get yourself a drink and sit down or jump in and give us a hand.'

'Where can I help?' Maureen asked, looking at the chaos around her.

'Wherever you can. Rachel is at the police station, so we're a pair of hands down.'

'At the police station ... why?'

'Long story. Alberto and Clinton have been arrested for that robbery at the distillery. Oh, hang on, here she is now, excuse me.'

Rachel had tears running down her cheeks and Carmen hurried over to her. Maureen stood on the spot, feeling that her feet were rooting through the floor and into the ground. The chatter of voices echoing around her, china cups clinking in saucers, water filling the sinks, childrens' laughter, the noise was echoing through her head, barely leaving room for the scream that was bouncing off the inside of her skull.

'Come with me,' Winnie said sharply, tugging her through the pub, behind the bar and then out into the quiet passageway that led to upstairs. 'Have you heard?' she asked.

Maureen nodded.

'You know that Brancher has done this, don't you?'

Again, she nodded and guilt swamped her.

'You've got to make this right, Maureen. You can't let Clinton and Alberto go down for something that they didn't do.'

'H-how? How can I make it right?'

'Talk to the police,' Winnie hissed. 'Tell them that you know it was Brancher.'

'But if he finds out that I've grassed him up, he'll go mad,' she blurted, shaking.

'So you'd see two innocent men be sent to prison rather than face the wrath of your husband?'

'No … but … Oh, Winnie, what a mess! I'm scared and I feel awful.'

Winnie's voice softened and she rubbed her hand up Maureen's arm. 'I know you are, love. I'd be scared too in your position. But you've got to do the right thing. Perhaps you could talk to Tommy Bradbury, eh? He's a good bloke and he'll be discreet.'

'I-I-I don't know, Winnie. I'm so confused.'

'Look, he's here now. Go up to my kitchen and I'll send him up.'

'Will you come with him … please?'

'I've got a pub full of folk, but yes, it's important that the police know the truth.'

Rachel came tearing through the passageway, her face wet with tears.

'What happened at the station?' Winnie asked.

Maureen stood back out of the way and leaned against the wall as Rachel sobbed, 'I met Alberto's *other* girlfriend, that's what happened!'

'What?' Winnie asked.

'He's been seeing another woman and when the police let him out, she ran into his arms!'

'Stone the crows! So Alberto and Clinton have been released?'

'Alberto has. I don't know about Clinton. I didn't hang around to find out,' Rachel sniffed.

'Good job an' all,' Tommy said, joining them in the passageway, 'or she might have been arrested.'

'What for?' Winnie quizzed him.

'For assault. She slapped the woman and then punched Alberto.'

Winnie looked at Rachel. 'Good for you, girl. It's no more than they deserved.'

'Winnie, I'm surprised at you,' Tommy said with a smile.

Winnie placed her arm over Rachel's shoulders and gave her a little squeeze. 'Listen, love, me and Maureen need to have a word with Tommy. You go up to your room, I'll come in and see you shortly.'

Rachel ran up the stairs, crying as she went.

'Poor girl,' Tommy said quietly. 'It wasn't a nice way for her to discover that Alberto had another woman.'

'I'll see to her soon, but tell me, are Alberto and Clinton in the clear now?'

Maureen held her breath, hoping they were. It would mean she wouldn't have to tell the police what she knew.

Tommy sighed heavily. 'Alberto is because Clinton has confessed to everything.'

Maureen felt her stomach lurch.

'What?' Winnie gasped.

'Yep, he was adamant that he did it and that it had nothing to do with Alberto.'

'You need to come upstairs, Tommy. Me and Maureen have to speak to you.'

As Maureen followed Winnie and Tommy, her mind turned. She couldn't understand why Clinton would confess to something he hadn't done ... unless Brancher was somehow putting pressure on him. She wanted to run back down the stairs and out of the pub, to curl up on her bed and hide from the world, but she knew she had to be brave, and as Winnie had said, she had to do the right thing.

Clinton laid on the wooden bench with one hand under his head, trying to accept the fact that this was his fate. He reckoned he'd probably serve about ten years, give or take, which was a harrowing thought, but the sacrifice of ten years of his life was worth it to save his sister's.

He heard the now familiar sound of PC Benson's boots thumping along the corridor. The copper stopped outside of Clinton's cell. Keys jangled and then the door opened.

'Get up. You've got a visitor.'

Clinton leapt to his feet, wincing from the pain of his bruised ribs, as he tried to think of who would be visiting him. He was led to the grey room again and, when he was unceremoniously pushed inside, he was stunned to see Maureen sat at the table.

'What are you doing here?' he asked.

'Sergeant Bradbury let me in, but I'm only allowed a few minutes with you.'

'It's good to see you … so good. But why are you here?'

'Sergeant Bradbury hopes that I can talk some sense into you.'

'What do you mean?'

'Clinton, we know that you didn't rob the distillery. It was Brancher, so why have you confessed?'

Clinton ran his hand through his hair and sat opposite Maureen. 'I had no choice.'

'Has Brancher threatened you?'

'No, Maureen, not'ing like that.'

'So, why, then? I don't understand.'

'I have a little sister, back home, and she's not very well.

243

She has a condition called diabetes and the only thing that keeps her alive is insulin.'

'Insulin?'

'Yes, bovine insulin. It's made from the pancreas of cows. My sister is sensitive to it, which sometimes makes her very poorly, and when that happens she needs another medicine to help. And, because she has diabetes, when the sandflies bite her, she gets bay sores, which take a long time to heal. They get infected, like ulcers, and then she needs penicillin to make her better.'

'The poor girl! I'm sorry, but what has this got to do with the robbery?'

'The medicines that my sister needs cost money. I can't work at the moment with a broken arm, but Alberto can and he will send money back home. I confessed so that Alberto could walk free.'

'But neither of you did the crime.'

'I know, but they have a lot of evidence that suggests we did. There's no point in both of us going to prison.'

'Neither of you should! You have to retract your confession. I've told Sergeant Bradbury the truth. He knows that it was Brancher.'

'Can he prove it?'

'No, not yet.'

'Well, if he proves it, maybe they will let me out of this hellhole, though I don't deserve that.'

'Of course you do. You're innocent.'

Clinton hung his head. 'No ... no I'm not. I didn't commit the crime that I'm charged with but ... I did a bad t'ing in Scotland.'

'What did you do?'

'I was desperate to send money home to my family, but after we were released from our tree-felling duties, I had no work. One day, I was in the post office with Alberto and the postmaster was called outside because a horse and cart had knocked over an old lady. I saw that the postmaster had left his money drawer unlocked. Alberto kept watch while I stole the cash. I had enough money to send home and to get me and Alberto to London. I'm not proud of what I did, but without that stolen money my sister would have died. So, you see, I'm paying for my crime now.'

'Oh, Clinton, we've all done desperate things in the past that we're ashamed of. Brancher made me do horrendous things, things that still haunt me now. Yes, you were wrong to rob the post office, but you don't deserve the sentence that you're going to get for this crime. The nightwatchman was badly injured. They'll throw the book at you!'

'Probably, but what else can I do? Is Alberto free? Have they let him go?'

'Yes. But Rachel found out about the other woman that he was seeing. She's ever so upset.'

'Maureen, please don't t'ink that I'm anyt'ing like him. I'm not, I swear. Alberto will never change. He left a wife and child in British Honduras and he helped me to steal the money from the post office because he wanted to get away from Scotland – from a woman carrying his child.'

'Oh my goodness! Rachel had a lucky escape.'

'She did. I didn't want to cover for Alberto, but when I lost my job, I needed him to send some of his wages back home. He's not a bad man. He just can't help himself with a pretty face.'

'I don't think that you're like him at all, which is all the more reason why you need to stop this confession before it goes in front of the judge.'

'I can't, Maureen. I can't risk Alberto going to prison too.'

'Then at least tell the police that you did the robbery with Brancher. It's not fair that he's going to get away with it.'

'No, no, no,' Clinton said emphatically. 'I did consider that, but I don't want to be locked up for years with Brancher. He'd make my life hell.'

The door swung open and PC Benson filled the frame. 'Your time's up,' he told Maureen.

Clinton could see in her eyes that she didn't want to leave him. He would have given anything to feel her in his arms. 'I'll be all right,' he reassured her, putting on a brave face.

Before walking out of the door, she turned to him and pleaded one last time. 'Please, tell them the truth. Tell them it wasn't you.'

Clinton could feel his eyes welling with tears and he lowered his head. He couldn't and wouldn't cry in front of a woman or the police. But it broke his heart to see Maureen go, knowing that he'd never see her again. Ten years. He might manage to get through ten years. But he'd never forget Maureen.

21

It was the day of Len and Renee's funerals. Winnie had squeezed her ample body into her black dress and wore a black pillbox hat. She stood behind the bar of her closed pub and breathed deeply, enjoying a rare moment of quiet. It had been a hectic few days, what with the bomb exploding a few doors down from the pub, Clinton being arrested, Rachel having her heart broken and, to top it all, Martha had caught mumps from the boy across the street. She rarely allowed things to get on top of her, but Winnie could feel the daily grind of life slowly wearing her down. Normal day-to-day living before the war had been hard enough, let alone dealing with the challenges they faced now. Explosions, deaths, shortages; it wasn't always easy to plaster on a big smile. Winnie often wished that she could escape from it all to somewhere peaceful.

She picked up Len's pewter tanker, shiny and looking pristine thanks to Rachel polishing it, and then placed it next to the till with a grainy black and white photo of Len and Renee that had been taken a few Christmases ago. She was sure that Maureen would appreciate them. After all, these two small items were all that the woman would have to remind her of her grandparents.

'It's a sad day,' Carmen said, her voice startling Winnie.

'It is, love, very sad. I thought Maureen would have been here by now.'

'Me too. She said she'd meet us here, but maybe she's gone straight to the church with Brancher.'

'I doubt that. She'd want to follow the hearse,' Winnie pointed out. Just hearing Brancher's name grated on Winnie. She knew she was going to find it challenging today and it would be a job to keep her mouth shut. There was so much she wanted to say to Brancher, but Len and Renee's funeral wasn't the place to air her anger.

'We can hold on for five more minutes and then we'd better get going,' Carmen said, checking the clock behind the bar.

Winnie nodded and then went to answer a knock on the door. 'That's probably Maureen. I've put signs up outside explaining that we're closed today.'

'Good idea.'

When she pulled the door open, Winnie was delighted to see Jan. 'Hello, love. I didn't think you'd be able to make it. Come in, we're almost ready to leave.'

'Hello, Mum. I can only be there for the service and then I'll have to get back to the hospital. But I had to come,' Jan said, holding out the lucky Touch Wud charm that Len had gifted to her when she and Terry had got engaged.

'Aw, you've kept it. I remember Len bringing that in here for you. It was good of you to come all this way to show your respect.' Winnie knew that Jan would be rushed off her feet at the hospital, nursing patients injured in the V1 attacks.

The weapons were lethal. Winnie didn't like to think of the dead and injured that Jan must see. She was so proud of the work her daughter did, but its toll was showing on Jan's face. She looked pale and dark circles ringed her sunken eyes. 'It's bloody good to see you, my girl. When I heard about that rocket landing on the hospital, well, you can imagine what was going through my mind. It was such a relief when you telephoned the brewery to let me know that you was all right.'

'It hit the B wing of the hospital, caused a fire and damaged about forty-odd houses nearby. It was a miracle that no one was killed.'

'We weren't so lucky with the one that landed up the road here, love. But no more talk of bombs today.'

'Where's Rachel?' Jan asked, looking around.

'She can't come. Martha has got the mumps. You should see her little face; she's swollen up like a squirrel stuffed with nuts. They're upstairs, but there's no time now to say hello.'

'Oh dear, poor Martha. I should check on her.'

'You're off duty, love, and there's no need. I've seen mumps plenty of times. She'll be fine.'

There was another knock on the door. Carmen answered it and came back with a plate of carrot cake. 'Mrs Burdin wanted to add this to the buffet.'

'She's a good egg. Everyone has been so generous; we've got a lovely spread to offer. Len and Renee would be proud. Pop the cake there, next to the pickled onions. I'll get the sandwiches out when we get back.'

Another tap on the door. It was Piano Pete, offering a gentle nudge, 'They're ready to leave, Winnie,' he said.

'We can't leave without Maureen,' Winnie protested.

'She may be outside,' Carmen suggested.

'I hope so,' Winnie said as they left the pub in a sombre fashion.

Winnie felt Jan's hand slip into hers and her daughter whispered, 'I hate funerals. You'd think that I'd be accustomed to dealing with death, the amount I see of it, but it's not something that you ever get used to.'

'I know, love, but it shows how much you care.'

Outside, there was no sign of Maureen, but Winnie was humbled by the display of affection for Len and Renee. The street was lined with people on both sides, men holding their flat caps in their hands, women dabbing at their eyes. The local housewives had spent two days sweeping the brick dust and rubble into neat piles, out of sight of the funeral cortège. There were no black horses or an elaborate cart to pull the coffins. That's not what Len would have wanted. Instead, the brewery cart, driven by the draymen and pulled by its magnificent shire horses, would carry Len and Renee the short distance to their final resting place.

The funeral director approached them and asked them to take their places. 'We can't leave yet. Renee and Len's granddaughter isn't here.'

'I'm sorry. I can't delay any longer. We have another funeral after this one.'

'Come on, Mum,' urged Jan. 'Maybe Maureen will join us on the way.'

Winnie couldn't believe that Maureen would miss her grandparents' funeral and feared that something had happened to delay her. They took their places behind the cart, Jan on one side of Winnie and Carmen on the other.

'Maureen should be here,' Carmen said through gritted teeth.

'I hope she's at the church,' Winnie replied.

As the procession slowly passed along the street, a chap called out, 'Gawd bless you, Len, Renee.'

And another shouted, 'Rest in peace, Mr Garwood, Mrs Garwood.'

The blessings were said with heartfelt emotion, which left Winnie fighting to retain her composure. She couldn't look at the coffins on the back of the cart for fear of breaking down in tears. She didn't want to think of Len with his craggy face, laid in a wooden box. Instead, she pictured him sat at the end of her bar, moaning about the weather or 'the youngsters nowadays who don't know they're born'. The thought brought a smile to her face.

Ten minutes later, they arrived at a full church. Winnie and Carmen looked around for Maureen, relieved when they saw her sitting on the front pew.

'We thought you were meeting us at the pub?' Carmen said quietly.

'I wanted to follow the hearse, but Brancher wanted to come straight here.'

'Selfish git,' Winnie ground out.

'He probably thought it would upset me too much.'

Yeah, and pigs might fly, Winnie thought as she glanced over her shoulder to see Brancher standing at the back of the church with a couple of his mates, all of them whispering and sniggering. Her temper rose. The man should be sat with his wife, offering her comfort and showing respect for Len and Renee.

Unable to contain herself, she marched over, her fists in

balls and her jaw tight. 'You're a disgrace, Brancher Fanning!' she hissed. 'You should be with Maureen, not playing silly beggars here.'

'Mind your own, Mrs Berry,' he retorted and turned to his mates, chuckling.

'In fact, you shouldn't even be here, you should be in prison! We all know it was you who robbed the distillery and you planted your filthy, dirty stolen money in Clinton's room. You're letting an innocent man pay for your crime. I don't know how you can live with yourself.'

Brancher's eyes darkened and he leaned in towards Winnie. 'Sod. Off. You batty old cow.'

Again, he laughed with his friends.

'That's enough of that,' Tommy growled, stepping in front of Winnie. 'You'd best apologise to Mrs Berry or I'll have you down the nick quicker than you can say Bob's your uncle.'

It was clear that Brancher wasn't intimidated by Tommy's threat, but he did at least say a very insincere 'Sorry.'

Tommy took hold of Winnie's arm and gently eased her back to the pew. 'Not here, Winnie. You can have your say, but not here.'

She knew that Tommy was right and slid along beside Maureen. 'Don't worry about him, love. We're all here for you,' she offered, giving Maureen's hand a gentle squeeze.

The service went smoothly and there were few dry eyes in the church. When it came to the time to congregate at the graveside, Maureen grabbed Winnie's hand. 'I can't do it ... I can't watch them put my dear gran and granddad in the ground ... I'm sorry, I just can't,' she sobbed.

Winnie placed her arm around Maureen's shoulders. 'It's

all right, love, you haven't got to. Your grandparents would understand and you've said your goodbyes. We'll sit here and maybe say a prayer and then go back to the pub.'

'Thank you' Maureen croaked, 'but Brancher…'

'You can leave him to me,' Winnie interrupted.

Maureen nodded and hung her head. Winnie didn't know if she was praying or not, but a few minutes later, she rose to her feet. They all did the same, but Winnie noticed that as Jan stood up, she seemed a bit unsteady and she reached out to hold onto the back of the pew. Winnie put it down to exhaustion. Jan never complained or said anything, but Winnie knew that her daughter was regularly working twelve- or even sixteen-hour shifts. But that's the way things were now. Folk did what was needed in times of crisis and just got on with it.

'There's a smashing spread laid on. You'd be surprised at how many people brought stuff round. Your grandparents were highly regarded,' Winnie said as they headed back to the Battersea Tavern. She glanced around, hoping that Brancher wasn't coming too and was pleased to see him sloping off with his mates.

Tommy caught them up and Winnie left Maureen to walk in front with Jan and Carmen. 'How's Clinton?' she asked.

'I couldn't say, Winnie. He's on remand in Wandsworth prison. He shouldn't be there, but all the while he sticks to his confession, there's nothing any of us can do about it.'

Winnie tutted. She wanted to wring Brancher's neck.

Jan turned around with an apologetic face. 'I'm sorry I can't stay. I really have to get back to the hospital.'

'That's all right, love. Give us a cuddle before you go,' Winnie said, outstretching her arms. Holding her daughter, she cooed in her ear, 'I miss you, my girl. Now, make sure you take care of yourself. You don't look well.'

'I'm fine, Mum, stop worrying.'

'I can't help it, it's my job to worry about you. Go on, off you go before you miss your bus.'

Winnie watched Jan walk away. She was sure that she saw her shoulders round as she clutched her stomach.

'My Jan's not right,' she said to Tommy.

'I should think she's worked off her feet. Those nurses are angels, every one of them, but especially your daughter.'

Winnie bustled, filling with pride. But she had a niggling feeling about Jan and hoped that she was fretting unnecessarily.

Maureen sat at home at the kitchen table, her eyes running over the plates of sandwiches and cakes left over from the funeral. It had been such a good turnout, but she'd been too wrapped up in sorrow to have taken much notice.

Tears pricked her eyes again, but she fought them back and sprung to her feet. As Winnie had said, *it was time to move on.* She'd always hold her grandparents' precious memories in a special place in her heart, but she couldn't dwell on their loss. She somehow had to be strong, just like all the mothers and wives of London who'd lost husbands and sons fighting against the Germans, and the poor orphaned children, their mothers killed by Adolf's bombs. Grief had to be buried with the dead bodies. Life had to continue. Morale needed to be kept up. Yet deep down, Maureen doubted she could ever be strong like Winnie. Brancher ruled her, and she was too afraid to stand up to him. Granted, she'd found the courage to tell Sergeant Bradbury what she knew about the distillery robbery, but she'd made it quite clear that she wouldn't speak out in court. So, without any evidence to convict Brancher, Clinton was still the only man being charged with the heinous crime.

She looked again at the leftover food and hoped that Brancher wouldn't complain about eating sandwiches instead of a hot meal. Mind you, with him coming home drunk most nights, she'd thrown more food in the bin than he'd eaten. It narked Maureen to waste good food, especially as there were shortages.

She went to the drawer and pulled out a writing pad and pen. Pushing the plates to one side, Maureen sat and stared at the blank page, searching for the words to tell her brother about how the funerals had gone.

Dear Stephen

She wasn't even sure if he'd received the last letter she'd sent, informing him of their grandparents' deaths. He was still fighting in Burma and she knew it was unlikely that he'd get compassionate leave. She'd been proved right. He'd said in his previous letter, he'd been granted one week's leave next month, but that was to be spent in Cairo. Maureen had never heard of Cairo and had looked it up on a map. When she'd seen that it was in Egypt, she wondered if Stephen would see the pyramids. Oh, she couldn't wait for this blasted war to be over and then her brother could come home.

Maureen sighed. She'd never seen outside of London and doubted she ever would. The closest that she'd been to the seaside was a few day trips to the 'beach' at Tower Bridge, the shore of the river Thames. Even that was closed to the public now. And from what Clinton had told her, the Thames was very different to the clear blue waters of the Caribbean Sea. She'd enjoyed hearing about British Honduras and the pictures in her mind that his stories had evoked. Thoughts of Clinton saddened her, leaving her heart feeling heavy with guilt. It was her husband's doing that had put Clinton behind bars. Yet she was powerless to get him out of prison.

When she heard the front door slam, Maureen leapt to her feet, quickly bunging the notepad and pen back in the drawer. Brancher didn't like her writing to Stephen and had no interest in hearing about Stephen's letters home.

She had just closed the drawer shut as Brancher steamed into the kitchen. She could tell from his expression that that his mood was dark. She'd been hoping that, today of all days, he'd at least be kind to her.

'I don't want you seeing that Mrs Berry again,' he snarled.

'Why?' Maureen asked, confused.

'Don't question me, Maureen, just do as I bloody well say.'

'Yes, Brancher.'

'That woman tried to show me up in the church today. I don't know who the flamin' hell she thinks she is! And it's none of her business. Anyway, what's for tea?'

'Take your pick,' she answered, trying to keep her voice light. 'There's egg sandwiches, fish paste or corned beef and brown sauce. And a nice bit of cake too. I'll get the kettle on and you can wash it down with a cup of coffee.'

'You're offering me leftovers?'

'It would be a shame to see it go to waste.'

Surprisingly, Brancher shrugged and started tucking into the food.

Phew, thought Maureen. She'd expected a slating.

'I suppose my name was dirt in the pub today?' he asked, and stuffed another sandwich triangle into his mouth.

'No, I never heard your name mentioned,' Maureen lied.

'Well, they can think what they like about me, I couldn't care less. I knew you'd be all right with them lot clucking around you. I'm here for you now, and that's what counts, eh?'

'Yes, Brancher.'

'A bit of gratitude wouldn't go amiss.'

'Thank you, Brancher.'

'You not eating?'

'I've had plenty.'

'Good, as I've said before, you could do with fattening up. I got you this.' Brancher reached into his jacket pocket and pulled out a very small package wrapped in brown paper. He placed it on the table, saying, 'Open it, then.'

Maureen picked up the package, wondering what was inside. She carefully unwrapped the paper and then stared agog at the gold, polished ring.

'It was your gran's. A fireman found it. I had it cleaned up for you.'

Silent tears streamed down Maureen's face. 'Oh, Brancher … I don't know what to say … thank you … thank you so much.'

'It ain't been easy for you, gal. I know you was close to them. Old Len never liked me, the moaning git,' Brancher said with a small chuckle. 'He never thought I was good enough for you.'

'My granddad rarely liked anyone.'

'Ha, yeah, that's true. I remember being in the pub years back, not long after we got married. These two fancy-looking blokes came in, done up to the nines. Turns out, one of 'em was an MP and they were celebrating winning the votes.

Though gawd knows how they ended up in the Battersea Tavern. Anyhow, Len starts giving this member of parliament a right ear-bashing. He was going on about the slums and better living conditions. Moaning about scabies, lice and bedbugs. Cor, your granddad was never one for saying much, but once he got going, there was no stopping him. These toffs, the MP and his mate, they were both on the merry side of sober, and in his posh voice, he started blabbing on about how the laziness of the drunken fathers and husbands was to blame for the poverty and their slovenly wives were just as bad. That tipped Len over the edge. He lumped that MP hard on the nose, put him on his arse. Mrs Berry picked him up by the scruff of the neck and slung him out.'

'Yeah, I remember. For months after that, my granddad went on and on about the rich and privileged,' she said, smiling with fond memories.

'More like years!'

'He never voted after that, said it was a waste of time and that they were all as bad as each other. He wouldn't let my gran vote neither, which put her nose right out of joint, especially as she'd fought hard to get the vote for women.'

'He was a card, was Len. I won't miss the old git, but I know you thought the world of him.'

'I did,' Maureen said tenderly, sniffing to hold back her tears.

'You keep your gran's ring safe, treacle, and I can promise you that it'll never end up in the pawn shop like your ring did.'

'Thank you, Brancher,' Maureen said, slipping the wedding band onto her finger, where her own had once been.

It was times like this, when Brancher showed his caring

side, that Maureen remembered how she'd first fallen in love with him. Now, though she was grateful for his efforts, the love had long since died, replaced with fear and resentment. And every time she looked at her husband, she saw Clinton's face, locked behind cold metal bars. Guilt coursed through her veins. She'd suggested to Brancher that he get rid of the stuff in the shed, but it had never occurred to her that he'd have put it in Clinton's lodgings. She should have known better. She knew what Brancher was like and what he was capable of. Maureen blamed herself for Clinton's imprisonment. Just as Brancher was always telling her: *she was useless.*

22

It had been nearly two weeks since Rachel had confronted Alberto in the police station. As the Soviets were making headway in Poland, gaining ground closer to Warsaw and forcing the Germans' withdrawal, Rachel's heart had hardened. She was no longer crying over Alberto's betrayal. In fact, since hearing about how he'd left a wife and child back home and another woman in Scotland carrying his baby, Rachel felt nothing but disgust towards the man.

Martha often asked after him, but now she was distracted by her new friend, Benny, the boy she'd caught mumps from. Rachel was also enjoying her new-found friendship with Benny's mum, Torrie, short for Victoria. The women spent most afternoons together while their children played happily and Cake lapped up the extra attention. Torrie, unlike many other women in the borough, wasn't bothered about Rachel being an unmarried mother and didn't judge her. She'd confided in Rachel that she'd married in a hurry with Benny in her belly. Torrie's husband, Benny senior, was in the navy, which caused Torrie no end of sleepless nights. Every morning, she'd rush to the newspaper hawker, who'd give her a shake of his head and Torrie would clap her hands with delight, knowing that there was no news of her husband's ship being torpedoed and sunk.

The women sat on a bench in Battersea Park, not far from where a doodlebug had recently landed on open ground, damaging a few flats nearby.

'My sister has asked me if I want to go to the dance at the town hall on Saturday. I can't say that I'm overly enthralled about the idea of it, but I'll go if you fancy coming too, lovey?'

Rachel couldn't remember the last time she'd been dancing, but it didn't appeal to her either. 'No, thanks.'

'I thought you'd be keen. There'll be plenty of fellas. My sister told me she got ever so friendly with an American chap. I warned her not to get into any trouble. She said she was keeping her hand on her ha'penny and just having a bit of slap and tickle, but I know he stayed the night at hers 'cos her neighbour told Mary opposite, who told Mrs Egan in the fish shop, who then told me.'

'Isn't your sister married?'

'She is, the dirty cow. Mind you, half the married women of Battersea are helping the Americans to keep their peckers up,' Torrie laughed.

Rachel laughed too. She found Torrie's company refreshing and it was nice to have a friend of her own age, though Torrie seemed much more worldly-wise than her. She looked older than Rachel too, with her chestnut hair nearly always curled around rollers under a scarf and a sweep of victory red lipstick on her lips. She also pencilled her eyebrows and her lashes were coated in castor oil. Torrie always wore high heels too, even when she was chalking her step or sweeping the pavement outside her house. 'I never know when my old man might turn up on leave,' she'd say. 'And I want to be looking me best when he does.'

'Ain't you bothered about finding yourself a nice fella?' Torrie asked.

'No. I've had it with men. I don't know what possessed me to fall for Alberto, but I did. It was a good lesson learned.'

'Granted, you've had your fingers burned a couple of times, but there are some good 'uns. Look at my Benny. He's a lovely bloke, you couldn't get better. He dotes on our boy and spoils me rotten. And he'd never even give another woman so much as a sideways glance.'

'Yeah, well, you got lucky. And even if I did want a fella, what's the chances of meeting one now? Nearly all the blokes are away fighting. Those at the dance will only be passing through. If, and that's a big *if*, I did meet a fella that I liked, I'd want more than just a bit of fun.'

'I know what you mean. I couldn't do what my Margaret does and then look my old man in the eye, but I can understand why she does it. This war … you never know if you're gonna see the dawn of the next day. My sister is all about living for the moment and making the most of what time she has. I get that, but *just a bit of fun* ain't for me and it's not for you neither.'

Martha and Benny came running over, Benny barefoot, his legs thigh-high in mud, and dirt smeared across his rosy-red cheeks.

'Bloomin' 'eck, what happened to you?' Torrie asked, her eyes bulging.

262

'Benny got stuck in the mud,' Martha giggled.

'For crying out loud, Benny, have you lost your shoes?'

Benny nodded and looked to be holding back tears.

'Great, that's all I need. I can't afford to be buying you new shoes. You'll have to go and find them. Go on, don't stand there snivelling like a big baby.'

Martha took Benny's hand, tugging him back to the sodden ground, urging, 'Come on, Benny, I'll help you.'

'Don't you get covered in mud too, young lady,' Rachel called after her.

'Come on, we'd better keep an eye on them,' Torrie said with a huff.

Half an hour later, and having used several large sticks, Benny's muddy shoes were finally retrieved.

'At last,' Rachel said. 'Home time. My stomach's telling me that it's time for dinner.'

They received plenty of funny looks on their journey home. Little Benny looked like he'd been dragged through the pigpens.

'You'll be getting a bucket of water over your head before you step on my clean lino,' Torrie admonished.

Outside the Battersea Tavern, the friends bid each other farewell and Rachel headed around to the back door. She stiffened when she saw Alberto. Martha ran towards him, squealing his name in delight.

'Hello, Rachel,' he said, sheepishly.

Rachel unlocked the back door and ushered Martha and Cake inside.

'But I want to see Alberto,' Martha protested.

'Inside, now. Don't give me any sauce,' Rachel told her firmly.

She pulled the door closed behind them and then turned to Alberto.

'You've got some cheek,' she spat.

'Please, Rachel, hear me out.'

'There's nothing that you can say that I want to hear.'

'Rachel, please, I'm sorry. I made a mistake.'

'Too right, you did!'

'Alberto misses his queen.'

'I'm not falling for all that flannel again. Clear off and don't come back.'

'Don't be like that, Rachel. Please, give me another chance to show you how good Alberto can be.'

'Not interested,' Rachel said, nonchalantly, then she spun around, walked inside and slammed the door closed in his face. She blew out a long breath and realised that her heart rate had doubled. But she felt good. Seeing Alberto hadn't left her running for her handkerchief. In fact, apart from being annoyed at his audacity, she was absolutely fine. And that's how she intended to stay. An unmarried mother, but a content one. And a mother who was taking control of her own destiny.

Spending time with Torrie made Rachel realise how much she wanted more from life for herself. Her new friend lived solely for her husband and son, which was perfectly acceptable and quite the norm. But since the war had started, Rachel had seen a new liberation in women: they were working in jobs that the men had done and had proved themselves capable, earning good wages too. Rachel had the notion of a career, something that would have sounded outrageous a few years ago. She'd been toying with the idea for a while now and, seeing that Martha would be starting school soon, she decided that it was time to get the ball rolling. For now though, until she had anything concrete to announce, Rachel intended on keeping her ambitious notion to herself.

'Hello, love,' Winnie said, half-smiling at Rachel when she came into the kitchen.

'You won't believe this,' Rachel blurted, pulling out a seat at the table.

'Try me.'

'Alberto was outside the back door, full of apologies and telling me that he misses me.'

'Huh, I can't say that I'm surprised. I hope you told him where to get off.'

'Yes, of course I did.'

'Good. Least said about him, soonest mended. Did you have a nice time at the park?'

Rachel began reiterating her day, but Winnie wasn't listening. Her mind had drifted back to Jan and her stomach knotted with worry.

'She sounds right saucy, don't you think?' Rachel asked, her voice breaking into Winnie's thoughts.

'Eh? Who does?'

'Torrie's sister, Margaret. Were you listening to me?'

Winnie shook her head. 'No, sorry, love, I wasn't.'

'What's wrong?'

'I'm worried sick about Jan. She was supposed to visit three days ago. I've rang the nurses' home every day, but I keep getting told that she's busy.'

'She probably is, Win. There's been hardly any let-up with those blinkin' doodlebugs landing on London.'

'Yes, I know, but I get the feeling that there's something she's keeping from me.'

'Like what?'

'I'm not sure, but I want to find out.'

'Have a word with Bill. See if he'll run you over to Westminster, then you can check on Jan for yourself. I'm sure he'll be happy to take the van for a drive if you give him the cost of the petrol, and you know that Flo won't mind.'

'I'm not sure. He was in here the other night moaning about petrol rations. He said he couldn't run his dress business if he couldn't get petrol. I don't think that he'll want to waste his fuel ferrying me around. But you're right, I need to see Jan and I won't rest easy until I do. I'll get the bus tomorrow.'

'Go now, Win, or you'll be fretting all night. Sod the bus. I've just walked past Bill and Flo's house. They're home, the van is parked outside.'

Winnie contemplated the idea. She'd done a lot for Bill and Flo over the years, even putting them up and inviting them to shelter in her cellar when their home was overflowing with a bombed-out family. Maybe asking Bill to drive her to St Thomas' Hospital wasn't too much of a big ask. 'I think I will. Can you let Carmen know that she'll be opening up by herself this evening?'

Winnie threw half a home-made cake into her basket, along with a fish paste sandwich and two plums. If she got to see Jan even for just a few minutes, at least she could give the girl something to eat.

266

Flo opened the front door, offering a genuine smile. 'Winnie, what a nice surprise. Come in.'

'Hello, Flo, I hope you don't mind me calling un-announced?'

'Course not, you know you're always welcome here and you should visit more often.'

'Thanks. Actually, it's Bill I wanted to see.'

'He's in the front room with his pipe and paper. Good luck getting more than a grunt out of him. Go through, I'll pop the kettle on.'

'Not on my account, Flo, I can't stop. I was hoping that Bill would be so kind as to run me up to the hospital to check on my Jan. Do you think he'd mind me asking?'

'He'd do anything for you, you know that. Is everything all right with Jan?'

'I don't know. I've not heard from her since Len and Renee's funeral. And I can't get hold of her on the telephone.'

'Follow me,' Flo said and walked briskly into the front room. She snatched away Bill's newspaper, picked up his shoes and placed them on the floor in front of his chair. 'Get them on your feet, you're taking Winnie to St Thomas',' she ordered.

Few people argued with Flo, least of all her husband. With her hair pulled back in a tight bun and thin lips that rarely smiled, it gave her a stern look. On the Northcote Road market where they sold dresses, she was known as a no-nonsense woman. Yet Winnie knew that Flo was a lot softer than she looked. She'd often brim with pride when she'd tell people that she used to buy dresses from Jan to sell on her stall and now Jan was a well-respected nurse. Flo's tale would always make Winnie smile. She was proud of her daughter, there was no doubt about that, but at times like this, when Jan worked in a hospital away from home, Winnie wished that her daughter was still making dresses with Hilda and selling them for a profit to Bill and Flo. Life had seemed simpler back then.

'Shall I pop to the telephone box and give her another call?' Flo offered.

'If you don't mind, I'd appreciate that. See if you have more joy than me, save Bill having to rush me up there.'

As Bill fumbled with his shoelaces, he asked, 'You're not poorly, are you Winnie?'

'No,' Flo answered as she left the room, 'Winnie is perfectly well. You're taking her to see Jan.'

'Righto,' Bill answered, without question.

He carried on reading his newspaper and Winnie tapped her foot impatiently as she waited for news from Flo.

Flo soon returned, coming into the front room, biting on the inside of her cheek. 'Hmm, the young lady I spoke to sounded a bit on edge. I think you're right to go and see for yourself.'

Winnie's stomach twisted. She'd been telling herself that she was being silly and worrying needlessly, but having Flo confirming her fears had further alarmed her.

At the front door, Flo spotted Winnie's food parcel in the basket. She placed a staying hand on Winnie's arm, saying, 'Just a mo,' before dashing towards the kitchen. Quickly returning, Flo placed a paper bag in the basket. 'Two Scotch eggs ... for Jan.'

'That's my supper,' Bill moaned.

'That *was* your supper and now it's Jan's. Go on, off you go, Godspeed.'

If Winnie hadn't been so worried about Jan, she might have chuckled at the disappointment on Bill's face. As she climbed into his van, she said, 'I'll see you're all right for petrol.'

'Don't worry about it, Winnie. Just hold on tight. I'll be putting me foot down on this old bone-rattler to get us there and back in double quick time. I don't want to be driving back in the blackout.'

Winnie was pleased to hear it. The sooner she got to the hospital, the better.

When they arrived on Lambeth Palace Road, she was horrified to see the damage that a doodlebug had caused a couple of weeks earlier. As Jan had told her, at least forty houses were damaged.

Bill dropped her at the entrance to the hospital and said that he'd find somewhere to park. He drove off, leaving Winnie standing outside. She clutched her fist to her chest and sucked in a long breath. The last time she'd been here, Jan had been buried under a pile of rubble and Winnie had thought she was dead. This time, it couldn't be nearly half as bad as that.

As she strode into the hospital, a tirade of thoughts crossed her mind. She even wondered if Jan had found herself with a bun in the oven and was hiding a swelling stomach. *Huh*, Winnie thought, *as if Jan would do anything like that!* But then again, women were doing all sorts of things that they wouldn't have dreamed of before the war.

'I'm here to see nurse Jan Card,' Winnie said decisively to a woman behind a desk. 'I'm her mother, Mrs Berry.'

'She works here?'

'Yes.'

'Take a seat, I'll see if I can locate her, but I hope you don't mind waiting. As you can see, we're rather busy.'

Winnie sat down with her basket on her lap. The woman behind the desk was on the telephone for quite some time and looked over at Winnie with very reticent eyes. Winnie could tell that something was wrong. She expected to be summoned back to the desk, but a nurse approached and gently said, 'Please, Mrs Berry, come with me.'

At last, Winnie thought: she was going to see Jan. She now felt rather silly for making such a fuss, though it would still be nice to give Jan the sandwich, cake and Scotch eggs. The last time Winnie had seen her, she'd looked as though she could do with a good meal!

The young nurse weaved through the hospital with Winnie following. She tried not to notice the fatigued faces on the medical staff, or the bandaged patients, cries of pain and general mayhem. *No wonder Jan hasn't been in touch for a while*, she thought, feeling selfish. *She must be run off her feet.*

At the end of a ward, the nurse opened a door to a side room. *How nice*, thought Winnie, assuming they were setting aside a private room for her and Jan to meet. But when she walked in, her stomach lurched and a cry of shock slipped past her lips.

'What are you doing in bed? What on earth is wrong with you?' she asked, rushing to Jan's bedside.

'Hello, Mum,' Jan replied weakly.

Winnie went to take her daughter's hand and that's when she noticed the tubes being fed into her. 'You don't look very well, my girl,' she mumbled, observing Jan's hollowed cheeks and pallid skin.

'I'm not.' A tear slid from Jan's eye, running down her temple and onto the pristine white pillowcase.

'Oh, darling, what is it? Did you get hurt?'

'No ... I'm so sorry, Mum ... so very sorry ...' she sobbed.

'Please, love, you're scaring me. Just tell me what's wrong with you.'

The nurse who had shown Winnie to the room said softly, 'I'll leave you alone.'

Winnie didn't look behind to acknowledge the nurse. Her eyes were firmly fixed on Jan and the yellowing whites of her eyes.

'Please don't be upset with me,' Jan cried.

'Never, love ... I could *never* be upset with you.'

Jan drew in a juddering breath, and then blurted, 'I've got cancer, Mum. Cancer in my stomach.'

The words hit Winnie like a sledgehammer, but she tried her hardest not to show any reaction. *Cancer.* She knew what that meant. Something evil was growing inside of her daughter and it needed to be cut out. 'Have they operated on you yet?' she asked, the crack in her voice evident.

Jan shook her head.

'Well, they need to, as soon as possible. Where's the doctor? I want to speak to him,' Winnie demanded.

'No, Mum ... it's inoperable,' Jan replied, weakly.

'What does that mean?'

'It means ... it means ... they can't make me better.'

'Don't talk daft, of course they can. You'll be all right, my girl, the doctors will fix you up,' Winnie insisted.

Jan sniffed and turned her head away.

'Come on, love, buck yourself up. You're young and fit. You can get better from a bit of cancer.'

'I'm dying, Mum,' Jan cried and turned back to look at Winnie.

Winnie gazed into her daughter's wet eyes searching for something that would make this not real. 'No ... no you're not. You're just scared, which is perfectly normal. But you're not dying and I won't have talk like that.'

'It's true, Mum ... I'm so sorry.'

Reality dawned on Winnie and punched the air out of her. She staggered backwards and slumped onto a hard hospital seat. 'Dying?'

'I didn't want you to know ... I'm really sorry.'

Winnie's legs felt weak and shaky, but she managed to stand up and rushed back to her daughter's side. 'You have *nothing* to be sorry for. Don't you dare apologise for this. But are you sure the doctors have got this right?'

Jan nodded sadly.

'I want a second opinion. I don't care how much it costs. I'll get the top specialists here to check you over.'

'Mum, please, stop ... it's too late. There's nothing that anyone can do. The cancer has spread to my liver, and it's probably in my bones too.'

Winnie couldn't hold back her tears any longer. 'How long have you known?'

'A few weeks. I didn't want you to find out. I couldn't bear the thought of seeing your pain as you watch me die.'

Winnie stroked hair from Jan's clammy forehead, crying now unashamedly, 'I'll be with you, *always*. I'm your mum, and it's my job to look after you. You're not going through this alone.' She leaned over the bed and hugged her daughter, feeling Jan's bones as her daughter's body jerked with painful sobs.

'I love you, Mum.'

'And I love you an' all, my girl.' Gently pulling away, she asked, 'Now, where's your doctor? I'd still like to have a word with him.'

Winnie went in search of the man and, with the help of the nurse, soon found him. She was surprised at how young he was. Though, like all the doctors and nurses, he looked weary and browbeaten.

The nurse made the introductions and, when the doctor realised who Winnie was, she saw his harassed expression change to one of sympathy.

'I'm very sorry, Mrs Berry, but there is little we can do for Jan except to make her as comfortable as possible.'

'It's true then? She's dying?'

Winnie was still holding on to hope, but the doctor knocked it out of her when he nodded his head.

With her chin jutting forward and choking back a sob in her throat, she asked, 'How long? How long does my Jan have left?'

The doctor and the nurse exchanged a quick awkward glance and then he said quietly, 'Weeks ... maybe days. It's difficult to be more precise than that, but the cancer is very advanced and aggressive.'

Winnie found herself unable to speak. A hard, aching rock of bile felt lodged in her chest. The whitewashed corridor seemed to be spinning around her.

'Are you all right, Mrs Berry?' the nurse asked, touching her arm.

No, of course she wasn't all right! She'd just been told

that her daughter had weeks or days to live! She wanted to collapse onto the floor, howling and screaming, but, as difficult as it was going to be, she had to be strong… for Jan.

Rachel ran from the room in tears and Carmen came to sit beside Winnie, who had just told them the devastating news about Jan.

'I don't know what to say, Win, I can't get my head round it,' Carmen mumbled. 'She's so young, it doesn't seem right.'

'I know. I can't stop bawling, but I've got to try to hold myself together for Jan's sake. As it was, she tried to keep the truth from me 'cos she didn't want to see me upset. I left her sleeping but cried me eyes out all the way home.'

'Is there anything that I can do to help?'

'Run the pub for me.'

'That goes without saying.'

'Thanks, love. I was thinking about bringing Jan home. I don't want her last breaths to be in that hospital. What do you think?'

'If that's what Jan wants, then I think it's a good idea. You'll get all the support from me and Rachel… I'm ever so sorry, Winnie, I wish I could make this better for you.'

'I know you do, love. I don't think I've accepted it yet. If you don't mind, I'm going for a lay down. I can't think straight.'

'Go and rest. I need to get back downstairs before Piano Pete gives away all our profits. He's great at keeping an eye on the bar, but he thinks that I don't know about him filling up his mates' glasses for free.'

Winnie tapped on Rachel's bedroom door. She could hear

muffled sobs and guessed that Rachel was crying into her pillow.

'Come in,' Rachel called quietly.

The room was in darkness, Martha sleeping soundly and Cake beside her.

Rachel pushed herself up from the bed. 'It's not fair,' she whispered. 'Jan is the nicest and kindest person that I know. She doesn't deserve this!'

Winnie sat on the edge of the bed and pulled Rachel close. 'I know, love. I've heard that Him upstairs takes the good people first. But you're right, it ain't fair.'

Martha stirred.

'Do you want a cuppa?' Rachel whispered. 'I know I could do with one.'

'Yeah, go on then. I was going to have a lay down, but there's something I'd like to discuss with you.'

In the kitchen, Winnie told Rachel about her plans to bring Jan home.

'It won't be an easy time for any of us, and I'm worried about how Martha will deal with it.'

'She'll be upset, the same as us, but nevertheless, Jan needs to come home,' Rachel agreed.

'All right. I'll make the arrangements tomorrow. Now, when Jan is here, I don't want any tears around her. There'll be plenty of time for tears once she's ... after ... Oh, Christ, I can't say the words,' Winnie said, throwing her hands over her mouth.

Rachel nodded. 'I know what you mean.'

Winnie swallowed down a lump in her throat. She was determined to keep her emotions in check. 'Come and give us a hand to get Jan's bed ready, there's a good girl.'

Keep busy and be practical, that was going to be the key. So long as Winnie could occupy herself with tasks, she'd be able to prevent her mind from dwelling on the inevitable. And as she'd tried to explain to Rachel, there'd be time for tears later.

23

Before Maureen closed the front door behind her, she remembered her gran's mantra: *Always keep a hankie up your sleeve and a packet of matches in your pocket*. There was a bit of a nip in the wind, so she'd worn her cardigan today. She tapped the pocket, checking for the packet of matches, noticing that there was something else in there. Slipping her hand inside, she pulled out a small, folded piece of paper. Maureen gasped. It was the note that Clinton had passed to her in the pub a few weeks back. Her eyes widened with fear and she quickly screwed it up and threw it away. She wondered how she could have been so careless and was grateful that Brancher hadn't been rummaging through her pockets for matches. Christ, he'd have lost his head if he'd found the note!

Brancher hadn't come home last night. Not that Maureen minded. She preferred it when he wasn't home. She didn't have to watch what she said around him or jump to do his bidding. And she didn't really care where he'd spent the night. In fact, she hoped he was with another woman, though if he was, she felt sorry for her.

Maureen headed to the shops. There wasn't anything that

she particularly needed, but it passed an hour or two of her otherwise dull day. With nothing but cooking, cleaning and washing to fill her time, Maureen was left feeling dead inside, her brain numbed through boredom. She'd have liked to pop into the Battersea Tavern and say hello to Winnie and Carmen, but Brancher had warned her to stay away. He'd also told her to keep herself to herself, which meant that she wasn't allowed to be friendly with the neighbours either.

As she plodded along the street, keeping her head down, her mind wandered to Clinton and, as it did, waves of guilt washed over her again. She still believed that she was partly to blame for his incarceration. If she hadn't told Brancher to get rid of the stuff in the shed, Clinton would be a free man. She wondered how he was faring and wished that it were Brancher behind bars instead. The awful wish added to her feelings of guilt, but then, she reasoned, why wouldn't she want to see Brancher locked up? Hadn't he made her life feel as though she was in a prison?

Maureen admired Winnie, Carmen, Rachel and Hilda too. She wished that she was more like them. She'd seen strength and bravery in those women. She doubted that any of them would put up with Brancher the way that she did. But Maureen didn't believe that she was made from the same stern stuff as them. She wasn't clever, neither was she skilled in anything. Brancher's words rang in her ears: *You're useless, you stupid cow.*

A dark cloud descended on Maureen, weighing heavy on her shoulders, draining her of energy. It was an effort to put one step in front of the other. She abandoned her idea of browsing the shops and started back towards home instead.

Two minutes after arriving indoors, Brancher crashed

through the front door, breathless and ashen-faced. 'The Old Bill are after me,' he announced.

'Why?'

'Don't ask questions. Just make sure that you tell them that I was home here with you last night. Got it?'

Maureen nodded, her mind racing, worrying what her husband had done this time.

'Where was I last night?'

'At home, with me, all night.'

'Good girl. Don't let me down,' and at the sound of thumping on the front door, he ordered, 'Go and let them in. Just act naturally.'

Her heart racing, Maureen rushed down the passage, un-surprised to find Sergeant Bradbury on her step and a police car at the kerb. She cringed, thinking of the neighbours' curtains twitching.

'We know he's home, Maureen, so let us in.'

Maureen pulled the door open wider and Sergeant Bradbury came in, followed by two other uniformed police-men. She led them to the kitchen to see Brancher looking rather blasé, sitting at the table.

'Brancher Fanning, you're accompanying me to the police station,' Sergeant Bradbury announced.

'What for?'

'To help us with our inquiries. Come on, laddie, be sensible and don't give us any trouble.'

'What enquiries?' Brancher asked, feigning innocence.

'You know full well. It was you who attacked one of my men last night during a robbery at Sarson's jewellery shop.'

'Leave off, Sarge, you're wasting your time. I weren't

anywhere near Lavender Hill last night. Ask Maureen, she'll tell you. Ain't that right, gal?'

Sergeant Bradbury looked at Maureen for an answer.

Oh, she *really* wanted to tell the policeman that she hadn't seen Brancher since yesterday teatime, but she could feel her husband's eyes boring into her. 'Yeah, that's right,' she answered shakily. 'Brancher was at home, here, all night.'

Tommy shook his head at her. She wasn't sure if it was disgust or pity that she saw in his eyes.

'See, told ya,' Brancher added smugly. 'Now clear off.'

'Take him away, lads,' Sergeant Bradbury ordered.

Brancher sprang to his feet, his fists clenched. Maureen edged back, steadying herself against the sink.

Sergeant Bradbury held out his hands in a bid to calm Brancher as he advanced towards him. 'Slow down, son. Don't do anything that you'll regret. Come quietly and we can get this all sorted out down at the station.'

Much to Maureen's relief, Brancher backed down and went with the policemen, moaning and cursing as they dragged him away.

Sergeant Bradbury held back. 'Was he really with you last night, Maureen?' he asked quietly.

'The policeman who got hurt ... is he all right?'

'He will be, but he was lucky.'

'I don't want to cover for my husband, but I ain't got a choice.'

'So, you are covering for him? Come on, tell me the truth.'

Maureen hesitated, but she'd had enough of fibbing for her brutal husband and nervously answered, 'Yeah. He ... He wasn't here, but if he finds out that I've told you that, my life won't be worth living.'

'Maureen, I appreciate you being honest. I'll do my best to charge him with the robbery last night and I promise that what you have just told me will remain between us. Your secret is safe with me.'

Maureen slumped with relief and, once Sergeant Bradbury left, she collapsed onto a seat at the table. She hoped that Brancher would finally get his just deserts. He had already stitched Clinton up, and he had now carried out another robbery, along with attacking a policeman. She hated the lies he forced her to tell and couldn't face living with him any longer.

Despite that, Maureen knew she'd never find the courage to leave him. Now all she could hope for was that the police would find proof that he'd carried out the robbery, and attacked a copper, then he'd be put away for a very long time. She'd be free then. Free to live her life without fear.

Rachel sat in Torrie's spotlessly clean and homely front room, while Martha and Benny played upstairs.

'Do want another cuppa, lovey?' Torrie asked.

'No, thanks. If I drink any more tea, I'll start to look like an urn. And thanks for letting me hide out here for a while.'

'You're welcome. I can understand why you don't want to be at home at the moment.'

'Can you? I feel really awful. I should be there, but I just can't face it, not yet.'

'Jan is a good friend of yours and Winnie is like a second mum to you. Don't feel bad about not wanting to see all the upset and pain. But you can't hide forever.'

'I know. It's just all happened so fast and I don't know what to say to Jan. Winnie's made it clear that there's not to be any tears around her, but I've hardly stopped crying since I found out.'

'It must have been such a shock.'

'It was. And I still haven't told Martha yet. How do you explain death to a child?'

'She probably understands death better than you think. She must have picked up on it. There's been enough of it around her. Death has been on our doorsteps since Hitler started bombing us.'

'You think that you're protecting your kids, but it's hard to know what to do for the best. Benny's nearly school age, like Martha. Will you send him away to keep him safe?'

'No, not on your nelly. When Benny was born, me and him were billeted to Somerset with a load of other evacuated mothers and babies. It was a bloomin' awful long train journey. And then when we arrived, the locals seemed surprised that us mums had turned up with our babies. I think that they were only expecting the kids, so there was a mad dash to find us spare rooms. I sat for hours waiting in the church hall, worn out, desperate to lay Benny down. Eventually, I was sent to a cottage on the edge of town with an old couple. I didn't feel comfortable from the off. About a week later, I noticed a small hole in our bedroom wall. Weird, it was. And then I caught the old man peeping through the hole at me. Well, I blew my top, packed me stuff and left. So no, I won't be having Benny sent anywhere. You never know who your kids will end up with.'

Rachel shuddered on hearing her friend's story and it firmly cemented her belief that she was doing the right thing by keeping Martha at home with her. 'They're awfully quiet upstairs,' she said.

'Yes, they are. That can only mean one thing… trouble! Shush, follow me, let's see what they're up to.'

Torrie led the way upstairs with Rachel sneaking closely behind. When they reached the landing, they stopped and listened. Martha was quietly giggling.

'They're up to no good,' Torrie whispered.

Flinging open the bedroom door, Rachel gasped at the mess that confronted them. Both children and the floor were covered in talcum powder. Martha had bright red lipstick over her face and, to Rachel's horror, she saw that Martha's beautiful golden locks were scattered around her, leaving uneven chunks of blonde hair standing on end from her scalp. Benny, who was in the process of clumsily painting Martha's nails with red nail varnish, jumped when he saw his mother.

'What the hell have you done?' Torrie screeched.

Benny's bottom lip began to quiver and the smile on Martha's face quickly vanished.

'We… we was playing pretty ladies,' Martha explained. 'I wanted to look like Torrie, so Benny cut off my hair and we was going to colour it in with brown shoe polish.'

'I can't be a pretty lady because I'm a boy, so Martha said I can have her hair to stick on my head, and then I can look like her mummy.'

Torrie looked at Rachel, stepped back from the doorway and quickly pulled the door closed. She clamped her hand over her mouth, stifling her mirth. 'How can I be angry with them?' she quietly laughed.

Rachel saw the funny side too. 'I suppose we should be flattered that our kids think that we're pretty,' she chuckled.

'My old man would blow a gasket if he knew that Benny was playing with make-up. But, oh my gawd, what a sight they are! I reckon there's more lipstick on Martha's face than what's on her lips. And I'm so sorry about her hair, she looks like a scarecrow,' Torrie giggled.

'And Benny, he looks like a ghost. Never mind about her hair, it'll grow back, but what a flippin' mess!' Rachel snickered. 'It's good to have a laugh though. I needed that. Come on, let's get them cleaned up. I think I'm ready to face Jan now.'

24

Winnie had hardly slept. She'd laid in the bed next to Jan's, listening to her daughter's shallow and laboured breathing. Every moan of pain from Jan's dry and cracked lips had felt like a stab in Winnie's heart.

She sat at the kitchen table, nursing a cup of tea and with her brow in her hand, fighting back the tears that were a now a constant threat.

Carmen padded into the kitchen and placed a comforting hand on Winnie's shoulder. 'Morning. Did she have a rough night?'

Winnie nodded, swallowing down a lump of agony in her throat that threatened to burst out.

'Did you manage to change her mind about telling Terry?'

'No. She's adamant that she doesn't want him to know. She's trying to protect him, but I think she's making a mistake. Terry's her husband; he has a right to know that his wife is …' Winnie couldn't finish the sentence. She couldn't say *that* word.

'Christ, it's going to be awful for him to come home to.'

'I know. She's asked me to help her to write a letter to give to him when he's back. I don't know if I can do it.'

Carmen sat at the table and placed her hand over Winnie's. 'You *can* do it, Win. There are going to be many things over the coming weeks that you don't want to do, or face. You're going to have to dig deep inside yourself to find the strength, but I know it's there.'

'I was feeling so blessed and thinking how lucky I've been that my family hasn't been killed, but then this... Honestly, Carmen, cancer is so cruel. It's wicked. I reckon Jan would have been better off if a bomb had landed on her instead of slowly wasting away in pain. She can barely even get any water down now.'

'At least you've been given the chance to say goodbye to her.'

'Yeah, I suppose so ... but I don't want to ... I can't ...' The sobs that Winnie had been holding in suddenly burst out. 'I said no tears ...' she cried. 'And look at the state of me now.'

'You're allowed to cry, Win. Better out than in.'

Winnie plucked a hankie from her sleeve and wiped her face before blowing her nose. She clenched her jaw and drew in a long breath. 'No tears,' she said firmly. 'Not yet.'

Martha toddled into the kitchen with Rachel in her wake. Winnie smiled at her granddaughter's head of hacked hair. It didn't look any better now than it had when Rachel had first brought her home. But at least the red nail varnish had wiped off easily with a bit of remover. 'Oh dear, my lovely, you're going to have to wear your bonnet or one of Mummy's scarves on your head.'

Martha looked quite dismayed, patting her head and crying, 'I want my hair back.'

Winnie scooped the child up onto her lap and kissed the top of her head. 'Don't you worry, my darling, you'll have your hair back soon. And even without it, you're still the prettiest girl in Battersea. Go and get Mummy's scarves, we'll see what we can do with them.'

Martha, placated, skipped off to her bedroom.

'She looks like she's been scalped because she's got nits!' Rachel said, rolling her eyes. 'I already get plenty of *looks* for being an unmarried mother. Now everyone's going to think that I'm dirty too.'

Carmen rolled her eyes too. 'No they won't and, if you keep a hat on her head, no one will notice.'

'How's Jan this morning?' Rachel asked.

'She didn't have a good night.'

'You look tired an' all, Win.'

'I am, but at least I don't have to work, Carmen is doing everything.'

'I'll muck in where I can too. In fact, Torrie won't mind looking after Martha so that I can help behind the bar.'

'Oh, that would be a great help. I'll pay her.'

'I can manage,' Carmen protested.

'I'm sure you can, love, but it won't hurt to have an extra pair of hands.'

'And Torrie would be grateful for an extra couple of bob,' Rachel added.

A long, arduous groan came from Winnie's bedroom. She stood up quickly and hurried in to see to Jan. She found her daughter writhing in pain, her bony hands gripping the bed sheets.

'It's all right, love, here you go, take this,' Winnie soothed, popping a codeine tablet in Jan's mouth and offering a glass of water to her lips, but she knew the girl would struggle to swallow it.

'It hurts so much … Oh, God, make the pain go away …'

'I wish I could, darling, I really wish I could. But the tablet will help to ease it soon.'

Carmen popped her head around the door. 'Can I help?'

Winnie looked over her shoulder and nodded her head. She'd never felt so helpless in her life. 'Fetch the doctor. She needs more than a tablet. And ask Rachel to bring me a bowl of water and a flannel.'

Looking back at Jan, it broke Winnie's heart to see her daughter's pale face contorted with crippling pain.

'The doctor is coming, love. He'll give you something stronger for the pain.'

'Morphine … I'm going to become a drug addict,' Jan said, managing a grim smile through her discomfort.

Winnie returned the smile, her eyes full of tenderness. 'Once you're feeling a bit better, we'll write that letter to Terry, eh?'

Jan nodded. She turned her agonised face and slowly groaned as Rachel tiptoed into the room with an enamel bowl and two small towels.

'Thanks, love,' Winnie said, taking the bowl and placing it on a small table between the beds. She dipped the towel into the water, rang it out and then gently dabbed Jan's sticky forehead. 'There, there, there,' she soothed. 'The doctor will be here at any minute.'

Maureen sat at her kitchen table with her hands locked together so tightly that her fingers were going white. Brancher hadn't come home, so she assumed that he was still at the police station. She was pleased of this but felt that hoping that he'd been charged was a betrayal to him.

Moments later, the front door flew open with such force, it whacked against the passageway wall. Maureen's back stiffened. She sat ramrod straight and stared in fear at Brancher's angry face. He thudded across the kitchen and shocked Maureen when he grabbed her by her hair.

'You're hurting me,' she yelped.

'Not as much as you've hurt me!'

'What, Brancher, what have I done?' she asked, desperately hoping he didn't know about the secret discussion she'd had with Sergeant Bradbury.

'I want to smash your ugly face through the wall,' Brancher growled. He yanked hard on her hair, but then released his grip and began pacing the small room.

Maureen sat trembling, tears rolling down her cheeks.

'You know how to make a fool out of me, but you're the one who's going to be sorry!'

'I-I-I'm sorry,' she stuttered.

'Sorry that I found out what a dirty slag you are!'

'W-what?'

'You're fucking good at playing dumb, Maureen, but it won't wash this time. Didn't you recognise Dean Benson when you went to visit that darkie in the police station? You remember Dean ... he was at our fucking wedding!'

Maureen couldn't breathe. She shook from head to toe, paralysed with fear. She'd never seen or heard Brancher as bad as this before.

'Penny dropped yet, has it? Dean Benson ... PC fucking Benson!'

She remembered – he was the policeman who'd taken her

in to see Clinton. Bile burned the back of Maureen's throat as it rose from her twisting stomach. She pushed the seat back and ran across the kitchen, violently vomiting in the sink.

'You filthy bitch,' Brancher snarled. 'I've gotta get out of here before I knock your stupid brain out.'

Leaning over the sink, trying to catch her breath, Maureen heard him stamp out of the house. The walls shook when he slammed the door behind him. She turned the tap on to clean the sink, her tears falling in big blobs and running down the plughole.

Brancher had walked out to calm himself down, but he'd be back and she was petrified of facing him. She couldn't deny that she'd visited Clinton now and couldn't think of a reasonable excuse for going to see him.

As Maureen splashed cold water on her face, she caught sight of her reflection in the window. The woman who gazed back at her looked scared for her life, her hair dishevelled and eyes red and puffy. She hardly recognised herself, an anxious shadow of the girl she'd been when she had married Brancher.

She cupped her face in her hands and, staring hard at reflection, said aloud, 'Run. Run for your life. Get out and don't look back.'

25

'She's been as good as gold, the pair of them have, no running amok like the last time they were together,' Torrie assured. 'She's kept my Benny entertained, which gave me a chance to clean me oven.'

Rachel flopped down onto Torrie's comfortable but sagging sofa. The cushions enveloped her like a warm hug. 'Thanks for having her.'

'Anytime, you know that. And I can't lie, the extra money is going to come in handy. I feel just awful accepting it, but it will go a long way to help me to look after me dear old mum, bless her. She's not been right since me dad died. I'd like to treat her to a nice day out and now I can, well, that's if she can manage it. How was your day?'

'Hard work! My feet are throbbing. I'd forgotten what it feels like to be on them all day.'

'And Jan?'

Rachel sighed heavily. 'Not good. She's in so much pain, Winnie had to call the doctor to administer morphine. It helps, for a while.'

'I can't imagine, the poor woman. And to know that you're going to die, it must be terrifying.'

'It's so difficult to know what to say. To be honest, I've avoided going in to see her as much as I can. Is that bad of me?'

'No, lovey. I'd be the same.'

'I suppose I'll have to put my plans on hold for a while.'

'Oh yeah, what plans are these then?'

Rachel reached across to the table for her cup of tea and grinned at Torrie. 'I'm going to be a teacher.'

Torrie gazed at her agog, 'A teacher, you reckon?'

'Yes. Martha will be at school soon, so I'm going to apply to teacher training,' Rachel admitted, pleased to finally announce her plans.

'But you have to be clever to be a teacher. I'm not saying that you ain't clever, but you need qualifications and to have been to a grammar school. Not only that, and I hate to say this, but I'm not convinced that they'd let you teach, you know, with you having a kiddy and not a husband. They'd say that you ain't morally right, if you know what I mean.'

Rachel wasn't offended by her friend's blunt talking, but she was determined to succeed. 'I'll get the qualifications and not having a husband is a bonus! I remember my teacher had to retire from her job when she got married. And as for being a single mother, well, I might have to tell a few fibs and say that my husband ran off and left me, or something like that.'

'Well, you seem to have it all worked out. I don't know what to say! Good for you for trying, but women from round here don't become teachers. What's wrong with cleaning work or the factories? That's the sort of jobs that the likes of us do.'

Rachel knew that she'd be faced with opposition and, feeling silly, she wished now that she hadn't divulged her plans to Torrie. 'I want more than domestic or factory work and I want to set a good example to Martha, to show her that anything is possible. Look what women have been doing since the men have gone … engineering and all sorts.'

'Yeah, I know, lovey, needs must, but you don't even speak like a toff.'

'I can learn to speak proper, that's easy enough.'

'I don't want to be the one to put a damper on your dreams, but you need to be realistic.'

'I've looked into it, Torrie. There's teaching training colleges, some that might accept me after an interview. I'm not shooting too high; I'm thinking of being a teacher to under elevens.'

'Well, good luck to you. You're going to be too hoity-toity for me to talk to,' Torrie laughed.

'I'll always be a Battersea girl at heart.'

Rachel called Martha down from upstairs and took her home, promising the girl that she could come back tomorrow to play with Benny.

The mood indoors was unsurprisingly sombre. Martha went to her room and Rachel found Winnie in the kitchen; her face etched with worry.

'You look done in, Win.'

'I am, love. Jan's sleeping at the moment. That injection that the doctor gave her seemed to knock her right out. At least she's not feeling any pain when she's asleep like that.'

'Why don't you go for a walk? Get some fresh air, it'll do you good and put a bit of colour back in your cheeks.'

'That's not a bad idea. You'll listen out for Jan, won't you?'

'Of course I will.'

Rachel wandered through to the front room and switched on the wireless but kept the volume low. With one ear listening to the broadcaster and another for Jan, her mind drifted back to the conversation that she'd had with Torrie. She'd seen in her friend's eyes that Torrie thought she was aiming for the impossible. It made Rachel doubt herself. Were her plans and ambitions too fanciful for a working-class girl from Battersea? Was she getting ideas above her station? Probably, she concluded, but she was still determined to give it her best shot.

Winnie trudged down the street feeling dazed and punch-drunk, her shoulders weary and her body aching as though she'd done ten rounds in a boxing ring. She tried to clear her head and, for just two minutes, not to think of Jan. But it was impossible. She couldn't stop worrying about her daughter and spun on her flat, sensible shoes to return home. After all, she didn't want to leave Jan, even if seeing her in pain tore Winnie apart.

Sergeant Bradbury walked towards her, looking very serious, but then on sight of her, his face broke into a wide smile. 'Hello, I was just on my way to see you.'

'Hello, Tommy.'

'I suppose you've heard about the robbery of Sarson's on Lavender Hill, the jewellery shop?'

'No, I can't say that I have.'

'I would have thought that all your customers were talking about it.'

Winnie didn't have time or space to think of anything

other than Jan. 'I've not been working in the pub. I'm sure Carmen would have heard.'

'Strictly between us, I hauled Brancher in for it, but I couldn't pin anything on him. But I'll have him, Winnie, I swear I will. It's just a matter of time.'

'Good.'

'I'm still trying to find some sort of proof that it was him behind the distillery robbery too. It's not right that Clinton is locked up for it. He's done so much for this country, leaving his family and home to travel thousands of miles to come here when we needed him, and this is how Britain repays him ... it's a diabolical liberty, Winnie, diabolical.'

'It is.'

'If you don't mind me saying, you don't seem your normal cheery self today.'

'I'm not.'

'Has something happened? Anything I should be aware of?'

'Jan's at home. She's ... she's not very well.'

'Oh dear, I'm sorry to hear that. Nothing too serious, I hope?'

'Cancer. She's riddled with it.'

The colour drained from Tommy's face. 'Flippin' 'eck, Winnie.'

'Inoperable, the doc says,' Winnie said flatly, sniffing as she began to cry.

'I'm sorry, very sorry.'

'I know, me an' all. So you'll excuse me not being very cheery today, but I can't find anything to smile or laugh about. My girl ... she's ... she's not gonna be here for much longer and I can't bear it, Tommy, I simply can't stand it,' Winnie spluttered through her tears.

Tommy pulled her to him and held her close.

Winnie instinctively wrapped her arms around him, finding much-needed comfort. 'Look at me making a spectacle of myself in the street,' she sobbed into his chest.

She went to pull away from him, but Tommy wouldn't let go of her. 'No one is here to see you, Winnie. That's it, woman, let it out. Have a bloody good cry and then you'll feel better to face Jan.'

Winnie's body jerked and trembled as her pent-up sorrow unloaded onto Tommy's smart uniform. She cried until her eyes were sore. 'I'm sorry,' she blubbed, composing herself eventually. 'But you're right, I do feel better.'

'Come on, let's get you back home to your girl.'

As they walked along the street in silence, Winnie felt Tommy wrap his large hand around hers. She didn't tug away from him or say anything. It just felt reassuring to know that he was there.

Maureen walked as fast as she could, trying to put as much distance between her and the house. Fear of running into Brancher made the blood pump around her body at a rate of knots and adrenaline coursed through her veins. She wasn't sure where she'd mustered the courage from, but she'd hurriedly thrown a few clothes into a cloth bag, slung it over her shoulder and then fled. But she hadn't thought through her escape and had no idea where to go. She was just running blindly, only knowing that she couldn't go back to Brancher.

Her legs moved so quickly she felt that they weren't attached to her body. *Just keep going*, she told herself. *Run, Maureen, run.* She dared not look behind and kept her head down, licking her dry lips and praying that she wouldn't bump into her husband.

'Oi, watch yourself,' a man barked as Maureen clashed shoulders with him.

'Sorry,' she mumbled and hastily hurried on her way.

She passed the shops, a pub, kids playing, a bus stop, a school, more shops, another pub, a bus stop, a pub, a church, up a hill, a bus stop, down a hill, shops, soldiers, mothers with prams, another bus stop ... yet she still didn't feel safe or far enough away from Brancher.

Maureen rummaged in her cloth bag and cursed, 'Damn!' In her haste to flee and in a panic, she'd forgotten her purse. She bit on her bottom lip, fighting the urge to cry. Brancher had been proven right again: she was useless!

Standing at the foot of Wandsworth Bridge, spanning the inky water of the Thames, she stopped and stared ahead at the dull blue, steel structure, camouflaged to avoid air strikes. Crossing it would take her over to Fulham, a place that was unfamiliar to her. But Battersea was behind her and she couldn't go back.

Run, Maureen, run. The words raced through her mind. But run to where? She had no money, no place to go and it dawned on her that she had no hope either.

You're useless, you stupid cow. Brancher had stripped away her confidence and destroyed her self-esteem. She couldn't live with him any longer, but she couldn't cope with life alone. She found herself standing on the middle of the bridge, her shaking hands resting on the cool steel, her gaze on the deep water below. As she realised what she had to do, a calm descended on her. Maureen, at last, found peace through her turmoil. She thought of her grandparents, of the baby she'd lost and of her mother and father who she barely remembered. Would they be waiting for her? She hoped so.

Resolute, her fear faded. As she leaned further over the edge of the bridge, she wondered if death would hurt. If it did, she knew that it wouldn't last long. Her cloth bag fell from her shoulder and dropped towards the river. Maureen watched it fall until it hit the water and was consumed by the river, swept under the bridge. This was to be her fate too.

She clung to the steel, pulling her legs up and throwing them over the edge. Now, sat with her legs dangling over the Thames, Maureen closed her eyes. She had one final ask of God, 'Please keep Stephen safe.' Then, ready to leave her pitiful life, she lunged forward.

She should be falling through the air, plummeting to the dirty water below, but instead she felt the hard ground beneath her and strong arms around her waist as a deep voice in her ear said, 'Oh no, missus, not on my watch. You're not meeting your maker today.'

Confused, and finding her feet, Maureen wriggled to free herself from the firm grip holding her steady.

'It's all right, missus, I've just saved your life. I won't hurt you.'

'You had no right!' she screamed.

The man let go of her and she spun to face him.

'You should have let me die,' she sobbed, and fell to her knees. *Useless, stupid cow.* She couldn't even end her life without messing it up!

The stout, middle-aged man, wearing dirty work clothes and a flat cap, reached down to offer his hand. Maureen batted it away and lifted her tear-stained face to see that a crowd had gathered around her.

An elderly woman stepped forward. 'Nothing can be that bad that can't be sorted,' she said kindly.

Another woman spoke, 'It's a sin what you was going to do. A sin! You'd rot in hell and you don't want that, do you?'

The sea of faces began to merge in Maureen's blurred vision. A strange sensation engulfed her and she felt herself drifting away, on a barge maybe, the undulating ground beneath her carrying her into an abyss.

A policeman's hand reached through the fog and a distant voice instructed, 'Come with me.'

And then the light went dark.

26

'Thanks, love, that's perfect,' Winnie said, forcing a smile that didn't reach her eyes.

'It was the fanciest paper and envelopes that I could find, just like you told me to get, but there wasn't much to choose from. That was the last pad,' Rachel said, handing the newly purchased writing set to Winnie.

'You did well to find any paper at all with these shortages.'

'Is it for Jan's letter to Terry?'

'Yes, love,' Winnie answered, and then straightening her back and pushing back her shoulders, she said resolutely, 'Right, let's get this done.'

In the bedroom, Jan looked somewhat relaxed, her eyes glazed. The doctor had been again this morning, but he'd given Jan only half of the dose that he'd administered the day before. It seemed to be keeping her pain at bay, though he had warned Winnie that as the cancer progressed, Jan would need more and more pain relief.

Winnie sat on the edge of her bed; the pen in her hand poised over the writing pad. 'All right, my love, tell me what you want to say to Terry.'

Jan smiled weakly. 'What do you say to your husband from beyond the grave?'

'I wouldn't know where to start. This has to come from you. Are you sure you won't change your mind and let me tell him that you're poorly?'

'I'm sure, Mum. I don't want him to watch me die. Let his last memories of me be good ones, not tragic ones.'

Winnie didn't agree with Jan's decision but said, 'Well, shall we start with *Dearest Terry*?'

Jan slowly nodded, tears welling in her bleary, sunken eyes.

'*Dearest Terry,*' she said. '*Please forgive me for leaving you. Believe me, I didn't want to. And please don't be angry with Winnie. I begged her to respect my dying wishes and to keep news of my cancer away from you.*

'*I realise that my death must have come as an awful shock to you. But understand, I couldn't allow you to watch me die. Now, your memories of me will be good and happy ones, instead of sad and sorry ones. And if you had been here in my final moments, it would have broken my heart to see your pain. It's selfish of me, I know, but I want to die remembering your smiling face. I couldn't go in peace if you were here, crying beside me.*

'*Please know, Terry, that you are the love of my life and the best thing that ever happened to me. You brought me so much happiness: for that, I thank you.*

'*Don't be sad for me, my darling. I'm not scared of death. I believe in God and heaven and I know that it will be beautiful. My only regret is that our future has been so cruelly cut short and that a tumour is growing in my stomach instead of our child. Oh, Terry, you will be such a good father, and one day, I hope that you will be. Please, I beg of you, do not allow my death to mar the rest of your life. You have so much love to give, you must give it to a deserving woman and find your happiness again.*

'I'm tired now. I have to go, my darling, sweetest husband. Remember me with fondness. Live your life to the full, for both of us.

'Eternally yours,

'Jan xxx'

Winnie had to keep wiping her eyes to stop her tears from falling on the paper and smudging the ink. 'That's beautiful, love,' she said, her voice cracking with emotion.

'Mum ... can you take this and put it in the envelope, please?'

Winnie saw that Jan was struggling to remove her wedding ring, too weak to pull it off. She jumped to her feet. 'Let me do that for you,' she offered and gently eased the gold band off Jan's finger.

'Do you think that you could snip off a bit of my hair too?'

'Yes, love, and I'll wrap it in a pretty ribbon.'

'Thanks, Mum. I know that wasn't easy for you.'

'It's done now.'

'And I'm sorry that it's going to be left to you to break the news to Terry.'

'Stop worrying about me, I'm a tough old bird. I'll be fine and I'll look after Terry, so you don't need to worry about him either.'

Jan's eyes had closed.

Winnie's heart leapt to her mouth, but then she saw the rise and fall of Jan's chest. 'Thank gawd,' she muttered.

Winnie knew the day was coming soon when Jan would take her final breath, but she wasn't ready for it yet. *I'm not prepared*, she thought, though she had no idea how she was supposed to prepare herself for the saddest day of her life.

The following day, Rachel glanced around the pub and shook her head. There were only three customers; two playing crib and one reading a newspaper, all drawing out the time their half-pints could last. 'It's really quiet today,' she said to Carmen.

'I know. I think word has spread about Jan and folk are feeling a bit awkward.'

'Do you reckon?'

'Yes. I mean, who wants to sit and enjoy a beer when you know that there is a young woman dying upstairs?'

Rachel looked down to the floor and bit her bottom lip. Carmen sounded harsh, but she'd probably hit the nail on the head.

The door opened and a tall, good-looking soldier came in. Carmen discreetly nudged Rachel. 'You can serve him,' she whispered and winked.

Rachel looked at the khaki-clad soldier as he came towards the bar and thought that there was something familiar about him. From under his cap, she could see that his brown hair had been highlighted by the sun and his skin glowed a healthy bronzed colour.

'Good afternoon,' he said in a low, deep voice. 'I wonder if you might know where my sister is: Maureen. Maureen Fanning.'

Rachel's eyes widened as she suddenly recognised him. 'Stephen!' she blurted, astonished. He'd been a skinny, pale-faced, shy young man when he'd left to join the army, yet had returned looking like a Greek god. Rachel could feel her cheeks burning at the notion of comparing him to Adonis.

'Yes, and you're Rachel, I believe?'

'I am. I'm, erm, sorry about your grandparents. Len was always one of my favourite customers. He's very much missed.'

'Thank you. He always spoke highly of this place and especially of Mrs Berry. So, do you know where Maureen is?'

Carmen, standing behind the bar beside Rachel, joined the conversation. 'Hello, young man. I'm Mrs Hampton, but you can call me Carmen. I have Maureen's address, but she's living on the other side of Battersea now.'

'Ah, Carmen, nice to meet you. Maureen told me about you in her letters. She said that you had been a great help to her, thank you very much.'

'I did what I could and you're welcome. One moment, I'll write the address down for you.'

'I've already got it, from Maureen's letters, and I called at the house this morning. There was no one home. The lady next door told me that Brancher was taken away in a police car and then came home slamming the door. And then she went on to say that she saw Maureen leaving with a bag over her shoulder. You don't know where she was going, do you?'

Carmen frowned. 'Winnie mentioned something about Brancher being taken in for questioning about a robbery. Perhaps Brancher has been taken to the station again and Maureen was taking some clothes for him.'

'But that doesn't explain where she is this morning. The neighbour said she was sure that Maureen didn't come home last night.'

'That sounds a bit odd,' Rachel mused.

'I'll go back and check the house again and then I'll be staying at this address,' Stephen said as he pulled out a scrap of paper from his pocket. 'Have you got a pencil?'

Rachel handed him one and Stephen wrote down his address.

Handing the paper to Carmen, he said, 'It's a boarding house a few streets back from here. If you see Maureen, will you tell her where I am, please?'

'Yes, of course. And will you pop back in later and let us know if she was at home?'

'Sure, and thanks.'

Rachel couldn't take her eyes of Stephen as he walked confidently out of the pub, but she was quick to tell herself to forget any romantic notions. She'd had enough of men and now it was *her* time. Regardless of what Torrie had said, she still intended to concentrate on building a career and making better a future for Martha.

Clinton sat on his hard, unforgiving bed with one scratchy, worn blanket beneath him and rested his head against the wall. The cell felt stiflingly hot and the slopping-out bucket for his ablutions was giving off a stink. The toilets in every cell had recently been removed to make way for more men in the overcrowded prison. Still awaiting trial, Clinton was aware that he was in the same prison where spies had recently been hung from the gallows and he'd heard talk of traitors to Britain being confined within the prison walls too.

No breeze wafted through the small, barred window located high on the wall. And no air seemed to be coming through the vented brick beside his bed. He covered his ears in a bid to block out the relentless screams, shouts and cries of his fellow inmates. There always seemed to be someone yelling for help or screeching profanities. Even after lights out, the noise was incessant. Locked up alone in cells not big enough to swing a cat, many a 'tough' man – murderers and rapists, fraudsters and thieves – had succumbed to lunacy.

Clinton closed his eyes and forced his mind to wander across the oceans and to the golden beaches of home. He tried to remember how the hot sand felt between his toes. The scorching sun on his skin. The thick green canopy of the forests and the squalls of tropical birds; the squeak of crickets rubbing their back legs together and the buzz of the cicadas. But most of all, he never wanted to forget the feeling of his mother's embrace.

Clanging and howling echoed around the prison, drowning out his memories, and hunger pains cramped his stomach. But it was the sheer boredom that really bothered Clinton. Day in, day out, hour after hour, nothing to do except stare at the walls or watch the bugs scuttling across the floor. The thought of spending years in Wandsworth Prison was a thought that he tried to avoid. But it would often pop up and confront him, especially at night when he'd be trying to sleep to shut out the despair of his life.

Clinton sat to attention when the cell door opened. His body rigid, he hoped that it wasn't the warden he'd met on his arrival. The short man with hooded eyes had taken an instant dislike to Clinton and, as he'd snarled abuse about the colour of Clinton's skin, the man had deliberately pushed him into a wall, hurting his already broken arm. It came as an instant relief when the prison chaplain walked in. With a thick mane of white hair, the man's nose glowed red, and the veins under his wrinkled cheeks were broken. It was clear that he liked a tipple of the altar wine. But he'd shown Clinton kindness, something that was rare within the confines of the prison.

'I've brought you this,' he said, handing Clinton a book. 'Not many of our guests request reading material of such a deep and thought-provoking nature. I hope it brings you peace and that the Holy Spirit touches you.'

Clinton bobbed his head at the chaplain as he accepted the Bible. 'T'ank you, sir. My mother is a God-fearing woman and raised me to respect the Church. She'd expect me to spend my time wisely in here. I can't fell trees, so I will reacquaint myself with the Lord.'

'Yes, indeed, good man. I've been looking into your background and case. It's quite exceptional. To come all this way from British Honduras as part of the war effort and to work tirelessly in the forests of Scotland, to then find yourself in here for a shameful crime. I'm curious... what led you to commit such an act?'

Clinton glanced past the chaplain to the warden standing just outside the cell door. The guard was looking up and down the corridor and didn't appear to be paying attention to their conversation. 'I didn't, sir,' he whispered. 'I've never hurt anyone in my wretched life. But I deserve to be here and will do my time without complaint or trouble.'

'You are a curious creature, and I would like to understand more. You will be in my prayers. God bless you.'

The chaplain left and the cell door slammed shut. Clinton hated that noise. He looked down at the brown leather-bound Bible in his hands and opened it to the first page. There, to his surprise, he saw a small inscription addressed to him. *You are a child of God; therefore, I will take you into my care. See you in the chapel on Sunday.*

Clinton smiled. He didn't feel quite so lonely or as scared

anymore. He had a friend and he intended to open his heart to Jesus.

But his smile turned sullen when he heard loud banging from the cell next door and a voice shouting, 'All your lot should be in here, lazy blacks, can't trust any of you.'

He sighed. It was going to be a very long and testing ten years.

27

After the pub had closed in the afternoon, Rachel had popped over to Torrie's to collect Martha. Once again, she felt herself sinking into the comfort of her friend's sofa and didn't want to leave.

'So, do you call your mum, Mum or Hilda?' Torrie asked, having been fascinated when she'd learned that Rachel had grown up believing that Hilda was her older sister.

'I've started calling her Mum recently, but it still feels odd. I haven't seen her for a couple of days. She normally calls in daily, but since Jan has come home, Hilda hasn't been to visit.'

'Well, I ain't being funny, but maybe she's having a hard time dealing with the situation too. I mean, you're spending more and more time here, not that I mind. You know you're always welcome.'

'Thanks, and yeah, you could be right. Are you sure you don't mind me being here so much?'

'Oh, lovey, you're me best mate, I love you being here.'

'I suppose I'd best get going though. I want to get Martha settled into bed before my evening shift.'

'You can always leave her with me for the night. She can top and tail with Benny.'

'Thanks, but I'd like to keep to her routine.'

'Well, the offer is there if you change your mind. I was thinking that I might visit my sister tomorrow. Margaret's got a lovely big garden. It's all right with you if I take Martha with me, isn't it?'

'Er, yes, I'm sure she'll enjoy herself,' Rachel answered, though she was a little concerned about what sort of influence Torrie's sister might have on her daughter. After all, Torrie had told Rachel some very racy stories about Margaret.

Back at home, Martha had something to eat and fell asleep soon after. Rachel managed to avoid going in to see Jan and was glad to be behind the sanctuary of the bar. She found that she was annoyed at herself for keeping her eyes on the door expectantly, hoping that Stephen would come through it. But the next customer to come in was Sergeant Bradbury, out of uniform and looking ghastly.

'You all right, Tommy?' Carmen asked.

'Yes, well, no, not really. Can I have a word with you both, in private?'

Carmen gestured to Tommy to follow her, and Rachel asked Piano Pete to keep an eye on the bar.

In the small back kitchen, Tommy rubbed his chin, his lips tight. 'I'm sorry, ladies, I know that it's a difficult time for you all at the moment, but another problem has arisen and I really don't know what to do for the best, other than to lay it at your door.'

'What's the problem?' Carmen asked.

'It's Maureen Fanning. I had a call from a colleague, who

informed me that Maureen attempted to throw herself off Wandsworth Bridge.'

'Oh my God! Is she all right?'

'She was stopped, just in time, and taken to the station, where they kept her in a cell overnight for her own safety. Now, we all know what could be coming next for her, and none of us wants to see that happen, do we?'

Carmen shook her head, 'Most certainly not!'

'What?' Rachel asked. 'What will happen to her?'

'She'll be locked up in a loony house,' Carmen explained. 'And they aren't good places to be.'

'Exactly,' Tommy said. 'She refuses to go home to Brancher, the hospital don't want her, the Women's Institute don't know what to do with her, so ...'

'Of course she can come and stay with us,' Carmen offered, 'and I'm sure Winnie will agree.' She then looked at Rachel for approval.

Rachel shrugged. 'Yes, she'll have to come here.'

'That's a weight off my mind,' Tommy said. 'I've left her with Iris from the W.I. while I've been trying to find somewhere for her to stay. I was worried about her being alone in case she tried to top herself again.'

'Don't worry, Tommy, we'll keep a close eye on her, and she'll be delighted to know that her brother, Stephen, is home,' Carmen assured.

'That's good to know. She could do with all the support that she can get. And to give you the heads-up, I expect that Brancher will come looking for her. I've tried to find him to let him know about his wife, but I can't locate the slippery swine anywhere.'

'If he comes here and creates a problem, we'll send for you immediately.'

'Make sure you do. I'd like to find a good reason to have him sent down, though I hope he doesn't cause any bother here. I'll go and pick Maureen up from Iris and bring her here. You're top women, all of you. How's Winnie?'

'Oh, you know, holding on.'

'Give her my best.'

Rachel went back to the bar, her mind turning. She couldn't imagine how low Maureen must have been feeling to have wanted to end her life and in such a terrifying way. But anger bubbled in her stomach. She thought of Jan, laying upstairs on the verge of death, the unjustness of it, yet Maureen had been willing to throw her precious life into the Thames. It wasn't fair and she hoped that Maureen realised how selfish her act had been.

Maureen was a mixed bag of emotions as Carmen led her upstairs. Though unbelievably grateful to the women for taking her in, she couldn't help feeling that she was a bother. She also felt ashamed, so deeply ashamed. Carmen must think her weak and feeble. And they must be laughing behind her back. After all, she couldn't even get her own suicide right. *Stupid, useless cow.*

Maureen slipped off the blanket that was around her shoulders and sat at the kitchen table. Carmen placed a cup of coffee in front of her. 'I've got some good news for you,' she said slowly.

Maureen thought that Carmen was speaking to her as if she was some sort of imbecile. They thought the same of her as Brancher did; she was thick.

'Maureen, your brother, Stephen … he's home. Isn't that wonderful! And he can't wait to see you.'

'Stephen … home … are you sure?'

'Yes, he's been in here looking for you.'

Tears of happiness sprang to Maureen's eyes. Her dear brother, home, at long last. But he'd returned to so much sadness: his former home that he'd shared with their grand–parents now burnt to the ground.

'He's staying in a boarding house not far from here. You'll see him soon; we've sent Piano Pete round to tell him that you're here.'

Maureen looked at her tears dripping onto the table.

'Do you understand what I'm telling you, Maureen?'

She lifted her head and smiled. 'Yes … does he know … about what I tried to do?'

'No, I don't think so.'

'Please, don't tell him. I don't want him thinking that I'm useless too.'

'Useless? What do you mean?'

'I'm so stupid! I can't do anything right. I always mess up everything, even my own death!'

'Well, firstly, you're far from useless. And secondly, I'm bloody glad that you didn't manage to kill yourself. So let's have a bit less of all this *feeling sorry for yourself* malarkey and get on with it, eh?'

Maureen didn't hear any sympathy in Carmen's voice, but she hadn't expected to. 'I'm sorry,' she sniffed.

'And so you bloody well should be! I feel for you, Maureen, I really do, but you've got to pull your socks up. Yes, it was tragic that you lost your grandparents, but people are being killed all over the country and you don't see their loved ones throwing themselves in the Thames. And we all know that Brancher is no good, but neither was my husband and Winnie's old man was even worse. So, no more of the doldrums, eh? There's a war on, Maureen, we've just got to get on with things the best we can.'

Carmen's tone was harsh, but Maureen knew that the woman meant well.

Her voice lowered and she continued, 'And another thing. Jan is in bed across the hallway dying of cancer. The woman doesn't want to die, it's not right. Life is precious, Maureen. You need to value yours more.'

Winnie's voice came from the kitchen doorway. 'Don't be too hard on her, Carmen.'

'Sorry, Win, but she needs telling.'

'You all right, love?' Winnie asked Maureen, sitting beside her.

'Yes ... I'm very sorry to hear about Jan.'

'I know. Do you want to tell us why you thought that chucking yourself off a bridge was a good idea?'

Maureen hung her head in shame. 'I didn't know what else to do. I'd run away from Brancher because he'd found out that I'd been to the police station to see Clinton. I convinced meself that he'd kill me, so I legged it, and then I realised I'd left my purse at home. When I got to the bridge ... I just ... I thought ... Oh, I feel so stupid.'

'Didn't you think to come here?'

'I knew that Brancher would find me here.'

'He wouldn't have got past us. Anyway, what's done is done. You're here now and we'll look after you. Rachel will sort you out a nightie and Carmen will get a bed ready for you on the sofa. After you've seen your brother, rest tonight, but I'll expect you to be pulling your weight tomorrow.'

Maureen nodded. 'Thank you,' and hearing her own flimsy explanation of why she had attempted suicide made her feel even more pathetic. She glanced from Winnie to Carmen and wished that she had their fortitude. Strong, admirable women, the complete opposite to her.

Rachel popped her head around the door, saying, 'Your brother is downstairs, Maureen.'

She smiled and shoved her seat back, desperate to see Stephen. As she walked across the kitchen, she stopped and turned back to the women at the table. 'Thank you again, and I'm sorry. But I'm going to be fine and I'm going to be better ... I'm going to try to be more like you.'

In Maureen's wake, Carmen tutted and said, 'She needs to sort herself out.'

'I'm sure she will now that she's here with us and away from Brancher.'

'Let's hope so. By the way, Tommy's downstairs. It's really quiet, Rachel can manage by herself, so why don't you have a break? I'll listen out for Jan and Martha.'

'Are you sure you don't mind?' Winnie asked, unsure.

'Go.'

As Winnie trudged down the stairs, she pinched her cheeks to put a bit of colour on her face and smoothed her hair. She couldn't remember when she'd last looked in a mirror and thought she must look frightful, yet, really, she was past caring.

In the bar, Tommy looked pleased to see her.

'Have you eaten?' he asked.

'Not much,' Winnie answered. The constant knot in her stomach and tightness in her chest suppressed her appetite.

'Come with me, I'll treat you to a bit of fish and chips. It's a smashing evening outside. We can find a bench and eat out of the newspaper. You look like you could do with a bit of fresh air and some good food.'

Winnie sighed. She didn't feel that she had the energy to go traipsing to the fish and chip shop or be good company for Tommy. But her stomach grumbled at the thought of chips with lashings of salt and vinegar. 'All right, but I'm not stopping out long.'

As they left the pub, she glanced at Maureen, sitting in a corner, smiling with her brother. *She'll be all right*, Winnie thought, which was one less thing to worry about.

Tommy chatted easily, going on about shortages and how it was a bonus that fish and chips weren't rationed. She listened but, understandably, her mind was on Jan.

As they passed a pub on the corner, the door opened and two fellas came out. Winnie absentmindedly looked into the pub and was disgusted to see a familiar figure sat at the bar. 'I don't bloody believe it,' she ground out through gritted teeth.

'What?'

'Hilda is in there!'

'Oh no. Wait here, Winnie, I'll go in and drag her out. She's got quite a reputation for being gobby when she's had a few.'

'I know, I've had to deal with her often enough. But she doesn't scare me,' Winnie said and marched into the pub with her arms swinging.

'What's your game?' she spat at Hilda.

The woman took her eyes from her half-drunk glass of

whisky and looked round at Winnie. There was no remorse on her face, just a sorry, blank expression.

The landlord stood behind the bar and nodded his head to Winnie. 'Evening, Mrs Berry.'

'Don't you *evening* me, Mr Thorpe. I told you not to serve her any drinks!'

'Oh, blimey, yeah, you did, ages ago. Sorry, I forgot.'

Winnie huffed. It had been a few years since she'd visited every local public house and warned them off serving Hilda. 'All right, well don't forget in future.'

Hilda clumsily spun on her bar stool and Winnie braced herself, expecting a tirade of abuse. But Hilda simply mumbled an apology.

'It's no good apologising, Hilda. You can't go down this track again. I'm taking you home.'

'Just leave me be, Winnie.'

'No, I can't. If I leave you be, you'll drink yourself into oblivion.'

'That's what I want. I just want to drown my sorrows.'

'Don't be ridiculous! What sorrows have you got, eh? Don't you think I've got enough on my plate at the moment without having to deal with you an' all! And where have you been since Jan came home? Getting pissed, I suppose? I've not seen hide nor hair of you. Well, thank you. Thank you very much. The amount of times that I've bolstered you up, and now, when I could do with a bit of support, you're too busy throwing whisky down your neck. And while I'm on the subject, your daughter is just as bad, she's hardly been in to see Jan neither.'

'It's hard, Winnie.'

'Jan ain't contagious. She's got cancer, not the bleedin' plague!'

Hilda still didn't shout and scream. She shrugged her shoulders, saying, 'Yeah, well, we can't all be as perfect as you.'

'What's that supposed to mean?'

'Look at you, the matriarch, the pillar of society. *Good ol' Mrs Berry. Winnie the wonder woman.* I'm not like you. I can't cope sometimes.'

'Pack it in, Hilda. You're stronger than most women I know. You're just looking for an excuse to drink. Well, let me spell it out for you ... There. Is. No. Excuse.'

Hilda picked up her glass and guzzled the rest of her drink. 'It makes me feel better.'

'Better about what?'

Hilda sniffed and ran her finger around the rim of her empty glass. 'I keep thinking, what if it was Rachel instead of Jan? And then I'm glad that it's Jan and not my daughter. Do you know how that makes me feel?'

'Pretty shitty, I should imagine, but you're right to be glad that it's not Rachel. What my Jan is going through, what I'm going though, I wouldn't wish it on my worst enemy. But I don't know how much more I can take, Hilda. I'm reaching breaking point and I can't deal with you on top of everything else. I need you. I need you to be sober and I need you to support me. Do you think that you can do that?'

Hilda finally showed some remorse, guilt etched her face. 'I want to ... I can try.'

'You'd better try damn bleedin' hard. Tommy will take you home. I expect to see you tomorrow morning in my kitchen and we won't mention this again.'

As Winnie fought back tears and marched out of the pub, she felt Tommy grab her arm.

'I'll walk you home and then come back for Hilda.'

'No. Just get her out of the pub and a get a cup of coffee in her. I'll see you soon.'

Winnie strode back to her pub and, for once, she was glad of the blackout. Nobody could see her crying in the dark.

28

'Stephen said that he'd pay for a room for me in the same boarding house,' Maureen announced with pride across the breakfast table. 'It's been ever so kind of you to put me up, but I don't want to be an imposition.'

'It's all well and good you staying there with him while he's on leave, but it could be some time before he's demobbed. I think you'd better come back here once Stephen's gone back,' Carmen said.

'I promise I won't try to do anything silly again.'

'All the same, I'd prefer you here. Anyway, we could do with you coming back to do your job.'

'Oh, well, if you're sure?'

'Very. The place could do with a good sweep through and the brass needs polishing. Not to mention the dust in the cellar. You'll be needing your wages too.'

Maureen smiled. She liked the idea of hard work and, for once, what she earned would go in her own pocket instead of Brancher's. 'Stephen is coming to collect me this morning. But I'll tell him that I'm staying here.'

'No, love, it's fine,' Winnie said. 'You spend some time with your brother and then come back here when you're ready. The dust can wait.'

'Thank you, but I'll be back this afternoon to start work.'

They heard a knock on the back door, which Carmen went down to answer. When she came back upstairs and into the kitchen, Hilda followed.

'Look what the cat's dragged in,' Carmen chuckled.

Maureen thought that Hilda looked rather haggard and she assumed that the woman had been on fire-watch duties all night. She'd liked to have done something similar, or worked in the factories or on the land. Brancher would never allow her to contribute to the war effort, but maybe she could now, and it was better late than never.

She slipped out of the kitchen and into the front room, where she checked her reflection in the mirror over the hearth and decided that she looked her usual dull self. But the colourful, floral dress that Rachel had given her brightened her up. She'd never worn such bold clothes and worried that the dress meant she wouldn't be able to fade into the background. And if Brancher found her wearing something so brazen, it would only add to his fury.

A while later, downstairs, as Carmen opened the pub, Maureen felt excited to see Stephen. When he walked in, she rushed towards him, grinning.

'Don't you look a picture in that dress,' Stephen smiled.

'Thanks. Rachel gave it to me. It's a bit bright.'

'It suits you. Are you ready?'

'Yes, sir! Lead on … left, right, left right left,' Maureen said, playfully saluting him.

The boarding house was only a ten-minute stroll from the

Battersea Tavern, but when they reached it, Maureen stopped on the middle of three steps that led up to the front door.

'Is something wrong?' Stephen asked.

'That sign,' Maureen answered, pointing to a notice in the window that was scrawled in large handwriting:

No blacks.
No Irish.
No dogs.

'Oh, that,' Stephen said. 'Horrible, ain't it?'

The sign had made her think of Brancher. It was exactly the dreadful attitude that he had. 'I don't understand. I've met a black fella called Clinton. He's a really smashing bloke.'

Stephen hitched himself up onto the low wall and sat down, tapping out a cigarette from a box. He lit it, the smoke curling around his face, as he said, 'I know, little Mo, prejudices are horrible, and it ain't just the Irish and blacks. I've heard terrible stories about the Germans persecuting the Jews. I don't know why we can't all rub along together nicely. What difference does skin colour make? Me and you, we weren't raised to judge a man on his colour. Granddad always used to say that a man should be judged on his hard work and honesty. I remember him taking me down the docks. There were loads of coloured men working there, Granddad was friends with a few of them, and like you said, smashing blokes. There's good and bad in all of us.'

'Yes, there is,' Maureen agreed, thinking that her husband was one of the bad ones.

'Did you know that all shades of people have lived in this country as far back as when the Romans invaded?' Stephen continued. 'And there's even talk of Queen Charlotte being of African descent.'

'Who's Queen Charlotte?'

'She was the wife of King George the third.'

'You're right clever, you are. How do you know stuff like this?'

'Books, little Mo. You should read more.'

'I dunno about that. I've got my job back at the Battersea Tavern so I won't have much time for reading.'

'Come on, let's get you booked in for the week. I'll warn you though, Mrs Richardson is a stickler for her rules. No women – in your case, no men – are allowed in your room. The front door is bolted at half-past nine. No smoking in the bathroom and no use of the kitchen. Breakfast is left on a tray outside your door at seven and dinner the same at six. Woe betide you if you return your plate with food on it!'

'Cor blimey, she sounds like a right battleaxe. But I don't care cos I'm going to have a lovely week with you. I'm so pleased that you're home.'

'Me an' all, little Mo, me an' all. And I can't say that I'm looking forward to going back.'

'I wish you didn't have to.'

'Me too, but I suppose I should be grateful that I got home this week. They don't normally allow compassionate leave for the death of a grandparent, but my commanding officer is a decent bloke. He managed to sort out the leave for me, but he had to pull in a few favours.'

Maureen wouldn't think about Stephen having to leave again, and neither would she allow herself to worry about Brancher. For now, her brother was home and she intended to enjoy every single minute with him.

The afternoon shift was coming to an end and Rachel was looking forward to collecting Martha and hearing about her adventures at Torrie's sister's house. As she wiped down the bar, she smiled at Tommy, asking, 'Enjoying your day off?'

'It's nice to have a beer.'

'What's that noise?' Carmen asked.

Rachel pricked her ears and heard the sound of a chugging engine. Her heart nearly punched out of her chest. 'It's not, is it? It can't be a flying bomb ... there's no sirens going off.'

The pub door burst open and Maureen rushed in with Stephen following. A dark shadow passed over the pub as Stephen shouted, 'Buzz bomb. Take cover!'

'Oh good God,' Carmen muttered. 'Right, down to the cellar everyone, make haste.'

'What about Winnie?' Tommy asked.

'She won't leave Jan. Come on, help me get everyone downstairs, quick.'

Rachel stood transfixed, her heart pounding in time with the thudding of ack-ack guns as she realised that she couldn't hear the V1 engine. It had cut out, which meant the bomb would be falling from the sky. 'Martha,' she cried and ran towards the door.

'Where are you going?' Stephen asked with urgency.

'My daughter. I have to make sure that Martha is safe.'

Running out onto the street, Rachel looked skyward and saw a strange black object gliding across the sky under the mare's tails clouds. No fire came out of the back. It was dropping down, nosediving in the direction of where Torrie's sister lived.

'No!' Rachel screamed and began rushing in panic towards Margaret's street.

Stephen grabbed her. 'You have to take cover.'

'I have to find Martha,' she shouted, tugging herself free of his grip.

She carried on running and noticed that Stephen was beside her. She'd lost sight of the rocket behind the rooftops at the end of the street, but, all of a sudden, a terrific boom blasted through the air and the ground trembled beneath her feet. Rachel fell backwards, Stephen did too. She sat on her haunches and watched in horror as a smoke and dust cloud mushroomed into the sky.

'Martha!' she shrieked, as debris began to fall on her.

Stephen helped her back to her feet and as she stumbled, he caught her, almost dragging her along the street. As they came closer to where the bomb had exploded, the air became thicker with acrid dust. Fire-engine bells sounded in the distance. Screams, cries and shouts for help carried on the light wind.

They turned a corner and both abruptly stopped. Rachel stared through the smoke and dust in horrified disbelief. 'The whole street … it's … it's almost gone,' she cried.

Feeling weak at the knees, and covering her mouth with a handkerchief, she staggered towards the fallen houses.

'She's dead, isn't she? My Martha's gone. There was no warning. No siren. They wouldn't have had time to shelter.'

She turned to Stephen, her eyes blazing with fear. He had a small trickle of blood running down his cheek from a cut on his temple. His brown hair, covered in the dust and dirt, was now grey and it had stuck to his skin too, making him look ghostly.

'We'll find her, Rachel. We'll find her,' he answered, breathlessly.

Ambulances began arriving in their droves, picking their way through the rubble. Firemen aimed their hoses at the flames. Men, women and even children began clambering over the wreckage on the outskirts of the impact site, calling out for survivors and listening for signs of life beneath the bricks and rubble.

'It's pandemonium. I don't know what house she was in. Oh, God, please, help me find my baby,' Rachel screamed. In a state of shock, no tears fell from her gritty eyes.

Stephen pulled her towards what was left of a house. The fireplace and chimney stack stood proud, but the front of the building had collapsed and the back door and back windows were blown out. 'We'll start here, and we won't stop looking for Martha until we find her.'

Rachel tentatively approached the unstable house, calling Martha's name. Tripping on bricks and twisted metal, she grazed her knee but felt no pain. 'Martha,' she called, over and over.

Stephen grabbed her arm. 'This isn't the house,' he said gravely.

'How do you know?'

She followed his eyeline and gulped at the sight of an old woman, half covered in bricks, her mouth hanging open in an unfinished scream. Rachel went to rush to the woman, but Stephen placed a staying hand on her arm and said solemnly, 'There's nothing we can do. She's dead.'

Clambering back over the debris, they tried the next house. The upper floor remained intact, but the roof, front and side walls were gone. Rachel could see the dark, art-deco style wallpaper on the back wall and the old-fashioned single, brass-frame bed in the bedroom. 'It's not this house either,' she said, knowing that Margaret's house would be modern.

At the next house, a woman stood holding onto what was left of a wooden picket fence. Her whole body was violently shaking and her hair was matted with dust and blood. She was staring at the remains of her house; just several timbers holding on precariously to a wall which looked like it was about to crumble.

'Which house is Margaret's?' Rachel asked urgently.

The woman didn't respond.

'Where does Margaret live?' she tried again desperately.

Nothing. The woman was in shock, mute.

Up ahead, Rachel could see that the Home Guard were trying to organise some sort of rescue operation. Men in tin hats and overalls were being directed to different houses. Women volunteers, also wearing tin hats, were mucking in too. Injured survivors were being ferried off to hospital, some sat on the ground, stunned and blackened with soot. People were rushing around with blankets, cups of tea, bandages. Rachel looked all around her, feeling helpless.

'We're not giving up,' Stephen reminded her. 'Look, there are plenty of walking wounded and there's a woman being pulled out alive over there. We *will* find Martha.'

Rachel's mouth was so dry from fear and brick dust that she could hardly swallow. But Stephen's words had given her hope and spurred her on. She saw another woman, her clothes in shreds, huddling a young, crying boy, walking towards an ambulance. Rachel rushed over.

'Do you know which house is Margaret's?'

The woman pointed and then hoisted the boy into an

ambulance. Rachel saw that his arm had been blown clean off, but it didn't register with her. Her eyes were fixed on the pile of bricks the woman had pointed at.

Stephen grabbed her by the shoulders, saying firmly, 'Stay here. I'll look for her.'

Rachel leaned to one side to see past Stephen and again stared at the demolished house. *She can't be in there*, her brain said. *Martha can't be in there.*

Stephen rushed off. Rachel ran behind him. As he climbed over the pile of bricks, Rachel screamed Martha's name, over and over until her throat felt raw.

A man, one of those in the tin hats and overalls, asked, 'Who's in the house, missus?'

'My daughter ... Martha ... she's only four years old ... she's a baby ...'

'Anyone else?'

'Er ... yes, two women and a boy ... Please ... find them ... help ...'

The man blew on a whistle and beckoned over a small group, then informing them, 'Two women, two kiddies.'

Several men scrambled over the ruins and a woman with a clipboard asked Rachel, 'Names of the missing.'

Before Rachel could answer, she heard Stephen shouting, 'Over here! Quick, over here!'

Rachel lost a shoe as she struggled across the loose blocks. Stephen threw a brick to one side, exposing an arm: a woman's arm. Rachel instantly recognised the elegant, red painted fingernails. 'Torrie,' she screamed and then hastily picked up bricks until they uncovered her purple and bloodied, battered face.

'Torrie … it's all right, we've got you,' Stephen said, somewhat calmly.

Rachel crouched beside her friend and used her handkerchief to sweep off the dust from Torrie's face and then her swollen eyes flickered open. 'The kids …' she said weakly.

'Do you know where they are, Torrie?' Rachel asked. 'I'll find them, but where were they?'

More men were pulling debris off Torrie and it soon became clear that she was pinned across her waist by a heavy ceiling joist.

She coughed, and a small dribble of blood oozed from her mouth. 'I can't feel nothing,' she groaned, her eyes glazing over.

'It's all right, Torrie, we'll get you out of there. Where are Martha and Benny?'

'I … I don't know … hide-and-seek … garden …'

'I'll find them, Torrie, they'll be all right,' Rachel assured, though panic surged through her trembling body.

Torrie wheezed, a guttural, rattling sound and her eyes widened. 'I'm dying … find them … look after my Benny … promise?'

Rachel had to try to keep the harrowing emotions from her voice as she soothed, 'You're not going to die. Look, they're lifting that thing off you now. I'll see you at the hospital.'

'Promise me …' She coughed and spluttered as more blood gushed from her mouth, choking her as her eyes rolled back in her head.

'Torrie … hold on … don't you dare die, do you hear me … hold on, please …'

Stephen grabbed Rachel's hand, his eyes lowered as he said, 'She's gone.'

'Oh my God ... No, this can't be happening!' Rachel screamed as she peered at her friend's lifeless face. There was no peace in her open, staring eyes, just fear and pain. 'I promise, Torrie. I'll look after Benny,' she cried, gulping down her sobs.

Stephen held Rachel's hand, helping her to manoeuvre through the bricks, metal and wood to what would have been the back of the house and into the back garden. Broken glass had cut into her shoeless foot and splintered wood had gauged her ankle. She shouted her daughter's name again and again, and Benny's, looking frantically around at the fallen trees and parts of houses that had been blasted into the garden.

'They've got to be here somewhere!' Stephen yelled, throwing roof tiles aside.

'There's a shelter ... they couldn't be in there, could they?' Rachel pointed at the buried Anderson, her heart filling with hope.

Stephen ran to the door of the shelter.

As he yanked it open, Rachel begged, 'Please, God, let them be inside.'

Light flooded into the Anderson. Rachel peered in, gasping at the sight of two terrified faces looking back at her.

'Mummy,' Martha cried, snot and tears running down her face.

Rachel held out her arms and both children ran into them.

'We was hiding in here from Torrie,' Martha bawled. 'And then there was a big bang and the ground shaked us.'

'I want my mummy,' Benny sobbed.

Rachel breathed in the scent of her daughter's hair, silently thanking God for keeping her safe. Tears of relief welled in her eyes, and tears of sorrow too. Somehow, she had to find the words to tell Benny that his mummy was dead and that she would be his new mummy until his daddy came home.

29

As always, the Battersea Tavern had opened its doors to offer tea and sympathy in the aftermath of the rocket attack just several streets away. Tommy had gone upstairs to check on Winnie and Jan. Hilda appeared to be calm and was organising whatever food she could rustle up. Carmen was fretting about Rachel and Martha but keeping herself busy. And Maureen was worried sick to the pit of her stomach about Stephen.

She looked outside the door again, glancing up and down the street for any sign of her brother. Shrapnel from the ack-ack gunfire littered the pavements. The sky over where the bomb had landed was dark with smoke and she could see that it was drifting across Battersea.

'Maureen ... Maureen ...' Hilda called.

She turned back in and saw Hilda at the tea urn.

'Go behind the bar and pour a brandy for anyone you see shaking. I can't work near the bar, Carmen is busy with ripping up sheets, so it'll be down to you, all right?'

Maureen nodded. She was grateful to have a purpose, anything that would distract her from worrying about Stephen.

Behind the bar, with her back to the pub, she placed several glasses on a tray with the bottle of brandy. She went to pick up the tray but noticed her hands were trembling. Quickly pouring a small drink for herself, she gulped down the liquid and drew in a long, steadying breath. *You're needed*, she told herself, *and you're not useless. Be strong, like Carmen and Winnie.*

With the tray in hand, when she turned around to look for anyone in shock, it fell from her hands at the sight of the person in front of her. Glass broke around her feet, the shattering sound bringing the pub to silence.

'Brancher,' she muttered, swallowing hard.

'I knew I'd find you here,' he sneered, his hands splayed on the bar top.

'What do you want?' she asked nervously.

'You, at home.'

'I'm not coming home, Brancher,' she said bravely, though inside, her stomach was doing somersaults.

'Yes, you are, even if I have to drag you home.'

Maureen didn't know what to say. She looked at him with contempt, her mind turning.

'Come on, Maureen, you're my wife, so it's time you started acting like one.'

Brancher's voice hid veiled threats and Maureen knew it. If she didn't do as he ordered, he'd turn nasty and she didn't want to create a scene in front of everyone. Yet she didn't want to go home with him either. Somehow she had to be strong, to be like Winnie and the others. If she didn't do it now, she never would.

'I'm staying here. You should go.'

He snarled and his eyes darkened with anger. 'Don't tell *me* what to do, you stupid cow. You're coming home whether you like it or not.'

Maureen hadn't seen Bill and Flo come into the pub, but now Bill placed a hand on Brancher's arm, saying, 'Now, now, Brancher. Maureen's fine where she is. Why don't you go and calm down, eh, mate?'

Brancher pulled his arm forward and then jabbed it backwards hard, his elbow smashing into Bill's face. Bill fell to the floor and covered his bleeding nose with his hands as Flo rushed to his side.

'Anyone else wanna have a go?' Brancher shouted, his crazed eyes scanning the pub.

Everyone stepped back, but Carmen came forward.

'Get out of this pub, Brancher Fanning. You're not to come back in here. Ever!' she shouted, pointing towards the door.

Brancher towered over her, looking down into her face. 'Sod off, you ridiculous old bag. It ain't even your pub.'

'I'm in charge and I'm telling you to get out ... or I'll call the police.'

'No need,' Tommy called. He'd come from upstairs. 'The police are already here.' Walking from behind the bar, his boots crunching on the broken glass, he stood in front of Brancher.

Maureen's heart was in her mouth. Out of uniform, Tommy looked like a short, aging man compared to Brancher.

'Now, son, don't give me any lip. You're under arrest.'

'Sod off, Tommy. You can't arrest me for taking my wife home to where she belongs.'

'No, but I can arrest you for that,' Tommy answered, pointing at Bill, who was now sitting at a table, nursing his broken nose.

'It was an accident.'

'You can argue your case at the station.'

Tommy took hold of Brancher's arm, but he yanked himself free.

'Don't make matters worse for yourself,' Tommy warned and grabbed Brancher's arm again.

Maureen wanted to close her eyes, to not see what was happening. She knew what was coming next and, just as she feared, Brancher retaliated. He threw his head forward and headbutted Tommy between the eyes.

Tommy staggered backwards but remained on his feet. 'That's it, Brancher, you're well and truly nicked, sunshine. You've assaulted a police officer and I'll make sure that you go down for a flippin' long time.'

Brancher ran towards Tommy, his fists clenched into threatening balls. Piano Pete, Bill and a couple of other men jumped to Tommy's defence and managed to wrestle Brancher to the floor. He fought back like a wild caged animal. Legs, fists and spittle were flying everywhere.

'No … no … no …' Maureen cried, concerned that someone would be hurt.

It came as a great relief when four uniformed constables ran into the pub.

'Ger off me!' Brancher yelled in his loud and booming voice as his arms were pulled behind his back and handcuffs were snapped onto his wrists. 'You're filth, the lot of ya. You can't do this to me!'

Tommy, smiling even though the skin around his eyes was already turning a shade of mauve, said smugly, 'I'll see you in court, Brancher. There are plenty of witnesses and when I give my evidence, it'll see you sent down for a good few years.'

As Brancher was dragged away to a waiting police car

outside, a woman leaned over the bar and whispered to Maureen, 'I sent my boy up the road to call the police.'

Maureen mumbled her thanks and saw an understanding in the woman's eyes; the same haunted look that was in her own. No doubt, another woman who'd been stripped of her self-esteem by a vile husband. But Maureen wasn't going to be bullied by hers any longer, she wouldn't allow it.

She was pleased to see the back of Brancher, but she was still worried about her brother. To take her mind off her fears, she found a dustpan and brush and swept up the broken glass, but she kept looking at the door, hoping that Stephen would walk in unharmed.

Joy filled her heart when he did.

As the day progressed, Jan's pain worsened. The morphine that the doctor had administered that morning hardly seemed to be touching her. It broke Winnie's heart to see her daughter weeping in agony.

'What can I do, love?' she asked in desperation.

'Take the blankets off me … get them off … they're hurting me … everything hurts …'

Winnie whipped back the bedcovers, shocked to see that Jan was laying on damp bed sheets, soaked with her own sweat.

'Oh, God … Mum … I can't take any more,' Jan cried, writhing and groaning.

'Here,' Winnie said, popping another codeine pill into her mouth and putting a glass to her cracked lips. Yet she knew that Jan's pain was beyond anything that the tablet could help to ease.

For the next hour, Winnie dabbed her daughter's head

with a cool, wet flannel and tried to offer soothing words of comfort, but she could see that Jan was exhausted and in unimaginable pain. She wondered if Jan would have been better off in the hospital and if bringing her home had been the wrong thing to do.

Carmen came in with a cup of tea for Winnie. When she saw the state of Jan, she asked, 'Shall I call the doctor?'

'Yes, I was just about to. Tell him to hurry.'

Jan didn't have the energy to scream, but Winnie had never seen anyone in so much agony. She wished that she could take it away. To stop it hurting. Watching her daughter struggling, it felt like hours until the doctor arrived, though it had only been just over twenty minutes.

'You've got to give her more morphine, Doctor. This is the worse I've seen her. It's dire, she's in agony.'

The doctor pulled Winnie to the other side of the room. 'I'm afraid it's only going to get worse. Jan's cancer is very aggressive and advancing quickly.'

'I can see that for myself, just give her something for the pain … Please, put her out of her misery,' Winnie urged.

'Mrs Berry, Jan is not going to improve. The morphine won't work, not unless I administer a very high dose, which is likely to be lethal. Do you understand what I am saying?'

Winnie looked at the doctor's face. A man about her age, though quite dashing with a pencil moustache and salt-and-pepper hair greased back off his face. What was he telling her?

'An animal wouldn't be left to suffer in the way that Jan is,' he said, very matter-of-fact.

His words sank in and Winnie's legs buckled. The doctor managed to break her fall and helped to ease her onto the dge of her bed. Jan lay in the next bed, begging for help, pleading for someone to make the pain go away.

Winnie couldn't bear to hear her daughter's distress any longer. 'Just stop my girl from hurting,' she said, a sob catching in her throat.

'Is there anyone who would like to speak to Jan?'

Winnie understood what he meant. It was time for them to say goodbye. But Jan's cries were becoming more desperate and Winnie just wanted her daughter to be at peace. 'No,' she answered, 'you can give her the medicine now.'

Her legs unsteady, her eyes glazed with unshed tears, Winnie went to Jan's bedside and held her daughter's hand.

'It's all right, my girl, the doctor is going to help you now.'

Jan's eyes blazed in pain. 'I can't do this, Mum... it hurts so much... I want to die,' she cried.

The doctor stood over Jan with the prepared needle in his hand. He paused for a moment and looked at Winnie. She knew that it was time for Jan to go and gave a quick nod of approval to the doctor.

As the needle went into Jan's arm, Winnie's heart broke and she looked away, gently stroking her daughter's cheek. 'Rest now, my love, rest. There's a good girl... just rest.'

Jan's eyes slowly closed and her rigid body went limp.

'You're all right now, my beautiful daughter, you're all right now. You can go, my love, it's all right, you can go,' Winnie soothed, tears streaming down her face.

Jan rattled three slow breaths and then her chest stopped rising and falling. As the doctor carefully placed his fingers on Jan's wrist to check for a pulse, Winnie knew that her daughter had passed.

She threw herself across Jan's lifeless body, holding her

close as she cried in her ear, 'Oh, Jan, my Jan, I love you...
My sweet, kind, beautiful girl... an angel on earth. I'm so
sorry... forgive me, but your pain is gone now... Goodbye,
my darling... goodbye.'

30

Five months later.
December 20, 1944.

Winnie's brave face had cracked a few times, though she'd always managed to keep a stiff upper lip in front of the children. As Martha and Benny skipped out of the kitchen, Winnie was grateful for the joy that they had brought into her home. Since Margaret had died alongside her sister, Torrie, and Benny's dad had been killed at sea, the boy was now a permanent and welcome part of the family. He'd settled in surprisingly well and Rachel had taken the boy under her wing as though he were her own flesh and blood.

Rachel collected the breakfast plates, taking them to the sink, lamenting, 'It's going to be an odd Christmas this year, with just us. I'm so used to being in the company of all and sundry downstairs.'

'It's too much to ask of Winnie to throw open her doors this Christmas,' Carmen said.

'My gran and granddad always used to talk about your Christmases, Winnie. They used to wax lyrical about them,' Maureen added with a reminiscing smile.

'We did have some fun,' Winnie said, remembering when Renee, after one too many sherries and before her legs were bad, had climbed onto a table and belted out a rendition of 'Hey Diddle-Diddle' with Piano Pete accompanying her on the piano. 'Do you know what… I reckon that we should put on a bit of a do after all.'

'Are you sure that you're up to it, Win?' Hilda asked, holding a saucer of tea to her lips.

'Yes, I think so. Jan would want me to. And anyway, it's not hard work with all of you mucking in to help.'

'The kiddies will love it,' Rachel beamed.

'I've not been putting money away all year like I would normally do, so how about rather than buying Christmas presents for each other, we buy things for the Christmas table instead?'

'I like that idea,' Carmen agreed.

Winnie smiled. 'And as long as you don't tell me where the stuff came from, I won't mind if you get what you can from any of the local spivs.'

'Ha, what Winnie means is *make sure* you get what you can from the spivs,' Hilda chortled.

'Well, I wouldn't want my table to be lacking or my guests to leave hungry,' Winnie said.

Carmen huffed. 'Tommy might have something to say about us serving up black-market food.'

'Not if we make sure that his mouth is stuffed with goodies. Right, I'd better write a list of what we'll need. Hilda, you let Flo and Bill know. Carmen, I'll leave it to you to do the invites. Rachel, you and the kids are in charge of Christmas decorations. And Maureen, I shall leave it up to you to make the Christmas pudding, just like Renee used to make, eh, love?'

'I'm not sure that mine will be as good as my gran's, but I'll give it a go.'

Winnie leaned back in her chair. 'This is just what we all need,' she said.

'Yeah, especially in light of these new bloomin' rockets firing at us from Holland, thanks to Hitler,' added Hilda with a shudder.

Rachel shook her head in disgust. 'It was bad enough when the Germans were flying over us night after night and dropping incendiaries and bombs from their planes. And then we had the Doodlebugs, but these … Christ, I've never been so scared. At least with the Doodlebugs, you could hear them coming. But there's no warning with the V2.'

'Evil things they are,' Carmen said and tutted. 'I used to hate the sound of the Doodlebug and I hated it even more when the engine would cut out and then you'd know the thing was on its way down. But the V2s are even more frightening. How can a thousand tons of explosives fall out of the sky so quietly with no warning?'

Winnie cleared her throat and said sternly, 'That's enough talk of bombs, thank you. We're supposed to be discussing Christmas, which is only five days away so we need to get cracking.'

'Sorry, Win,' Rachel said.

'Right, chop chop, let's make a start, and I know I say it every year, but this Christmas is going to be the best Christmas that the Battersea Tavern has ever put on,' Winnie said, and she meant it. She hadn't mentioned anything to the others, but her wishful thinking of a life elsewhere had re-emerged, even more so now that Hitler was sending his most powerful and deadliest weapons to London. So, yes indeed, this Christmas party might be the last one that she would host in the Battersea Tavern. And if it was, Winnie would ensure that it would be one to remember.

Rachel glanced around the table and bit on her bottom lip. She'd been waiting for the right moment to make her announcement and now seemed as good a time as any. Taking a deep breath, she said, 'Erm, before you all go rushing off… there's something I'd like to say.'

Winnie, Carmen, Hilda and Maureen looked at her expectantly.

'Go on then, tell us,' Hilda encouraged.

'You know that little bit of money that Benny's grand-parents gave me to help care for him?'

'Yes,' Winnie said.

'I've bought a stall with it.'

'What sort of stall?' Hilda asked.

'One on wheels. A big, posh barrow, really, I suppose.'

'And what are you going to do with it?' Winnie asked.

'Well, with your permission, I'm going to sell cockles and winkles, outside the pub, and then I can wheel the stall round the back at night. What do you think?'

'I love a winkle, me, with plenty of vinegar,' Hilda smiled, 'I'll be a regular customer.'

'I think it's a smashing idea,' Winnie agreed.

'Aren't you the proper little businesswoman?' Carmen smiled.

'See, the thing is … I wanted a career. I had dreams of becoming a teacher. But Torrie was right. She told me that they'd never allow an unmarried mother to teach children. And then… well… now I've got two kids and to be honest, since, you know, what happened, when I thought I'd lost Martha… I can't stand the idea of her being out of my sight.'

'Yeah, well, that's understandable,' Winnie said.

'I looked at you, Win. You've got your own business, and it inspired me to want to achieve something too. A stall outside is just the ticket and who knows what it might lead to. I want Martha to know that she can do well in life, you know, set a good example.'

'Good for you. I reckon you'll make a good go of it. My customers will love a pint of cockles or winkles. Will you sell whelks, prawns and jellied eels too?'

'Yep, and brown bread an' all… when I can.'

Hilda folded her arms across her chest. 'Well, well, well… I had no idea that my girl was so ambitious and had fancy ideas of becoming a teacher. And now she's going to have her own business. Well done, darling, I'm proud of you.'

'Yeah, maybe the whole *teacher* thing was a bit too ambitious. But I can't wait to show you my stall. It needs doing up a bit, painting mostly, and I'm going to have a sign across the top that reads, *Pick-a-Winkle*. What do you think?'

Winnie threw her hands in the air, enthusing, 'Brilliant! You're a clever girl, Rachel.'

'Thanks. It's good to know that I've got your support. I thought you all might laugh at me. But the thing is, I'm going to need to put in long hours, and I was wondering if—'

'Yes,' Winnie interrupted. 'I can't speak for Carmen, but I'd be happy to help with the children.'

'Me too,' Carmen added.

'And me, when I can,' Hilda agreed.

Martha and Benny came running back into the kitchen, both giggling. Benny was carrying the dog's lead and Cake jumped around him, excited at the prospect of going for a walk.

'Can we take Cake out, Mummy?' Benny asked.

Rachel gulped and gazed lovingly at the boy. He'd called her *Mummy* and it had sounded so natural. 'Yes, but put your coats on, it's a bit nippy outside.'

The children ran back to the bedroom and Rachel turned to the women at the table.

'Did you hear that?'

'Yes, love, we did. Bless his little cotton socks. I'll never forget the first time that Jan called me *Mum*, so I know how you're feeling right now.'

'I won't let him ever forget Torrie, but it was lovely to hear that. And it's good for Martha to have a brother.'

Winnie then suggested, 'I think we need to make a bit more space up here for us all. After Christmas, let's rearrange things a bit.'

'What do you have in mind?' Carmen asked.

'I was thinking that you could come in with me. Then Rachel can have your room. The kids will have their own room and I'll get someone in to put a portioning wall up in the front room so that Maureen can have her own room an' all.'

Carmen nodded. 'Great idea. We hardly use the front room. We're nearly always sat round this table. But if I'm going to be sharing with you, I'd better get meself a pair of earplugs.'

'You cheeky moo,' Winnie laughed.

Rachel, her heart warmed, smiled and placed her hand on Hilda's. 'I'm so lucky. I've got the best family,' she said, thinking, *Please, God, keep them safe.* The fear of a V2 rocket landing on the Battersea Tavern was never far from her mind.

31

Winnie stood at the Christmas table holding a glass of port aloft. 'To our loved and absent friends and family,' she said, thinking of Jan. But there were few sat around her table who hadn't lost someone close in the dreadful war.

She spotted Maureen quickly dash away a tear and knew the woman was thinking about her grandparents. And Rachel, with an enigmatic smile, remembering Torrie. Mrs Sturgess from around the corner had lost two sons oversees and Mr Webber had buried his wife and daughter after a bomb had exploded at the school where his wife had been a dinner lady.

Winnie nodded to Piano Pete, who took his cue and played a cheerful tune. Carmen topped up everyone's glasses, but only half filled them as the pub was low on stocks of alcohol and it was a struggle to find replenishments. The shortages were affecting just about everything now, including booze. And there had been no turkey or goose to carve for lunch, instead they had made do with two joints of slowly cooked mutton.

'It's a fine party, Winnie,' Tommy said, clinking her glass with his own.

'Let's hope that this year is the last we see of rationing, eh. There's a lot of optimism that the war will end in forty-five.'

'I'll drink to that,' Tommy said, clinking her glass again. 'By the way, I've got some good news to share with you soon. I can't say too much about it now, but you'll be pleased with the work that I've been doing.'

'Sounds intriguing. I shall look forward to hearing about it. Can't you even give me a hint?'

Tommy tapped the side of his nose. 'Let's just say that justice is being done.'

Hilda sidled up to the piano and whispered something in Pete's ear. Then Piano Pete, with an unlit roll-up stuck on his bottom lip, began playing a melody, but hit a few wrong notes and had to start again from the beginning. To Winnie's surprise, Hilda began singing along, and beautiful it was too! Everyone stopped talking and turned to look and listen to Hilda as she crooned 'Have Yourself a Merry Little Christmas', a song sung by Judy Garland from a film that had been released that year.

Rachel swayed and hummed along. Maureen sat with her head cocked to one side and her eyes closed. Carmen rested her chin on her hands and smiled. The words, so delicately sang by Hilda, felt so appropriate and touched every person in the pub: *From now on our troubles will be out of sight*. Winnie hoped so.

When Hilda had finished the song, the children rushed over and hugged her as the pub broke into a round of applause.

'I didn't know you could sing like that,' Winnie called.

'Well, if you want an entertainer, you know who to ask,' Hilda joked.

Bill called over the din, 'There's someone knocking on the door.'

'Let 'em, in, love, the more, the merrier,' Winnie answered.

Her jaw dropped open when a world-beaten looking soldier ambled in, his khaki uniform looked tired, as did his gaunt face.

'Terry!' she exclaimed and leapt to her feet, rushing over to embrace him.

Terry fell into her arms and squeezed her so tightly that she could hardly breathe.

'What on earth are you doing here?' she asked.

'I got your letter,' he said sadly. 'I've been travelling for nearly a week. I'm only here for two days and then I've got to return, but not to the front line.'

Winnie had gone against her daughter's last wishes and had written to Terry to inform him of Jan's death. She'd felt it was the right and proper thing to do and Carmen, Hilda and Rachel had agreed.

'Come and sit down, love, you must be knackered. Carmen, get Terry a plate of food. Rachel, fetch him a drink.'

Terry took his kitbag off his shoulder and placed it on the floor. 'Actually, Winnie, if it's all the same to you, can we go upstairs for a while?'

Winnie nodded, knowing exactly what Terry wanted: the letter that Jan had written him. She had one too, Carmen had handed it to her after Jan's funeral. But Winnie hadn't been able to open it. Instead, she'd placed it in a drawer with Terry's letter and had decided that they would read them together.

Trudging wearily up the stairs, Terry said, 'I shouldn't be here, Winnie. My captain managed to get me on a special envoy with some returning men from Africa.'

349

'What did you mean about not going back to the front line?'

'I've been put on light duties. I got shot, Winnie, in my back. The bullet is lodged near my spine. It could shift at any time and cause me a right lot of damage.'

'Good grief, Terry, why didn't you write and tell me?'

'You had enough to deal with.'

'Can't the doctors take the bullet out?'

'Possibly, but it needs to be done by a specialist.'

'Blimey, that's a bit of a worry. Sit down, love, I'll get you a drink. You will get it seen to, won't you?'

'Yeah, I hope so.'

Winnie poured Terry a bottle of beer and then she went to her room and collected the letters, one for Terry and one for her, in the identical special envelopes that Rachel had been sent out to buy.

She poured the tea and sat opposite Terry, handing him the letter, saying softly, 'She loved you very much, Terry.'

Terry peered at the envelope, his eyes welling with tears. 'I should have been here for her.'

'That's not what she wanted and I can understand why. It wasn't nice to see her dying, love. She wanted to save you from it.'

'You've got a letter too?'

'Yes. I've not read it. I'm not sure that I can.'

'We'll do it together,' Terry said and squeezed her hand.

Winnie's hands trembled as she pulled the note from the envelope. Seeing Jan's spoken words written in black ink on the white embossed paper was almost like hearing her voice again. Tears pricked her eyes and then streamed down her face as she read the words of love.

Dearest Mum,

I'm leaving this world soon, but I want you to know that I'll be all right. And if I can, once I'm gone, I'll try to let you know that I'm still there with you and I always will be.

You saved me, Mum. You gave me a home, a life and unconditional love. I know that you were very proud of me, but I am all that I am because of your love. You believed in me and you showed me how to believe in myself. Your strength gave me courage. Your words inspired me and your arms comforted me. Thank you, Mum, for always supporting me and for making my life the best that it could be.

I hope you're not too sad. The only part of dying that scares me is the thought of the pain for those left behind; for you and Terry. I'm so sorry that I've put you through this, but please, for my sake, grieve but don't dwell on my death. Instead, remember the special and happy times.

I love you.

Listen for me. Watch for me. I'll be there with you.

Your loving daughter,

Jan xxx

Winnie swallowed hard and looked over to Terry, who was silently crying too.

'As sad as this is, as heartbreaking as it feels ... to read my girl's words, and on Christmas Day, well, it's just about the most special and cherished gift ever.'

Terry shook his head. 'I wish that bullet in me back had killed me and then I'd be with her.'

'I know how you feel, love, but that's not what Jan would have wanted. She told you to live your life to the full. I hope you're not going to let her down?'

Terry shrugged. 'It hurts, Winnie, it hurts so bloody much. I wish that I could see her just one more time.'

'I know, love, me an' all. I wish it every day.'

As Terry carefully slipped his letter back into the envelope, Winnie glanced out of the window at the light flurry of snow that was falling.

'Bugger me,' she said, getting up from the table and going to the window.

'What?' Terry asked.

'There's a butterfly flapping at the window. Look, and at this time of the year, that's extraordinary!'

Terry didn't make any response; he was clearly too wrapped up in his own grief.

But as the colourful and delicate wings of the butterfly flitted in front of Winnie, she smiled through the glass and whispered, 'Hello, Jan.'

Her shattered heart felt as though just one of the tiny pieces had been put back together.

Clinton's broken arm had healed well, but, thanks to Brancher and a warden who was willing to turn a blind eye, Clinton now had two broken ribs, as well as half an ear and two teeth missing. When he'd first set eyes on Brancher in the prison, he couldn't believe his own misfortune, and Brancher had made it clear that he was out to get him. At least Clinton had found some solace in God. Though he wasn't much in the mood for celebrating Christmas and didn't feel that he had much to thank the Lord for. Nonetheless, he'd gone along to the prison church service, if only to get out of his cell for an hour.

As the prisoners were led back to their cells, the chaplain

pulled Clinton to one side and handed him a book of psalms. 'Read psalm one hundred and nineteen. It has a special meaning.'

Clinton had no idea why the chaplain had singled him out, or instructed him what to read, but he accepted the book and thanked the man of God.

Once back in his cold and damp cell, he sat on the hard bed and turned the pages to the specific psalm. It was the longest of all the psalms, starting with *Blessed are those whose ways are blameless.* Clinton rolled his eyes. He was blameless for the crime that he was serving time for, but he certainly didn't feel blessed. He read the psalm three times until his eyelids began to feel heavy. Laying back, the words went around and around in his head. He had tried to live by God's word and to be a good person, but he'd let himself and the Lord down when he'd stolen money from the post office in Scotland. This was his penance and he accepted it. He vowed to himself and to God that he'd never commit a crime again.

Thoughts of a white, sandy beach and a red sun setting over a warm ocean drifted into his mind. He could feel himself swaying lazily in a hammock and he could see his mother's smile. His mouth watered at the memory of the taste of a suckling pig that his mother had roasted under the ground. It was a rare treat in their poor household, but even the thought of rice and beans made his mouth salivate.

As sleep eventually came, Clinton's dreams were shattered when he realised that when he awoke he'd still be incarcerated in the prison and doubted that he'd ever see his home country again. His only comfort came from knowing that at least Alberto was still sending money home that would help to keep his little sister alive.

32

Rachel stood back and admired her work. She'd spent days painting the *Pick-a-Winkle* stall and it now looked bright and cheerful. It was much heavier than she'd expected and she had soon realised that wheeling it to and from the back of the pub wasn't going to be an easy task. *I'll have muscles like an Irish navvy*, she thought, flexing her biceps.

Maureen came out of the back door and handed her a cup of beef broth. 'Wow, that looks like a shiny new button,' she said admiringly.

'Thanks. I'm hoping the rain leaves off until the paint has dried,' Rachel said, looking up at the ominous grey clouds above.

'I had a letter from Stephen today,' Maureen smiled. 'He said to give you his regards.'

'That was nice of him.'

'I think he's sweet on you.'

'I doubt it. There aren't many blokes who'd lumber themselves with a woman with two kids. He's a nice fella, your brother, but he's just being polite.'

'What are you on about? You're a catch.'

'Leave off, Maureen.'

'No, I'm serious. Look at you, you're an attractive woman and now you've got your own business too. I'd be ever so proud to call you my sister-in-law.'

Rachel baulked. 'Hey, slow down, girl. Your brother sends me his regards and now you're marrying us off,' she laughed.

'Would you consider it?'

'No,' Rachel blurted, feeling herself blush. She had to admit to herself that she found Stephen attractive, but men, dating and marriage were out of the question. 'Look, nothing against your brother, but I'm really not interested in getting involved with a fella.'

'I understand, I'm the same. I'm dreading the day when Brancher gets out of prison.'

'That judge was a bit too lenient. Brancher should have got a much longer sentence than eighteen months, especially for headbutting a copper.'

Maureen sighed. 'I agree, but the prisons are becoming overcrowded. There's been some harsh sentences handed down for looting and loads of people have taken advantage of the blackouts, but then come unstuck with the law.'

'Yeah, I suppose so, but thank gawd we can have the lights back on now. It was lovely to see the stained-glass windows in the church lit up and I feel much safer after dark.'

'Yeah, me an' all. Though I don't think I'll be feeling very safe when Brancher gets out.'

'Try not to worry, Maureen. We'll all look after you.'

'I know, thanks. I don't know what I would have done without you all. And I'll be eternally grateful to you and Carmen for going to my house and collecting my things, especially my granddad's tankard.'

'You're welcome and, I must say, you're like a different person to the woman who first turned up here. You've got your confidence back. It's lovely to see.'

Carmen popped her head through the back door. 'Ah, there you are, Maureen. Tommy's here, he'd like a word.'

Maureen threw Rachel an anxious look and asked, 'Will you come with me?'

'Of course,' Rachel answered, wiping paint from her hands onto an old rag.

She followed Maureen upstairs and into the kitchen, where Tommy, in his uniform, was sitting at the table with a cup of tea.

'Wait until you hear this,' Winnie said, smiling widely.

Rachel stood near the sink as Maureen pulled out a seat at the table and sat down.

'I've got some good news for you, Maureen,' Tommy announced. 'Your husband will be going to court again, charged with the robbery and assault on the nightwatchman at the distillery and the assault on one of my men during the robbery of the jewellery shop. I'll expect that his sentence will be lengthened by quite some time.'

'I-I-I don't understand?'

'Unfortunately for Brancher, he finds it difficult to keep his mouth shut and was heard boasting about his crimes. It seems that he was rather proud of what him and his mates had got away with. Also, unfortunately for him, he was very vocal and named the other culprits. It was brought to my attention, so I dragged in his mates and they sang like canaries, putting Brancher in the frame for the crimes.'

'Will I have to go to court?' Maureen asked anxiously.

'No, Maureen, we have all the evidence we need without

you being called as a witness. Anyway, you'll be protected from having to go to court by law, Spousal Privilege.'

'Thank goodness. How long will he get?'

'I'm not a judge, I couldn't say, but I reckon a good seven to twelve years.'

Rachel stepped forward and asked, 'What about Clinton? If Brancher is being charged with the crime at the distillery, surely Clinton will be released?'

'Yes, Rachel, that's a very good point and, from what I know, Clinton's release is imminent.'

'And so it should be!' Winnie piped up. 'We all knew that Clinton didn't rob that distillery.'

'That's right,' Rachel agreed. 'Alberto was a swine, but neither him nor Clinton deserved to be arrested for a crime that they didn't commit.'

'Excuse me,' Maureen mumbled. She shoved her seat back and fled from the room.

'What's wrong with her?' Tommy asked, bewildered.

'I'll see to her,' Rachel replied and hurried after Maureen.

The bathroom door was closed, so Rachel gently tapped on it and asked, 'Are you in there, Maureen?'

'Yes.'

'Are you all right?'

'I think so,' Maureen answered, pulling open the door.

Rachel could see that Maureen's face was wet with tears. 'You don't look all right. I thought you'd be pleased to hear that Brancher will be going down for many years.'

'I am ... it's such a relief ... but I feel so guilty that Clinton has spent all this time locked away.'

'Come on, cheer up, it's not your fault and you heard

Tommy; Clinton will be a free man soon. Did you and him … did you, erm, get close?'

'He was a good friend when I needed one. I spent a day with him once. Of course, Brancher never knew. I liked Clinton, but I was … still am, a married woman.'

A loud clap of thunder roared outside. 'Oh flippin' 'ell, my stall,' Rachel said, alarmed, hoping that the paint had dried and that the rain wouldn't ruin her hard work. She dashed down the stairs and out of the back door, relieved to find that the clouds above were keeping hold of their water.

Surveying her brightly coloured stall, she admired the paintings that she'd done of Martha's and Benny's smiling faces, one on each side. She thought about Maureen, how the woman had almost been destroyed by her husband and was only just regaining some of her confidence. She thought of Torrie too, her life dedicated to her husband, child and her home. Winnie had once been reliant on Mr Berry and Carmen had been left destitute when Harry had died. Rachel took a step back from her barrow and folded her arms across her chest, beaming with pride. This was a venture of her own doing. She'd never be reliant on a man. She had proved to herself that was capable of making her own way in life and she was determined to make it a success, not just for her but also for her two children.

The cell door opened and a prison warden motioned to Clinton, ordering him, 'Get out.'

Clinton winced, his ribs hurting, as he pushed himself to his feet. 'I don't understand?'

'You heard. You're free to leave.'

'Leave where?'

'This shithole. You're a free man. You've got two minutes to collect your stuff.'

Clinton stared at the pale-faced, balding man, wondering if this was some sort of cruel joke.

'Are you stupid? Get your stuff. You're leaving here,' the guard reiterated.

Snapping into action, Clinton glanced at his few belongings and quickly gathered the Bible and the book of psalms before standing in front of the guard.

'Is that it?' the warden asked, looking over Clinton's shoulder.

'It's all I need.'

'Come on then.'

Clinton kept his head down as he was led through the prison. Insults from fellow prisoners were shouted at him, metal cups clanged on metal bars, but someone called, 'Good luck.' He still couldn't believe that he was going to be freed and was convinced that there must be some sort of mistake.

After signing some papers, he was handed a parcel containing the clothes he'd arrived in. He was shown to a room where he could change, and then he gladly handed back the prison overalls. His own clothes felt strange and everything still felt unreal.

'This way,' the guard said, leading him through several locked doors and then across a yard until they reached a huge set of locked gates.

Clinton knew that liberty lay behind them and finally started to believe that he was about to step into his freedom.

'You've got the chaplain to thank for this,' the guard said. 'He overheard Brancher Fanning talking about the robberies and pushed for an investigation. He always felt that you were an innocent man.'

'Can you t'ank him for me?'

The guard didn't reply and, after several checks, a smaller door within one of the large ones was opened and Clinton took a last glance behind before stepping outside.

'You can thank him yourself,' the guard said, nodding to where the chaplain was standing.

As Clinton walked towards the chaplain, he heard the door close behind him and was grateful that he'd never again hear that sound.

'I only have a bicycle, so I'm afraid I can't offer you a lift anywhere.'

'T'ank you, sir. I understand that you helped to get me out of prison.'

'No need for thanks, young man. God works in mysterious ways. He could see that your heart is pure. And I'm pleased to see that you brought with you the books that I gave you.'

'Yes. They have kept me in good faith, sir.'

'Where will you go now?'

'Home, sir.'

'To British Honduras?'

'No, to Battersea.'

'Well, God bless and keep safe.'

'T'ank you, sir, t'ank you for everyt'ing.'

As Clinton made his way to Battersea, he thought the grass had never looked greener, nor the air smelled fresher. Even if rain were to fall from the grey clouds overhead, he knew that he'd enjoy the taste of it on his tongue. His step was light and speedy, and he soon arrived at his old lodgings.

With no key, he sat on the step and waited for Alberto to arrive home from work.

To while away the time, Clinton looked again at the psalm that the chaplain had told him to read and now the words made sense. *I will walk about in freedom.* He was! He was free, and he didn't have to fear running into Brancher.

Another thought crossed his mind, something that he'd thought about a thousand times since walking out of the prison; should he pay Maureen a visit? And would she be welcoming? There was only one way to find out, Clinton thought and, leaping to his feet, he eagerly made his way to the Battersea Tavern. He appreciated every second of how wonderful it felt to be free, and even his ribs didn't seem to hurt so much now.

33

Winnie kept one eye on her customers and the other on Maureen. Carmen had gone to Balham to visit her daughter, so Maureen was working behind the bar. Though Winnie thought the word *working* could be used loosely. Granted, she had just received some big news from Tommy, but Winnie couldn't understand why Maureen looked so sad and distracted. She'd have expected the woman to be singing with joy.

The door swung open and through the smoky haze that lingered midway in the air, Winnie saw Clinton walk in. With a smile on his face and a spring in his step, his happiness was undeniable and a pleasure to see.

Tommy, on his way out of the pub, stood in front of Clinton with his arm outstretched. 'Let me shake your hand, laddie. I sincerely apologise on behalf of the Metropolitan Police, our King and Great Britain. It was a travesty that you were put behind bars. I'm glad to see that the right man is now serving time and you're free.'

'Er, t'ank you, sir.'

'And you've no need to fear Brancher Fanning. He will be spending a long time in prison. Though looking at the state of you, I reckon you've already had a run-in with him.'

'Yes, sir, I did.'

'Onwards and upwards, lad, onwards and upwards.'

Tommy waved goodbye and Clinton came to the bar.

'Hello, Mrs Berry,' he smiled.

Winnie could see that he'd had a couple of his teeth knocked out. She guessed that he'd had a hard time in prison, singled out because of his dark skin. 'You're a sight for sore eyes, love. It's really good to see you. Would you like your usual?'

'I, erm, haven't come in for a drink,' he answered sheepishly.

Winnie guessed that his pockets were empty, but she also knew exactly what he'd come in for. 'Go and sit yourself down. Maureen will bring you a drink, on the house.' She glanced over at Maureen, who was gawping at Clinton and looking uneasy. 'And she'll keep you company for a while. After all, she's not much bloomin' use behind the bar today.'

'T'ank you, Mrs Berry,' Clinton smiled, keeping his eyes on Maureen.

'Oi, Maureen,' Winnie said, her voice slightly raised. 'Get Clinton and yourself a drink. You can have the rest of the afternoon off.'

'But ... I'm, erm, supposed to be working.'

'You're like a tit in a trance, love. But don't worry, I'll have you working doubly hard tomorrow,' Winnie said with a chuckle. *Tit in a trance* had been one of Len's favourite sayings. She looked round to his empty stool at the end of the bar, still half expecting to see his craggy face. He would have been so pleased about Brancher being put away for a long time. Winnie peered up to the gap in the shelf where Len's tankard had always sat, and whispered, 'Don't worry, Len. I'll look after your Maureen. She's part of the family now.'

Awash with guilt, Maureen couldn't meet Clinton in the eyes. She sat beside him and murmured how sorry she was.

'It wasn't your fault, Maureen, don't be sorry.'

Clinton placed his hand over hers, but she quickly pulled away. She knew that Brancher was locked in Wandsworth Prison, but she couldn't shake the feeling that he might walk in at any moment and catch her sitting with Clinton. Years of her husband controlling her couldn't be overcome in only a few months. Even with the clothes she chose to wear each morning, her brain still thought, *What would Brancher think? Would he approve?*

'Have you seen anyt'ing of Alberto?' Clinton asked.

'No, he's not been brave or stupid enough to come in here since Rachel caught him out.'

'I hope he's still at the lodgings and working at the power station, but you never know with Alberto, he tends to go where the wind takes him ... or a pretty face.'

'But didn't he promise to send money to your family?'

'Yes, and he will keep his word about that, I know he will. Are you living here now?'

'Yes. Winnie very kindly took me in,' Maureen replied, looking down at the table. She wouldn't mention the fact that Sergeant Bradbury had brought her here because she'd attempted to throw herself off of a bridge. 'What will you do, now that you're a free man?'

'Look for work. But being in prison gave me time to t'ink

and I found God again. I'd like to visit the local church and become part of the congregation. Would you come with me?'

'Oh, I don't think so ... I'm not religious or nothing like that.'

'Maybe if you came to church with me, you might hear the good Lord's voice.'

'I doubt it,' Maureen replied, shaking her head. She believed that God was for good people and that she was bad. Well, at least, she'd done bad things. Things that she was deeply ashamed of. The horrific memory of tugging at the dead woman's finger to remove her wedding ring flashed through her mind. She'd never forgive herself for allowing Brancher to make her do it, so she couldn't expect God to forgive her either.

'Do you know what else I t'ought about a lot while in prison?'

Maureen shook her head.

'You,' Clinton smiled, revealing his missing teeth.

'You shouldn't have ... I'm not worth wasting time on.'

'Yes, you are. I kept t'inking about the day we spent together. Do you ever t'ink about it?'

Again, Maureen looked at the table. She shrugged. 'Sometimes, I suppose.'

'It's going to take me some time to get back on my feet. But once I've found a job, will you consider allowing me to court you?'

Maureen's lips pursed as she stared at her drink, eventually replying, 'I don't think so, Clinton.'

'You don't have to worry about Brancher anymore.'

'I know ... but he's still in here,' she spat, jabbing her finger at her temple. 'I'm not like other women ... I'm damaged.'

'Let me help to fix you.'

'I have to go.'

As Maureen rose to her feet, Clinton asked, 'Can I see you again?'

Her eyes finally met his and she felt herself melting into them. 'Maybe … No … Oh, I don't know. I don't think that I'm ready for this.'

'It's fine, Maureen. I'll be patient. I can wait until you are ready. Perhaps we can still be friends?'

She shrugged again, saying, 'I really have to go.'

Dashing through the bar and then upstairs, Maureen ran into the bathroom, closed the door and stood over the sink. She splashed cold water on her face, and then dabbed her cheeks with a towel while she looked at her reflection in the mirror. She studied with contempt her dull complexion, lank mousy hair and plain features; as Brancher had often told her, she was ugly. And she felt ugly inside too.

She could put on an act around Winnie, Carmen, Rachel and Hilda. She had them convinced that she was doing well and gaining confidence. But she couldn't fool herself. Deep within, she knew that Brancher would always have a hold on her and she would always be a stupid, useless cow. But hearing that he was going to be in prison for many years had sent a shockwave through Maureen, and now she was beginning to doubt that she could cope without him.

34

Three days later, Rachel stood behind her shellfish stall, stamping her feet to put some feeling back into her numb toes and blowing on her hands to warm them. But she was happy to brave the cold weather in order to sell her wares. Business had been remarkably good so far – in fact, better than she'd anticipated.

An old fella came out of the pub and nodded his head, tugging his flat cap at Rachel.

'Pint of prawns to take home with you?' she called, 'Or how about a tub of winkles smothered in malt vinegar. Makes your mouth water, don't it?'

'Go on then,' the old chap answered with a gummy smile. 'I'll have a pint of prawns. You could sell snow to an Eskimo.'

'Or sand to an Arab,' Rachel laughed.

'I'll have some of those jellied eels too. That'll do nicely for me supper tonight.'

As the fella walked off with his purchases, Winnie came out of the pub, pulling her cardigan around herself. 'Cor blimey, it's taters out here. How are you getting on, love?'

'I'm fine, Win, you don't need to check on me every ten minutes.'

'I can't help it. I don't like to think of you all alone out here in the cold. Why don't you bring your stock inside and sell it over the bar? You'll be a lot warmer.'

'Thanks, Win, but I'd miss a lot of passing trade. Anyway, the cold doesn't bother me ... it wouldn't feel like *my* business if I was working from your pub.'

'I can see where Martha gets her stubbornness from,' Winnie chortled, 'but I admire you.'

'Thanks, Win. Are Martha and Benny all right?'

'Yes, as far as I know. Maureen is upstairs watching them. Last time I checked, she was making a right old mess, covering their hands in paint and pressing them onto old newspapers. The kids seem to be enjoying it though. Right, bugger this cold, I'm going back inside. Good luck, love.'

Five minutes later, Rachel saw two middle-aged women coming along, both with knitted cloche hats on and over-sized, scratchy-looking wool coats. 'Winkles, whelks, prawns, crayfish tails, jellied eels ... any of it take your fancy?'

The women stopped in front of the stall, oohing and ahhing. 'Oh, I say, Gerty, I haven't had a winkle in ages.'

'Me neither, Pat, not since my old man put his back out,' Gerty answered, and then both women roared with laughter.

Rachel laughed at the innuendo too. She'd heard plenty of jokes about winkles over the past couple of days, yet surprisingly, it was mostly her women customers who had the dirty minds. She could see Winnie out of the corner of her eye, standing in the pub doorway being nosey.

Gerty looked from one bowl to another, smacking her lips together. 'I'll have half a pint of winkles and half of cockles, to take home. I've got a special brooch indoors that me mum gave me, specially for picking winkles. It'll be lovely to use it, sat in front of the fire and warming me cockles.'

Both women laughed again.

'I'll have the same, and half a pint of prawns too. Cor, my girls are in for a treat tonight.'

'I've not seen you here before. Are you permanent?' Gerty asked.

'Yes, I opened two days ago,' Rachel answered proudly.

'You'll do well here. I'll let all the girls down the knitting club know, and I'll get my old man to spread the word at the working man's club. This is just what we need here, and all the more so now that Mr Coggin's shop has gone.'

'Thank you, I'd appreciate that.'

Rachel didn't mind not spending as much time with the children. Her mind was at peace because she knew where they were and that they were close by. She didn't care that she was stiff with cold, or that she smelled fishy. She wasn't bothered that she had to get up at the crack of dawn to buy her goods, or that by the end of the day her feet ached and she was dog-tired. As far as she was concerned, it was all worth it. She was her own boss, earning her own money, and she already had ideas for expanding the business.

'I know you're there,' she called to Winnie.

'No, I'm not,' Winnie shouted back.

Rachel smiled, calling, 'I want to say a big thank you to you for being such a good example of a successful business-woman. Now go inside and get out of the cold, you mad moo.'

★

Winnie went back into the warmth of her pub, relieved to be out of the cold and happy to see that Rachel was doing well. She'd worried that the stall wouldn't get enough customers, especially as it was bitterly cold outside, but Rachel looked to be making it successful. She shouldn't have fretted. After all, the girl was bright and wasn't afraid of hard work.

Winnie chuckled to herself; she wouldn't be surprised if Rachel soon had a string of *Pick-a-Winkle* stalls all over the borough. It was comforting for Winnie to know that if she decided to move away, Rachel had set herself up with a good business and could take care of herself and the children. Though Winnie hoped that wherever she went, her family would come too.

She glanced around, wondering where Carmen was, and saw that Piano Pete was stood behind the bar with his customary roll-up stuck on his bottom lip.

He rolled his eyes at Winnie and said, 'There was a right commotion upstairs. Carmen went to sort it out.'

'What sort of commotion?'

'Dunno. Maureen was screaming.'

Winnie's heart thumped harder and faster as she hurried upstairs. The sound of Martha bawling reached her ears, and then she heard Benny coughing.

'What's going on?' she demanded as she burst into the front room and looked around.

Maureen was sat on the sofa with her face in her hands, apologising repeatedly. Carmen was patting Benny's back and Martha looked purple in the face from howling.

'Benny couldn't breathe,' Martha cried. 'I thought he was going to die.'

'Well he didn't, Martha, he's fine, so stop crying,' Carmen ordered. 'It's all right, Win, there was just a bit of an accident.'

'It was my fault,' Maureen sobbed. 'I'm sorry, I was supposed to be watching them. I'm useless ... a stupid, useless cow.'

'Pull yourself together, Maureen, and get Benny a glass of water,' Carmen snapped. Winnie looked at her for an explanation and Carmen explained, 'Benny swallowed a button. It got lodged in his throat. But it's out now and I think we all NEED TO CALM DOWN!'

Carmen's raised voice made Maureen cry harder, Benny's bottom lip wobble and Martha howl louder.

Winnie could see that she needed to take control of the situation. 'Maureen, go and wash your face and get a grip of yourself because you're upsetting the children. Benny, show me the button ... we'll give it a good telling-off, and Martha, come here and give your old nan a big cuddle.'

Maureen scampered out of the room.

Carmen sucked in a long breath. 'Sorry about shouting. It was just bedlam in here.'

'I know, I wondered what I'd walked in on,' Winnie said, wrapping her arms around Martha, who had quietened down.

'This is the button,' Benny said, holding a large, blue-painted wooden button on the palm of his small hand.

Winnie wagged her finger at the button, saying sternly, 'You naughty button! I'm going to spank your backside.'

Benny laughed. 'A button hasn't got a backside.'

'All right, then I shall spank the back of its legs,' Winnie said, crossly.

Martha laughed too. 'Nanny, a button doesn't have legs.'

Humour had done the trick. Calm had been restored.

'I'll get back downstairs,' Carmen whispered.

'Hang on a minute,' Winnie said, and then she told the children to go to their room. Once alone with Carmen, she quietly asked, 'How did Benny get a button stuck in his throat?'

'I'm not sure, you'll have to ask Maureen. When I came up, Benny's lips were turning blue and Maureen was screaming and pulling on her hair.'

'What, she didn't do anything to get the button out of his throat?' Winnie asked incredulously.

'Not that I saw. I picked him up and laid him across my lap. Two slaps on his back and the button shot out of his mouth. You saw for yourself, he's as right as rain, no harm done.'

'I hope Rachel sees it that way. You know how protective she is over the kids and they are bound to tell her what happened.'

Carmen went back down to the pub and Winnie looked around the room. She saw a notepad and pencil on the table next to the armchair. Picking it up, her brow creased as she read the scribbled words.

Dear Brancher,

I don't suppose that you was expecting to hear from me and I hope you don't mind me writing to you.

I've been thinking a lot about our lives together and about you. Once, a long time ago, we used to be happy together. I miss that. I know it's my fault that things started going wrong with our marriage. I'm useless, a stupid cow. If I'd been a better wife, you wouldn't have had to keep having a go at me. I'm sorry.

Being away from you has showed me how useless I really

am. It's so hard to live without you. I can't think for myself.
I don't know what I'm supposed to think. I need you, I can
see that now, and I should never have run away like I did. I
wish

The letter was unfinished but Winnie was shocked and had read enough to know that Maureen needed help, though she wasn't sure how to support the woman.

An idea struck her. She'd call a meeting with Carmen, Rachel and Hilda. Between them, Winnie was sure that they could come up with something. And in the meantime, just in case Maureen tried to end her life again, she'd be keeping a very close eye on her.

35

On Saturday morning, Winnie had sent Maureen to the Northcote Road market with an extensive shopping list, the plan being that she'd be out for hours. She had then asked the others to join her at the kitchen table.

Winnie had barely got started, saying she worried about Maureen's state of mind, when Rachel scraped her chair back.

'I'm sorry, Win, but I haven't got time for this. I feel sorry for her, I do, but I've got a stall to open. Whatever you three decide, I'm telling you this much: Maureen is not looking after my children again. Winnie, Carmen, you'll have to take turns behind the bar and watching the kids.'

' 'Ark at her,' Winnie said. 'She's running her own business and now giving out her orders to *us*.'

'Keeping an eye on the kids, isn't a problem, is it? Only, when I told you about setting up my stall, you all agreed that you'd help with Martha and Benny. And they'll be starting school soon.'

'No, love, it's not a problem. In fact, it's a pleasure. And you're quite right. Me and Carmen can take it in turns and

Maureen can stay behind the bar. There, sorted, now go and open up your stall.'

Rachel said her thanks and hurried away, leaving Winnie taken aback by Rachel's lack of empathy for Maureen. But, she reasoned, the girl was busy with making a success of her business and didn't have time to be dealing with Maureen's problems too.

'I think we need to make Maureen feel worthwhile,' Carmen said thoughtfully. 'Brancher's worn her down so much, she doesn't have any faith in herself.'

'I agree, love, but how do we make her feel useful again?'

'I know that feeling,' Hilda said. 'Believe you me, I've been there.'

'What made you feel better about yourself?' Winnie asked.

'Packing in the drink, for one. But that aside, I think Maureen needs some responsibility. Sewing helps me. I take pride in my work and when I've made a nice outfit or done a good repair on the soldiers' uniforms, I feel that I've achieved something.'

'Yes, I can see your point. I know that my Jan got a lot out of sewing with you, it did her the world of good.'

'How would you feel about Maureen using Jan's sewing machine?' Carmen asked gently.

Winnie felt a pain like a hot poker stabbing through her guts and up into her heart. She didn't think she could bear seeing Maureen sat at Jan's sewing machine, but then Martha came trotting into the kitchen.

'Look, Nanny ... we made you a picture.'

Winnie smiled down at her granddaughter's angelic smile as she took the picture from her small hands. Unfolding the paper, she blinked hard in amazement at the colourful butterfly. Tears stung her eyes that she managed to hold back. 'Thank you, love, it's beautiful. I'll pin it on my wardrobe door and then I can look at it every morning. How about you and Benny make Nanna Hilda a picture too.'

'Oh, yes please,' Hilda encouraged. 'And then after that, get your coats, hats, gloves and scarves because we'll take Cake to Battersea Park.'

As Martha skipped off happily, Winnie looked at the picture again, a butterfly; Jan was there with her, she could feel her, just as Jan had said that she would be.

'What do you think then, Win? Would it be all right for Maureen to use Jan's machine?' Hilda probed.

'Yes, it's what Jan would have wanted,' Winnie answered resolutely.

'Great. If she's unsure about using it, I'd be happy to give her a few pointers,' Hilda offered.

Carmen clicked her finger, as if just remembering something. 'I've got some material in a box under my bed that she's welcome to.'

'Good. To be honest, Maureen isn't really cut out for bar work, so once the kids are at school, she can sew away to her heart's content. I think it's a smashing idea, Hilda. It will give her a purpose, especially if she can sell any dresses she makes to Flo and Bill, just like Jan did.'

It was a small step, but Winnie believed that if they bolstered Maureen up and gave her a purpose, it might help to restore some self-worth in the girl.

Maureen was pleased that she'd managed to purchase everything that was on Winnie's shopping list, though the seven pounds of potatoes in the bag that she carried in her left hand were beginning to feel heavy. Maureen's feeling of satisfaction at getting something right for a change was short-lived as, once again, the image of Benny struggling for breath flashed through her mind. She hated herself for just standing there in panic instead of acting. Thankfully, Carmen had saved the day and Benny's life. As Maureen trudged through the market, laden with shopping, she shook her head. She'd never have forgiven herself if Benny had come to any harm. And she wasn't convinced that Rachel had accepted her apology.

She'd only taken her eyes off the children for a few minutes, but there was no excuse. She should have been watching them, not writing a letter to Brancher. Maureen cringed. When she'd gone back into the front room, the notepad with her half-written letter had gone. She knew that Winnie had found it and must be disgusted with her. If only she could turn back time, but once again, Maureen knew she had messed up. *Stupid, useless cow.* It was true, but Brancher's words still stung.

In a world of her own, a man's hollering voice pierced her thoughts.

'STOP ... THIEF!'

Maureen turned around to see a lanky, young man charging towards her, an older fella giving chase.

The older fella yelled again, 'Stop that man ... Thief!'

As the thief went to dodge her, Maureen acted instinctively. She swung the bag of potatoes round and clunked the bloke in the ribs. He fell sideways, the blow knocking him clean off his feet, and the bag of potatoes split open, spilling everywhere.

While the man lay on the ground, groaning and dazed, with potatoes scattered around him, Maureen saw that he'd dropped a purse. In case he managed to get back onto his feet, she quickly grabbed at it and held the purse securely to her chest.

The older fella caught up, and holding onto his sides as he tried to catch his breath, he looked at Maureen bemused. 'Well done,' he grinned. 'I've never seen nothing like that before!'

The costermongers and shoppers began to applaud. Maureen's eyes flitted around and she realised that they were clapping her, cheering too.

The older fella placed his booted foot on the thief, pinning him to the ground, and said to Maureen, 'Cor, that was a knockout and an 'alf. He deserves everything he gets. The thieving low-life pinched an old woman's purse.'

'It's here,' Maureen said, holding it out.

'You keep hold of it, give it to the police. 'Ere they come, a bit late, mind, you've already done their job for 'em.'

A couple of women who'd seen everything started to collect the spilled potatoes for Maureen, but a costermonger from the fruit and veg stall approached and handed her a cloth bag. 'Spuds. You'll be needing these, especially if your old man gives you any jip. You can whack him round his swede with 'em.'

Maureen smiled, embarrassed. 'Thank you.'

When the two policemen came through the crowd, Maureen recognised Sergeant Bradbury. The old man told them what had happened and as the copper arrested the thief, Sergeant Bradbury turned to Maureen.

'Superb work, Maureen. That was very brave of you.'

Maureen shrugged.

'Are you on your way home?'

'Yes.'

'I'll catch you up.'

As Maureen walked through the market, the applauds followed her. She could feel herself blushing and looked up from the ground every now and then to offer an uncomfortable smile.

Ten minutes later, Sergeant Bradbury walked beside her. 'The thief has been taken to the station. Well done, Maureen, I mean it, that was a quick thinking and a courageous thing that you did back there.'

'Not really. I wasn't thinking … I just did it. I'm not quick thinking and I'm certainly not courageous.'

'Give me them bags and stop undermining yourself.'

Sergeant Bradbury seemed to know everyone in Battersea. Almost each person that they passed said hello to him.

When they arrived back at the Battersea Tavern, he walked in behind Maureen and announced, 'This woman is a hero.'

'Stop it,' Maureen hissed, lowering her head.

'What's she done?' Winnie asked.

Sergeant Bradbury spoke loudly enough that everyone in the pub could hear. 'She single-handedly stopped a thief in his tracks, enabling us to arrest him.'

'Oh, I say, Maureen,' said Carmen, her eyebrows raised in surprise. 'How did you manage that?'

'She knocked him over with a bag of spuds. Potatoes everywhere, there was.'

'You never did!' Winnie exclaimed.

Maureen gulped. 'Your potatoes are fine, I was given some new ones.'

'I'm not worried about me spuds, love. I'm more worried

about you … are you all right? You wasn't hurt or nothing? Did someone try to rob you?'

'No, no, nothing like that and, yes, I'm fine, thank you.'

'You look a bit shaken. I'll get you a brandy.'

'No, really, I don't need one, thank you.'

'A cup of tea then. Come on, out the back, the pair of you, I want to hear all the details.'

Maureen followed Winnie as she bustled through to the back kitchen, and Carmen took the shopping bags from Tommy. As the kettle boiled, Maureen sat at the table and Tommy relayed the morning's events.

'Good grief, Maureen,' Winnie said, 'That was ever such a brave thing to do!'

Maureen shook her head. She didn't feel brave. In fact, all the fuss that everyone was making only made her feel more like a fraud. 'I only did what anyone else would have done.'

'No, love, you did something exceptional. I certainly wouldn't have been swinging my bags at a man. And there ain't many who would have been so quick off the mark.'

'Honestly, I didn't have time to think. I just, well, reacted, I suppose.'

'Good reactions, Maureen, good reactions. I wish some of my blokes on the force had reactions as quick as you,' Sergeant Bradbury said. 'I can't stop, I'll be back tonight. See you later, Winnie, and well done, Maureen.'

Winnie waved him off and then sat at the table, saying seriously, 'Now, young lady. Me and you are going to have a very good talk.'

Maureen nodded, biting on the inside of her cheek. She could guess that this was going to be about the letter that she'd started to write to Brancher. She wanted the earth to open up and swallow her, but she knew that she couldn't run and hide. Bracing herself, Maureen prepared for a proper telling-off.

'No, man, you can't come in with me,' Clinton told Alberto, around the corner from the Battersea Tavern.

'It's a public house, which means it's a house that is open to the public,' Alberto argued.

'Open to the public, yes, but not to you.'

'But I like the Battersea Tavern, I always get a friendly welcome.'

'I guarantee you, there won't be any friendly welcome extended to you after what you did to Rachel.'

'Fine, you go in without me and waste your time chasing Maureen. I'll see you later.'

'Where are you going?'

'To have a drink in a pub where I *will* be welcomed.'

Alberto swaggered off, leaving Clinton feeling relieved that his good friend hadn't insisted on accompanying him into the pub. He turned the corner and saw a stall outside and was surprised to find Rachel behind the counter.

'Hello, Clinton. How are you?'

'Good, t'anks. What's this?'

'My new business. I'm selling shellfish. Have you ever tried a winkle?'

Clinton looked at the bowls of winkles, cockles and jellied eels, wrinkling his nose at the unappetising sight. 'No, I can't say that I have. But we eat a lot of shrimp and lobster back home.'

'I have crayfish tails and prawns, if you'd like some?'

'No, t'ank you, maybe next week after I've earned myself some honest wages.'

'I'll hold you to that,' Rachel smiled.

'Is Maureen in the pub?'

'Yes. She's become a bit of a local celebrity.'

'Maureen?'

'Yes. This morning, down the market, she caught a pickpocket. She knocked him out with a bag of spuds. Everyone is talking about it.'

Clinton's eyes widened in surprise. He couldn't imagine Maureen being so bold.

The cold began to bite at him, so he said a quick goodbye to Rachel. Inside the pub, he was grateful for the warmth. Though London wasn't nearly as cold as Scotland, Clinton knew that he'd never acclimatise to the British winters. He missed home and longed to be back there, but London offered opportunities of work and money which he needed for his family.

He searched the pub for Maureen but could only see Mrs Hampton behind the bar. She smiled, pulled half a pint and, placing it on the counter in front of him, she said, 'On me. I'm ashamed of the way that you were treated. Anyway, I suppose you're looking for Maureen?'

'T'ank you, and yes.'

'She's out the back with Winnie. They shouldn't be much longer. I'll let her know that you're here.'

Clinton sat at the bar, sipping his ale, appreciative of the generosity from the women of the Battersea Tavern. He thought it was a damn shame that Alberto had ruined things with Rachel and could no longer enjoy Mrs Berry's and Mrs Hampton's hospitality. But at least Alberto's girlfriend had promised to talk to her father about getting Clinton's job at the power station back. He couldn't believe that the fancy woman still wanted anything to do with Alberto, but she had, and Clinton hoped that she'd manage to persuade her father. He hadn't mentioned his cracked ribs but felt sure that he could manage the work.

He felt a rush of cold air as the pub door swung open and then he heard the joviality of a group of men with American accents and a distinct Southern drawl. Clinton glimpsed down the bar, his heart sinking when he saw four white soldiers, full of swagger. He hoped they wouldn't notice him and he quickly looked the other way.

'Maureen will be out shortly,' Mrs Hampton said, and then she wandered down to the Americans at the other end of the bar, asking, 'Yes, gentlemen, what can I get you?'

'Well, ma'am, I was going to ask you for four bottles of your finest liquid amber, but I see you're keeping unsavoury company.'

Clinton instantly knew that the American GI was referring to him. Rather than face a confrontation, he stood up and was about to walk out when Mrs Hampton said loudly, 'Stay exactly where you are, Clinton.'

Clinton sat back down, tentatively waiting to be hurled abuse. *Ignore them*, he told himself, keeping his head down, his pulse racing.

'If you don't like the company we keep in here, then I suggest you move on. You'll find plenty more pubs in the area that are more to your liking.'

'We've travelled over the bridge from the King's Road on an invite from a very good lady friend of mine. She assured me that Battersea folk are mighty friendly and obliging, ma'am. Now, I'm assuming that there's been an oversight here, on your part. See, where I'm from, we don't drink with negroes. I surely would be grateful if you'd change your mind and ask that coloured down there to vacate the premises so that us good, white folk don't have to lower our standards.'

'With respect, young man, I won't be asking him to leave. Now, can I get you a drink or not?'

Another soldier, almost twice the size of the one who had been doing the talking, growled, 'I'll make him leave.'

From the corner of his eye, Clinton saw the soldier stomping across the pub towards him. He jumped off his stool, but the soldier was already in front of him, blocking his path. Seeing the man's aggressive scowl and clenched fists, Clinton pushed himself backwards against the bar, holding his hands defensively in front of his face. He cowered, waiting to feel the force of the soldier's blows. But out of nowhere, Maureen appeared and somehow she managed to squeeze in between Clinton and the soldier.

'You'll have to get past me first,' she said boldly to the soldier.

'No, Maureen, please, stay out of this,' Clinton urged.

The soldier sniggered. 'You heard the negro. Step aside, ma'am.'

'I won't. And if you lay a finger on him, I'll chop your bleedin' crown jewels off!'

'*Crown jewels* ... I have no idea what you're talking about, little lady, but I hope you're not threatening me?'

Mrs Berry's voice carried from behind the bar. 'Oi, you and your mates ... clear off. I don't have *your sort* in my pub.'

'I beg your pardon, ma'am?'

'You heard me. Get out. I don't welcome *white* American soldiers, so bugger off or I'll call the police.'

As Mrs Berry spoke, Sergeant Bradbury walked in and immediately registered the situation. 'Did someone call the police?' he asked.

'No, sir, we were just leaving,' the shorter, smaller soldier said.

'And good riddance to you,' Mrs Berry shouted as they left.

When the door closed behind them, Clinton's knees were knocking together. He climbed back on the stool to steady himself, saying to Maureen, 'You shouldn't have done that, you could have been hurt.'

Sergeant Bradbury laughed. 'Talk about good timing, eh! I walked in just at the right moment. I bet they were wondering how the police turned up so quickly.'

Mrs Berry laughed too. 'That was funny, like something out of one of those black and white silent movies. Their faces were a picture.'

'I see Maureen was quite the hero for the second time today and this time without a bag of spuds,' Sergeant Bradbury smiled.

Mrs Berry looked proudly at her. 'Yes, she was. She takes after her grandfather. Len stuck up for me when I needed him to, and he stepped in on many a brawl in here. See, I told you, Maureen, there's a lot more to you than you give yourself credit for.'

Sergeant Bradbury placed his hand on Maureen's shoulder. 'You were very brave, Maureen, but next time, leave it to the police.' Then he turned to Clinton, asking, 'Are you all right, laddie?'

'Yes, sir, t'ank you.'

'I can't flippin' stand the way some of the Americans treat their comrades, just because of a different skin colour, it's appalling,' Mrs Berry moaned. She turned to Maureen. 'Tommy's right, though, love, you did a good job, but you shouldn't be putting yourself in danger. Though when you threatened his crown jewels, he didn't know what you were talking about. It did make me laugh.'

'Well, I thought threatening his crown jewels was the right thing to do. You've heard what everyone says about the Americans: *overpaid, oversexed and over here.*'

'Yes, indeed, love. And as they say about us: *underpaid, undersexed and under Eisenhower.*'

'Yeah, well, I'm quite happy to be undersexed, thank you very much,' Mrs Hampton piped up haughtily, which made Mrs Berry and Sergeant Bradbury chuckle again.

As the laughter died down, Mrs Berry leaned over the bar and said quietly to Maureen, 'See, you can stick up for other people. Now I want to see you sticking up for yourself too.'

Maureen looked embarrassed, but her smile appeared to be more confident than he'd seen before now.

Clinton's nerves were beginning to calm. He whispered to Maureen, 'I t'ink I may be getting my old job back at the power station. I'll soon be a man of means. Will you let me take you out to dinner next week? To say t'ank you for what you just did for me.'

To Clinton's delight, she smiled and nodded. There was something very different about her persona compared to the awkward, anxious exchange they'd had yesterday. She seemed more relaxed, more confident.

Maybe pushing his luck, he asked, 'Can we go for a walk together?'

'Brrr,' she answered, shivering. 'It's freezing outside. But I was just about to have a bite to eat. You can join me, if you like?'

'Yes, I'd like that very much.'

She leaned closer and said quietly, 'I won't invite you upstairs, it's not my place to ask guests up, but I'll bring us down a sandwich.'

While Maureen was upstairs, Clinton overheard Mrs Berry asking Sergeant Bradbury why he had come back to the pub. The man told her that he'd popped back to invite her out for a meal this evening. She readily agreed and he said that he'd pick her up at seven.

Clinton smiled to himself. Romance was in the air; he could feel it. And not just for him, but for Mrs Berry and the friendly policeman too.

36

It was Saturday the twenty-seventh of January: a couple of weeks had passed since Winnie had sat Maureen down and given her a good talking-to. She was pleased to see the effect that it had on the woman. Or maybe it was the incident in the market with the pickpocket or the run-in with the white American soldier that had boosted the young woman's confidence. Whatever it was, since that day, Maureen seemed much happier and had shown herself to be an accomplished seamstress too. It was good to see the old Maureen back, the Maureen that Winnie remembered before she'd married Brancher.

Sipping her tea, in the unusually quiet kitchen, Winnie raised her eyes towards the ceiling. 'We did it, Len. I told you that I'd look after your Maureen. She's fine now, love. I don't know what you're doing up there, knowing you, you're probably moaning about something, but you can rest in peace now.'

'Who are you talking to?' Rachel asked, coming into the kitchen pulling her apron around her waist.

'No one, love, just meself. You off to open up your stall?'

'Yes. Hilda will be here any minute to take the kids.'

'They're thriving at that school. Martha's been reading to me, you know. She's such a bright girl. I reckon she takes after you.'

'Ha, I hope so. Benny's doing well too. But he asked about his mum and dad last night. I still don't think that he's fully grasped the idea of never seeing them again.'

'The poor love. He's too young to understand. He's lucky to have you.'

'Hilda is taking them both to see Benny's grandparents today. They dote on him. I suppose he's their only link to their son. Oh, that's probably her now, knocking on the back door. See you later, Win.'

As Rachel dashed out, Maureen wandered in.

'Good morning, love. There's tea in the pot. Got any plans for today?'

'I don't know. Flo has put an order in for a posh evening dress for one of her customers. I suppose I should make a start on it, but I quite fancy a day off, doing nothing.' Maureen stretched her arms and yawned.

Winnie liked seeing her looking so relaxed. The tension in her face, the way she carried herself with her head lowered and shoulders rounded, all that had gone. Now, Maureen walked tall and her eyes sparkled with energy.

'Oooh, a day off sounds inviting. You should have one. You've not stopped lately.'

'Yeah, I know, but my granddad taught me the value of hard work.'

'A day off will do you good. We could go out for lunch together.'

'I'd like that. And … I've been thinking about something lately that I'd like to run by you.'

'Go on, I'm all ears.'

Carmen came into the kitchen. 'Have I missed something?' she asked as she sat at the table.

'No, not yet. Maureen was just about to tell me something.'

'Actually, I'm glad you're both here. Two heads are better than one … You can laugh, or you can tell me that I'm being daft … but Flo and Bill were telling me about a pitch on the market that's coming up for grabs. And, well … I was thinking of putting my name down for it. What do you think?'

Winnie looked towards the ceiling again, saying in her head, *Told you, Len, she's as right as rain.* 'What are you thinking of selling? Only I don't think Flo and Bill will to be happy if you set up in competition with their business and you'll never have enough ration coupons to buy the material that you'd need.'

'Oh, no … not dresses … well, yes, dresses, but baby clothes. I could sell a new range that I'd make myself. I know it sounds like a silly idea at the moment, but there seems to be a lot of optimism that the war will end soon and when it does, so will rationing. Gertrude, she's one of Rachel's regular customers and runs the knitting club, she told me that once the war is over, they won't be knitting balaclavas and scarves for the troops anymore, but they're going to keep their club going and will knit baby clothes instead, which I can buy from them and sell on.'

Winnie frowned, thoughtful for a moment, and then said, 'I don't want to sound like the voice of doom and gloom, but we don't know for sure that the war will end soon. And you know that most of the kiddies' clothes go to the exchanges set up by the Women's Voluntary Service. I think you've got a smashing idea, love, but the timing's all wrong. I know for a fact that Mrs Callard has made her girl's white school blouses from pillowcases. And Mrs Hellier bought some old utility clothes to make her boy's shorts. I just can't see how you'll make any money, at least not at the moment.'

Winnie saw Maureen's face drop with disappointment.

Carmen said, 'Winnie's right. Material is hard to come by and we're all still living on rations. Couldn't you put your plan on hold for a while? It would be something to look forward to, eh?'

Maureen sighed. 'I suppose so. But you don't think it's a silly pipe dream?'

'No, love, not at all. I think it's something that you should work towards, but not just yet.'

Maureen's smile returned and she said brightly, 'You're right. And I can wait. But one day, I'm going to open my own babywear business and Battersea will have the smartest-looking babies in London. I never imagined that I'd even so much as think about working for myself, but seeing Rachel doing so well has really inspired me. You've both helped me to see that I'm not useless or stupid.'

'Good, because you definitely aren't and I never want to hear you speak those words again, Maureen. In fact, I admire you,' Carmen said.

'Me?'

'Yes. All of you … Winnie's got her own pub, Rachel her stall and now you're planning on setting up a business too. I don't know if I'd ever be brave enough to do something like that or have the wherewithal to do it. So, yes, I admire you. You should be very proud of yourself.'

Winnie reached out and patted the back of Carmen's hand. 'You're our backbone, love. You organise the kids, our dinners, the stock for the pub and so much more besides. I reckon we'd fall apart without you.'

'Leave off, Win, we're a team.'

'We're a family,' Winnie said firmly. 'And talking of which, are you off to see your Cheryl today?'

'No, I've been invited to Sunday lunch tomorrow instead.'

'Well, you're behind the bar by yourself today then, 'cos me and Maureen are having a day off.'

'Are you, indeed?'

'Yep, and we're going up the high street for lunch: pie, mash and eels. Only don't tell Rachel. She'll get the right hump if she finds out that I'm having jellied eels that ain't from her stall,' Winnie chuckled.

Winnie smiled across the table to Maureen. She was looking forward to spending some time with her and she intended on finding out how Maureen felt about Clinton. The pair had been spending quite a bit of time together, though Winnie wasn't sure if they were just friends or if the relationship ran deeper. Either way, Winnie was pleased that it was one up on Brancher.

Maureen spooned the last mouthful of mashed potato and liquor into her mouth. Her stomach was full and she felt fit to burst.

'Did you enjoy that, love?'

'Cor, yeah, thanks, Winnie.'

'So, tell me, is it serious with you and Clinton?'

Maureen's eyes widened, though she didn't know why she

was surprised by Winnie's question as the woman was always direct. 'Erm, no, we're not dating or anything like that.'

'Really? You're just friends, then?'

'Yes. I think that Clinton would like us to be more than that, but it's not what I want.'

'I'm surprised. I thought you liked him.'

'Oh, I do, he's a smashing fella. So thoughtful and kind. He's like my best mate, but I can't get involved with him, not in *that* way.'

'Why not? I hope you're not worried about Brancher?'

'No, I'm never going to worry about him again. But it's Clinton: he wants to go back to British Honduras one day, for good, so there's no point in me letting meself get carried away with how I feel about him.'

'Oh, I see. But couldn't you go with him?'

'Me ... Halfway around the world? No, never. I've not been outside of London. I'd be terrified at the thought of being on a boat for all that time.'

'It would be an adventure.'

Maureen shook her head. 'No, I'm not adventurous. And I don't think I'd be able to cope with the heat. Or the food they eat. I'll be staying put.'

'And he definitely wants to go home?'

'Yes, he talks about it all the time. He misses his family.'

'I can understand that. Right, you ready? We should head back before it starts getting dark.'

Maureen looked at a large, round clock on the back wall. It was nearly four 'o'clock, they'd been out for hours. 'Yes, I'm ready, though I might need a barrow to carry my belly. I'm stuffed!'

As they ambled out of the shop and along the high street,

both content and relaxed, a huge boom echoed through the air. Maureen screamed as the ground beneath her feet trembled and a gush of dusty, gritty air rushed past her. She closed her eyes and turned her face, covering her mouth with her hand. Shop windows shattered, women and children screamed, some dropped to the ground with their hands over their heads for cover.

'What was that?' Maureen cried, searching the skies.

Winnie's hand shook as she pointed towards the end of York Road, where a cloud of smoke and debris had risen high into the sky.

'Oh my God, a V2 ... it came out of nowhere.'

'It came from Holland, sent by Adolf,' Winnie said with disgust. 'Are you all right?'

'Yes, I think so ... are you?'

'Yes, love, but gawd knows about the poor blighters under that bomb. Come on, we'd better get back sharpish. Carmen and Rachel will be worrying themselves sick about us.'

Maureen didn't realise that she was crying until Winnie pulled a handkerchief from her coat pocket and handed it to her.

'Sorry,' she sniffed. 'It's just so ... shocking. I used to get meself in a right old state when the German planes came over, loaded with bombs. My gran used to calm me down. But these rockets ... there's no warning. Nothing. It was so close. It could have landed on us!'

'But it didn't. We're alive and well. Just thank your lucky stars for that, eh.'

Maureen tried to think positively as fire engines whizzed past. She couldn't bring herself to look behind towards the devastation and willed her trembling legs to carry her forward.

A woman, lowly stooped, covering her head with a newspaper, ran past. On the corner, an old man stood shaking his walking stick towards the darkened sky, swearing and daring the Hun to try again. *The world has gone mad*, Maureen thought amid the mayhem.

When they arrived at the Battersea Tavern, Rachel and Carmen were waiting in the doorway.

'Thank gawd,' Carmen sighed, her face as white as the snow that had melted.

'You're covered in dust,' Rachel said, sounding alarmed.

'We're both fine, but it was bloody terrifying. I don't think I've ever needed a cup of tea quite as much as I do now,' Winnie said, her voice cracking with pent-up emotion.

Carmen ushered them inside. 'We heard it and thought the high street had been hit.'

'No, it was York Road, towards Wandsworth,' Winnie replied.

Maureen slumped onto a seat at one of the tables.

Winnie joined her. 'Cor, I'm out of breath.' Then she asked Rachel, 'Where are Martha and Benny?'

'They're upstairs with Hilda. She's put them both in the bath. They came home cold through to their bones, so she's warming them up with some hot water.'

'Sod the tea, get us both a brandy, love, bring it upstairs, please, I need to wash me face.'

When Maureen accepted the glass from Carmen, she was pleased to see that her hand had stopped shaking, though she still felt that she might burst out crying. 'Winnie was so brave. I wasn't, I was scared stiff.'

'Anyone would have been scared. Winnie was too, she just

hides her fear better. Get that brandy down your neck, you'll soon feel better.'

'Thanks, Carmen.'

Maureen sipped the drink, not enjoying the pungent taste, and found herself thinking about Clinton. She could have been killed today and if she had been, he would never have known how she felt about him. Life was too short to leave things unsaid. She was in love with him but had held back to protect herself from the heartbreak of one day having to say goodbye. It was time to lay her cards on the table. He had to choose: a life in Britain with her or the dream of one day returning to his home.

She couldn't believe it when she saw him walk into the pub. It was almost as if she'd conjured him up. He looked around and, when he saw her, rushed over, and blurted, 'I had to know that you weren't anywhere near that explosion.'

Maureen took his hand in hers. 'Sit down,' she said. Mustering all her courage, she was about to pour out her heart to Clinton and force him make the biggest decision of his life.

Winnie came back downstairs, her face now clean, and poured herself another brandy, steadying herself on the bar. She'd put on a brave face, as she always did, but inside she felt like a quivering bowl of jelly. The rocket had been so unexpected and the blast had scared her more than she'd let on. It had been far too close for comfort!

Tommy came in and walked straight up to the bar. 'Blimey, Winnie, what happened to you?' he asked.

Winnie realised that she must look a sight, her hair still

covered in dust. 'I was just coming out of the pie and mash shop when that rocket landed.'

'Stone the crows! But you're all right?'

'Yes, all in one piece. It was blinkin' close though, Tommy.'

'I've heard that it was up at Usk Road, near York Road. At least a dozen people have been killed, God rest their souls, and twenty-odd houses demolished.'

'It felt like the whole world blew up!'

'My timing is probably out, but can I have a word with you?' he asked, his tone serious.

'Come and sit down. I'm in no state to be standing behind the bar.'

'In private, if you don't mind?'

Winnie flicked her head towards the back kitchen. 'I'll put the kettle on,' she said.

Tea poured, Winnie sat at the table but wondered why Tommy was pacing back and forth.

'What did you want to talk to me about?' she asked, beginning to wonder if he had bad news about David or something similar.

Tommy pulled out a seat and sat adjacent to her. He removed his helmet and placed it on the table, and then pinched the bridge of his nose between his finger and thumb. 'I'm due to retire from the police force next month.'

'That'll be lovely for you.'

'Yes, I'm looking forward to it, and a quieter, slower pace of life. I've got a small cottage in Cornwall that belonged to my aunt. She left it to me when she died. Pretty little place, it is, with a thatched roof and thick stone walls. Views that go on for miles, green meadows, big skies. It's breathtaking.'

'Sounds idyllic.'

'Oh, it is, Winnie, it is. You'd love it.'

'Are you planning on moving there?'

'Yes. I want to enjoy my retirement in clean air, pottering around my vegetable patch and bringing fresh carrots and peas to the table for my wife to cook us a wholesome meal.'

'What wife?'

Tommy suddenly dropped onto one knee, taking Winnie by surprise.

'Will you marry me, Winnie?' he blurted, fumbling in his pocket until he pulled out a gold band with a small diamond centrepiece.

'Oh my goodness,' Winnie gasped, her hands flying over her mouth.

'Is that a yes?'

Winnie found that she was gobsmacked and couldn't answer. Instead, she stared wide-eyed at Tommy as her mind raced.

'I don't mean to hurry you, Winnie, but can you give me an answer before I do meself a mischief here.'

'Erm – er – I wasn't expecting a marriage proposal, Tommy. You've been a good friend to me, but this is so out of the blue. I don't know what to say.'

'Yes, would be a good answer.'

'I don't know, I'm not sure, it's just so unexpected. And you want me to move to Cornwall with you?'

'Yes. You could sell this place or leave it to Carmen to manage, whatever you like. But … hang on, I'm think I'm stuck … give me a hand up.'

Winnie pulled Tommy back to his feet. He sat at the table again and continued.

'Think about it, Winnie. A quaint village, a quiet life. We'd

398

be great companions for each other. Grow old together and look after each other in our dotage. I'm not talking about any, you know, *how's your father.* Bloomin' eck, I'm no good at this. I don't mean to make you feel uncomfortable. What I'm trying to say, in my own clumsy way … well, we'll play it however suits you, if you get me drift?'

Winnie looked at him quizzically. 'I think I know what you're saying.'

'So, what do you think? Do you reckon that you could be my wife? Live in Cornwall?'

'I don't know, Tommy. I'm sorry, but I'm going to have to think about it.'

'That's fair enough. No pressure. But I hope you'll agree. I'll, erm, leave you to mull it over. See you tomorrow.'

'Yes, see you Tommy.'

Winnie sat agog as Tommy slipped away. She'd never considered marriage to him, but she imagined selling her pub. A country life in Cornwall had its appeal, it was everything that she'd dreamed of, handed to her on a plate. And she thought a lot of Tommy, he had proved himself to be good company and a caring man. But, the tug of her family was strong. She had a lot of thinking to do before she made any life-changing decisions.

37

Winnie's sleep had been restless as she'd struggled with Tommy's marriage proposal. And now, as she pulled open her bedroom curtains and gazed across the familiar sight of rooftops with chimneys bellowing smoke, she was still undecided.

In the kitchen, Carmen was munching on a slice of toast, Rachel was washing up the children's breakfast plates and Maureen was staring into space.

Winnie heard a knock on the back door and knew that it would be Hilda. Rachel rushed past her to answer the door, and Hilda greeted them with a chirpy, 'Good morning.'

Sitting at the table, Carmen poured her a cup of tea. 'It's a bit stewed,' she said, 'but it's wet and warm.'

Hilda said to Maureen, 'I've just seen Clinton on his way to church. He looked very smart but seemed a bit down in the dumps. Is everything all right with him?'

Maureen shrugged. 'We're not seeing each other anymore.'

'Oh, I'm sorry to hear that, sweetheart. You must be upset?'

'No, funnily enough, I'm not. In fact, I've never felt better.'

'Care to elaborate?' Carmen asked.

'Well, I thought that I loved him, but I was holding back because I knew that he wanted to return to British Honduras one day. Then after that bomb yesterday, it gave me the shock of my life, and I started thinking about how life can be snuffed out in an instant. So, I sat him down and told him he had to choose either a life with me or the dream of going home.'

'Blimey, that's out of character for you,' Rachel said.

'I know, you lot must be rubbing off on me,' Maureen laughed.

'I assume he chose home?' Hilda asked.

'Yes. But do you know what, I don't blame him. I mean, I could never leave my home, here, with you all.'

'You don't seem very upset,' Carmen noted.

'No, I'm not. I thought I would be, but then realised that I'm not really in love with him. I think I *needed* him more than actually loving him. And now, well, I'm free. I've never felt like this before, and do you know what? It feels flippin' amazing.'

'You're definitely one of us,' Rachel laughed. 'And now that you're a single woman, you'll have more spare time on your hands. So how do you feel about helping out with Martha and Benny?'

'What do you mean?' Maureen asked.

'Taking them over the park now and then, picking them up from school, keeping an eye on them.'

Maureen looked pleasantly surprised but a little awkward. 'Oh, I'd, erm, love to, thank you.'

'Don't thank me, you'll be doing me a favour. Look, what happened before, with Benny and the button … it could have happened to any one of us. You can't watch them every second of every day. And I'm not sure if I wouldn't have reacted in exactly the same was as you did. I think I would have panicked too, so don't worry about it. I overreacted and I'm sorry.'

Winnie had been sitting back, listening, and thinking.

'You're quiet, Win,' Hilda remarked.

'Hmm, yes, I am.'

'Something on your mind?'

'You could say that,' she answered.

'Are you going to share?' Carmen asked.

Winnie looked from one woman to the other, swallowed hard and announced, 'I had a bit of a surprise yesterday; Tommy asked me to marry him.'

'You're kidding?' Carmen blurted, coughing on the tea that caught in her throat.

'No, I'm not. On my life, he got down on one knee and offered me a ring.'

'It's not on your finger, so I take it that you said no?' Hilda quizzed.

'I told him I'd think about it. He's retiring next month and wants to move to a cottage down in Cornwall.'

'You're leaving us?' Rachel asked, looking hurt.

There was a long, silent pause. Winnie could feel the tension around the table as they waited for her answer. She knew that accepting Tommy's offer would have massive ramifications for them. If she sold the Battersea Tavern, they'd be homeless and Carmen would be jobless too. But Winnie's decision wasn't based on the effect that it would have on everyone else. She'd made her choice based solely on what she wanted, and she finally answered, 'No, I'm not leaving to live in Cornwall and I'm not marrying Tommy.'

'Oh, thank goodness for that,' Rachel gushed. 'Call me selfish, but I couldn't stand the thought of you moving away.'

'I second that,' Carmen said. 'Though you have to do what makes you happy and we'd all support you either way.'

Winnie smiled. 'I am happy.'

'Are you sure?' Hilda asked. 'You're not turning down Tommy's offer for the sake of us lot?'

'No, I'm turning Tommy down because I don't want to marry him. He's offering me companionship in my old age, but I've got that here, with all of you. And the only way you'll get me out of this pub is by carrying me out in a wooden box. He caught me on the hop, but I've made my decision and I'm staying put, here where I belong, the landlady of the Battersea Tavern, and with my family.'

'I'm chuffed, Winnie, but aw, you're gonna break Tommy's heart,' Hilda said.

'I doubt that. I'm sure he'll be fine without me and find the companionship he wants in the local village. Though I'm not looking forward to letting him down.'

'I can understand that,' Carmen commented. 'Tommy's one of the good ones.'

'Yes, he is.'

'Talking of romance,' Maureen smiled. 'I received another letter from Stephen. He asked after you again, Rachel. I'm sure he's sweet on you.'

'Oooh,' Winnie cooed, 'What's all this about? It's the first I've heard of it.'

Rachel's cheeks pinked as she answered, 'It's nothing, just Maureen trying to play Cupid between me and her brother.'

'He's a nice young man, maybe you could write to him?' Winnie suggested.

'Maybe,' Rachel replied coyly. 'But gawd knows when he'll be home.'

Winnie shrugged, 'Well, there's a lot of talk of the war being won soon. I reckon that the end is in sight.'

'Do you really think so?' Hilda asked.

Winnie nodded adamantly. 'Yes, I do. I can feel it in me water. And I'll tell you what... bugger Cornwall. I need to be here because when Britain defeats those Nazi monsters, I'm going to throw the biggest party that the Battersea Tavern has ever seen. We'll welcome the troops home in proper style.'

'I like the sound of that!' Carmen agreed. 'A good old knees-up to cheer our boys. And it wouldn't be the same without you here, Win.'

'Well, I'll be honest... I've thought about moving away. Believe you me, the idea of leaving Battersea has crossed my mind many times. But I couldn't leave, not ever; all my memories are here. Not the bad ones, I've let them go, but my special, dearest memories are in this place, in my heart and all around me,' she said, choking back tears as she thought of Jan. And as Winnie spoke, she was sure that she could feel the gentle flutter of delicate butterfly wings brushing against her cheek. *I can feel you my girl*, she thought. *I know you're here with me.*

In that moment, Winnie knew that her decision to stay in the Battersea Tavern, her home, was absolutely the right one.

Acknowledgements

Thank you to Deryl Easton. Your fascinating family stories have inspired many of the characters in this series.

Thank you to Tracy Robinson, Beverley Ann Hopper, Sandra Blower and Lucy Gibson for running the Kitty Neale and Sam Michaels fan group on Facebook.

Thank you to all my special friends on social media for your support. I love seeing your photographs, your post shares and smashing comments.

Thank you to the wonderful team at Orion. I've enjoyed every minute of working with you and I'm looking forward to many more books to come!

Thank you to my amazing hubby. I can't remember the last time that I had my hands in the kitchen sink or used the washing machine! Love you darling.

And thank you to my lovely readers. I hope you've enjoyed this book series as much as I've enjoyed writing it!

Love and rainbows, Kitty xxx

Credits

Kitty Neale and Orion Fiction would like to thank everyone at Orion who worked on the publication of *A Wife's Courage* in the UK.

Editorial
Rhea Kurien
Sanah Ahmed

Copyeditor
Jade Craddock

Proofreader
Laura Gerrard

Audio
Paul Stark
Jake Alderson

Marketing
Brittany Sankey

Contracts
Anne Goddard
Humayra Ahmed
Ellie Bowker

Design
Charlotte Abrams-Simpson
Joanna Ridley
Nick Shah

Editorial Management
Charlie Panayiotou
Jane Hughes
Bartley Shaw
Tamara Morriss

Finance
Jasdip Nandra
Sue Baker

Production
Ruth Sharvell

Operations
Jo Jacobs
Sharon Willis

Publicity
Becca Bryant

Sales
Jen Wilson
Esther Waters
Victoria Laws
Rachael Hum
Anna Egelstaff
Frances Doyle
Georgina Cutler

Discover how Winnie's story began with the heart-wrenching first book in the *Battersea Tavern* saga

Can she put right the secrets of the past?

London, 1939. Winnie Berry has been the landlady of the Battersea Tavern for nearly twenty-five years, and the pub is like home to her – a place of tears and laughter, full of customers that feel like family. A place where she's learned to avoid the quick fists of her husband, and where she's raised her beloved son, David.

He's inherited his father's lazy streak and can't seem to hold down a job, but when war is declared Winnie is determined to keep her son safe. She's still haunted by the choice she made years ago as a desperate young woman, and she won't make the same mistake of letting her family be taken from her ...

But when a young woman crosses her path, the secrets of Winnie's past threaten to turn her world upside down. There's nothing stronger than a mother's love – but can it ever have a second chance?

And follow up with the second book in the *Battersea Tavern* saga ...

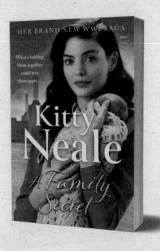

In a time of war, what's holding them together could tear them all apart ...

London, 1949. Winnie Berry is at the heart of the community in her pub, The Battersea Tavern. Her door is always open to those in need of a cup of tea and sympathy.

Winnie's abusive husband has left and she finds herself foolishly falling in love with black-market trader, Have-it Harry Hampton. But Harry is married and Winnie soon finds herself tied up in his web of secrets.

Meanwhile Winnie's son is back in London – not to visit his own child, but to charm the latest barmaid at the Battersea Tavern, which will lead to devastating consequences for the family.

With bombs dropping all around them, is it too late for Winnie to uncover the secrets of those closest to her in order to protect her true family?